Praise for Rebecca Chance

'Family secrets, revenge, diamonds and lots and lots of saucy scenes. What's not to love?'   *Sun*

'With lies, theft and even murder, *Killer Diamonds* sizzles with glamour, romance and revenge!'   *OK!*

'Sex, glamour, betrayal and murder – all the ingredients of a classic bonkbuster . . . irresistibly readable'   *Sunday Mirror*

'If you're a fan of Jilly Cooper, you'll LOVE Rebecca Chance'
Vina Jackson

'Sizzles with glamour, romance and revenge. Unputdown-able. A glittering page-turner . . . had me hooked from the first page'   Louise Bagshawe

'This is a pacy read, dripping in diamonds, stuffed full of sex and most definitely not for prudes. It's occasionally outra-geous and always entertaining'   *Daily Mail*

'This one will have you glued to the sun lounger'
Cosmopolitan

'Glitzy, scandalous and hedonistic, this compelling read is a real page-turner'   *Closer*

'If you want sex and scandal, you won't go wrong with this gem'   )*wn*

Killer Affair

Rebecca Chance is the pseudonym under which Lauren Henderson writes bonkbusters. Under her own name, she has written seven detective novels in her Sam Jones mystery series and three romantic comedies. Her non-fiction book *Jane Austen's Guide to Dating* has been optioned as a feature film, and her four-book young adult mystery series, published in the US, is Anthony-nominated. As Rebecca Chance, she has written the *Sunday Times* bestselling bonkbusters *Divas*, *Bad Girls*, *Bad Sisters*, *Killer Heels*, *Bad Angels*, *Killer Queens*, *Bad Brides*, *Mile High*, *Killer Diamonds* and now *Killer Affair*, which feature her signature mix of social satire, racy sex and roller-coaster thriller plots. Rebecca also writes for many major publications, including the *Telegraph*, the *Guardian*, *Cosmopolitan* and *Grazia*.

Born in London, she has lived in Tuscany and New York, and she travels extensively to research glamorous locations for the books. She is now settled in London, where she lives with her husband. Her website is www.rebeccachance.co.uk. She has a devoted following on social media: you can find her on Facebook as Rebecca.Chance.Author, and on Twitter and Instagram as @MsRebeccaChance. Her interests include cocktail-drinking, men's gymnastics and the Real Housewives series.

By Rebecca Chance

Divas
Bad Girls
Bad Sisters
Killer Heels
Bad Angels
Killer Queens
Bad Brides
Mile High
Killer Diamonds
Killer Affair

Killer Affair
REBECCA
CHANCE

PAN BOOKS

First published 2017 by Pan Books
an imprint of Pan Macmillan
20 New Wharf Road, London N1 9RR
Associated companies throughout the world
www.panmacmillan.com

ISBN 978-1-4472-8291-4

1 3 5 7 9 8 6 4 2

A CIP catalogue record for this book is available from the British Library.

Typeset in Minion Pro 11.5/15 pt by Palimpsest Book Production Limited, Falkirk, Stirlingshire
Printed and bound by CPI Group (UK) Ltd, Croydon, CR0 4YY

Visit **www.panmacmillan.com** to read more about all our books
and to buy them. You will also find features, author interviews and
news of any author events, and you can sign up for e-newsletters
so that you're always first to hear about our new releases.

For three wonderful, supportive, loyal friends,
Greg Herren, Laura Lippman and Chloe Saxby
(who strongly feels she deserves it 'for just being fabulous')

Prologue

It was an ocean liner come to rest in the heart of London, its glittering, prow-shaped facade jutting towards the Thames. From its terraces and balconies, the view was unparalleled: the beautiful curve of the Playhouse Theatre with its glowing lights, the flow of boats along the wide river, the sprawl of the South Bank beyond, London's bounty spread like a fabulous offering of endless possibilities to the gilded, privileged guests who occupied the penthouse suites.

However, the young woman who was climbing out of the black cab outside the hotel entrance on Whitehall was in no mood for relaxing on a private balcony with a glass of champagne, resting her arms on the rail, gazing down over the glittering city as she made plans for that evening. Her jaw was set determinedly, her eyes hard. The liveried doorman, reaching into the cab for her two suitcases, asked if she was a guest at the hotel, to which she responded curtly that no, she had a booking at the spa and needed to check her luggage.

If the doorman thought it was strange for a day spa visitor to arrive with a pair of large, battered suitcases, there was not a hint of that reaction on his face; his demeanour remained entirely polite and neutral as he carried them inside. Privately, he speculated that, judging by the airline tags on the cases, she had come straight from the airport. Her deep tan, together with the dark shadows under her eyes and her air of jet-lagged exhaustion, were clear indications that it had been a long-haul flight. Perhaps she was heading for the spa to restore herself after a taxing trip; but then, he asked himself, why did she look like a woman on a mission, rather than one who couldn't wait to float in the swimming pool, gazing up at the flickering, hypnotic waves reflected on the dove-grey ceiling, after sweating out the stress of the trip in the steam room?

And then, as he handed her the cloakroom ticket for the suitcases, the doorman looked her directly in the face for the first time and realized who she was. It took all of his professionalism not to acknowledge that he had recognized her as he wished her a pleasant visit to the spa.

'Was that—' the other doorman asked under his breath.

'Yes!' he said, just as quietly; any public discussion of famous hotel guests was grounds for instant dismissal.

The second doorman shook his head.

'That was *rough*,' he said sympathetically. They were standing side by side, no guests needing assistance with doors or luggage; it was a perfect moment for a swift exchange of gossip. 'Going through that on live TV – everyone watching you get totally shafted—'

'She got no sympathy from my missis, I can tell you,' the first doorman said. 'Thinks it's no more'n she deserved. Practically threw a party to celebrate.'

His colleague grinned.

'Yeah, the wives're bound to feel that way, eh?' he said. 'All things considered!'

Upstairs in the spa, the young woman was explaining that she had rung an hour ago to book a day pass, and the receptionist, a very attractive Eastern European called Irina with a strong accent but perfect command of English, was asking if she would like to add on any massage treatments. Irina found the young woman just as brusque, as oddly determined, as the doorman had done. As Irina explained to her that her day pass, costing a hundred and forty-five pounds, included full gym access and a light lunch, the young woman seemed entirely uninterested in what she was purchasing for that considerable amount of money, apart from the spa access itself.

That was unusual enough. Even more so was her indifference to the elegant foyer, with its open line of flickering flames set into a curving black glass surround, its white walls and even whiter floor, polished to a glossy, mirror-like sheen. Guests almost always commented on the fireplace, or at least glanced around, appreciating the sheer luxury of the surroundings. This one, however, might have been standing in a council gym smelling of chlorine and gym bags.

Irina, however, was far too professional to show a flicker of surprise at the visitor's unusual affect; she processed her credit card, showed her to the lavish women's changing room, handed her a robe and slippers, and left her with a smile, wishing her a relaxing visit to the spa. When Irina returned to reception her colleague Karen was on the computer, staring avidly at the details that had just been entered about the recent guest.

'Do you *know* who that was?' Karen babbled. 'She must just have got back from Australia! She looked weird, didn't she? Like, really wound up?'

Irina shook her head. She recognized the internationally famous guests – film stars and athletes – but rather than watching British television, she spent her free time either at the gym or studying for her personal trainer certificate, and as a result she rarely knew who many celebrities were. If anything, this was an asset, as it meant that she could deal with them in an entirely professional way, without any temptation to blurt out that she was their biggest fan.

'She's actually prettier than I thought she would be,' Karen said, very excited. 'Wow, I wonder how she's coping with – oh my *God*, Irina!'

Karen clapped her hands to her mouth, a reaction she would never have permitted herself if anyone else had been present.

'Do you know who else is *here*?' she blurted out. 'She came in a couple of hours ago! Oh my *God*, should we do something?'

Irina stared at Karen, baffled, as the latter started to spill out a flood of information about the guest who was already in the spa and the one who had just entered.

'But there are four floors,' Irina broke in, trying to re-assure her. 'They maybe will not even see each other! So one gets her nails done, or is in the steam room – even if they are both in the thermal spa, it is dark in there, they could be very close by and still not recognize the other one—'

'No, you don't get it!' Karen interrupted. 'I think she's here deliberately! *That's* why she looked so weird!'

'*Oh.*' Irina finally understood. 'Oh no, that is not good. What should we do?'

'I don't know!' Karen said, picking up the phone. 'I'm going to check!'

The young woman, meanwhile, had stuffed her creased, travel-stained clothes into her locker, and donned the hotel robe over her bra and knickers. She hadn't bothered to retrieve a swimsuit from her suitcases: she had no intention of actually using the lavish facilities. As the receptionist had guessed, she was searching for another guest. She hadn't realized how dark it would be inside the spa; black floors, black walls, soft lighting. Irina had been quite right: it was possible for two people to pass each other without any flicker of recognition.

The young woman stopped just inside the entrance, waiting for her eyes to adjust. Her gaze was caught by the flames set into a black glass wall to her right. The image was like something from a dream, beautiful and hypnotic. No wonder it was placed in front of a row of white marble loungers, clearly the final resting place where spa visitors, having completed the circuit of all the steam rooms and pools and saunas and whirlpools that the huge floor could offer, arrived at last, worn out by sheer physical pleasure and ready to collapse happily, probably lulled into sleep by the sight of the flickering fire, the sound of the water jets bubbling in the pool beyond . . .

And there she was: the person the young woman had come to find. It was that easy. Her target was stretched out on the far lounger, her black hair flowing over the white towelling cushion, her eyes closed, her breath slow and even.

The young woman looked round for a water dispenser, but spotted something even better at the far end of the gigantic space, beyond the space-age sauna: a huge, curved stack of flaked ice piled in a coppery bowl the size of a fountain, gradually replenished by more ice slowly dropping onto the sculpture from a slanted tube above.

Marching over as fast as she could in the hotel slippers, she dug both her hands into the ice, heaping her palms as full as possible. Then she stalked back to the lounger area. There were only a few other visitors to the spa, and they were all much too happily focused on their own relaxation to notice one young woman on the warpath.

Her target was asleep, or at least in a deep trance. The young woman stood over her, quite unaware of the cold biting into her palms, the ice dripping slowly to the marble floor as it started to melt. So many emotions were roiling inside her that she could not have said which one was uppermost. But as she lifted her hands and dumped their contents into the sleeping woman's face, she felt a rush of wild savagery that was as hot as her palms were freezing.

The ice tumbled onto the woman's eyes and nose and mouth, a series of brutal shocks: first the impact of the sharp slivered edges, then the cold burning into her skin. She shrieked in fear and panic, scrambling to sit up, not yet realizing what had happened. Her hands flew up to her cheeks, scrabbling frantically to push the ice away; she screamed again as she realized what had cascaded onto her face.

Just then, the main door of the spa swung open, and the manager entered, followed by a very excited Karen, whose head was turning back and forth as eagerly as a Labrador trying to spot a rabbit. They stopped dead at the sight of the woman on the lounger, her hands working on her face as if she were trying to fend off an invisible swarm of bees.

'What the *fuck*?' the woman blurted out, her eyes finally opening now that she knew it was safe to do so, that it was only water that had landed on her, nothing more dangerous; but her lashes were wet and heavy, her vision blurred, and she couldn't make out the features of the woman standing over her.

She recognized the voice, though.

'You *bitch*!' the young woman hissed. 'You've completely ruined my life!'

PART ONE

PART ONE

Chapter One

Sexy Lexy was on the warpath. Her target was Frank Callis, striker for Kensington, top of the Premier League table, and come hell or high water, she was going to make sure she took him up the aisle . . .

Caroline paused, fingers fractionally raised from her laptop keys, considering what she had just typed. Had she pushed it too far? Would Lexy think it was funny, or that it sounded too much as if she had chased Frank till she let him catch her, as Caroline's grandmother had said disapprovingly when she thought a woman was setting her sights too blatantly on a man?

And what about the style? Caroline wanted to flatter Lexy, make her sound clever and sophisticated. Was this opening a little too crude for that?

She tried a spin on one of the most famous lines to ever begin a novel:

It is a truth universally acknowledged that a glamour model in possession of a great pair of boobs must be in want of a footballer husband . . .

But regretfully, she deleted it. Lexy wasn't likely to recognize the start of Jane Austen's *Pride and Prejudice*, and nor

11

were her fans. It was a shame, though; this actually worked very well. Maybe Caroline could use it for her blog?

She retrieved the line, cutting and pasting it over to a blank document, then switching back to her draft of Lexy's life story. The woman sitting next to her cast a desultory glance at the screen of Caroline's laptop, saw that it was just boring text, no tweets or gossip, and looked away again, scrolling down the *Daily Mail* website on her phone.

Caroline had checked the *Daily Mail* earlier this morning: there was, as usual, a piece about Lexy in the sidebar that ran down the right side of the page. Lexy's management team was indefatigable, conjuring up stories about their most prominent client from practically nothing, but this one was a genuine triumph of the publicist's art.

'*Sexy Lexy's Near Miss!*' the headline shrieked.

It was a royal dilemma for Queen Elizabeth I when she found a puddle in her way – and Lexy O'Brien, reigning queen of reality TV, had exactly the same problem yesterday.

Sir Walter Raleigh famously laid down his cloak for the monarch to keep her feet dry but Frank Callis, Lexy's heartthrob footballer hubby, was nowhere to be seen.

With her favourite high-heeled suede Gina stilettos costing £390 (see box for Get the Look for Less), Lexy couldn't afford to ruin them.

Luckily she spotted the puddle in time and a short skip to the left was all she needed to avoid a watery disaster.

Carrying one of her many Birkin bags, the reality star and entrepreneur flaunted her famous curves in skintight jeans, those Gina heels, and a low-cut tee showcasing her latest boob job.

Caroline usually hated press descriptions of women 'flaunting' or 'showcasing' their bodies, but in Lexy's case, she had to admit that the verb was perfectly justified.

The article continued breathlessly:

Lexy recently confessed to boosting her bust from a 34C to a 34DD cup, admitting that breastfeeding and previous surgeries had left her breasts 'a bit shit'.

In her weekly column for Lovely! *magazine, Lexy shared that her operation, costing £7,500, had 'perked up her boobs', restoring them to the size and shape of her glamour-modelling days.*

'They're back to their prime,' the star wrote. 'I'm over the moon. I've got my volume back and there's no more sagging. It's a real confidence boost!'

Fashion editor: We know Lexy loves her Ginas and this pair's a particular fave! Remember her Instagram caption last year: 'In my Ginas 4 my b'day gonna dance all night #killerheels #ginalove #becauseImworthit #soglam'! Get the look for cheap with these fab ASOS stilettos at just £24.99!

Caroline had read the story in reluctant admiration, which was blended with envy at how striking Lexy looked in the candid photos. Of course Lexy had seen the paparazzo's camera: she was playing up to it, exaggerating her side-step round the puddle, first pulling a comic face of panic, and then flashing her best smile when she side-stepped the obstacle.

She was a relentless self-publicist. It was the secret of her success.

Many aspiring glamour models, all teeth, tits and hair, had tried to parlay their youthful, plump-cheeked prettiness into marriage to a high-earning sportsman, and quite a few had succeeded. However, Lexy had achieved the Holy Grail:

although she had snagged a footballer, she had, uniquely, surpassed him in the fame stakes. Frank had a regular presenting gig giving sports commentary on Sky TV, as well as various guest slots on radio shows, but he was as modest and retiring as Lexy was outgoing and attention-seeking, and it was Lexy who dominated the tabloids, Lexy who kept rolling out new products, all relentlessly branded with multiple photos of her famous face and equally famous cleavage.

Sensibly, Lexy made no secret of the fact that both face and cleavage had had surgical interventions over the years. They had been well done, however – Lexy was too self-protective to overdo the injectable fillers, a particular danger – and her teenage prettiness had evolved into the striking good looks of a confident woman in her prime.

She was thirty-seven, and in considerably better shape than Caroline, who was ten years younger than her. It was an unpleasant observation for the latter, who was squashed uncomfortably into a seat on the South West Trains 9:35 a.m. service to Bournemouth. Caroline wasn't fat, precisely, but she was no sylph, and it wasn't easy for her to cross her legs under the table for any length of time, which would have reduced the space they took up. She felt that she was spilling over normal boundaries with not only her body but her laptop, which was taking up more than a quarter of the four-seater table and garnering annoyed glances from the man opposite her, who was compensating by shoving his knees aggressively into hers.

Caroline couldn't even dream of being Lexy's size, a slim 8–10. It was impossible, unattainable. She would be ecstatic if she could fit into a 12 – not a Marks and Spencer or Wallis

12, however, with such a generous cut they were effectively vanity sizing! No, she wanted to be a Topshop or River Island 12. If she were that enviably slim, she could kick off her shoes, curl up in her window seat, remove her knees entirely from contact with the man facing her. Lexy would be able to manage that without any effort at all . . .

Caroline couldn't picture Lexy on this train service, however. Not even in the first-class section, which was near-identical to standard class apart from the fact that it was slightly less crowded. Lexy was surely whisked back and forth from London in a chauffeured limo, rather than waiting, shivering, on the wind-whipped, ugly platform at Waterloo in a throng of intent, narrow-eyed travellers who, knowing exactly where the train doors would open, were poised to dash on and claim their preferred seat. The term for this, *Metro* had said that morning, was 'pre-boarding'.

Caroline hadn't thought this journey would be so crowded, but the previous train had apparently been cancelled, and this one was a carriage short, so the result was a series of overstuffed sardine cans packed with a lot of extremely unhappy sardines.

The man opposite her pushed his knees further forward, pretending that he didn't realize he was butting against her, his head buried pointedly in his copy of the *Guardian*. One of those types who was all sharing and caring in public – above the table, with his lefty newspaper – but was quite happy to shove her underneath where no one could see. Another observation for the blog! Doing her best to squash her thighs to one side, Caroline opened another document and noted it down before switching back to the Lexy draft, praying that, unlike her, the man wasn't travelling all the way to Bournemouth . . .

Bubblier than a magnum of Cristal, bouncier than a tennis ball smashed by Rafael Nadal, Lexy flirted her way into the nation's heart the moment she appeared on ITV's Who's My Date?. *With her big blue eyes, tumbling dark ringlets and swift-witted banter with the suitors vying to take her out, Lexy was an instant sensation. Offers from men's magazines to pose for them flooded in, and a producer from the show pitched a special to ITV:* Love Me Lexy!, *in which members of Lexy's army of admirers would go through a series of challenges for the chance to spend a weekend away with her in Marbella.*

The viewers watched agog – bookies even gave odds on who Lexy would choose. But though the public's hearts were on fire, Lexy's was not. No matter how many hoops they jumped through, Lexy was never going to settle down with a plumber from Portsmouth or a brickie from Bognor. She was on her way up, and she wouldn't stop till she reached the heights.

As soon as Love Me Lexy! *aired, Lexy dumped the winner of the show, selling a tell-all story to the* Sun *about that weekend in Marbella, spilling saucy gossip about his lack of endowment. But that was only Part One of her publicity coup. Outrageously, just days afterwards, she stepped out on the arm of Darrell Rose, the presenter of* Love Me Lexy! *himself – with Darrell's long-term girlfriend nowhere to be seen.*

It was a genius move, cementing Lexy's position as a C-list celebrity. The scandal of Darrell dumping his girlfriend for her, plus the fact that he'd presented the very show on which Lexy was supposed to find love, meant that Lexy was no longer the nation's sweetheart. She'd become something even better, even more attractive to the media: controversial. People could project what they wanted onto her. For some, Lexy was the sex bomb they fantasized about being, wild and fun and uninhibited. For others, she was a slut, a homewrecker, just like the younger woman who had run off with their husband, and they could conveniently offload all the hate for that man-stealer onto her.

Lexy and Darrell were splashed over the tabloids and gossip sites, Lexy dazzling in a series of very revealing outfits, Darrell apparently dazed by the entire turn of events. After Lexy left him for a more famous rugby player, Darrell described her bitterly as a tornado who had whirled him up in the air, spun him around and jettisoned him when she had no more use for him.

The rugby player was merely the second celebrity boyfriend in a long male beauty parade. Even when Lexy dated a 'civilian' – a sexy barman, a stripper she'd met at a friend's hen night – she transformed him into a celebrity, polished him up and got the maximum value from him that she could.

In short, for almost twenty years, ever since she exploded into the spotlight, Lexy's been a publicist's dream client. Her life has been non-stop drama, keeping her fans on tenterhooks to see what's coming next.

But now . . .

Caroline's fingers, which had been flying over her laptop keys, finally paused. She wasn't quite sure what she was writing: a pitch for Lexy to read? An attempt to prove to herself that she could pull off the sort of fun, breathless style that would work in a book? Or should she be trying to tell the story as Lexy would, capture Lexy's distinctive voice?

Over the last two days, Caroline had spent all her spare

time researching her potential subject, but had been too nervous to start writing anything. As soon as the train had pulled out of Waterloo, however, she had learned something that many established authors already knew: travel was very stimulating to the creative impulses. Typing busily away, she did not even notice when the *Guardian* reader opposite alighted from the train at Basingstoke, barely registering the fact that she could lean over the keyboard without getting knobbly-kneed pushbacks under the table.

Finally, the words were flowing! She would have something to show Lexy at today's meeting, something to demonstrate that she was actually capable of the job for which she was pitching: ghostwriting a memoir for Lexy. Caroline had not realized initially why the agent had got in touch with her. The email had simply been one curt line, mentioning Caroline's blog and asking her to get in touch. It hadn't even come from the agent herself, who was far too important to contact Caroline directly, but her assistant, a very posh-sounding girl called, implausibly, Campaspe Norton-Brown.

Heart pounding, thinking that she was being offered an opportunity to discuss the novel she had always dreamed of writing, Caroline had completely failed to play it cool. She had rung the agency as soon as the email pinged onto her screen, and only when someone answered, his accent impeccably upper-class, had she realized that she had absolutely no idea how to pronounce the name of the person she was calling.

But she had stumbled through the syllables and been connected to the ineffably bored-sounding Campaspe. To Caroline's great disappointment, however, the assistant did not even bother to begin by telling her how much she loved her blog, let alone ask if she'd ever thought about expanding some of her short stories and blog entries into a novel. Instead, she had asked Caroline if she knew who Lexy O'Brien was, and, having received a positive response, proceeded to sound her out as to whether she would 'care', as Campaspe put it, 'to consider' ghostwriting for Lexy.

'It's a fixed fee, no royalties,' Campaspe had drawled. 'Standard drill. Full confidentiality agreement, of course.'

'Of course,' Caroline had said, so taken aback that she could only parrot what Campaspe was saying.

'Ideally, we want someone who can write a blend of autobiography and fiction,' Campaspe said, her tone, Caroline thought, slightly quizzical. 'That's Lexy's concept, anyway. She wants her story told as a novel. Don't worry if you don't have the faintest idea what that means – she'll tell you exactly what she has in mind. We need someone who'll get her voice, obviously, but also someone who'll sort of embed herself in the family, to an extent. I don't know how much you know about ghosting, but it's standard practice to spend a good deal of time with the subject, at least at the start, so Lexy has to get on with whoever it is.'

Unable to repeat 'whoever it is', Caroline fell back on 'Of course' again.

'Having said that, she's seeing this collaboration as a source of future book ideas too,' Campaspe continued. 'I'll let her explain what she means, but basically she's suggesting that a fiction writer will be able to help her come up with real-life stories that'll feed into projected books and be fodder for the tabloids at the same time . . .'

And that was the central issue. Even before embarking on her frantic two-day Lexy research binge, Caroline had read the *Mail Online* as much as the next woman. Caroline was aware of the way Lexy and her publicists contrived to get herself, Frank and her children into the press on a very regular basis. Look at that puddle story – in its way, it was a triumph of the genre, a much-ado-about-nothing that still kept Lexy's face in the press.

Clearly, however, Lexy was wary of being reduced to that kind of wisp-thin newspaper filler. The familiar faces who regularly appeared in the tabloids generated constant lurid stories – broken engagements, torrid affairs, betrayal by close friends, lawsuits over libel, weight loss and gain, three-somes, drug use, even husbands who turned out to be transgender – that kept their fans perpetually enthralled by their real-life soap operas.

Lexy's problem, Caroline assumed, was that she was now, by all accounts, happily settled down with Frank and the kids. The older one, Laylah, was from a previous marriage of Lexy's; Frank had adopted her, and they were bringing her up together with London, the little boy fathered by Frank. Now that Lexy was in a long-term, solid marriage, the titil-lating stories would dry up. Was Campaspe hinting that Lexy wanted a writer to help her concoct fake news items so that she could stay in the news forever?

There had been no point asking Campaspe that question: she had made it clear that Lexy would be briefing Caroline.

'*But now . . .*'

Caroline looked at the last words she had written as the train pulled into Bournemouth station.

Nothing follows a happy ever after, she thought. *The prince and princess get married and have some babies and that's it. End of the line. Just like the train announcement, we terminate here and start reading about a new princess instead. If Lexy wants to keep herself in the papers for the next ten years, she'll have to come up with a whole new storyline, and how's she going to manage that?*

She packed away her laptop in her shoulder bag, unwedged herself from under the table and shuffled off the train with the rest of the passengers, hoping the bus stop would be easy to find. Campaspe had told her that Sandbanks, where Lexy lived, was equidistant to Bournemouth and Poole stations, but that the former was preferable as it had a taxi rank. Caroline had waited eagerly on hearing this piece of information, but no offer of compensation for train ticket or cab ride had followed, and she couldn't possibly afford to pay for a cab herself.

Caroline was quite aware that if she had been an established writer, not just a nobody blogger, expenses would have been offered. Ironic, of course, because a proper writer would surely need the money much less than she did. Caroline had had to buy an open return, having no idea how long the interview would take. At least she'd been able to get an off-peak ticket, but it had cost over fifty pounds, and she had had to take the day off from her job. Her boss had sounded thoroughly pissed off when she rang in that morning, pleading flu: half the department had recently been sacked and the survivors were working double time to catch up.

It was too far to walk to Sandbanks; Google had told her that Bournemouth was also a better choice for the bus service. But the bus was running late, and then she got off at the wrong stop because she was so stressed about the delay. When she realized her error, she launched into an awkward half-run to get there faster. Caroline never ran, was totally unfit, and by the time she arrived at the big security gates of Lexy's mansion she was not only clammy with sweat and out of breath, but her hair and coat were damp because a light rain was falling and she hadn't thought to bring an umbrella.

Caroline felt disgusting. And as she gave her name to the tinny voice answering the intercom, the access door in the gate buzzing open, the sight of The Gables, Lexy's multi-million pound mansion, was so intimidating that she almost turned on the scuffed plastic heels of her cheap boots and ran away.

Chapter Two

Sandbanks, the peninsula on which Caroline was standing, was known as the British Palm Beach. Unbelievably, it had the fourth highest property values in the world. The forty or so houses that ran around the outside of the sand spur, having direct access to the sea, were worth seven- to eight-figure sums. It was a millionaire's playground, and a tiny one; it measured just half a square mile.

Looking at the house – no, the mansion – awestruck and daunted, Caroline could quite believe that it had cost a fortune. It was colonial-style, pale blue wood siding with white trim, its roof gabled, its matching white balconies and terraces delicately carved, composed of one long central building with wings on either side reaching away from the entrance gate towards Poole Harbour beyond. What she was looking at was clearly the rear of the house, despite the imposing marble staircase that led up to the large front door; and that was even more intimidating, because the back of this house was more impressive than the front of any other she had visited in her life.

The most elegant of backs, Caroline thought. *A supermodel walking away down a catwalk. A ballet dancer gliding offstage.*

Having been writing for two hours straight, her brain was creatively fired up, primed to find metaphors. Then, as she walked up the marble steps, the big front door swung open, and the vista in front of her made her gasp in appreciation, her brain racing even faster to think of how she would describe it. The mansion, like so many other Sandbanks houses, had been designed to face the sea, making the most of the superb panorama over Poole Harbour and the marina. Its wings opened like arms to frame the view.

A double staircase curved up either side of the huge entrance hall, encircling the vista. Glass walls beyond gave an open perspective all the way through the house to a rich green lawn sloping down to a jetty that reached out into the grey, wind-flecked English Channel. The sky beyond was equally grey, rain falling with increasing strength, creating a veil of water between clouds and sea.

It had a bleak, hypnotic beauty. Caroline imagined herself owning this house, curled up in an oversized armchair, watching the rain beat gently against the windowpanes as classical music played. It was such a compelling picture that for a moment she lost herself inside it, and jumped when the young woman who had let her in said briskly:

'You leave your coat. Outside is wet.'

The young woman had a light foreign accent, an impressive head of thick black curly hair contained in a heavy plait, and a no-nonsense attitude. As Caroline took off her thin, cheap wool coat, she flinched in horror: someone had started screaming upstairs, the screeches at a near eardrum-piercing level. The young woman, who was opening the hallway closet, paid not the slightest attention. Footsteps

24

sounded above, and a small child dressed from head to toe in pink dashed along the landing, screeching 'I won't, I won't, *I won't!*' so loudly that a recording of her could have been used at riots to disperse crowds. All Caroline's instincts were to clap her hands over her ears and duck for cover.

The little girl skidded to a halt, pressed a button and stepped into a glass box against one side of the hall at landing level, a lift that Caroline had not previously noticed. As the lift began to descend, the little girl kept screaming, hands clenched into fists, cheeks as fuchsia as her stripy tights, her blue eyes round and bulging. The lift was demonstrably not sound-proof: the screeching was muffled but still audible.

It was an extraordinary sight. Caroline goggled at the child as she sank to ground level, her eyes sliding over Caroline and her companion without a flicker of interest, dismissing them as utterly unimportant. She was screaming all the while, barely taking a breath, the noise persisting even after she had disappeared from sight into the depths of the house.

'I don't like children,' the young woman said flatly, nodding at Caroline to hang her coat up in the closet. 'There are two here. The boy is not as bad as the girl. But I only like cats.'

No response seemed to be required, which was lucky, as Caroline had no idea what to say. A dispirited-looking, dowdy, drooping young woman came along the upper hallway, glancing at the steel and glass lift shaft as she started to head down one wing of the staircase.

'I know what you're going to say, Carmen,' she said wearily. 'Kittens are better than children.'

'Kittens are so fluffy!' Carmen said, coming fully to life. 'And they don't talk! I keep saying to you, you should get a job looking after kittens!'

'Please don't make me cry,' said the young woman, reaching the ground floor. 'I just hope she hasn't thrown herself into the swimming pool by now.'

Carmen shrugged with superb nonchalance.

'She will float,' she said. 'In my country we say that. Witches float.'

The nanny snorted out through her nose and went through a side door which presumably led to a staircase to the basement and the swimming pool in which the small child would be floating.

'Are you the housekeeper?' Caroline asked her politely, closing the cupboard door.

'I am the cleaning lady,' Carmen corrected her. 'That was the nanny. But she won't be here long. She's weak. Her hair is thin. It's because she is vegetarian. I tell her many times what to do about her hair, but she won't listen.'

'What should she do?' Caroline asked, fascinated. 'Eat meat?'

'Of course,' Carmen said, looking at her with mingled contempt and pity. 'But also, when you brush your hair, you must always leave the hair outside for the birds, to make their nests. Then your hair will grow long and thick like mine.'

She tossed her plait back over her shoulder complacently and pointed ahead, towards the view.

'You go there,' she said. 'Lexy is in there.'

Tentatively, her nerves on edge, not knowing how to react

to the scene she had just witnessed or whether she should mention to Lexy that her daughter might be floating – or sinking – in the swimming pool, Caroline crossed the hallway. It was a long walk, and she was acutely aware of Carmen's eyes on her back as she went, judging everything about her. God knew what comments Carmen would be making about her to the nanny in due course, but she already guessed that they wouldn't be positive.

Caroline had seen multiple photographs of the huge sitting room online. It had featured in spreads for weekly magazines for which Lexy, Frank, London and Laylah had posed, modelling clothes from Lexy's fashion line. Running the entire length of the main part of the house, it was even more spectacular than it had appeared in pictures, partly because it was visually extended by the stone terrace beyond, which also ran the length of the house and was fully visible through the glass back wall.

Like the sitting room, the terrace had groups of square, modern furniture composed into conversational areas, interspersed with decorative planters or vases. The sofas and armchairs inside were grey suede, the ones outside pale grey with white cushions, all neatly protected against the rain by transparent covers. The effect was to double the size of the already enormous room. It was like walking into the lounge of a generously proportioned boutique hotel rather than that of a private home. On the various glass coffee tables were bowls of flowers, platters of fruit, and fanned-out magazines, which only increased the resemblance to a chic hotel.

'Over here!' instructed a very familiar voice, and Caroline turned to see Lexy reclining on a chaise longue, a tablet in her lap and a pile of magazines scattered next to her. 'It's Caroline, yeah?' she said, not waiting for confirmation. 'Find it okay?'

'Yes, thank you,' Caroline said, her heels clattering across the expanse of beautifully polished wooden floor.

As she had known she would, she felt hugely self-conscious about her walk, her outfit, her hair, her make-up. She had spent a considerable amount of time debating what to wear for this crucial meeting, and decided that there was no point her trying to look like a less attractive, much fatter clone of Lexy, dressed in tight jeans, with cascading hair and cleavage popping out of an animal-print T-shirt, the look finished off with shiny jewellery and heavy eye make-up. Instead, Caroline was positively dowdy in her grey jersey top and long black skirt. She had tonged her hair into loose waves that morning, but the rain had put paid to those, and it was hanging limply on her shoulders. After her sweaty dash from the bus stop, her BB cream felt greasy on her cheeks, but she didn't dare blot it, in case she rubbed it off and revealed her rosacea.

Lexy's eyes flickered up and down Caroline's body as she approached. And Caroline, a born observer, could tell straight away that she presented no threat to Lexy, none at all. Caroline had very enterprisingly found back copies of *Lovely!* magazine at her local library, in which Lexy had a weekly column; she had soon noticed how often Lexy feuded with women she saw as her rivals, how rarely she complimented or spoke positively of them. In all her research, Caroline could barely find photographs of Lexy smiling and posing with fellow glamour models or other footballers' wives. She seemed to have no real female friends, nor feel any need for them.

So, in choosing her outfit, Caroline had avoided any suggestion that she might be on Lexy's level, any presentation of herself as a potential equal with whom Lexy might form a bond. Caroline's outfit and bearing were humble and self-effacing, presenting herself as a person who would be easy to have around, who would not seek attention or put herself forward. Someone to whom you could tell your stories; someone who would structure them into books. Someone who wouldn't dream, however, of bothering you with their own stories in return; someone who had no pretensions to anything like friendship with you.

I'm like a governess, Caroline thought with a quick flash of inner amusement, *in a nineteenth-century novel by the Brontë sisters. Jane Eyre or Agnes Grey. Quiet, retiring, unobtrusive, there when you want me, slipping away like a shadow when you don't. Look at me! I'm even dressed in grey, just like the governesses in those books!*

And as Lexy gestured at Caroline to sit in an armchair facing the chaise longue, she gave a small nod of approval. This could have been a set-up for therapy, the therapist sitting while the patient stretched out on a sofa, vulnerable and open. But there was nothing vulnerable about Lexy in her black velour diamante-trimmed onesie, unzipped enough to show off the upper curves of those recently plumped and lifted 34DD cups. She adjusted the zebra-print faux fur cushions behind her, swivelling to fix Caroline with those famously big blue eyes that were identical to Laylah's.

'I saw your daughter just now,' Caroline said, lowering herself into the armchair. 'She's really pretty.'

'She's a right little madam,' Lexy said with unabashed frankness. 'Goes through nannies like a knife through butter. And not a butterknife, either. A steak one. Fuck knows what we're going to do with her – she's always kicking off at school too. They'll be telling us we've got to take her out if she carries on like this. Wouldn't be the first one she's been chucked out of.'

Caroline had no idea how to respond to this, and she was sensible enough not to try. Lexy continued almost immediately:

'So you're a blogger, yeah?'

Caroline nodded, unable to stop staring at Lexy. Her face and body were so familiar and so beautiful, her skin extraordinarily smooth and clear; her eyes were outlined with black pencil and carefully shaded and highlighted, her eyebrows perfectly shaped, thick and dark. Even in the unforgiving clear cold daylight, her skin had a smooth texture which made her look ten years younger than she was.

Her lips were clearly enhanced. There was that tell-tale fullness to their outer corners, a shape that never occurred in nature, indicating the presence of injectable fillers. Her forehead was Botoxed, and the corners of her eyes too. From a distance, it looked as if Lexy had been frozen in time at the age of twenty; closer up, one could see that parts of her face were fighting silently with others, the nose wrinkling too much because the forehead couldn't, the mouth fractionally stretched against the cheeks when she smiled.

But these were tiny flaws, and only noticeable if you were

Caroline, accustomed to sitting quietly in a crowded room, people-watching. By any standard, Lexy was breathtakingly pretty, with those huge blue eyes, the tightly curling dark ringlets which were pinned up today on the crown of her head, the cupid's-bow mouth and pale creamy skin.

She held herself, too, with the air of a woman who knew exactly how lovely she was. She might have been a queen reclining on that chaise longue, talking to a lowly lady in waiting. But her confidence was even higher than that, because Lexy hadn't been born to this celebrity royalty status: she had created it herself. Plenty of very pretty girls had sat on the *Who's My Date?* stool over the course of the series, girls with quick wits and good personalities. But only one of them had ever broken out as Lexy had so successfully done. Only one girl had ever managed to forge an entire career on the charisma she had projected sitting there, chatting to Darrell Rose, making a nation fall in love with her.

Lexy's fashionably heavy eyebrows were raised. Caroline snapped out of her reverie, realizing that there was a question that required answering.

'Yes, I'm a blogger,' she said, and was about to elaborate when Lexy continued:

'But it's not your day job, right? You're not one of those people who make money from blogging?'

'No,' Caroline admitted. 'That works if you do recipes, or run a gossip site, something that you can sell ads for. Book reviewers do it for love and free copies, but me putting up my writing is basically a pitch to get a book deal. That's the dream.'

Lexy nodded.

'Money in writing books, is there?' she asked.

'I don't really know,' Caroline said honestly. 'I've never published one. Everyone in the online writers' groups says it's really hard to make a living doing it. The big names make loads, but what they call the mid-list doesn't. And romance novels – the branded ones – don't pay much at all, apparently. You'd need to write loads a year to make a living.'

'I hope you're not expecting to get rich writing for me,' Lexy said. 'I'm really tight. Everyone knows that.'

'Well, if they read your column about your vaginal surgery, they do,' Caroline blurted out, and then went cold with horror. She literally could not believe what she had just done: she'd referred to the fact that Lexy had told anyone who'd care to listen that after the birth of London she had had vaginal rejuvenation surgery.

Lexy stared at her, mouth falling open, and Caroline's entire body tensed, going as taut as, presumably, Lexy's now-restored vagina.

'You are fucking *kidding* me,' Lexy said, and if Caroline could have got up and fled the room, clumsily, stumbling over the edge of her long cankle-hiding skirt in her cheap boots, she would have done. But her muscles were cramped too rigidly for her to be able to move, and she sat there mutely as Lexy went on:

'That's fucking funny. I'm going to put that in my column. Nice one.'

'Thanks,' Caroline said, her voice a faint thread of relief, fresh sweat puddling in the small of her back.

Lexy's eyes were narrowed now.

'Do you think I write my column myself?' she asked Caroline.

'Um, I don't know,' Caroline said carefully.

'Well, I don't! Not a word of it!' Lexy flashed her a beautiful smile. 'None of us do! Honestly, some of the other bitches are so fucking thick they can barely even sign their own names! Some poor editor rings us up, same time each week, tells us what's been in the news and what the latest jealous wannabes are saying about us, and then we mouth off about them and what we think of the name the latest silly slag gave her baby, and they write it all up and put "Love, Lexy!" at the end with a lot of kisses. Pretty much like what I'll be doing with this book.'

She lay back on the chaise longue.

'You're just filler,' she continued. 'You know that, right? They only sent you 'cause I didn't like anyone they sent so far, and I was kicking off about wasting my time with writers who were really posh and up themselves, or thick as planks. They must have panicked – gone googling for people on the internet and found you in some random search. I've got two more bloggers coming in the next couple of days.'

Unflattering as this was, it did not come as a surprise to Caroline. She couldn't flatter herself that she would have been anyone's first, or even tenth, choice for a ghostwriter. Although she hadn't known much about the profession until Campaspe's email, she had researched it on the internet with the same dedication she had invested in finding out about Lexy's vivid life story to date.

Ghostwriters for sports stars' autobiographies, apparently, could make a great deal of money. The good ones were in high demand, and the use of them was an open secret, as no one expected a cricketer or rugby player who could barely talk in full sentences to produce an entire book on their own. Writing autobiographies for other celebrities, however, was a more ambiguous affair, as was the authorship of the novels to which they put their names.

Generally, the celebrities liked to pretend that they had written the book themselves, with the most minimal amount of 'help' from someone hired by the publisher to, as they tended to phrase it in interviews or book acknowledgements, 'put together the novel'. A pop star had recently been exposed as not having written her own bestselling novel, and the young woman who had actually done the work had apparently been paid very little. From online newspaper reports Caroline had googled, it looked as if the book had been written in under two months and the writer had been paid a measly flat fee, just eight thousand pounds, with no stake in the millions the novel had made. Exposed, the pop star had insisted that the 'story and characters' were hers, but had refrained from adding that she now felt that the person who had done the work should be getting a proportion of the royalties.

It was shockingly low pay. But Caroline would have leapt at the offer to ghostwrite for the pop star as eagerly as the novelist had probably done. Caroline had done the annual challenge to write a novel in the month of November, NaNoWriMo, the year before, and despite the demands of her day job, she'd pulled it off. It hadn't been much good, but it had had a beginning, a middle and an end, and she was sure that if she were offered eight thousand pounds, a fortune to her, she could manage a novel in two months . . .

Campaspe had made it clear already that there wasn't much money on offer. Lexy's frankness hadn't been a surprise. The only celebrity who openly acknowledged her ghostwriter, as far as Caroline could see, was Katie Price, and hers had apparently been paid very well; but that seemed to be an exception to the normal rule. Caroline had no expectation of getting rich if she were lucky enough to be chosen to write Lexy's novel-cum-autobiography. But her hope was that if she did a good job, Campaspe or some other agent would read the book and take her on as a client, get her a publishing deal to write a novel of her own.

Caroline didn't know why Lexy had just challenged her about her lowly status. But she sensed that Lexy wanted to see whether Caroline had a backbone.

'I'm surprised you even wanted to meet me, then,' Caroline answered. 'You're surely too busy to bother with someone who's just filler.'

'It's not much trouble for me,' Lexy said nonchalantly. 'I just have to lie around in my own cosy house. You're the one that had to trudge here from wherever you live.'

'London,' Caroline said equably. 'It wasn't like I had to come from the Hebrides. And I quite fancied a nice day out by the seaside.'

Lexy grinned at this.

'Bad luck for you with the rain,' she said.

'It's good for the skin, my grandma used to say,' Caroline countered, and hoped that her BB cream was still doing its job well enough so that Lexy wouldn't observe her rosacea and comment that her skin could do with all the help it could get.

'Yeah, I've heard that too,' Lexy said. 'It's the way all the British people make themselves feel better about the shitty weather. I'd be in Dubai right now if I could. You know what's really good for skin? The absolute fucking fortune I spend on vitamins and omega oils and facials and mineral make-up. Costs me a shitload of money, even with my VIP discount. But it's totally worth it.'

She glanced at Caroline.

'Think I should put that in my book? What I spend on my skin?'

'Definitely,' Caroline said without hesitation. 'Your skin's lovely. I noticed it already. People will be really keen to know what your regime is.'

'My *regime*,' Lexy repeated, and Caroline thought that she was being mocked.

'It means—' she started hurriedly.

'Yeah, I know,' Lexy said. 'The beauty places always talk about regimes. It's a good word. Like something out of a book.'

She was still staring at Caroline, those big blue eyes penetrating.

'How do you know you can write a book?' she asked.

Caroline took a deep breath and prayed that her hands weren't shaking. She couldn't mention that NaNoWriMo novel; it wasn't good enough to show anyone.

'I don't yet,' she said. 'But it sounds like you didn't like any of the people who've proved they can.'

Lexy tilted her head a little to the side. Caroline would come to know that this gesture meant she was thinking hard.

'Some of them had a go at writing stuff,' she said. 'I read bits of what they wrote, and it didn't sound like me.'

Caroline frowned.

'I don't think my stuff would sound like you either, though,' she said honestly. 'That comes after, surely? I mean, someone needs to sit down with you for a while, talk to you, see what story you want to tell, and then work on it till you feel they've got your voice.'

She paused, wondering if she should say what was on the tip of her tongue. Being direct with Lexy had worked well before, but still . . .

'Spit it out,' Lexy said, reading her mind with disconcerting accuracy.

'Well, I was thinking that they'd have to cut out a lot of your swearing,' Caroline said. 'I don't think a publisher wants a book full of effing and blinding, unless it's an East End gangster novel.'

'That's fucking funny,' Lexy said for the second time, nodding in approval. 'I could use that in my column too. I want to give updates about the book as I write it –' she had the decency to raise her hands and pantomime quotation marks around the word 'write' – 'to fire up the fans on my social media, too. Make them excited for it as I go along, get them pre-ordering online.'

'That's a great idea,' Caroline said, but Lexy wasn't listening to her; the doorbell had rung, and the clattering of equipment, bustle and overlapping voices filled the hall.

'Here we go,' Lexy said, swinging her legs over the side of the chaise longue and standing up, pulling the bunched-up crotch of the onesie out of her own with an absolute lack of embarrassment. 'Time to get to work. I'm filming my show this afternoon. We're doing a scene where I get my anal bleaching done.'

She grinned at Caroline, not in an entirely friendly way.

'Tell you what. You watch the whole thing, then write it up like it was in a book, happening to me, but me telling it. I'll have a read and see what I think. That's further than any of the other writers got with me. I see your writing, you get to see my arsehole. Looks like this is your lucky day, eh?'

Chapter Three

You know what real fame is? It's being known by your first name only. It's everyone knowing who you are as you walk into a restaurant, not just your hardcore fans. It's being in the sidebar of the Daily Mail *because you nearly walked in a puddle, but didn't.*

But if I had to pick a single example of what real fame means, it'd be not having to hold open your own bum cheeks when you get anally bleached.

In the old days, for waxing and bleaching, it was always me reaching back like I was doing some sort of mental yoga pose, grabbing my bum and trying not to wince while some Russian cow with an advanced degree in KGB interrogation techniques smeared hot wax on me and then ripped all the hairs off while I screamed and swore and said I'd tell her anything she wanted as long as she'd just effing stop. Nowadays, I know to take a handful of ibuprofen an hour or so before, never schedule this sort of thing when you're premenstrual as it's even more bloody painful then (excuse the pun!), and have a nice glass of champers before you get started, to take the edge off.

Plus, get someone else to do the bum-cheek holding so you can relax and breathe your way through it as best you can.

Right now, I'm stark naked on the treatment table while my make-up artist and my fake tanner are stood on each side of me. Each one of them's got a handful of what I must say are my very impressively firm round buttocks – all those lunges my bastard trainer makes me do three times a week – and they're hauling their side towards them so that the technician can get a good old look at my bum hole.

It's ironic, because Jay and Nathan are totally gay, and couldn't give a shit about a woman's arse (yeah, I like my puns!). God knows what the technician fancies, but all I can say is that if she's gay she's in heaven with her job. She must see more women's bits in a day than a gynaecologist – they only get to do the front part, right?

Normally, of course, I'd be on my knees, shoving my bum back at her. But because I'm being filmed for my reality show, I'm having to lie down. Apparently it's 'too real' to film me naked on all fours screeching 'cause I'm getting acid rubbed into me back there . . .

'You want front done too?' asked the bleaching technician, as she had been prompted to do by the producer of *All About Lexy*. And as they had rehearsed, Lexy squealed with laughter.

'Nah, love!' she said. Her head was raised, propped on her hands, so that the camera directly in front of her could capture her facial expression. Eyes dancing with amusement, full lips curved, she added:

'Frank likes it pink! If he fancied copping off with an albino chick he should've done it before he got married, shouldn't he?'

'God, the hell you women have to put up with!' Nathan

said, shuddering theatrically. 'Do some of you actually bleach your vadges?'

'Mental, isn't it,' Lexy said casually. 'What some needy desperado bitches do to snag a man. Hey, Ghost Mouse, don't put "desperado" in! I know it's wrong, I just like using it.'

Everyone looked over at Caroline, who was sitting tucked away in one corner of Lexy's sprawling bathroom. She was ensconced on the loo seat, a suitably humble position for a lowly blogger who was lucky even to be interviewing for this job, scribbling away on a notepad, since tapping on her laptop keys had been banned by the TV crew on the grounds of background noise.

'Cut,' the director said, sighing. 'Lexy—'

'Yeah, yeah, I'll pick it up, no worries.'

Caroline's cheeks were tingling, that unpleasant feeling when all her little rosacea nodules became activated. She hated attention, and even though the anal bleaching technician, the make-up and hair artists and the crew had only glanced her way for a moment, as Lexy mentioned her, it had made her extremely self-conscious. Absurd, of course. There was Lexy, not only naked but positively splayed open to one of her cores, and it was the fully-dressed Caroline who was shrinking from being stared at.

'Okay to go again?' the director said to Lexy.

'In three,' she said, leaving a pause. Then, with the skill of long practice, in just the same tone as she had used before, she repeated:

'Mental, isn't it. What some needy desperado bitches do

to snag a man.' She paused. 'Oi, Nathan! You got to keep opening up my area so she can get to it!'

Nathan tightened his grip on Lexy's left buttock.

'You're in good nick, babes,' he said. 'Nice and plumptious.'

'Got to have something for Frank to hold on to!' Lexy said. 'Oh, look, speak of the devil.'

'*You're* the devil,' Jay commented, his pre-scripted dialogue for the scene. 'Frank's the angel, if you ask me.'

Once more ignored in the far corner of the room, quite removed from the angles of the cameras, which had been carefully positioned to avoid unwanted reflections in the many mirrors, Caroline looked over as Frank Callis, Lexy's husband, walked into the room. This was scripted too, of course. Caroline had been privy to the whole planning and choreography of this scene, the producer and Lexy conferring on the shape of it, feeding Nathan and Jay their catchy lines, deciding that Frank should enter and feign shock at Lexy's latest beauty treatment to give the scene some drama.

'What you doing to yourself now, Lex?' Frank asked, one of the cameras turning to capture his entrance, though naturally it would be reshot as well. His delivery was not lively, but it wasn't wooden either; apart from several seasons of his wife's reality show, having been a sports commentator for years he was very used to the demands of television by now.

'Bleaching me arsehole for your pleasure!' Lexy said, blowing him a kiss. 'I hope you're happy!'

Tucked away on the toilet seat, Caroline had a clear view of Frank. His wife's tanned, hairless, naked body was stretched out on a treatment table covered with white towelling. The contrast made Lexy's skin glow luminously against the white background. Her dark hair was pinned up on the crown of her head, elongating her neck; it looked positively swanlike as Lexy swivelled to address him directly: she was breathtakingly attractive

But it was Frank who was holding all Caroline's attention. He'd never been a classically handsome heartthrob, pursued by adverts keen to use him for underwear or aftershave campaigns: he was no David Beckham or Freddie Ljungberg. However, Caroline was realizing, this must be due to the fact that he did not photograph well. It was her first experience of the capricious gift that nature bestows on some people but not others, the magic of being born photogenic. Lexy had it in spades. Frank did not.

His features were blunt, his forehead too low. But the dark curls clustering over it gave him a very youthful appearance, and his almond-shaped black eyes were luminous and compelling. He was taller than Caroline had expected, his shoulders wider, his stomach flatter. It was amazing to her, staring at him, that Frank had never had a fan club of admirers, never been considered anything but a safe pair of hands, a very reliable winger, a thoughtful and considered TV pundit. The television cameras did not capture the softness of those wonderful dark eyes, the quiet confidence of his demeanour, and most of all, the luminosity of his skin.

Lexy glowed because of her excellent and expensive fake tan, but Frank's colour was all his own. Caroline had copyedited a press release for a luxury wood company the year before, and still remembered some of the more exotic varieties. Cherrywood, fruitwood, Ipswich pine, red mahogany, colonial maple: poetic names. Well, Frank's skin made her feel poetic: it looked like the burnished golden pecan about which the press release had waxed lyrical, the heart of a fire against which you could warm your hands. Frank might have been planed down and then oiled deeply, just like the wood; Caroline imagined that if she ran her hand down his chest, which was partly visible at the neckline of his open shirt, it would feel just as smooth . . .

She caught herself, swallowing so hard it was almost painful. But she simply hadn't expected Frank to be so handsome. On TV, on Lexy's show, he came across as – not bland, exactly. But . . . nice. Dependable. The voice of reason on every panel discussion, the foil to Lexy's high-spirited, attention-seeking loudmouth. Good husband material, a man who had unquestioningly taken on Laylah, Lexy's daughter, raising her as his own. Laylah's biological father, a basketball player with whom Lexy had had a famously tempestuous affair, had walked out when she told him she was pregnant. Frank was, in every way but genetic, Laylah's father.

Good husband material: that phrase was never used to describe a man who was sexually attractive. But as Caroline, her face on fire now, ducked her head to hide it, she was so dazzled by Frank that all she could manage was to make squiggles in her notebook so that anyone who looked over would think she was writing. She had never seen a man who she had found more compelling.

Frank said the line fed him by the producer: 'Babes, you know I like you a bit more natural.'

Even his voice sounded different than it did on television. Charming, gentle, amused. Sexy.

He really cares about her, Caroline thought. *You can tell he loves her in their series, but in real life . . . he doesn't just love her, he likes her. That's just as important.*

'Oh, come on, Frank, you love it when I'm all nice and smooth!' Lexy was saying flirtatiously.

Frank raised one big hand and wiped it over his face as if he were trying to block out the image of his wife lying naked in front of him with two gay men pulling her buttocks apart, a young woman with a white plastic spatula smearing gel between them, and a camera crew surrounding her, with bright lights illuminating the entire scene.

'Sometimes, Lex,' he said, lowering his hand again, 'I wonder where this is all going to end, y'know?'

Lexy paused. This wasn't what he had been supposed to say, and she wasn't sure whether to make an unscripted joke about him and one of her ends; their show was re-run in the daytime, and she couldn't say anything too explicit.

Although she was being filmed in the nude, the viewers would see nothing but the blurred curve of her bottom. It was commonplace now on reality shows for female cast members to get their private parts waxed. The network, however, was increasingly strict with Lexy about her swearing and sexual innuendo, and she knew that if she made a joke that was too risqué it would be cut.

And yet Frank's reaction, though unscripted, had been so good, so honest, that it would work fantastically on TV – if she could find something light and funny to respond with . . .

'Mummy!'

Laylah tore into the bathroom, her plaits bouncing on her shoulders, her blue eyes wide as she took in the sight of her mother splayed on the beauty therapist's table. She skidded to a halt beside her father as, following in her footsteps, her little brother London, a stocky four-year-old, tumbled in behind her. With his tight dark curls and burnished skin, his slanting eyes and square jaw, he was the image of his father, apart from the light eyes that were clearly from his mother's gene pool. Suddenly shy at the number of people present, he slipped behind Laylah, aware that all the attention would be on her as soon as she entered a room.

And he was perfectly right. Laylah stole the scene.

'Oh *no*, Mummy!' she said, nailing that world-weary tone that small children can sometimes assume. Playing for the cameras, as she had been taught, she folded her arms over her chest and stuck out her small pointed chin. 'Why have you taken all your clothes off for the men *again*?'

'And *cut*,' the director said gratefully.

Chapter Four

He was blindfolded, helpless, his sweat beginning to soak into the silk bonds that held him strapped, spread-eagled on the mattress. No wonder the Marquis had had him escorted to this room, with its four-poster bed whose curlicued mahogany pillars looked as heavy as marble. No matter how much he thrashed, trying to loosen the woven cords around his wrists and ankles, the wood to which they were fastened barely even creaked; and not only was he a strong young man, his muscles were not merely for show. He was the son and apprentice of a blacksmith, his biceps mighty, his stomach thick and solid for balance, to hold his back safe against the swing of the forging hammer: no footman, hired for height and decoration, no young Regency buck who sparred with Gentleman Jackson at the latter's Bond Street boxing salon for sport.

That last image made his blood stir. None other than Lord Byron had recorded in his diary that, after pugilistic instruction from Jackson, the two men had enjoyed an encounter just as sweaty, just as intense, but even more stripped down and private. Byron swore that he had had carnal knowledge of Jackson, and whether it were true or not, the vivid picture that this conjured up, the Champion of England and the famous poet, the one all muscle and sinew, the other a beauty for the ages, naked, wrestling for physical supremacy, on a bed identical to this, the sound of their panting as they struggled one to conquer the other with urgent cocks rather than clenched fists – not just the sounds of them gasping for breath, but the slick of sweating flesh against flesh, the quick spit of saliva into a palm, the moist slick of that fluid, enhanced by thick drops eagerly released in anticipation, up and down a thrusting shaft, the final gushing rush of release into mouth or arsehole, the groans of both men as they gave and received in turn . . .

His cock was straining now. If his hands had been free – even one hand, even his less-favoured left hand, which lacked the long expertise in pulling his own cock with the exquisite torture that would inevitably lead to the longed-for explosion – he would have come immediately at the picture of those two men. It was their physical competition that excited him so much, the element of constraint, of force, one compelling the other to a surrender that was so desired but also so erotically resisted to prolong delight.

This was what he craved: the being forced, the forcing in turn. This was why he found himself now, here, oil worked into his body as if he were a harem slave, tied to a bed, desperate for satisfaction, but longing to greet the Marquis with a stiff cock whenever he deigned to enter this bedroom, rather than a belly smeared with his own almond-scented liquid.

It was agony, this waiting, this anticipation. When, finally, after God knew how much time had passed, his tears wetting the silk blindfold that kept him in delicious darkness, he heard footsteps in the passage, the doorknob turn, his balls tightened, his cock sprang even fuller, even more erect, its tumescence now more pain than pleasure . . .

Oh, heaven help him! No – heaven would scorn to reach out and save him from what awaited him. It was his punishment for being who and what he was, not just for desiring men, but for his need of restraint and restraining. For it was not just the Marquis who had entered the room, who was staring at his naked and aroused body. There had been more than one set of boot heels stepping heavily down the corridor, into this bedroom. One man closed the door while another walked to the bed, stood beside the mattress, his gaze as hot on the young man strapped down there as if it were a flambeau held by a footman, so close it could burn the skin.

'You filthy catamite,' the Marquis said softly, and more tears dampened the blindfold even as, to his humiliation, his hips thrust upwards at the insult, silently showing his submission. 'You deserve more punishment than I alone can give you for your disgusting lusts.'

And even as the Marquis's leather-gloved hand closed around his cock, other hands unfastened the cords around his ankles, freeing them, pushing them up towards his chest. The mattress sagged with the heavy weight of a man climbing onto it, up between his spread legs, still in riding boots, the squeak of the leather unmistakeable. He was to be fucked by a gentleman who did not even deign to strip before he drove his cock in, just loosened his breeches, spat on his hand and went to work.

It was glorious. It was all he could do not to shoot straight away into the Marquis's calfskin glove. He grit his teeth, threw back his head, held out as long as he could, and his reward, *on feeling the stranger's hot eager come flood his arsehole, finally, was to yield his own to the Marquis's mouth, which was now tightly sealed around his cock, lapping up every drop of the catamite's filthy, sinful, forbidden spunk.*

'You *wrote* this?' Lexy stared at Caroline, turning over the pages of print-out to see if there was any more of the story. '*You* wrote this?'

Caroline nodded, pressing her lips together to control her fear, as she couldn't tell from Lexy's stunned reaction whether she loved or hated the Regency gay sex scene, and it was crucial that she did. This was the second test: Caroline had passed the first, as Lexy had liked the first-person narrative that she had challenged Caroline to write about the anal bleaching scene. Lexy didn't know yet, she had said, what she thought the book should be; a novel, a biography, a combination of the two. But she had pronounced the piece to be easy to read, full of personality, and not pompous or patronizing. From the way she'd delivered the last words, it was clear that some of the other potential ghostwriters had been exactly that.

So Caroline had demonstrated that she could write in a way that appealed to Lexy. And her attitude was clearly acceptable; in fact, Caroline's deference provided Lexy with a great deal of amusement. Lexy had a way of looking at Caroline with lightly concealed mockery every time Caroline acted too humbly or seemed intimidated by Lexy's sheer physical confidence.

They were meeting today in the bar of a Bloomsbury hotel, all black leather sofas and parchment-toned orchids on polished silver tables, and Lexy had already laughed out loud at Caroline's insistence that she was perfectly fine just drinking tap water. Lexy was on Pinot Grigio, which she had ordered with a slice of lemon in it. The nervous waiter had brought the lemon on the side, and Lexy, tutting loudly, had plonked it into her glass, commenting on how annoying it was when people couldn't listen properly. The waiter, not knowing where to look – her famous face, her famous breasts and her famous legs were all very much on display – retreated backwards as if she had been the Queen, bowing and mumbling apologies.

'*Well*,' Lexy finally said, putting down the pages once she had confirmed that the Regency bondage and buggery scene ended at the point that two out of the three participants reached their climax. 'I'd never have guessed it! You don't look the type at *all*. But they say the quiet ones are always the filthiest, don't they? Fuck me, I need a drink after that!'

She picked up her glass, drained the wine, sucked enthusiastically on the lemon, and waved over to the barman to order another. Then she turned back to fix Caroline with a stare that, for the first time in their acquaintance, had respect in it. Caroline had emailed Lexy the anal bleaching scene a couple of days after the meeting in Sandbanks, and though Lexy had rung her up that very day to convey her approval, she had added that she had a big question which needed to be resolved. As far as Caroline was concerned, that could have been almost anything, and she held her breath until she heard what Lexy was about to say.

'No offence,' Lexy had said breezily, which naturally meant that something very likely to insult was coming down the pipeline. 'But can you be sexy?'

Caroline – who was at work, in her usual uniform of Next

grey skirt and M&S polyester crepe shirt – looked down at herself instinctively and winced.

'I could *try*, I suppose,' she said feebly.

'Hah!' Lexy laughed. 'Don't worry, I'm not going to make you get on a pole and give me a twirl! I mean your writing, Ghost Mouse! Can you *write* sexy?'

'Oh!' Caroline let out a sigh of relief. Was bated breath the same as holding it? If so, hers was unbated now. 'Yes,' she said confidently, careful not to repeat the word 'sexy' so that her colleagues didn't realize this wasn't a work call. 'Yes, I can definitely do that. You don't need to worry.'

'Okay, but I can't just take your word for it,' Lexy pointed out.

'I've already written, um, quite a lot of material in that area,' Caroline said, glancing around at her co-workers to make sure they didn't notice anything unusual in this conversation.

'Great! You got something I can read?'

'Yes. I could email it—'

'Nah. Bring it along this afternoon,' Lexy said briskly. 'The Bloomsbury Square Hotel, three o'clock, in the lobby bar. Print it out, yeah? My editor says it's better to read stuff on paper than screen. Fuck knows why.'

And without bothering to say goodbye, Lexy had hung up, leaving Caroline impaled on the horns of a dilemma. If she ducked out of work that early, her boss would be livid; the day she had taken off to go to Sandbanks last week was still being held against her because of the lack of notice. And walking out in the middle of the day was even more extreme.

Caroline would have to plead a family emergency – after

she'd surreptitiously printed off a sex scene for Lexy, of course, a sackable offence in itself to use office equipment for private purposes – but she was dreading how this would be received. She was quite right to be worried. Her boss threw a massive wobbly: to placate her, Caroline had to promise to come in an hour early for the rest of the week and stay an hour late, effectively tripling the time she would be taking off this afternoon.

It wasn't fair. But no one in their twenties expected the job market to be fair. You didn't go to HR to complain, you didn't point out that you had holiday days or sick days coming against which you could set this afternoon. You were desperate to keep your job, pathetic and low-paid and prospect-free though it was. So you kept your mouth shut and apologized and agreed to anything your boss demanded, then grabbed your cheap plastic knockoff handbag from under your desk and slunk out with your head hanging, pantomiming guilt, mumbling a string of *sorrys* to the colleague who was going to have to finish your proofing work as well as her own . . .

And having to meet Lexy while dressed in ugly work clothes was an extra punishment. Caroline had been staring miserably at her handbag on the tube, mortified at the state of it. Threads were coming off the stitching all round the handle, and when she tried pulling at one to break it off, it just kept coming till she got scared it would all pull free. She ended up wrapping the thread clumsily around the base, trying to knot it as best she could so it wouldn't keep working itself loose. The bag, bought from a market stall a couple of years ago, was in a terrible state. She had known it was very bashed up, but it was only now, sitting with it on her lap, that she took in how badly the plastic was cracked and curling away from the corners, the threads on the side seams fraying as well.

She had strategically pulled out the book extract for Lexy before entering the hotel, bunching the handbag up under her arm and then dropping it onto the armchair, practically sitting on it to conceal its decrepitude. The waiter brought Lexy her second glass of Pinot Grigio, this time with not only a slice of lemon in it but a decorative curl of peel perched on the rim, and she nodded at him in thanks as he set it down.

'So what's with the gay stuff?' Lexy asked Caroline, picking up the glass. 'Don't get me wrong, I like gay porn as much as the next girl! The only thing better than one naked hot guy is two or three naked hot guys, right?'

Having lived her adult life under the glare of TV cameras, Lexy was entirely nonchalant about making sexual or revealing comments in front of staff. The waiter's ears were bright red as he withdrew to the bar once more, and Caroline, much shyer, waited until he was out of earshot before she answered.

'I wrote a novel last year,' she said. 'That's an extract from it. It's about a blacksmith who falls in love with the son of an earl. In the end they run off to be pirates together on the South Seas—'

'Cool, but why the gay stuff?' Lexy was inexorable. 'Why not girls and boys?'

Because I don't feel sexually confident enough to write straight sex scenes, Caroline thought. *Because describing women's bodies that are way better than mine – women who don't have any problems getting on top of a guy because their tummies are flat, or doing reverse cowgirl because their bums are smooth and not spotty or pocked with cellulite – makes me feel incredibly sad about my own really boring sex life. I'm too embarrassed to try anything but missionary. Or doggy, but only in the dark.*

I bet that's why women write male gay porn novels, she thought suddenly. *I bet it's because it doesn't make them depressed at the contrast between the perfect figures they're describing and the state of their own belly fat. If you're creating hot guys with washboard abs and bulging biceps and bums like twin peaches, guys who would never look at you in real life, it's much easier to have them fancy each other. That way you don't have to deal with the cold hard truth that you'll never, ever, shag a man that hot and sexy . . .*

'Lots of women write this kind of thing,' she told Lexy. 'They use their initials, or men's names, otherwise the gay guys wouldn't buy it. Or the women readers, I suppose – the fantasy is that it's a sexy man telling the story. There isn't loads of money in it, though, because only gay guys and some women buy them, which doesn't add up to a huge amount of people.'

'I didn't even *know* there were books like this!' Lexy said. 'I'd definitely give this one a go, though! Hot gay porn! And I don't even *read* books much.'

She glanced at the pages spread out on the table, nodding approvingly.

'I didn't understand some of the words, honestly, but that doesn't matter, 'cause you can totally work out what's going on,' she commented. 'It makes you sound really clever. Plus it makes the reader feel clever too, reading a dirty sex scene with long words and all that posh history stuff in it, Lord Byron and that. It's much classier than . . . I dunno, those porn novels with the black and white photos on the cover.'

'Thanks!'

Caroline went pink at this praise. The part about making the reader feel clever was the best part of all.

'Could you do something that was sexy like this? In the same sort of style as that bit you sent me about me getting my bum bleached?' Lexy asked. 'Ugh, Frank wasn't joking about liking me more natural, by the way. He hasn't gone near my arse since. I even googled "how long does it take anal bleaching to fade?" but couldn't get an answer.'

'You should try Reddit,' Caroline suggested.

As Lexy had already learned, Caroline was swift at repartee, and she was a fast learner, aware now that when Lexy said something outrageous, the best response was not to become embarrassed but to assume a poker face and a dry retort.

'What's that, then?'

Lexy was almost through her second glass of wine, but she didn't sound remotely affected by it.

'It's online,' Caroline explained. 'People ask questions and everyone chimes in to help and answer them. It can be really funny. Celebrities do it too, for interviews in real time. It's called an AMA – Ask Me Anything. Seriously, you should definitely do it when you've got something to promote – you're good at banter and thinking on your feet.'

'So are you, eh?' Lexy said, setting down her now-empty glass. 'You don't look it, but you are.'

She surveyed Caroline, who cringed, knowing what was coming.

'I don't mean to be rude,' Lexy began, 'but what you're wearing is fucking criminal. You look like you work behind the counter at a bank. *Do* you work at a bank?'

'No, I write and copy-edit press releases for a media company,' Caroline said, noticing with pleasure that Lexy was folding the A4 sheets of her book extract and dropping them into her extremely expensive-looking leather bag, covered in buckles and studs and unnecessary hardware. 'We do publicity for trade organizations and—'

But Lexy was calling for the bill, pulling out her wallet, ignoring Caroline's answer.

'Come on, then!' she said, standing up. 'We've got a meeting at four. I'm not promising anything, yeah? But you might as well come along. It's just round the corner.'

'What is?'

Caroline's heartbeat juddered irregularly as she waited for the answer.

'My publishers, of course!' Lexy said impatiently.

Her eyes widened as she saw Caroline stand up and fish out her bag from the armchair.

'Fuck me,' she said. 'What *is* that thing? Looks like you nicked it off a skip on the way over here!'

Chapter Five

'What a fun read! Sizzling hot!' carolled Lexy's editor Gareth, refolding the pages of Caroline's Regency bondage gay porn extract and looking at her with twinkling eyes. 'You've got *quite* the imagination, babes!'

Caroline knew she was unprettily red in the face. She was both excited and mortified by the fact that a gay man had, for the first time ever, read one of these sex scenes – and an editor, to boot! It was embarrassing to acknowledge, but she had no close gay friends, something she attributed to her lack of chicness and sophistication, together with her boring job. Neither gave her opportunities to meet the kind of gay men she would love to befriend.

Caroline wasn't completely unconfident; she knew that her quick wit was something gay men would appreciate. Lexy and her gay entourage were deliberately, knowingly camp for the TV cameras, but when that scene with the anal bleaching had finished shooting, they had visibly relaxed into a more natural friendship, teasing each other in a way that was more intimate than any coos of mutual support could possibly have been.

Caroline had envied her so much for that. In so many

ways, Lexy had exactly what Caroline wanted. It was quite unexpected: before meeting her, Lexy would not even have been on Caroline's top ten list of women in whose shoes she would love to walk. Yet having seen Lexy's house, her lifestyle, her genuine beauty, her children – Caroline wasn't *that* keen on children, but obviously planned to have them one day – and most of all, her gorgeous and devoted and surprisingly sexy husband . . . yes, it was very hard not to picture herself at the centre of that world, a famous novelist, like Jackie Collins, doing interviews in slinky jersey dresses that showed off her fantastic figure, advised on her hairstyle and make-up by a cabal of witty, wise gay men.

Ones like Gareth. It was the most enormous relief that he had called her sex scene 'sizzling hot'. Caroline had based it entirely on gay porn and other 'man on man' novels, probably, as she had explained to Lexy, written by women like her. She'd never even *had* anal sex, mortifying though that was to acknowledge.

'*But*, that said, obviously this isn't the kind of thing that'll work for Lexy,' Gareth continued, handing the pages to Lexy's agent Miranda, who had been texting while he read. She put down her phone and started to peruse them in turn. 'We can't expect her audience to believe that she's been secretly writing historical homo smut all this time.'

Lexy sniggered. 'But Gazza,' she observed teasingly, 'my fan base is women who like sexy stuff, plus gay guys – it's on brand, you know? And the writing's really classy! Full of big words!'

Gareth shot a speaking glance at Lexy's agent, a very slim, chic woman dressed entirely in expensive fitted black. Gratifyingly, this was exactly how Caroline had imagined a literary agent to look. Miranda turned to Lexy, leaning a little forward in her seat, and said:

'Fun idea, Lexy, but we really need to—'

'I was joking!' Lexy looked from Gareth to Miranda, flashing her beautiful smile. 'You lot don't know me that well, do you? Come on! I want to make a ton of money off these books, yeah? Of course I'm taking the piss!'

Miranda visibly relaxed. Gareth made a show of wiping his brow theatrically.

'Well, *that's* a relief!' he commented. 'We were panicking there for a moment! We want you to make a ton of money too. Don't worry about that, babes. I'm thinking what we talked about in the initial meeting – something closely based on your wild, fabulous existence. You're having a fantastic life shagging around, you fall pregnant and have to deal with the fact that the father is never going to be around for you and the baby – *so* relatable! – heartbreak, etc. etc. – you're a sexy, brave, battling TV star who's a single mum. Like so many women, just a lot more glam! Then you find true love to cap it all off!'

'That sounds *very* commercial,' Miranda said approvingly.

'And because we want *all* the goss on all your guys,' Gareth said, eyes gleaming, 'if there's stuff you could get sued for – drugs, threesomes, perviness – we'll create fictional characters instead. We can drop clues so the readers will guess who they are, but change some details so the guys can't start dialling their lawyers. *Roman à clef*, they call it in France. Nice to see my degree was good for something!'

Lexy nodded. 'Sounds just right,' she said cheerfully. 'And I think Caroline's the one to do it.'

They were sitting in a small conference room at Bailey

and Hart, Lexy's publishers, which was located in a large 1970s block off Russell Square. It was much more modern than Caroline had imagined; she had had a vague idea that publishers' offices were located in creaky old townhouses, with stacks of papers piled everywhere. Instead, the decor was the office version of an All Bar One – light wood, bright lighting, glass panels instead of walls.

The staff, however – slim, youngish women in bright fashionable dresses, called Emma and Katie and Lucy and Helena – sounded like they belonged more in a Fulham gastropub full of young men in stripy shirts and bright cord trousers. The ones to whom Caroline had been introduced had all greeted her in friendly tones as clear and bright as the lighting, shaking her hand politely, but she had been very conscious of how dowdy her clothes were compared to theirs.

Lexy had insisted they stop at the first shop they passed that sold handbags, and forced Caroline to buy a basic leather tote into which she dumped the contents of her previous bag; Lexy herself had bundled that up and thrown it into the shop bin with superb contempt. But Caroline's outfit was still cheap polyester, her accent notably unrefined compared to those of the Emmas and Katies.

Oh well, Caroline had reflected for consolation, *a posh girl wouldn't be able to ghostwrite for Lexy. She couldn't write how Lexy talks. Plus, Lexy would think she was patronizing her.*

Gareth had been initially bemused by Caroline's presence; Miranda, who strode in shortly afterwards in a whirl of expensive perfume and the glitter of diamond stud earrings, had been more direct, giving Caroline a swift, deeply unimpressed glance and asking Gareth in a tone of barely veiled incredulity if she was his new assistant. Lexy had said cheerfully that no, Caroline had actually been sent to her by Miranda's agency as a possible ghostwriter, and Miranda's double take had been so unintentionally comical that everyone had pretended it didn't happen.

After all, what are writers supposed *to look like?* Caroline wondered tetchily. *You'd think that not being glamorous would be a good thing for a ghostwriter, wouldn't you? Self-effacing, willing to bury their own personality so that they can tell someone else's story – surely that sounds like the ideal candidate for the job?*

Now, however, as every head in the room turned to look at Caroline, this argument seemed much less convincing. She felt, instead, exactly like what Lexy had said she resembled: someone who worked behind the counter of a bank, her hair the colour of a muddy river, pulled inexpertly back with a cheap plastic clip, her skin muddy too and bumpy with acne and roseacea to boot.

She wanted to sag in her chair to avoid the looks of frank concern on Miranda and Gareth's faces, the amused grin on Lexy's. Lexy was obviously not going to say anything else; she was waiting for Caroline to step up, show that she had the nerve to push for what she wanted.

And in desperation, feeling that everyone's eyes on her might as well have been the barrels of three shotguns, a question popped into Caroline's head.

What would Lexy do?

This was the first time that, prompted by panic and desperation, Caroline heard those four words challenge her for an answer. It would by no means be the last.

And the answer was simple.

Lexy would not flinch. Lexy would sit up straight in her chair, delighted that the attention was on her. Lexy would smile confidently, set her shoulders back and launch into her pitch to be taken seriously in whatever it was she wanted to achieve. After all, what had she done after her unexpected lightning strike of success on *Who's My Date*? She had taken meetings with TV executives and managed to convince them that she could parlay a single TV appearance into a whole series, to be carried entirely by her charm and quick wit.

Lexy couldn't possibly have known then that she could pull that off; she just assumed that she could. Just as Caroline should assume that she could most definitely write the Romana Clay-type book that Gareth wanted to commission. She'd have to look that term up somehow – she had the feeling that *roman à clef* wasn't spelled quite like that . . .

'I'm really excited to tell Lexy's story,' Caroline said, happy to hear that her voice was strong and confident. 'I think we'll work very well together. It's been very successful so far – we have a good rapport and she liked my writing style.'

'Right! You read her bit about me getting my bumhole waxed? It's really funny!' Lexy said enthusiastically.

Caroline was sure that Lexy was testing Miranda and Gareth to see if they would flinch at the word 'bumhole'. If so, she was disappointed. Caroline was later to find out that the pair of them represented and published many reality stars' biographies and 'novels' and that Lexy, compared to some of their other clients, was a model of articulacy and sophistication.

Instead, to Caroline's absolute delight, both Miranda and Gareth nodded in agreement.

'Loved the voice,' Gareth said. 'Very lively. I'd do some tweaking, sit down and work out the parameters, but overall yes, it was a nice little scene.'

'It certainly brought the, ah, event to life,' Miranda added drily.

'But – and I mean this kindly –' Gareth smiled at Caroline, who managed a smile back – 'there's a reason we don't commission new fiction authors based on a chapter or two. Agents need to see the whole novel, too.'

Miranda nodded.

'I was on a panel a while ago with Val McDermid, a very famous crime author,' she said. 'During the question part of the session, an aspiring writer asked us what was the key to becoming a professional writer. Before anyone else could answer, Val said: "One word. Finishing." The rest of us applauded. Do you *know* how many people, when they hear I'm an agent, tell me they've started a book and do I want to read it? I absolutely won't if it isn't already finished! Doesn't mean I'm going to read to the end, but there needs to *be* an end.'

'We have a strict timetable on this book,' Gareth chimed in. 'Ideally, it'll come out when the next series of Lexy's show premieres. And that means it needs to be written in four to five months so it can go into production. It's a quick turn-around.'

Caroline nodded, trying to look unpanicked by this; actually, she couldn't talk because of the gigantic lump which had just formed in her throat.

'Normally we need a manuscript a year in advance,' Gareth explained, aware that neither Lexy nor Caroline knew how publishing worked. 'But for celebs with books that are really time-specific, we can do a major rush job. Remember when that cat that did the swimming obstacle course won *Britain's Finest*? We got his "autobiography" out in two months. The guy wrote it in a week, start to finish, holed up in his garden shed. His boyfriend brought him food three times a day – he only left that shed to use the loo and sleep. But don't tell everyone we can do it that fast!' he added ruefully. 'I have enough trouble wrangling some of the lazy trollops who write for me to get their books in on time . . .'

'So you see the issue, Lexy,' Miranda said, pushing back her sleek blonde-streaked shoulder-length hair with both hands, a gesture that signified seriousness of intent. 'We just can't risk someone with no experience taking this on and then not delivering on time. She's an unproven quantity. I do know it was Campaspe who sent you along to see Lexy,' she said, turning to Caroline. 'She found your blog and thought it was nicely done, and Lexy was pressing her to find more ghostwriting candidates. Believe me, I ticked her off for not consulting me first.'

'Yeah, well, Caroline's here now and I like her,' Lexy said, unabashed. 'Caroline, can you write the book in four to five months?'

I'll have to quit my job, Caroline thought, petrified. *There's no way they'll give me a leave of absence. I'm not remotely important enough for that.*

But what if I can't do this book in a few months? I'll never get my job back if it doesn't work out! And even if it does, there's no guarantee I'll get more work ghostwriting. I could make a success of Lexy's book and still not have enough to pay the rent. Plus, Lexy told me in Sandbanks that she's famously tight.

She opened her mouth to admit that she couldn't manage it; that this would be a huge personal risk for her, biting off much more than she could chew.

What would Lexy do?

'I can definitely do it!' Caroline heard herself say, again in the Lexy voice – strong, confident, sure of herself. 'Though I won't be locking myself in a garden shed to do it. Apart from anything else, I haven't got one.'

Chapter Six

Caroline could not stop shaking with fear and excitement all the way home. Victoria line to Seven Sisters, overground to Edmonton Green, bus to the high street and a short walk back to the house she shared with four other 'young professionals', as the lettings agent had called them, an expression Caroline thought profoundly stupid. They weren't doctors or lawyers or anything that could be counted as a proper profession. They worked in IT, in call centres, in insurance; ironically, Caroline was considered by the housemates to have the most aspirational-sounding job, as writing press releases, even for timber firms, gave her a tenuous claim to be connected with the media.

They worked long days, commuting on three modes of transport twice a day to get to their jobs – apart from Stewart, the smug urban cyclist who did not have showers at work so washed himself with wet wipes in his office's handicapped loo, something he bitched about every single weekday on his equally sweaty return home – and, after having paid their extortionate rent and Oyster travel passes, they were left with just enough for their share of the utilities and day-to-day needs. None of them could put a penny aside to save for a down payment on a mortgage; all of them were servicing student loans, and the majority had credit card debt accrued at college to pay off too.

The dilapidated terraced house didn't even, technically, have five bedrooms. Stewart slept in what should have been the back half of the lounge, which had been divided by the landlord into two rooms, leaving the tenants the front part as an abbreviated sitting room. There was only one bathroom, small and cramped on the half-landing, because it had been located above the kitchen to keep all the plumbing close together. The saving grace was the downstairs loo. That, more than anything, meant that they were able to cope with living in such cramped quarters, especially as most of them hadn't known each other before sharing the house. They'd trickled in through Gumtree ads as one tenant left and a fresh candidate went through a humiliating interview process in order to gain the privilege of paying off someone else's mortgage on a shabby house in Zone 5 whose roof needed complete retiling.

It was seven by the time Caroline got home to Enfield Drive. Stewart and Marko and Veronika were in the lounge, watching a US comedy they were streaming from the internet. After the flat-screen TV had been cracked in an accident for which no one would take responsibility, Stewart had rigged up a projector directed onto the back wall of the room for streaming. It was effective, if you were tech-savvy enough to know how to make it work. Caroline wasn't, but she was perfectly happy to watch TV on her laptop in her bedroom, as most of them did anyway.

'I've got champagne!' she called, going past them into the kitchen, plonking down the carrier bag she had lugged back from the Tesco Express next to the bus stop. She took four chipped tumblers from the draining board and started filling them. Riz clattered downstairs and appeared in the kitchen doorway.

'We celebrating?' he said, as Caroline reached for a fifth glass. 'What's up?'

The sound of the TV show stopped abruptly as she popped the cork: Stewart, Marko and Veronika were on Riz's heels, everyone crowding into the kitchen at the offer of free alcohol. Caroline, wanting her moment of glory, waited until they all had glasses in their hands. She had given herself the actual champagne flute, the only one in the house. Holding it up, she announced:

'I'm going to write a novel with Lexy O'Brien! I'm leaving my job and writing a novel that's going to be published! Under her name, but still – published!'

As she finished, she felt the Taittinger she had drunk earlier with Lexy to celebrate turn over in her stomach, stale bubbles acid and sour at the back of her throat. It was the taste of fear.

'Oh my God!' Marko exclaimed incredulously as they all clinked glasses. 'What the actual fuck! Have you *met* her?'

'I've been to her house!' Caroline boasted. 'I've met her husband and today I went to her publishers with her and we've been drinking champagne just now to celebrate!'

'*Fuck*,' Marko said devoutly. 'I would *so* give her one.'

'Me too,' Stewart said. 'Even if she is getting on a bit. She's still well fit. Does she look like she does in her pics, Caz?'

'Even better, actually,' Caroline said, swilling down the cheap champagne. 'Her skin's amazing.'

'What about her tits?' Marko said, and sniggered immoderately.

'You guys,' Veronika said crossly, her Ukranian accent strong but her English perfect, 'you're being so rude! You should tell Caroline how cool this is – she's going to write a book!'

'Oh yeah, congrats,' Stewart and Marko chorused dutifully, as Veronika, beaming, came round the kitchen table to give Caroline a quick hug. Riz, always quiet, clinked his glass with Caroline's again, his eyes meeting hers momentarily above the rims.

'Cool,' he said. 'Def something to celebrate, yeah?'

Caroline knew exactly what he meant by that, and the champagne was very effective in speeding up the process. After finishing it off and then doing a couple of vodka shots from a bottle Marko had produced from his bedroom to 'keep the party going', a mere hour and a half later Caroline was flat on her back on her bed with Riz pumping away diligently on top of her. They usually hooked up more discreetly, well after dark; it was the first time this had happened so spontaneously, and in daylight – or at least dusk.

It had started late one night, when Riz and Caroline happened to be the only two housemates still up, streaming *Deadpool* in the lounge. The film had turned out to be much sexier than they had realized: the erotic dirty talk and sheer hotness of the two actors, plus the cheap box of wine sitting on the coffee table, had combined to form an increasing atmosphere of sexual tension. Riz had executed the time-honoured manoeuvre of putting his arm casually behind Caroline on the back of the sofa, and, not expecting this at all, she had turned to look at him in some surprise. As his face was much closer than she expected, they had started kissing rather inexpertly, almost out of reflex. After a clumsy makeout session on the sofa the projector had been switched off and, in unspoken agreement, Riz and Caroline had made their way up the stairs and into Caroline's bedroom.

Since then, the pattern had been for Riz to knock on Caroline's door a couple of nights a week at bedtime to see if she 'fancied a visit', happy to take no for an answer if she wasn't feeling like it. But she usually was. She liked sex. It connected her directly to her body in a way nothing else did; she didn't exercise, so sex was the only physical activity that had that effect. Though she would have to admit that for her it was scarcely an athletic endeavour, as ninety per cent of the time she was lying down in order to minimize the swell of her stomach.

Riz never seemed to mind their lack of inventiveness, however. He was just happy, like Caroline, to have a reliable, regular, stress-free source of sex. They had never tried to define what was happening between them, but Caroline thought of Riz as her fuck buddy, remembering the old episode of *Sex and the City* with that title.

In that episode, however, Carrie tried to have a dinner date with her fuck buddy and it turned out they had nothing to say to each other beyond sex talk. Riz and Caroline were the other way round. They had always been able to chat perfectly easily, sit and share a takeaway pizza for dinner if no one else was around. But the sex banter was non-existent. They fucked quietly, wanting, in silent consensus, to be as discreet as possible for the other housemates. When their clothes came off, the talking stopped.

Besides, Caroline reflected a little gloomily, *Carrie's fuck buddy was really hot. Flat abs, great pecs. While Riz is . . . well, he's the guy next door, literally. He'd rather sit on the sofa eating Wotsits and Ginsters pies than go to the gym.*

Caroline wasn't a hypocrite. She knew that she couldn't criticize Riz for his slightly pot belly and plumpish chest, his pimply cheeks and wispy attempt at a beard, when she herself was no hard-bodied Lexy Barbie, with a taut stomach, buns of steel and unfeasibly large breasts. Sometimes, as Riz thrust more vigorously, their stomachs rubbed against each other, sweaty flab against sweaty flab, an audible smack, a visible wobble. Riz never seemed to care, but it made Caroline mortified; when it happened, she would be taken completely out of the moment, trying desperately to suck in her gut, a line burnt into her memory ever since Janice Dickinson had shrieked it at a contestant on *America's Next Top Model*.

Though Caroline enjoyed the sex, she never came. She would take care of herself after Riz left. He always licked his fingers and paddled around between her legs dutifully before he busied himself pulling on the condom and getting down to the main event, and though that was fine, it wasn't going to bring her to any sort of climax. Caroline couldn't criticize him for that either; if she wasn't going to tell him what she wanted, how could she expect him to know? And she had always been embarrassed to articulate what she wanted in bed, partly because she wasn't quite sure what it was. She watched porn, of course, liked all kinds of scenarios, but she had never really clarified what her specific tastes were in real life . . .

Liar, a clear cold voice inside her head informed her. *You're such a liar. You know what you want! Of course you do! The truth is that you think you're lucky to be having sex at all, and you're scared that if you ask for something, the guy will get turned off and not want to fuck you any more. You're a liar and a coward and you're lazy – you lie there while a guy does all the work, you're basically encouraging him to treat you like a hole in the mattress – is that what you want?*

No, it wasn't. Not at all.

For the third time that day, she found herself asking the question that was genuinely beginning to transform her life.

What would Lexy do?

'Fuck me harder!' Caroline blurted out.

The words flew out much more loudly than she intended. Riz paused mid-thrust, his expression comically surprised.

'*Really?*' he said, sounding nervous. Clearly he did not quite trust this totally unexpected command.

'Yes!' Caroline said, dizzy with her own bravery. She was holding on to his shoulders, and she made herself look up into his face, meeting his eyes. 'Fuck me harder. And squeeze my boobs.'

'Oh, okay. Like, more porny?' he asked, sounding downright hopeful now. 'Just to make sure . . .'

'Yes! More porny!'

She arched her back, offering her breasts up towards him so there could be no doubt at all that she was giving him full consent. Caroline was lucky enough not to be one of those women who were overweight but who had comparatively small breasts; her bra size was a very respectable 38F, and Riz's hands could barely contain their fullness as he clasped them with great enthusiasm. Caroline heard herself moan, a guttural, completely uninhibited groan of sheer pleasure.

'Really squeeze them?' he asked, wanting to be absolutely sure.

'Yes!' she squealed. 'Do it, squeeze them hard and fuck me hard . . . *do it* . . .'

'*Fuck* yeah!' Riz said, starting to pump away much harder, much faster, his groin slamming into hers. It wasn't enough to make her come, but the stimulation against her clitoris was much more powerful, and Caroline's moans rose in volume.

'Like that?' he panted.

Caroline didn't bother to answer; the sounds she was making could not be misunderstood.

'This is hot!' Riz said enthusiastically. 'Hey, can I talk dirty?'

'Yes!' she managed. '*Please!*'

'I'm fucking your pussy,' Riz groaned. 'Oh yeah, I'm fucking your pussy and squeezing your tits, your big tits . . . yeah, I'm fucking you and squeezing your tits . . .'

It was neither subtle nor inspired, but it did the job. Caroline's body was heaving now as she shoved her torso up towards him, her pelvis into his, trying to maximize the contact, the wildness of the ride; she wanted him to lick and bite her nipples, maybe even pinch them, but Riz was well into his rhythm now and she didn't want to throw him off by adding extra commands.

'Fucking your pussy, your wet pussy . . .' he was chanting now.

The headboard was starting to thud against the wall, on the other side of which was Marko's bedroom. Normally Caroline would have been mortified at this clear evidence that she and Riz were having sex. She didn't know if anyone in the house knew that they hooked up every so often, but it had never been mentioned, either because the other housemates were ignorant of it, or because they preferred to turn a blind eye. Either would have been very easy to do: Riz's slow and steady pumping gently rocking the bed, his muted grunt when he came, Caroline softly whimpering in subdued pleasure, had been the sum total of the noise they made.

Now, however, they were going at it like animals. Caroline had lost all her inhibitions. Their bellies were slapping against each other noisily, their bodies were covered with sweat, and she didn't even care; she just wanted her tits squeezed and her pussy fucked hard . . .

'I'm fucking coming – shit, I'm shooting in your pussy so hard!' Riz yelled, suiting his action to his words.

Damn. It was over. She could have taken another ten minutes of this; she wanted to feel utterly worked over, her body thoroughly fucked. But it was the first time she had truly relished watching Riz's face contort, his cock buck inside her as the orgasm took him. Before, she had closed her eyes when he came, embarrassed by the sight of him losing control. Now she could tell exactly what an effect she had on him, and it made her excited. The contortions of his features, the gaping mouth, were ugly but as powerfully sensual as the hammer strokes of his groin thudding against hers with the last spasms of release.

You don't see men's faces in straight porn when they come, she realized. *Because it's made for straight men, and they don't want to see other men. They want to see the spunk dribble over the girl's face or tits. But in gay porn you can watch them come, and I've always really liked it – and now, apparently, I like it in real life too . . .*

Riz collapsed on top of her, heavy, sticky with sweat. Before, she would have thought it claustrophobic, crushing; now, she enjoyed even this too.

I did this. I made this guy limp and helpless from fucking me. It feels really, really good.

'Aah, the condom . . .' Riz complained. 'Shit, I don't want to move, but I've got to . . . sorry . . .'

Slowly, reluctantly, he rolled off her, sat up, and, carefully sliding off the condom, reached for the tissues by the bed to wipe himself off. This would be the cue, based on their previous encounters, for him to bend over, kiss her awkwardly, and say, 'Nice one,' before pulling his clothes on and returning to his own room for the night.

Now, however, he hesitated, still sitting on the edge of the mattress, his back turned to her.

'Uh, that was good,' he said tentatively.

Caroline, luxuriating in post-coital relaxation, stretched her arms back above her, her legs out, toes pointed. She had never felt sexy before, she realized. Not till this moment.

'It *was*,' she agreed.

'It was cool that you told me, you know,' Riz mumbled. 'What you wanted.'

Finally! Caroline thought, amazed at how easy it had been, at how cowardly she had been not only with Riz, but the handful of men she had had sex with before him. *Wow, what a waste of time and fucks that was!*

'You were great,' she said enthusiastically. 'You could maybe lick my nipples next time. Even bite them a bit.'

'Fuck, yeah. I could do that. You have great tits. I just didn't know if . . . I didn't want to, in case you didn't like it . . . but yeah, it was very hot to be squeezing them. It really got me off.'

Riz turned to look at her, the healthy glow in his cheeks from vigorous activity diminishing the visibility of his pimples, the light in his eyes new to her.

'Uh, I could sleep here, if you like?' he said very tentatively. 'Then we could wake up and do it tomorrow morning as well?'

Caroline didn't answer straight away, but it was not out of reluctance. She was first taken aback, then hugely flattered that Riz wanted to have sex again so soon. And then she was swept with excitement as she pictured them fucking as the grey light of dawn filtered in through her inadequate curtains. That would make waking up, for the first time in her adult life, something she actively looked forward to doing.

'But not if you don't want!' he said, misunderstanding her silence and turning away, standing up, throwing the tissues in the bin. 'Sorry – it's too much – I just thought – but if you don't fancy it—'

'No, no! You can sleep here,' Caroline said, sitting up and not even bothering to pull a sheet over her naked body to conceal her fat rolls. 'It's okay! I was just thinking that you could wake me up by, um, going down on me.'

Riz swivelled to look at her once more.

'Oh!' he said, his cheeks getting pinker. 'Yeah! I could do that. Like in the films.'

This was exactly what Caroline had been imagining. It was the scene in romantic comedies where you first saw the heroine's face in close-up, her eyes opening, looking briefly surprised before a smile blossomed on her face, the sheets pulled up to her neck; then the camera tracked down, showed the outline of a head between her legs, discreetly concealed under the sheet, as the music swelled and the camera coyly angled back upwards . . .

She was embarrassed to admit that her fantasy had such a corny origin, rather than the porn on which, in her generation, it was completely socially acceptable to base your sex life. More than that, actually: positively required, if you didn't want to seem like a total prude.

Riz didn't seem to mind the romcom scenario, however. He was picking up his T-shirt and stepping into his boxers with a grin plastered across his face.

'I'll go and shower, eh?' he said. 'So I don't pong. And then I'll get in my PJs and come back. We could maybe stream an episode of something before we go to sleep – that okay? I usually do that to get me nodding off.'

'Yeah, fine,' Caroline said; he seemed to have it all planned out. 'Um, I'll use the bathroom after you.'

'Cool. I'll bring my laptop, yeah?'

Caroline nodded. She had one too, of course, on which they could stream a show, newer and better than Riz's. But she knew how much men liked to be in charge of technology. The male housemates got genuinely upset if she or Veronika even touched the projector.

Riz shut the door quietly behind him, as if their house-mates might be disturbed by the sound, as if he and Caroline hadn't just made enough noise in the last fifteen minutes to be audible to everyone under this roof. Caroline stared at the ceiling for a moment, processing everything that had just happened. Then she jumped up and started tearing through her chest of drawers, looking for a pretty nightie she could wear to sleep in, already picturing Riz pushing up the hem and getting to work on her with his mouth the next morning. She would shower after him, trim her pubes, maybe even shave them so he wouldn't get hairs caught in his mouth. She'd slather on her Clinique Happy perfumed hand and body lotion so she smelt nice to sleep next to as well – she should put some on her hand first and lick it before she applied it anywhere near her crotch though, in case it tasted funny . . .

As she extracted from the back of a drawer a silky poly-ester strappy babydoll nightie she had owned for years, bought for a previous sort-of-boyfriend who'd never even seen her in it, because she hadn't had the nerve to present herself as overtly sexy in case he laughed at her aspirations, Caroline fretted that she might turn into a monster. All those years of pent-up desire, now surging up! She'd better be careful, she decided, not to ask too much of Riz all at once, in case she put him off . . .

But the next morning, the silky nightie balled around her waist, her hands clutching as much of Riz's hair as she could grasp, her cries of orgasm rising as Marko, woken early by the racket, started to bang on the wall in protest, no such worries preoccupied Caroline. Riz was not very experienced at giving head, but he was undeniably enthusiastic, and did not seem at all put off by the way Caroline was thrashing her crotch against the lower part of his face.

When, finally, he lifted his head, breathing hard, licking lips smeared with his saliva and her juices, he was delighted to see her roll over, grab all the pillows on the bed and raise her hips to shove them underneath her belly.

'Fuck me from behind,' she said. 'Do it hard and pull me right onto your cock.'

'Wow,' he groaned in anticipation, grabbing a condom off the bedside table and unwrapping it. 'What the fuck's *happened* to you? It's like we're in a porno all of a sudden!'

And Caroline, bare arse raised in the air, the nightie inelegantly tangled around her breasts, her face shoved in the mattress, her panting breath dampening the sheet as she waited for him to do what she had told him, not caring that her stomach had by no means been flat while he ate her out, nor that his belly was about to slap against her wide bottom with every stroke, could not have imagined any higher compliment.

Chapter Seven

Caroline had noticed very smugly that Riz had not said 'Nice one' after their morning bout either. Instead, that grin back on his face, he had wiped himself off, dropped a much more enthusiastic kiss than usual on Caroline's lips, and left her room with the words 'Congrats again on the book job, yeah? Very cool. Um . . . see you later?'

Caroline managed a nod. She was lying splayed on her mattress, her chest still heaving from their exertions. As the door closed behind him, she realized that she was shaking her head gently from side to side in sheer disbelief at how swiftly her life had changed. Yesterday she had a boring full-time job and regular bad sex. Today she was self-employed, with a book to write and, presumably, regular very satisfying sex.

Lexy's 'novel' was not going to make Caroline rich. She would be paid, Lexy had told her, five thousand pounds on delivery of a manuscript, if it were deemed of suitable quality to be published. Caroline had not noticed the flickering glance of amusement that Miranda had exchanged with Gareth on this announcement; it was common knowledge in the publishing world that if the client negotiated the ghostwriter's pay, they were much more stingy than the editor would have been.

A thousand would be advanced to Caroline as soon as she signed the contract. She had managed to negotiate travel expenses, too, after pointing out how much of her pay would otherwise be eaten up by them. Bailey and Hart had agreed to pay for a season ticket for her between London and Bournemouth for the next four to five months, plus local taxis in Bournemouth, if someone in Lexy's entourage couldn't give her a lift to and from the station.

It would be a scary few months for Caroline, living as cheaply as she possibly could, working all hours of the day and night with no assurance that she'd manage to pull off the feat of writing a novel in such a short time, and only four thousand pounds awaiting her if Gareth decided it was good enough to be published. She was anticipating doing a lot of writing on the train, as the words had flowed so freely on her initial trip to see Lexy.

At first she would be travelling to Sandbanks almost every weekday, interviewing Lexy intensively to get as much material as possible. Although Lexy had a show to film, promotional events to attend, photoshoots to do – a whole raft of her usual activities – she had committed to carving out a morning or afternoon for Caroline each day. They would also meet in London when Lexy visited for work. Frank and Lexy maintained a pied-à-terre in Chelsea Harbour, and the interviews could be conducted there.

Additionally, Lexy's manager would be sending Caroline what would probably be an avalanche of press clippings about Lexy. The book was to be a slightly fictionalized romp through Lexy's wild life and times; as many of Lexy's affairs as she was willing to spill the beans about, the birth of Laylah, the rebound into Frank's arms and the pregnancy with London. It would end triumphantly on Lexy and Frank's star-studded, very over-the-top wedding at a stately home, for which Lexy, naturally, had worn an eighteenth-century hoop-skirted dress and full powdered wig, her breasts spilling over the top of her corset.

She had made Frank wear breeches. He had not been happy, but he had done it anyway. And *Wow!* magazine had paid half a million for exclusive magazine rights to the photos, so, as Lexy had pointed out, he'd got paid plenty for it. Naturally the photographs would feature in the book, including a very tasteful black and white shot of Lexy breast-feeding one-and-a-half-year-old London after the ceremony, with one boob hoicked entirely out of the corset.

The song 'These Words' by Natasha Bedingfield started to play by the bed. For a moment Caroline, still sex-dazed, was baffled as to why, before she remembered that in her elation yesterday at having pulled off the incredible feat of being hired as Lexy's ghostwriter, she had downloaded the song on the bus home to celebrate. It was about writing, the struggle to get the right words down on paper; Caroline had sung along to it many times working on her blog. After all, it had been Bedingfeld's debut album, and both 'These Words' and 'Unwritten' had chronicled the scary and exciting process of getting her first creative project out to the world. What could possibly be more inspirational?

She grabbed for the phone and answered the call. The man on the other end of the line identified himself briskly as Jason, Lexy's manager, needing Caroline's address for the courier to send over the stack of Lexy's press clippings.

'There are boxes and boxes,' Jason said. 'And boxes. Be prepared. I'll send you the link and password to our online archives too, but Miranda told me you'll work faster going through them on paper. I'll book the courier now – that'll give you enough time to get them into your place before you meet Lexy this afternoon. She's having a facial and she wants you to go along to make notes. Says you think readers will want to read all about her beauty regime.'

'Her skin's really good,' Caroline said, feeling that Jason might mean this sarcastically. 'You realize it when you meet her. I thought her fans would be interested in—'

'Oh yes, it's a great idea!' Jason said quite unironically. 'Considering how much she drinks and smokes, it's a miracle how good she looks, trust me!'

Lexy was already at Skin3, the salon, when Caroline arrived. Caroline had taken the overground to Swiss Cottage, walking down from the Finchley Road, and the change in atmosphere during the short descent was palpable. Once she turned away from the chain stores and charity shops on the parade, the ugly 1970s council flats above them with their heavy steel doors and graffitied balconies, the architecture shifted almost immediately into huge and beautiful, wedding-cake, white-painted mansions with pillared entrances and charming modern mews-style houses, set back from the road behind tree-lined drives.

Many were as pretty as New Orleans carriage houses, with their little balconies and cascading greenery reminiscent of Louisiana Spanish moss. Caroline couldn't even imagine how many millions each house must cost, but the BMWs, Mini Cooper convertibles and Range Rover Evoques, all as gleaming as if they were fresh from the dealers' forecourts, indicated that the homeowners had considerable disposable incomes.

The Skin3 salon was very clearly the latter rather than the former, its facade sleek and expensively designed, transparent glass with pops of deep pink and white, intended to both attract and reassure its female clients. *Look*, it said, *how smooth and clear I am! This is what your skin will look like once you step through these doors and let my skilled beauticians go to work on you!* Ranks of cosmetics and creams were arranged in illuminated recesses inside the salon; lavish orchids stood in an elegant vase on a side table. Beside the flowers were two jugs of water, one full of lemon slices, one of cucumber, the pale yellow and green refreshing against the pink and white of the salon. And on a smart grey sofa Lexy, wearing a cashmere onesie, was holding court.

'So I said, I don't care if her clothes are all classy now, I remember her back in the day with the fake boobs and the fake hair and the fake voice – 'cause she can't sing and she knows it – and for all those tabloid pics of them playing Happy Families with their kids, that husband of hers's been shagging around for*ever*. And not just with the ladies either, like she wants to make you think!' she was saying to a couple of beauty therapists, who were giggling at Lexy's salacious gossip.

The therapists were young, very pretty and utterly intimidating. Skincare employees at department stores could look eerily perfect, but Caroline could always console herself that they had plastered on so much make-up that morning that it was impossible to tell what they really looked like. With the Skin3 beauticians, however, that excuse wouldn't work. Their skin was, magically, both luminous and matte, which seemed impossible until you saw it for yourself; and they were wearing very minimal make-up.

Additionally, they were both very slim and immaculate, with elegant dark uniforms and smooth hair. Caroline could only be grateful that she had the memory of the excellent sex she had had that morning to bolster her confidence. If not, with her self-consciousness about her skin and weight issues, it would have been very hard for her to feel that she had any right to be in a place like this.

'Oh hey, Caroline!' Lexy said as her ghostwriter entered. 'Don't get comfy, I'm just getting up. You wanted to see what I do to get my skin all glowy and gorgeous, yeah? Well, brace yourself. You've never seen anything like this before, trust me.'

'Lexy was just telling us about the book you're writing together,' one of the young women said, smiling at Caroline. Her eyes were wide-set, her nose delicate and with a slight ski-jump tilt at the tip: she looked like a Disney princess. 'Hi, I'm Davina. It's so exciting. I really wish I could write.'

'Caroline writes *amazing* filthy stuff,' Lexy said gleefully, standing up and reaching for her Birkin bag. 'You wouldn't think it to look at her, but she's got a dirty, dirty mind. The book's going to be scorchio.'

'Ooh, that sounds brilliant!' the other young woman said. 'I can't wait to read it! I'm Eva, by the way.'

She held out her hand for Caroline to shake.

'I do Lexy's treatments,' she said. 'Feel free to ask me anything you want about them for the book – I'm more than happy to answer any questions you have. Lexy asked me to tell you what I'm doing as we go along.'

As Eva led Lexy and Caroline downstairs to a treatment room, Caroline was given yet another lesson on how the top one per cent lived. She had, with online discount vouchers, bought plenty of facials in an attempt to tame her rosacea and her period spots. But she was used to cut-price high-street salons, decorated with cheap flock wallpaper in baroque curlicues of silver, black and fuchsia; so cramped that you had to wriggle past a drying rack of towels imperfectly concealed behind a screen if you needed to use the tiny, not very clean loo; the treatment rooms narrow and partitioned by MDF sliding doors which swung and rattled loudly in their cheap channels every time they were opened or closed.

None of the facials, unsurprisingly, had worked. But she could see why. They had been the Poundland version of the beauty salon world, while this was Harvey Nichols. Its white paint was immaculately clean, its walls hung with huge black and white photographs of women's flawless faces; outside each treatment room was a bud vase affixed to the wall, each filled with a single perfect yellow rose. The bed in the room into which Eva ushered Lexy was not a rickety massage table with a flimsy paper cover and a lone towel which was never big enough to cover both boobs and bum if you were getting a full-body treatment.

No, this looked like an actual, proper single bed, the kind you got in First Class airline seats – white leather, with wide adjustable arms. It was made up with a dark grey bottom sheet, with matching towels laid on top; it had not only a proper pillow, but an actual duvet, all in the same elegant shade of charcoal. Caroline's eyes were wide. A *duvet*! She couldn't begin to imagine how much all of this would cost. And when Eva started Lexy's facial, explaining to Caroline the scientific research behind the salon's approach, the reasons for the various supplements Lexy took daily, Caroline realized that she should have brought a Dictaphone, or whatever recording device journalists used. This was the Rolls-Royce of beauty regimes, and there was simply too much information for her to process, even making frantic notes. She had been going to buy one for her interviews with Lexy; she'd bring it back next time Lexy visited Skin3.

Eva put a heating pad behind Lexy's neck for extra comfort; she cleansed and moisturized Lexy's face and décolletage; she applied terrifying-looking twin oversized plastic forks the size and shape of salad servers, attached by wires to a machine she wheeled out from a built-in cupboard, to Lexy's neck and lower face.

'This is our Precision Lift treatment,' she said, pinching the forks onto what would be jowls if Lexy had them. 'It's a microcurrent therapy called CACI, originally developed to treat facial palsy – you know, after a stroke your face gets saggy on one side? They worked out they could bring back muscle tone by running microcurrents on the saggy bits. Lots of cosmetic improvements come from medical innovations, actually. We call it a non-surgical facelift – lots of ladies get it because they'd rather tone up than get plastic surgery. We really promote alternatives to that here.'

'Doesn't it hurt?' Caroline was unable to resist asking, watching the forks dig into another section of jawline.

'Like buggery,' Lexy said, as best she could with the forks deep in her skin. 'But that's how you know it's working. I don't know why they say "Like buggery", eh? That's *much* more fun!'

Caroline and Eva both sensibly decided not to respond to this last statement, though Caroline scribbled it down so that she could use it for the book; it was so very Lexy.

'And you can feel the current going through?' Caroline asked.

'*Oh* yeah. It buzzes a lot.' Lexy produced a little giggle. 'She's got no idea what's coming next, does she, Eva? Hope she doesn't freak out!'

Eva smiled, a perfect professional smile; she was clearly used to Lexy's teasing ways. The CACI treatment completed, the machine was returned to the cupboard and Eva started to mix up a facial mask, thick and gelatinous. To Caroline's amazement, Eva applied this to Lexy's entire face and neck. Eyes vanished entirely under the viscous white substance, as did lips, till only Lexy's nostrils were visible. Caroline felt a palpable sense of panic on Lexy's behalf, which only increased when Eva wheeled out a second machine, and, incredibly, attached electrodes on clips to the edge of the mask, which had already jellified enough for this to be feasible.

'The current drives the nutrients in the mask much deeper into the lower layers of the skin, where they're really needed. We use very fresh Vitamin A and C, plus anti-oxidants,' Eva told Caroline. 'This will stimulate her collagen production and increase her hydration, making her skin much smoother. Without the machine to force those nutrients into the lower dermis, it's all just cosmetic. You get a nice glow for the day, but that's all it achieves.'

Caroline heaved a sigh.

'That's exactly what happened when I had facials. I looked nice and shiny afterwards, but my spots never got any better,' she said gloomily.

'Nothing that you can get over the counter or in a beauty salon will make a difference deep down where the skin needs it,' Eva explained, now massaging Lexy's arm with long flowing strokes. When she had had facials, Caroline had always been left alone in the room while the face mask sank in, but this, again, was not a discount voucher beauty treatment. Clients were tended to every moment they were in the treatment room.

'That's why our clients take their vitamins and omegas every day,' she added. 'We treat the skin from inside and outside. It's called Feed, Fortify, Finish.'

As Caroline scribbled this down, the machine beeped. Eva unfastened the electrodes, took hold of one side of the mask and lifted the whole thing off in one smooth go. It had set to a rubbery consistency now, like something from a science fiction film, the underside moulded to Lexy's features. Eva disposed of it and started working a light oil into Lexy's face to finish off.

'Hey, Eva,' Lexy said once this was done, 'while I'm getting dressed, why don't you take Caroline upstairs and give her the skin consultation? Then she can write about that for the book, too.'

The consultation entailed Caroline sticking her face into a light-filled machine so that her skin could be scanned and photographs could be taken of the condition of her dermis. Then she had to look at one terrifying scan after another covered with ominous-looking coloured dots, and be told by the lovely and smooth-skinned Eva about the bacteria and lack of hydration that was adversely affecting her rosacea and period acne. This was particularly hard as she knew there was nothing she could do about it; the treatments Lexy had just undergone, with all the expensive machines and gadgets, were far beyond the reach of a self-employed ghost-writer who had to live on a thousand pounds for four to five months and would have to negotiate an overdraft to cover her rent and food, as her meagre savings certainly wouldn't cover those expenses . . .

As Lexy came upstairs again, Eva slipped away to do her make-up. Caroline remained in the consultation room, filling her notepad with information for the book. After all, Lexy sold herself so much on her appearance. There were photoshoots and press launches for which she wore eye-grabbing costumes and hairdos for the rollout of each of her new products; modelling gigs for her various clothing lines; spreads in weekly gossip magazines; endless pap photos in the dailies and tabloids and gossip sites; videos for her You-Tube vlogging channel.

And in all of these Lexy needed to look wonderful, her skin smooth and glowing, her hair thick and glossy. Her fans and haters alike pored over her images, eagerly dissecting them, both ripping her apart and getting tips on how to dress, how to do their own hair and make-up like hers.

Brands she talked about on social media saw instant spikes in their internet traffic: Caroline knew it was Jane Iredale make-up Eva was applying to Lexy because she had seen Lexy enthusing about it repeatedly on her Instagram. Clothes from Lexy's brand sold out instantly if she was photographed wearing them.

'Oi, Caroline!'

Lexy's head popped round the corner of the room. Caroline blinked. Lexy's skin, post-BB cream, hydrating spray and powder, was even more eerily perfect than usual.

'Davina's had a cancellation,' Lexy announced. 'Aren't you the lucky one? I said you should take the appointment. My treat,' she added before Caroline could panic at how much this would cost her.

Caroline was struck dumb with shock and gratitude. She was to learn that this kind of impulsive gesture was typical of Lexy. As she had already told Caroline, she was very tight, quite happy to take a quarter-million advance on her book while only paying the ghostwriter who would actually do the work a tiny five-grand flat fee, with no percentage of any royalties that might be earned.

The flip side of her fierce economizing, however, was an impulse to spontaneous generosity. This had been suppressed during the years she'd been building her career, fighting her way ruthlessly up the ladder, refusing to be just a flash in the pan, the latest pretty face/pair of tits combo, to be discarded after a few years by the media as fresher female meat came along.

Now, however, having heard the wistfulness in Caroline's voice as she commented on her facials not having done anything for her, seeing Caroline's bumpy rosacea cheeks and the scarring on her chin from past acne breakouts, Lexy had yielded to her better instincts. She was pleased to see Caroline's flush of happiness, her smile of delight; it was very pleasant to be generous, but it was even more rewarding to see the recipients showing gratitude.

Caroline was stammering a fervent '*Thank* you!' as Lexy carried on:

'Oh yeah, and why don't you get a train down tomorrow morning and bring a suitcase? You could stay in the guest suite for a few days. We can do tons of work, you get an inside view of the whole setup, kids and all – what do you say? It'd turbo-charge getting started on the book, yeah?'

'I – yes – that sounds—'

'Frank's around tomorrow,' Lexy swept on. 'If you text me to let me know what train you're on, he can pick you up. And bring a swimsuit. We've got a pool, sauna, Jacuzzi, rainforest shower with colour change, the works. You might as well make the most of it. There's a gym too, if you fancy working out.'

I am never, ever, ever wearing a swimsuit around Lexy, was Caroline's first thought. But her second, and the one that made her feel hot all over, was:

Oh my God – Frank! If he saw me in my swimsuit I think I'd genuinely drop dead from mortification!

And that image hit her with a positive flash of self-revelation, a white light illuminating a hidden corner of her subconscious. She was forced to admit to herself that while she and Riz had been fucking yesterday and today, the image she had seen whenever she closed her eyes had not been slightly pudgy, palest brown, sparse-bearded Riz. It had been golden-pecan-skinned, curly-haired, taut-muscled Frank.

Lexy's husband. The man she was going to be sharing a car with tomorrow, making conversation as best she could, smelling his aftershave . . . whose house she would be staying in, who she might – God help her! – see in the gym sweating as he pounded the treadmill, as he lifted weights or did lengths in the pool, effortlessly levering himself out from the deep end with his strong upper body, drops of water pouring from his muscled frame . . .

Caroline closed her eyes briefly, telling herself to get a grip. She knew, of course, that she was quite safe. Frank wouldn't glance her way for a moment. She could indulge herself in fantasies as much as she wanted without any fear that she would get into trouble for flirting with her boss's husband.

Even if Lexy guesses how much I fancy him, she thought sadly, *I won't get the sack – she'd laugh her head off instead. She'd think it was hilarious that a spotty chubster like me would have a crush on her gorgeous husband.*

Flicking through her notes, making sure that everything was committed to paper before she had her facial and completely zoned out, Caroline read the scribble of Lexy joking about buggery being fun, and another image flashed vividly before her eyes: Riz, doing precisely that, as she smushed her face against a pillow and imagined it was Frank kneeling on the bed behind her.

Riz, she reflected, wasn't going to *believe* his luck when she got back to Edmonton that evening.

Chapter Eight

Want to know how Frank and I met? He gets really embarrassed when I tell this story, but that's Frank, so fuck it. He gets embarrassed by tons of stuff anyway and if I worried about that I'd never tell anybody anything! So, I was on Twitter just messing around and this fan tweeted me with 'Hey, did you know that Frank Callis fancies you?'

Frank's not on Twitter, obviously. He's the least chatty person ever. So though they hashtagged him in the tweet he didn't see it or anything. But they posted a link – apparently some journo from the Sun *asked him who his celebrity crush was and he said me. I've got a suspicion that he was hoping I might hear about it – Frank would never normally tell a journo who he fancied, he's very private!*

Now, here's something I've found out over the years to get a bloke interested in you. Trust me on this. It works. If you're crushing on someone, and you don't look like the backside of a bus, tell some of your mates that you fancy him. It's bound to get back to him, and when it does, he'll think: 'Oh, really? I wouldn't mind giving that a go!' It's human nature to sit up a bit when you hear that someone likes you and think: 'Well, what about it then?'

I must admit that Frank hadn't been on my radar. I usually go for the more outgoing types. Ones who are naughty like me, if you know what I mean. I knew his name, of course, but I couldn't give a shit about sport, which is ironic considering how many footballers and basketball players I've been out with.

Oh, talking about that, here's another bit of advice: if you're going out with men who play sport for a living, but you don't watch it, don't fake it and be all, 'Oh I thought the ref was really out of order with you on Saturday' or, 'They should've been playing 4-4-2' or anything like that. I've seen endless girls do this to suck up and try to show that they'll be good girlfriend or wife material, but trust me, the guys can smell it from a mile away. They might fuck you but they'll take the piss out of you behind your back. It's much better to go, 'Hey, I don't know WTF you do apart from the fact that the ball needs to go into the net, but show me those ripped abs again, why don't you?'

Anyway, I googled Frank and I liked what I saw. He was a bit different, and to be honest I thought I needed a total change from Jamal. God, Jamal was a massive slag. He couldn't keep his dick in his pants for longer than thirty seconds and he partied so hard he made me look like an amateur – trust me, that's not easy! Going after Frank wasn't a big deal. I didn't think, Oh yay, this guy is my future husband, which is just common sense. I've known girls picturing the ring before they even shag the guy, and it never ends well.

I'd've tweeted him, started flirting, but like I said, Frank and social media are like carbs and bikinis, you know? They just don't go together. And honestly I had my hands full with a few other guys . . . But a couple of months later I was at this launch for a new restaurant – I'm not going to name it because the drinks were rubbish and the VIP area was a fucking joke, so I'm not going to give them publicity – and guess who was there too! So I rolled up to him from behind, pinched his bum and went, 'Hey, sexy, I read in the Sun *that you fancy me! When are you taking me out?'*

His bum was amazing. Like that bit from Blackadder – *'Ooh, Nursie, I like 'em firm and fruity'. And then he turned round and frankly – haha – I was a bit dumbstruck, and that never bloody happens. He's taken, so don't all you bitches start getting ideas, but Frank is so gorgeous in person, you have no idea. I'd've done him then and there if he'd been up for a leg-trembler in the loos.*

But that's not Frank at all. He's a serious person. I had to practically drag him to bed on the third date. And as it turned out, serious was exactly what I needed to balance me out. I'm a party girl, he's a family man. I like clubs and parties, he likes the sofa at home and his kids around him.

Trust me, my team was over the fucking moon about me getting together with Frank! Jason, my manager, had been banging on about my reputation ever since I got knocked up by Jamal. I was all, 'Look, Jason, you're being sexist, it's a modern world and I don't have to get married to have a baby', but he'd get all snappy and say I was wrong and that a male celeb who puts it about gets flack from the papers too. Sponsors want someone with a pretty wife and a couple of kids.

'Look at David Beckham,' Jason said. 'He had an affair years ago, no one liked that, and now he's repositioned and rebranded himself as a devoted family man. He even had a

baby daughter after the affair to show his wife's forgiven him. Plus Victoria's a career woman now, which makes him a modern husband supporting his partner's ambitions. You've got to think differently now you've got a kid.'

The way Jason put it, everyone was okay with me having lots of notches on my bedpost when I didn't have Laylah. My fans really enjoyed seeing what I was up to and reading all the hot gossip in my column – who's a selfish wham-bam-that's-me-done-ma'am shagger, who's hung like a dormouse, who can do it five times a night and still wake up in the morning with a big smile and a tent in the sheets. But now I've got a little girl, people aren't so keen on pap shots of me staggering out of nightclubs at three a.m., falling into limos with my skirt round my waist, some guy I only met that night getting in with me. I mean, I can see it's not exactly the best image for a mum.

It took a while to sink in, though. At the time I got pissed off and said: 'Laylah's being very well looked after and that's no one's business but mine,' but Jason went, 'Well yeah but you want more kids, don't you? Sooner rather than later? And what if it doesn't work out with the next guy, and the next – d'you really want to be a three-by-three or a four-by four?'

Pretty harsh. But I don't keep Jason around because he's warm and cuddly. That whole four-by-four thing's scary – for anyone who's been living under a rock, it means having four kids by four different dads. I can sort of see how three could be possible, but four's just bloody sloppy.

And Jason was right. I did want more kids, and it's not exactly fun dealing with your daughter's dad not being around. So here comes Frank, getting on with Laylah like a *house on fire, telling me after a month he was in love with me, making it clear he wanted kids – just what the doctor ordered. Time to settle down – plus, I could throw a huge, over-the-top wedding, get a ton of sponsors for it and sell the photos to a weekly for a massive great whacking sum.*

And don't go thinking I was conning Frank! He knew who I was right from the start. I didn't pretend to be a reformed character or promise that I'd never go out clubbing again once that wedding ring was on my finger. Actually, I sat down with him and went, 'Look, if you're taking me on, you know I'm always going to want to do my reality show and a ton of appearances for publicity, that's never going to change.' He was okay with being on the show, as long as he didn't have to do anything embarrassing – he said he was on TV anyway, so it wasn't a big deal.

He said he wanted to live in Sandbanks, not London, and I was okay with that. It's not like we can't afford a driver or anything. But of course we got a place in town and I need to spend a lot of time there, what with everything I've got on – meetings for my product ranges, promo stuff, shopping and yeah, going out to launches and premieres and seeing my mates. After all, I've got a rock-solid husband at home now with the kids, so who cares if I go out with the girls every so often and let my hair down?

Well, Frank does, unfortunately. He's not over the moon about my staying over in London – he keeps saying it's not every so often, but all the flipping time. He wants to get a dog or two to keep him company, but I've put my foot down on that. I know him. If he gets the pair of golden Labs he keeps banging on about, he'll spend all his free time walking them on the beach, use them as an excuse never to go up to London with me for charity auctions, awards shows, red-carpet dos – he just doesn't get that we need to be photographed together at that kind of thing!

Plus, he wants more kids, ASAP, and he keeps nagging on about getting started. I must admit I did make a promise on that one – I said we'd try for a houseful. But I ate like a starving pig when I was knocked up with London and I'm still not ready to go through that slog of diet and exercise and How I Got My Bikini Body Back photos for the tabs again quite yet . . .

Caroline stopped, staring at what she had just written. What was she *thinking*? Where on earth was she going with this? For starters, the book was supposed to stop at Lexy and Frank's triumphant wedding, not cover their marriage at all. Today's writing session had started out really well, with a flow like a river in spate; it was out of sequence, of course, a section that would come towards the end of the book. But Caroline had already learned that it was best to let Lexy talk about whatever subject she wanted to that day; that was how she came out with the most personal, revealing information, like her fear of turning into a three-by-three or a four-by-four.

God knew what Lexy would think of that particular line when she read it over. But over the fortnight that she had been working on the book, Caroline had discovered that her employer did not react badly when faced with her own words turned into prose. Lexy was no hypocrite. She wouldn't deny that she'd said something shocking or self-revelatory after knocking back plenty of white wine with a slice of lemon: at the worst, she would comment, with an easy shrug: 'Cut that bit. My fans won't like it.'

Well, her fans certainly wouldn't appreciate Lexy confessing that she was refusing her husband both the kids and the dogs he wanted! Additionally, this information had not all originated with Lexy. Although Caroline was not interviewing Frank for the book, she had already forged a rapport with him. The cook/housekeeper prepared lunch every day for the household at one, and when Caroline knew Frank would be at home that day, she made a point of setting her alarm twenty minutes before so that she could put on some make-up, brush her hair, apply some eau de toilette, before heading down for, hopefully, a rendezvous with him.

That was by no means the only time they spent together, however. As Caroline was staying there during the week to make a push on the novel, she had already shared a pizza with him and the kids several times on the nights that Lexy was out in London. And, chatting over lunch, or clearing up as the nanny put the kids to bed, it was very natural that Frank should mention his wish to expand his family and get a couple of dogs, fill the house with activity, have his wife home more than a few nights a week . . .

Caroline pushed back her chair and stood up. She needed to reset her brain, get Frank's perspective out of it and Lexy's back in. Crossing the living room of her suite, she stopped in front of the picture window, staring out at the breathtaking view. The chainlink ferry that crossed between the Sandbanks peninsula and the Studland nature reserve on the other side of the narrow mouth of Poole Harbour was making its way over to their side of the water, the clanking noise of its mechanism now so familiar to Caroline that she no longer noticed it. Far out to sea, a much larger boat was heading away from the English coast, making for one of the Channel Islands or for Cherbourg. It was beautiful, hypnotic, the sight of the ferries voyaging back and forth as fishing boats, sailing yachts and motorboats wove around them in a slow, gracious saraband.

In high season, Frank had told Caroline, she would be amazed at how full the waters around the coastline became, how packed the beaches were. But it was early spring, still chilly, and the sea was more steel-grey than blue. The sandy shores of the nature reserve, across the harbour mouth, were only sparsely populated by dog walkers and the occasional jogger.

That should be me, Caroline thought suddenly. *I should be out there every day, getting fit. Toning up. Losing weight. I need a break from work anyway. I've obviously got onto the wrong track . . .*

Before she could talk herself out of it, she went into the bedroom and pulled on her trainers. Though she had bought them at Sports Direct, she had never actually used them for any form of exercise; she had no idea if they were even running shoes. But if she could walk in them, maybe she could run in them too? God knew she wouldn't last long at it!

Caroline was already wearing tracksuit bottoms and a loose T-shirt. Perfect exercise wear: ironic again that she was dressed for it, that nowadays everyone wore loose-waisted exercise gear while rarely using it for the purpose for which it was intended. But it meant that she couldn't delay by making excuses about not having clothes in which she could work out. Grabbing a fleece top and some change for the chainlink ferry ticket, she made her way from the guest suite along the corridor to the main wing of the house and down the central staircase.

As she came down the stairs, Frank was crossing the hallway, fresh from a vigorous workout session in the basement gym. He was lightly sheened with sweat, his curls damp; his pecs, delineated by his tightly clinging Under Armour T-shirt, were swollen and pumped, the nipples pointed. He must have been lifting weights. Caroline stopped in her tracks, clinging to the rail of the staircase for support at the sight of Frank's body so very clearly outlined by his tight workout gear, the healthy flush on his tawny skin.

'Hey!' he said with a friendly smile, pulling off the towel round his neck and wiping his face down with it. 'You going out?'

Caroline hesitated. With Frank standing in front of her, a perfect physical specimen, she was embarrassed to admit what she was planning. It was like a five-year-old informing Albert Einstein that she had just learned how to add two plus two.

Ooh, she thought, *that's a nice little line! I should remember that!*

She was finding, after a fortnight of doing very little else but eat, sleep and write, that clever one-liners or observations kept popping into her head, funny little comparisons that were perfect for the book. It was as if she had been tuning up an engine she'd rarely used before, working it, oiling it, so that it ran more and more smoothly, turning over by itself now without help, throwing off creative sparks.

'I was going to go for a run,' she blurted out.

'That's great!' Frank's eyes lit up. 'Good for you! I didn't know you ran, Caroline.'

'I don't,' she admitted. 'It's my first time.'

'Wow. Brilliant. Are you going to use the treadmill?'

'No. I'm going over to Studland so I can run along the sand.'

Frank's heroic effort to keep his face straight made her heart sink to the soles of her cheap trainers.

'Don't put me off!' she heard herself begging. 'I want to do this! I've got it into my head and if I don't go and do it now, I might never manage it!'

'I got it,' Frank said gravely, draping the towel around his neck again. 'Okay, can I give you two pieces of advice?'

'Um, yeah. But please don't scare me . . .'

Caroline was fidgeting like a restless horse, wanting to get going before she lost her nerve.

'Stretch your calves a lot before and after,' Frank said, walking over to the front door and gesturing to her to follow him. 'You can hang off the edge of the stairs on the ferry going over and coming back. Have you got a watch?'

Caroline shook her head. Frank unfastened his own and handed it to her.

'Walk fast for five minutes to warm up,' he instructed. 'Run thirty seconds, walk for two minutes, repeat. Try to do that for half an hour if you can. If you need to run for a shorter time, okay, but make sure you alternate actual running with the walking, even if you only manage a few steps. Then walk for at least fifteen minutes afterwards, as slow as you want, to cool your muscles down and stop lactic acid buildup. Can you keep all of that in your head?'

Caroline nodded.

'And when you get back, come and find me and we'll get

you stretched,' Frank finished, crossing the hall to open the door for her like the gentleman he was.

Yeah, that is not going to happen, Caroline thought, even as she smiled at him and stepped outside into the fresh, cool spring air. *No way is Frank getting his hands on my bulgy, sweaty, post-exercise body.*

She walked briskly along the pavement of the curving road towards the tip of the spit of land where the Ferry Hotel stood next to the sloping dock of the ferry. Lexy was fond of unleashing her wit on the subject of the hotel, which she felt, considering how smart Sandbanks was, needed a full revamp; she described it with great relish as 'Fawlty Towers designed by Travelodge'.

The ferry was coming in, a local bus sitting on its deck; it was still amusing to Caroline to see a double-decker being ferried across the water. A line of cyclists in tight Lycra and cleated shoes had formed already, waiting on the dock, ready to ride a big loop around the nature reserve. Caroline followed them onboard and obeyed Frank's instructions, putting her toes on one step and hanging her heels down below to lengthen her calf muscles. Then she did a stretch she'd seen runners perform, standing on one leg, grabbing the heel of the other and pushing it as tightly into her buttock as she could.

She felt the pull at the front of her thighs, one after the other, and was pleased with herself. She could do this. She was ready. She was going to time herself just as Frank had suggested. After all, how hard could it be to run for just thirty seconds at a stretch, with a generous two-minute walk to recover each time? The watch was heavy in the pocket of her tracksuit bottoms, still warm from his body. She had heroically resisted the urge to lift it to her nose and sniff Frank's sweat on the leather strap. She was a grown-up woman out for a run, not some stupid teenager crushing on a married man.

The links of the chain groaned heavily, pulling taut as the ferry reached the far side of the harbour mouth. The cyclists pedalled off down the road; the beach was right there, on the far side of a low sandy wall. In a few steps Caroline was on the sand, walking briskly to warm up. She could *totally* do this.

Only a few minutes later, she knew that she couldn't. Not at all. Merely walking fast left her breathless, and by the time it came to running she was panting like a dog. The wind whipped slices of sand off the top of the beach and drove them into her face as if she were moving across the Sahara in a scirocco. It made it even harder to catch her breath, because every time she breathed in she inhaled grains of sand with the salty air.

Additionally, it had dawned on her almost immediately that she had entirely failed to consider the issue of adequate support for her breasts. Even in her full-coverage bra, they were bouncing around like a pair of melons in a thin mesh bag. It was so uncomfortable that she had to press them to her chest with her hands to stop them moving as much as possible, her palms not big enough to contain them, their sheer weight making her realize how much excess flesh she was carrying around, why it was so hard for her to move fast.

Not being able to use her arms to help propel her forward made jogging even more difficult. In no time at all, Caroline was both winded and coughing.

No wonder Frank had been trying to control his expression! She had seen people on TV shows running with seemingly effortless ease along Santa Monica Beach, barefoot, hair blowing in the wind, but the reality was slogging along as if wading through mud, her feet dragging, the flanges on the bottoms of her trainers struggling to work free with every step. The thirty seconds of running slowed down to twenty, the two minutes of walking lengthened to three, then four. Whenever the inexorable watch display told her it was time to run again, she wanted to cry with sheer misery.

To add insult to injury, the beach was much harder to traverse than it looked from the far side of the water. It was impossible simply to run, or walk, along it. Rivulets of water remaining from high tide trailed from the low dunes right down to the water's edge, wide enough in many places to make it impossible for Caroline to jump over the broad gullies. She had to go right up to the dunes, hop and skip around the channels and puddles of water, the effort truly painful when she was running and needed to keep moving. She knew, from the way other people on the beach tactfully averted their gazes, that she looked ridiculous. A chubby madwoman, holding her own chest, clumsily trying to ford the pools of standing water at a stumbling run.

Eventually she noticed a little path rising up through the thick grass of the dunes. At least that would be easier to run on than a deep layer of sand that yielded beneath her feet and made every step much harder to manage. Chest heaving, every breath by now a sharp wheeze of agony, she scrambled painfully up the side of the dune and found herself in front of a mauve-painted stake in the ground with a small sign on it indicating that it was a 'heather path'.

Alas, the heather path brought its own set of challenges. Yes, the terrain was much easier to run on, but the path was so narrow and bumpy that her feet kept getting caught in the grass that bordered it. She was terrified of twisting an ankle, having to limp back to the ferry landing, her first attempt at exercise ending in utter humiliation . . .

The intervals of jogging became speed-walking, and the walking itself slowed practically to a standstill. She had turned around to retrace her route when she was about half-way, but she hadn't calculated for the fact that she was moving so much more slowly now. The fifteen minutes of cool-down stretched into thirty, maybe even more; she couldn't bear to look at the watch, to fully take in how long she had been lumbering through this landscape of waist-high heather in bloom, the wind turning the grasses into a rippling sea. It seemed to take forever for the road which led to the ferry landing to come into view.

Caroline knew she shouldn't stop moving. Frank had mentioned the lactic acid issue. So she shifted from one foot to another repeatedly while waiting for the ferry, as if she had drunk too much Red Bull and couldn't stand still. Her entire lower body felt as if it had been beaten with hammers, her lungs were on fire, and a glimpse of herself in the wing mirror of a lorry waiting to drive on board showed that her face was both turkey red and sallow in unattractive patches. Her hips were aching badly, and when she made it off the ferry at the Sandbanks side she found herself limping back to Lexy and Frank's mansion as gracelessly as if she had advanced osteoporosis, fighting the urge to burst into tears at how out of shape she was.

It took her last shred of energy to climb the marble stairs that led up to the front door, leaning heavily on the balustrade. Her only hope was that she could get back to her room and into the shower before Frank could see the state she was in.

So when the front door swung open as she was fumbling for her keys, she screamed in shock and clapped her hands to her face in a vain attempt to shield her ugly blotched skin, dripping with sweat, from the sight of the man about whom she was now fantasizing on a nightly basis.

Chapter Nine

'It's an ambush!' Frank said, beaming. 'I didn't trust you to come back and stretch on your own!'

He had showered and changed into jeans and a V-neck sweater, worn without a T-shirt underneath, the scent of ferns and bergamot from his body wash rising from his warm golden skin.

'I feel so awful,' Caroline whimpered. 'I can't breathe and I'm all sweaty.'

'Great – that means you really did it – you went for it! Good girl! Go have a quick shower and put on something loose. Even pjs are fine if you don't have a change of workout gear. I'll wait for you in the gym to show you some basic stretches, otherwise you'll stiffen up like a piece of board. I'll give you fifteen minutes. Don't make me come up there and get you!'

Only a man as well-intentioned and as much in love with his own wife as Frank could have threatened, even jokingly, to haul a young woman staying in his house out of her own bedroom. He stood back and watched her crossing the hall to the lift, looking back in mortification to say:

'I can't go up the stairs . . . it hurt so much coming up the entrance ones . . .'

Frank threw back his head and laughed, a full-throated laugh that held no hint of mockery.

'We've all been there!' he said reassuringly. 'Feel like you've got iron rods shooting up into your bum cheeks every time you take a step?'

'That's *exactly* what it feels like,' she said as the lift doors opened.

'Don't worry,' Frank said. 'We're going to stretch out your glutes. It'll really help. And I can teach you how to do it on your own after a run if I'm not around.'

Caroline was horrified at the sight of herself in the bathroom mirror. She did cry a little as she stripped off her sodden clothes. The mottling on her face reached down her neck all the way to her collarbones, and her hair had frizzed up unattractively. She looked like a madwoman, a bag lady, and the fact that her bra, under extreme stress, had partially given up the struggle to support her breasts only added to that impression. At least she could change into a fresh one after the shower, and she tightened the straps to pull her boobs as high as was feasible . . .

'Okay!' Frank said, as she limped out of the lift and into the gym. 'You're in pain, but that's fine. It's normal. No pain, no gain. We just have to minimize it as much as we can, and work on your flexibility so you don't tear anything. You're bound to stiffen up, and that's where you're most at risk of damaging yourself. Let's start with that glute stretch.'

Caroline promptly found herself lying on her back on an exercise mat, the ankle of one leg crossed over the knee of the other, the leg folded as if in a half-lotus yoga position; her other foot was resting high up on Frank's thigh, pressing firmly into it as he stood in front of her. Her foot was close enough to his crotch that she couldn't even look at it; Frank had anchored it there without a hint of embarrassment, as befitted a professional sportsman who had spent decades being stretched out by a whole bevy of coaches and physios.

'Okay,' he said cheerfully. 'I'm going to lean in. I want you to take the stretch in your bum and hip as much as you can bear it. If it goes into your knee, tell me and we'll back off. Knee bad, bum good. Got it?'

'Yes,' Caroline said in a tiny voice, staring at her own boobs to avoid looking at him.

Frank started to walk a little forward and she realized exactly what he had meant. As his thigh pressed harder against her foot, the buttock of that leg was forced further downwards, into the mat, and the fibres of its gluteal muscles, which had tautened up with the effort of walking and running on damp sand, were required to stretch out again. The hip joint screamed in pain as it opened up.

'Ow!' she yelled.

'Bum or knee?' Frank said mercilessly.

'Bum,' she admitted, wishing she had the nerve to lie.

He kept going. She wailed. He stopped, but held the position, letting her body, which had tensed up against the pain of the stretch, adjust, realize that it wasn't going to rip apart, let it happen.

'Breathe in,' he said. 'Then breathe out loudly.'

It was a trap. He was a bastard. As soon as she exhaled, he pushed a little further, and to her horror, Caroline heard a stream of curses, mostly 'fucks', pouring from her mouth at the pain of the stretch.

Frank laughed again, his hands on his hips for balance.

'Like I said, we've all been there!' he said cheerfully. 'And I've heard everything, don't you worry! Some of the lads make death threats to their physios, turn the air blue. You swear as much as you want – it's water straight off my back.'

To her eternal relief, he eased off now, stepping back slowly. It hurt, in quite a different way; and then he was nodding at her to switch legs. Simply taking the crossed leg off the other one, setting up for the stretch on the other side, was horrendous in itself.

'I feel like I'll never walk again,' Caroline said helplessly.

'Yeah, I know,' Frank said sympathetically. 'You were pretty ambitious there with that beach jogging. Good for you. After this you should go and get in a hot bath with lots of Epsom salts. Tomorrow it'll be worse. I'm not going to lie to you. But if you've got the guts to keep going, you'll be surprised how much better it gets.'

The sight of her face when he mentioned going back to Studland tomorrow to repeat the agony of today was enough to set him off again.

'I hope you don't think I'm laughing at you,' he said contritely. 'It's just the faces you pull. I can't help it. You should be doing comedy on the telly – you'd have everyone in stitches.'

'I'm glad my suffering amuses you,' Caroline managed, as the door of the gym swung open and Laylah's high, piping voice asked:

'Daddy, what are you *doing* to Caroline? Do me next! Do me!'

Laylah threw herself down by Caroline on the mat, crossing her legs in imitation of Caroline's contorted position.

'It's so easy for kids, isn't it?' Frank said to Caroline, and she couldn't help a half-smile, half-grimace; it was exactly what she had been thinking, Laylah's rubbery, bendy little legs were instantly able to fold into any shape she wanted.

'No, *me*! Daddy, do me!' London insisted, following suit.

'I have to finish stretching Caroline,' Frank said patiently. 'She's done a really cool thing today – she's started to jog on sand, which, let me tell you two, is not an easy thing at all. Laylah, why don't you be me and stretch out your brother, and London, you can be Caroline?'

'I don't want to be the girl,' London said sullenly, shaking back his dark head of curls, so like his father's, even as Laylah leaped to her feet, excited to follow her father's suggestion.

'London! We're not sexist in this house!'

Frank knuckled his fists and put them on his waist, staring down at his son with a deep frown.

'Girls can do anything boys can!' Laylah said, sticking her tongue out at London. 'Like Corinne in *Barbie and the Three Musketeers*! They told her she couldn't be a musketeer but she *could*, and her friends were ones too!'

'That's a stupid film,' London muttered.

'Oh yeah? So why do you watch it all the time? And *Barbie: A Mermaid's Tale* too? You watch that again and again and *again and again*—'

Laylah's voice was rising ominously; Caroline fought the impulse to clap her hands over her ears. London threw himself at his sister in an attempt to silence her, going straight for the throat.

'Shut *up*, shut *up!*' he yelled. 'I hate you!'

'GUYS! STOP IT AT ONCE!'

But Frank's yelled command did nothing to stop his children fighting. They were struggling madly; Laylah tried to push London off and he fell to the ground, taking her with him, his hands tightly clasping the collar of her blouse. They rolled over and over each other on the mats. Caroline had to scramble clumsily to her feet to avoid their thrashing feet as Frank stood impotently over them, begging them to pack it in, unable to get a grip on them to separate them: by now they were a mass of tossing curls and writhing limbs. Though only four, London clearly took after his father in build. He was a stocky, solid child who was more than able to give his skinny nine-year-old sister a run for her money in a wrestling match.

Every morning the housekeeper brought a fresh pitcher of filtered water down to the gym, as the environmentally conscious Frank was very keen on avoiding plastic bottles where at all possible. Caroline, heroically ignoring the agony in her legs and buttocks, strode over to the table on which the pitcher and several glasses stood next to a pile of neatly folded hand towels. Peeling off the lid of the pitcher, she went back to the kidfight. London's hands were now wound in his sister's hair; she was shrieking with pain, pulling her knees up to her chest and wriggling to get the right angle to kick him in the balls. Frank was almost sobbing with frustration.

Leaning over, Caroline dumped the entire contents of the pitcher onto the two squirming and screaming children. Absolute silence descended on the gym for a long moment as Laylah and London froze in shock. Then they started spluttering for breath, their hands coming up to wipe the water off their faces. This gave Frank the opportunity to bend down and grab both by the scruffs of their necks, hauling them to their feet.

'I hope you don't mind –' Caroline stammered, shocked by what she had just done. It completely exceeded the bounds of any normal guest behaviour. 'My mum used to do it when we were scrapping and it always works, but . . .'

Frank turned to her, a child practically depending from each big hand, holding them as far apart as possible so nothing could start up again.

'Genius,' he said simply. 'Genius. Wish I'd thought of it myself. Kids, say sorry *now* to Caroline for kicking off like that in front of her.'

'Sorry,' Laylah and London mumbled in unison. London sneezed, a very cute little cat-like sound that made both Laylah and Caroline giggle.

'The water went up my nose, Daddy,' he said in a small voice. 'It hurts.'

'You deserved it,' Frank said sternly. 'Where's Lina? Why's she letting you two run around like wild animals?'

'She said she had a headache,' Laylah said, beginning to wriggle. 'She picked me up from school and she said London was naughty at his Monty Saury and she was already cross, and then when we got home she said she had to go and take a pill for her headache.'

Lina was not the nanny whom Caroline had met on her first visit to Sandbanks, just a few weeks ago; the children apparently went through caregivers as fast as they consumed the contents of a tube of Smarties. She had initially seemed a phlegmatic, unemotional young woman, but the task of dealing with Laylah and London seemed to have defeated her only a short time into her job.

'Is Carmen around?' Frank asked hopelessly. 'Could she look after you if Lina's not feeling well?'

'No, Carmen doesn't like us,' Laylah said pertly, wriggling free of her father's clasp. 'She says we're loud and annoying and make a mess.'

'Well, she's got a point there,' Frank muttered.

'She only likes cats,' London added. 'But she likes me better than Laylah. She told me so.'

'She didn't!' Laylah stamped her foot. 'She said she doesn't mind you as much! She didn't say she *likes* you!'

'Look, Laylah,' Caroline said, seeing that Frank had no ability to control his own children's behaviour, 'I have to go and have a bath because I just went for a run and I hurt all over. But would you like to watch a film with me afterwards in my room? I've finished work for the day now. You can pick which film. We could make it a pyjama party.'

Laylah shrugged.

'Yeah, okay,' she said ungraciously. 'Not a Barbie one though. I'm too old for them now. They're for little kids like—'

'UGH!'

London tried to wrestle free to throw himself bodily on his sister once more.

'Could you take her upstairs with you and tell Lina to do her bloody – um, the job that we pay her good money to do?' Frank asked Caroline, looking hapless. 'I'm sorry, I just think we need to keep 'em apart at the moment . . .'

'Of course,' Caroline said. 'Come on, Laylah. Let's go find Lina.'

She held her hand out to Laylah, who, to her surprise, considering that Caroline had just showered her with water, took it without hesitation. Caroline was not one of those people who particularly like the company of children, but the feeling of Laylah's small hand trustingly closing around hers was very pleasant.

'You need to do your nails,' Laylah said, looking at Caroline's fingers. 'I could do them for you if you want. I have a whole nail polish wall in my room.'

'That sounds great,' Caroline said quite sincerely; her nails could definitely do with some help.

'London bit another little boy at Monty Saury,' Laylah confided as they left the gym, Frank shooting Caroline a look of such gratitude that it made her feel warm all over. 'Don't tell Daddy. And then he bit Lina too when she made him get in his car seat.'

Caroline pulled a face.

'I won't tell him, but I'm sure Lina will,' she said, pressing the button for the lift. 'The nursery will want to know what your mummy and daddy did about it.'

'They won't,' Laylah said airily. ''Cause the lady who runs it gets all googly when she sees Daddy. She complained about London last year and Mummy said that if they didn't want him there, she'd move him to another nursery and the lady got upset because she likes Daddy, so she said it was okay and he could stay. Mummy told me in the car coming home. She was laughing. She said London could flush another kid's head down the loo and that lady still wouldn't make him leave.'

The lift came, and Caroline was grateful, as she was so taken aback at Lexy talking so frankly to her small daughter that she couldn't muster up the right words to say for a minute or so.

'I'm sure Mummy was just joking,' she managed eventually.

'No, she meant it,' Laylah assured her. 'The lady goes bright red whenever she sees Daddy and she starts forgetting her words. Mummy says it's hilarious as she's so old and fat that Daddy'd never want to kiss or cuddle her.'

'Um, it's not really nice to call people fat, or old, especially if it's in a mean kind of way . . .' Caroline said as the lift rose up.

She couldn't help but take this comment personally. Lexy would doubtless categorize Caroline as too fat to interest Frank. Caroline had noticed that, though the previous nanny and Lina were in their early twenties, neither of them could be considered in any way attractive: the one she had met on her first visit had been as limp as a wet noodle, while Lina had a positive moustache. And Carmen, though she was young and striking with her thick mane of curly black hair and flashing dark eyes, had such a paralyzingly direct manner of expressing her thoughts that ninety-nine men in a hundred would be much too terrified of her to make a pass.

Caroline was sure that Lexy had hired them all with a view to avoiding the classic mistake made by a lot of wives – installing a young, pretty woman under her roof, a caring, apparently sweet-natured creature to whom the husband would naturally turn for sympathy when he had the inevitable fight with his wife. It was a lesson painfully learned by both Gwen Stefani and Jennifer Garner, whose husbands had notoriously had flings with their children's nannies. Jude Law had cheated on Sienna Miller with his kids' nanny; Robin Williams and Ethan Hawke had even married theirs.

Frank didn't remotely seem the type to cheat, but still, Lexy wasn't taking any chances. Did that mean she would have refused a ghostwriter who looked like a younger version of herself? For all Caroline knew, that might have been the reason Lexy rejected the other candidates. Maybe the agent had assumed that Lexy would want someone who was young and pretty, chic and trendy, someone with whom Lexy might be able to identify, who would render Lexy's stories of drinking and partying and being the prettiest girl in the room with extra accuracy because she shared the same kind of experiences.

Instead, Lexy had selected a dowdy Plain Jane who would always be inferior to her, whom she had nicknamed Ghost Mouse the first day they met. One to whom she could even play Lady Bountiful – because Lexy had not only paid for Caroline's consultation and facial at Skin3, she had thrown in the vitamins and omega-plus fish oils which Davina had recommended Caroline take daily, bought her a starter kit of cleanser, toner and facial oil, and told them to schedule Caroline for a monthly treatment on Lexy's account while she was writing the book. That first facial had been transformative, disconcerting though it had been to lie there under the heavy mask, feeling the electrical current running through it; Caroline genuinely felt her skin was already smoother, her rosacea less irritated.

But what if she's just being generous because she looks

down on me from such a great height? Caroline thought bitterly. *She can afford to help me sort my skin out, because she knows that even when I do, I'll never be her equal!*

I thought she was so nice saying I could live in the guest suite during the week. But what if Lexy only feels okay with me staying in her house because I'm overweight and not that pretty?

The questions were coming thick and fast now.

Has she noticed my crush on Frank? Does she laugh at me behind my back and say it's hilarious, like she does with the poor woman who runs the Montessori?

As Caroline stared at her bare, un-made-up face in the mirrored doors of the lift, she realized that resentment towards Lexy was slowly building inside her, displacing the sheer gratitude she had felt up until this moment.

How I wish that in one way, even a very small one, Lexy would see me as some sort of a rival . . .

It was the first time this idea had ever entered Caroline's mind. But it would most definitely not be the last.

Chapter Ten

Two weeks later

'Ghost Mouse's losing weight!' Lexy said, flopping down next to Frank on their king-size bed. 'Have you noticed? She's slogging over to the nature reserve and lugging up and down the beach every day, apparently!'

'Yes, good for her,' Frank said, clicking off the TV and putting an arm around his wife. 'I've been showing her how to stretch. She was limping around for a week after she started.'

'Was she?' Lexy said incuriously.

'Seriously, did you not even notice the poor thing couldn't get up the stairs! Lucky for her we've got a lift.'

He looked down at Lexy, who, as usual, was scrolling through her Instagram account on her rose-gold iPhone, seeing how many likes she had garnered with the photos she had uploaded that day.

'Did you not notice she was moving like a lame donkey?' he asked, and shook his head in amazement at his wife's obliviousness as she said:

'No, was she? She's always sitting down when we do our sessions, so . . .'

Lexy trailed off, her attention captured by the comments on a selfie of her in the shower that morning, which she had

122

artfully angled to show off her curves without actually being naked.

'You're unbelievable, Lex,' Frank said. 'Do you notice *anything* that's not about you? Do you realize that Laylah's got no sense of discipline? She'll talk back to anyone and think she can get away with it because you laugh whenever she says something cheeky, instead of ticking her off for it. And did you know that London's been biting kids at his Montessori? Not just kids! Lina says she's going to give her notice if he goes after her again, the little horror.'

'Just tell her to wear extra clothes for padding. We'll up her rate a bit,' Lexy said airily.

'Lex, you're joking, right?' her husband snapped. 'Can you put that phone down for once so we can talk?'

'I can think of other stuff to do than talk,' Lexy said, still scrolling on her phone, but one-handed now, as she was sliding the other one down to stroke Frank's penis through the pyjama trousers he was wearing. 'Can't you? *Much* more fun!'

'Lex . . .' Frank gently removed her hand from his genitals, winding his fingers through hers. 'You go for my dick any time I want to talk about something you want to avoid. It's not that I don't like it, but sometimes we need to look at what's a priority.'

'Sucking you off is always a priority,' Lexy said, raising their linked hands to her mouth and starting to lick the tips of his fingers, while still, however, continuing to survey her social media on her iPhone. 'I'll get on to that in just a sec.'

Frank's dick started to stiffen at these promising words; its owner muttered a curse at it to settle it down again.

'Hey, Caroline's knocking out some really hot sex scenes, by the way,' Lexy commented. 'I should read you one to get you in the mood. They're a massive turn-on.'

Frank dragged his hand away from his wife's, and his arm from behind her. Pulling back, he sat up straight on the bed, crossing his legs.

'Lexy,' he said. 'Did you just suggest that you read scenes that Caroline's written about you *having sex with other men*? Are you completely crazy?'

When Lexy didn't answer immediately, Frank reached out and put one large hand over the screen of the iPhone.

'Lex, this is beyond a joke!' he said, his voice deepening with resentment.

Lexy sighed, dropping her phone to the elaborate satin bedspread, turning to look her outraged husband full in the face.

'Some of them are partly made up,' she said, 'because . . .' Her voice trailed off as she realized that was because they described experiences so racy that her editor was concerned she might be sued if the identities of the other participants were revealed. 'Um, I could change the names when I read them to you?' she suggested.

'They're still about you and another man!' Frank writhed in embarrassment and anger. 'I *never* want to think about that kind of thing! You know I don't!'

Another man? Lexy thought. *Oh babes, you have no idea – you think I only ever shagged one guy at a time?*

Never mind. It's not like he's ever going to read the book.

'Okay,' she went on, 'what about Caroline's Regency porn threesome thing? It turned into a foursome, actually. I got her to put the whole thing up on her blog – it's brilliant. Want to have a read?'

She picked up her phone again. If she couldn't distract him with sex, she was eager to place an electronic barrier of some sort between herself and her husband, who was trying to have a conversation about awkward subjects in which she had no interest. Lexy was fully occupied with her one over-riding priority: her career.

'No! Put that phone down *now*, Lex!'

'Ooh!' Lexy tried for a flirtatious tone as she obeyed his command. 'You sound so butch, I love it. Here I am – all yours!'

She put the phone down on the bedside table, theatrically pushing it away from her, and flapped her faux eyelashes in a way that usually made him melt. Lexy had, practically from birth, learned the technique of flirting her way out of any awkward situation. The only daughter of a doting father, with three older brothers who all adored and spoilt her almost as much as her parents, she had learned that a toss of her curls and a bat of her lashes was almost always a Get Out of Jail Free card.

Lexy's mother had been the lone voice trying to hold her daughter accountable for her actions, wanting her to take responsibility and make amends if she misbehaved, rather than just charm her way out of it. But Mrs O'Brien would be the first to admit that she had failed. The tricks Lexy had perfected on her father and brothers worked just as well on her teachers, the male ones in particular. Female teachers made valiant attempts to force Lexy to take her studies seriously, use her brain rather than her charisma, but Lexy had been too busy achieving her status as the Queen Bee of her school, the one all the boys wanted and all the girls wanted to be.

She knew fairly early on that the status she craved would not be attained by using her brain and going to college. Lexy dreamed of having her own reality show, presenting stints on *Loose Women*, product lines, endorsement deals and a loaded footballer husband. None of those goals would be achieved by getting the BA in Media Studies her teachers were suggesting. She'd be too old by then – twenty-one, twenty-two! Over the hill! No, she needed to get her body out there on TV when it was as young and fresh as possible, so by the time she hit her thirties – which to her, back then, meant that she would practically be on her deathbed – she had the career and the social media followers and the man all in place.

And Lexy's grand plan had worked out more perfectly than she could have imagined. However, she hadn't bargained for the fact that when you married a decent family man, rather than a perpetual slag about town, he'd expect you to sit down with him and have serious conversations about your kids cheeking and biting people, rather than taking sexy photos of the two of you cuddling in your designer bedroom which could promptly be uploaded to Instagram.

She could tell from the way Frank's full lips were pursed into a straight line, the firmness in his dark brown eyes, that emergency measures were called for. Reaching up, she took hold of the lapels of her Kiki de Montparnasse silk satin butterfly-patterned robe and slipped it off her shoulders, revealing that she was naked underneath it, and freshly waxed to boot. Her new boob job was so perky her tits were almost nudging her chin. They'd settle down a little with time, just as her nose had done – shit, that month where its tip was Miss-Piggy-meets-a-ski-jump had had her freaking out, but her surgeon kept assuring her that gravity would sort it out, and now it was perfect . . .

Despite himself, Frank's lips softened as he stared at his naked wife. To him, Lexy was the most attractive woman in the world. She might have knocked out two kids, but with the help of a very good plastic surgeon, a diet of cigarettes and chicken slices, plus a hardcore personal trainer, she was perfectly comfortable posing even in a semi-recumbent position, which inevitably made anyone's tummy pooch out a bit, unless you were a gym bunny with a body-fat ratio of six per cent.

Sensing that Frank was still struggling, brain versus cock – which was visibly butting against the fly of his pyjama trousers once again – Lexy decided to tip the balance in her favour. Knowing very well that Frank was very much a breast man, she cupped her 34DDs in her hands, pressing them together to create an eye-popping cleavage as she said saucily:

'Right, big boy, you've got my full attention. Still want to talk about the kids, or do you fancy letting off a bit of steam?'

It was with considerable smugness that she heard her husband groan, 'Okay . . . but we still need to talk . . . after . . .', as he reached out to cover her hands with his own, his head lowering to start kissing the plastic surgeon's latest twin masterpieces. Hopefully all he'd be good for afterwards would be sleep.

Chapter Eleven

He was utterly drained, thoroughly fucked. His cock had shot its load into the Marquis's eager mouth, his arse had been drilled by the gentleman the Marquis had brought in to take his pleasure of the blacksmith's boy who was their latest plaything – spotted as the Marquis rode through the village with his beautiful sister, Lady Maria, and summoned to the Abbey to be used in any way that might give pleasure to the lord of the manor and his friends. Sprawling on the feather mattress and the silken sheets, collapsed in a comfort he had never even been able to imagine, Jim's eyes closed as he drifted off in exquisite release.

It was not just the physical satisfaction that was flooding through him, calming him even more than the effects of sinking a couple of pints of the powerful cider they served in the Northam Arms after a hard day's shoeing recalcitrant stallions. It was that finally he was able to be himself – be recognized for the licentious, filthy pervert he truly was. Somehow, the Marquis had seen him, seen not the easy-going, hail-fellow-well-met, cheerfully lusty Jim who every father in Northam village wanted to marry his daughter; the Marquis had known in a flash, just looking in his eyes for a moment, what Jim really wanted to do not only with that daughter, but her brother too, and at the same time if they'd let him.

He had spent eighteen years of his life hiding from his desires, ashamed of them, treating the young women of Northam as delicately as if they were made of fine china, when what he was craving was to crack their arses with a strap and then have them do the same to him. And in his fantasies, the woman he dreamed of strapping him more than any of the others was the Lady Maria, with her white skin, willow-slim body, luxuriant blonde hair and tiny pointed breasts like—

'Caroline! Carmen has a scarf made out of her own hair *and* her mummy's!' Laylah blurted out as she burst into Caroline's living room. 'Did you know that?'

Caroline slammed her laptop shut so fast that the desk bounced with the impact.

'Laylah!' she said, her heart pounding, partly from the sexual charge that had built up while she read her own extremely saucy writing, and partly from the terror that Laylah might have caught a glimpse of it as she tore into the room. 'You can't just come into my room without knocking! We all need privacy! What if I was on the loo or something?'

'Well, you weren't!' Laylah said, putting her hands on her hips and tilting her head with a pert smile. 'So what? *Anyway . . .*'

'What time is it?'

Caroline looked at her phone. She had been getting ready to write a sex scene between Lexy and her babydaddy, Jamal, involving bondage, whipped cream, a douche and pegging. Jamal's name had been changed, but it was very clear from the context which of Lexy's previous sex partners had been a six-foot-five, two-hundred-and-fifty-pound bottom to her top.

Jamal was a basketball player, and Caroline had had the brilliant idea to make the character in the book a wide receiver, an American football term that she had always thought very funny. Lexy had loved it, and had given Caroline so much detail about exactly how Jamal liked to widely receive that Caroline had had to listen back to it on headphones rather than just playing it back, in case anyone happened to come in.

Thank God I took that precaution! she thought, pulling out her earbuds. She hadn't actually had Lexy's narrative running; she'd just finished listening to it, and had thought that the best way to get into the swing, as it were, of writing a big sex scene was to warm up with one of her own.

And it had worked all too well. Caroline was distinctly hot and bothered, not at all prepared for the incursion of a small, bratty child at nine in the evening wearing mini-Uggs and a nightie with *Me Princess, You Whoever* emblazoned across her skinny chest in bright pink glittery lettering.

'Carmen's mum's hair is lighter than hers so it's in stripes on the scarf,' Laylah babbled. 'And she has a winter headband made out of her own hair, and mittens. Those are stripy too. Carmen's mum tried to knit gloves but she said the fingers were too hard. You should put that in the book, about Carmen. No one else has a head scarf made out of her own hair and her mum's, do they? Carmen says not.'

'No, I don't think they do,' Caroline said in a daze. 'It's not really the kind of thing that—'

'Mummy and Daddy are fighting,' Laylah said, abruptly shifting tack and throwing herself down on the sofa.

The sitting room of the guest suite was generously proportioned, with a sofa and armchair set arranged around a coffee table to face out to the sea. Even if life at The Gables hadn't included the delicious proximity of the handsome Frank in gym gear, it would have been an increasingly hard wrench for Caroline to leave the suite every Friday afternoon to head back to her London houseshare, with its grotty bathroom, mouldy windows, and the communal lounge that lacked enough sofas and armchairs for all the housemates to sit down comfortably at once.

'You ought to be in bed,' Caroline said. 'Does Lina know you're up?'

Laylah made a loud farting noise.

'Course not,' she said. 'She's Skyping her boyfriend and crying, like she always does in the evenings. I got bored and couldn't sleep so I went out of my room, and I heard Mummy and Daddy shouting. Daddy said that me and London are out of control and Mummy said I'm just like she was when she was little and Daddy said that's a nightmare 'cause Grandpa Don spoilt her so much this is why she's like she is now, and Mummy got really cross and shouted that Grandpa loves her best in the world and not to talk about him like that, and Daddy said that Grandma Margaret's the brains of that operation if you ask him, and *she* should come here and whip us into shape instead of useless Lina, and Mummy said over her dead body as Grandma Margaret's always so mean about me and London and our high spirits and Daddy said he agrees with every word that Grandma

Margaret says and it's not high spirits, we're tearaways and we need a short sharp shock –' Laylah finally ran out of breath.

Caroline commented, eyebrows raised: 'You don't seem very bothered! If my dad was saying I needed a short sharp shock—'

'Oh, it'll never happen,' Laylah said breezily. 'Mummy always wins.'

'Laylah!'

Both Caroline and Laylah turned to the sound of Frank's voice; he was standing in the open doorway, hands on hips, brow furrowed.

'What are you doing up?' he demanded. 'You should be in bed by now! We kissed you goodnight and tucked you in!'

'I couldn't sleep,' Laylah said, shrugging. 'So I came to see what Caroline was doing.'

'You're not supposed to be bothering her!' Frank said, throwing an apologetic glance at Caroline. 'Come on, now, back to bed –'

But just then Lexy swept into the room, wearing a silk robe in shades of peacock blue and green which whirled around her slender limbs. The garment was so elegant, and clearly so expensive, that Caroline could not avoid sighing in envy.

'Laylah darling,' Lexy said loudly, bending down to hoist the little girl into her arms, 'Daddy thinks I don't spend enough time with you! So you're going to sleep in my bed tonight and Daddy can go and sleep in yours, or wherever he bloody well wants, but he can't share with us, because it's girls only, okay?'

'Okay, Mummy!'

Frank had to jump aside to avoid being whacked by Laylah's feet as Lexy whisked their daughter triumphantly from the sitting room, her tone light but her eyes flashing and her jaw set in fury. The little girl looked equally smug, pushing back her hair from her face so she could pull a defiant grimace at her father, proving the point she had just made: that Lexy always won.

Frank stood there, half-leaning now against the door jamb, head lowered, his shoulders sagging. He looked utterly defeated. Caroline stared at him helplessly, not knowing what to say. She hated to see him so unhappy. But nastily, selfishly, she was also glorying in the sight of Frank brought so low by Lexy, who, Caroline was more convinced with each passing day, was not at all worthy to be the wife of such a wonderful man.

Frank pushed slowly off the door frame, his eyes blank. But then he stopped again, clearly blocked; he wasn't sure where he was going, now that his wife had banned him from their bedroom. It was almost like watching the tall woman at the party in *Breakfast at Tiffany's* start to topple over, the moment where Holly Golightly famously puts her hands to her mouth and yells '*Timber!*' as her friend crashes to the ground.

Frank wasn't going to fall, but he was swaying on his feet as if he had been punched. And when Caroline saw that, she got up and practically ran towards him, wrapping her arms around him, embracing him, breaking through all her inhibitions, because against him were pressing her oversize boobs and her protruding stomach, not to mention the roll of fat between them on her upper torso. She hugged him as if he were her boyfriend and he had just been told that his parents had been killed in a freak accident.

Frank was only wearing a T-shirt and pyjama bottoms, soft, well-washed fabric, nothing that could disguise the hard contours of his body. He felt like a bronze sculpture sheathed in velvet, and when his arms came round her, returning the hug, the smell of him was overwhelming. His curls tickled her ear and his body hair, twining over the neck of the T-shirt, rubbed against her skin. There was a light perfume of expensive herbal soap which, mingled with his own scent, made Caroline's head swim and her limbs tremble as if she had drunk a whole pot of black coffee.

'I'm sorry this is happening to you,' she mumbled into his chest. 'You don't deserve it. I'm so sorry, Frank.'

His arms tightened even more. She could feel almost the whole length of him now, the long muscles of his thighs pressing into her much soggier ones. And he seemed not to mind at all, not to be repulsed by her body, even though it was so much less perky and tight and taut than Lexy's.

'You're a really good friend, Caroline,' he said, and to her shock, one big hand came up and stroked her hair. 'A really good friend. We're all so lucky to have you.'

He heaved a long sigh.

'Fantastic with the kids, so easy to hang out with, great company . . . sometimes I honestly don't know what I'd do without you.'

Caroline didn't think that Frank was aware he had switched from 'we' to 'I'. And the fact that the transition had been involuntary made her cherish it even more. She knew she had to be the first one to pull back, so that Frank wouldn't suspect she had an ulterior motive for the hug, but it took tremendous willpower to manage it.

Smiling up at him, she said:

'It's funny to think I've only been here a few weeks, isn't it? It's silly, but I'm already feeling a bit sad to think of the book getting finished and not being around all of you any more!'

And in those wonderful dark brown eyes, she saw, to her considerable delight, that Frank's feelings about this eventuality were exactly the same as hers.

Chapter Twelve

'You look *amazing*,' Riz said, staring at Caroline as she walked in the door on Friday evening; he dashed to help her with her laptop case, something that he had never done before. 'Have you been working out?'

'Oh, a little bit,' Caroline said nonchalantly, yielding the case to him even as she thought how ironic this was. She was noticeably tighter, stronger, slimmer, and now a man was rushing to take her luggage: surely, logically, he should have done it before, when she looked like she was too out of shape to carry anything?

She had definitely lost weight over the course of the last few weeks, a combination of arduous runs on the Studland beach from Tuesday to Friday mornings and limiting herself to the diet meals that Lexy's cook prepared for her boss. Portion control, only a tiny amount of dressing, practically no dairy or carbs. It was horrible, nibbling on dryish slices of roast chicken while looking wistfully at the mayonnaise into which the kids were dipping their chips for dinner, or forking up a stir-fried prawn with no rice to go with it. She hadn't realized before how stringent a proper dieting regime was. Up to now, Caroline's idea of a diet had been to replace white rice with brown, buy low-fat hummus, avoid butter on her bread; she hadn't realized that, for her to have anything close to Lexy's figure, she would need to go much further, cutting out carbs almost entirely.

At first she had barely lost a pound, which she had found very discouraging. Frank had been a rock of support, however, explaining that the jogging was building up her muscle, which weighed more than fat, and that she should stay off the scales. Instead, she should watch for signs that her clothes were looser, that she felt lighter as she hauled her body over the sand. This week had been a breakthrough: finally daring to weigh herself, she had realized that she had lost half a stone, and that revelation made her almost as happy as the memory of hugging Frank two nights ago and the lovely chat that had followed, the two of them sitting on the sofa of her suite for a good half hour.

Caroline still didn't know how she'd managed to avoid giving herself away. Frank's thigh had been so close to hers that it was almost pressing against her. The words poured out of him as he confided that Lexy broke his heart when she tried to use sex to distract him instead of working on their marriage and parenting their kids. Frank was very discreet; he didn't even say the word 'sex', but Caroline was sharp and intuitive, and it took only the subtlest reference to 'intimacy' for her to understand the situation.

Very sensibly, she didn't offer advice, but just curled up and listened, murmuring sympathetic words from time to time. Eventually Frank headed to the spare room to sleep, but not before telling Caroline how grateful he was for letting him bother her with his troubles. It wasn't the kind of thing he could talk about to his mates, he had explained; without his going into any more detail, Caroline quite understood that a husband complaining that his wife kept distracting him from serious conversations by offering sex would bring the same amount of sympathy as if he had tried to elicit it by lamenting that his cock was oversized.

It was highly unpleasant to think of Lexy regularly seducing Frank. So Caroline pushed those images away and basked instead in the revelation that Frank and Lexy's seemingly happy marriage had problems significant enough for them not only to fight openly in front of Caroline, but for Lexy to declare that Frank wasn't welcome in the marital bed that night. The day afterwards, the very honest Frank had told Lexy over morning coffee that he had stayed up for a while after she stormed out, telling his troubles to Caroline. By chance, Caroline had been about to enter the kitchen, and she had paused just outside to hear Lexy's response. Lexy had laughed and commented that Ghost Mouse wasn't getting paid enough if she had to listen to Frank's shit as well as her own.

No shred of insecurity. No hint that Lexy felt threatened in any way by her husband sitting in the cosy atmosphere of Caroline's living room after a marital fight, confiding his troubles to her. Caroline had been absolutely right. Lexy had indeed put her ghostwriter firmly in the no-risk-to-my-marriage category, along with the limp-noodle nanny and moustachioed Lina.

Caroline had spent the last two days, when not working, brooding very heavily and with great resentment on the words 'Ghost Mouse'. When Lexy had coined the nickname the day they met, Caroline had actually liked it: she had focused almost entirely on the first word, as a sign that Lexy might genuinely be considering her for the coveted job. Now, however, she was giving much more attention to the second.

She did not let the resentment show in her behaviour around Lexy, of course. Even though, as Caroline was all too vividly aware, Lexy's self-obsession was so all-encompassing that she would have been oblivious to any change in Caroline's demeanour – short of Caroline throwing her laptop at her while screaming that she was very far from being a mouse . . .

'Looks like you've lost more than just a little bit!' Riz commented now, staring at her with obvious appreciation. 'Congratulations! Have you been—'

Caroline cut him off. 'You know what?' she said, leaning in. 'We can talk later. But right now I'm a bit sweaty from the journey and I want to have a shower. Why don't you come in and join me?'

Riz's face went pink, and he blinked madly.

'I was just meaning to tell you,' he said under his breath, nodding to the lounge in which Stewart and Veronika were visible on the sofa, watching *The One Show*, 'people have been saying to me that we need not to make so much noise when, you know, when we—'

'So gag me with my knickers and then fuck me while the water's running,' Caroline hissed back.

Riz's eyes went wide. Caroline was taken aback herself at her frankness before she realized that this idea had come straight from an anecdote of Lexy's that she had spent all yesterday evening writing up. Jamal might have wanted Lexy to peg him, but Sean, a celebrity cricketer famous for his wild partying ways, had been quite the other way round, enjoying nothing more than to tie Lexy up in all sorts of eccentric positions and have his way with her.

This was the first time Caroline hadn't actually had to ask herself what Lexy would do. She realized, staring at Riz's now very red face, that she seemed to have internalized the question: now she was popping out the answer almost as easily as Lexy herself.

Ten minutes later, she was naked and facing the shower, water pouring down on the crown of her head as Riz, precariously balanced behind her in the bathtub, tried to slip his cock into her; she could hear him slipping around as the head butted against her and then retreated again.

'I'm scared I'm going to fall on top of you and we'll both smash our faces in,' he said urgently. 'I can't really get a good stance back here, the bath's so narrow . . .'

Caroline thought of the big walk-in shower in her guest suite at The Gables, of Lexy and Frank's huge wet room with waist-high wraparound jets, of the rainforest shower in the gym with fragranced oils to match its colour-change programmes. How much sexier it would be if they were fucking in one of those, rather than this narrow, cramped bathroom!

Of course, if she were having sex under one of the many luxurious, state-of-the-art showers in the Sandbanks mansion, it would not be with Riz. Even as the two of them climbed out of the bath, clinging to each other and bracing themselves against the bath edge so they didn't slip and fall, as she took up position in front of the sink, hands flat on the chipped tiles behind it, not daring to cling to the rickety sink itself in case it came out of the wall, even as Riz started sliding his fingers into her, making sure she was ready, and she groaned to show him she was – she hadn't reminded him about gagging her with her knickers, as on reflection she really hadn't fancied it after having worn them all day – even as Riz's cock entered her and he started to get a rhythm going, she closed her eyes so she didn't have to see the dirty grouting between the tiles, the broken cord on the cheap window blind, the various housemates' stained bits of soap ranged along the crusted edge of the sink.

Caroline wasn't in London any more. She was back at The Gables, showering after her run, in the big bathroom off the basement gym, immersed in a beautiful fantasy in which Frank, somehow failing to hear the running water, would open the door to the circular shower room, step in, and promptly babble apologies at the sight of Caroline in the nude, water dripping down her, soaping herself. She would turn and look at him, the soap held at her breast.

But she wouldn't say a word. She wouldn't try to seduce him in any way; she wanted Frank to do everything, initiate the entire sexual encounter. That way, not only would she have nothing to feel guilty about, it would be the most flattering scenario imaginable, because it would be all about Frank being attracted to her naked body.

He would shut the door behind him, slowly, and then tear off his clothes, all in one go. This would happen unrealistically fast, without the usual awkward moments when one tried to pull off socks and trainers, hopping from one foot to the other, so that neither Frank nor Caroline could have second thoughts or an attack of guilt. Like all culminating moments in the best romance novels, they would be swept away on an overpowering tide of passion.

And then he would be upon her. Much as Caroline would have loved to fantasize about Frank lifting her up in one effortless swoop, her legs wrapping around his waist as he pressed her back against the tiny, opalescent, extremely expensive gold-flecked mica tiles of the curved shower wall, not even her very vivid imagination could stretch to that. Some days ago Lexy had recounted a hilarious story of another basketball player trying to pick her up and fuck her against the wall of a hotel bathroom: according to her, it had been incredibly tricky. Although he had had the strength to hold her up, his feet had kept slipping on the tiled floor, and though he had taken a pause to stand on a bathmat instead, it had barely helped. Eventually, they had given up; he'd put her down and she'd turned round instead, bracing herself against the wall, with much joking about getting the hotel to send up one of those old-people rubber shower mats to stand on next time.

So, in Caroline's fantasy, Frank would be kissing her neck and sliding into her from behind. With her eyes closed, Caroline could picture that it was Frank behind her, not Riz. Frank's golden-brown hands on her hips; Frank's handsome face contorted as he tried to hold on as long as possible, to keep the bliss of this encounter going for at least ten minutes; Frank's thick hairy fingers, snaking around to start stroking her clit. The workings of lust, she thought hazily, were fascinating; she wouldn't have dreamed of fantasizing about hairy fingers before she met Frank, and now, in her fantasies, she couldn't stop picturing them all over her . . .

Riz was making her come, and as she did, trying to be quiet for the housemates, images of not only Frank but the sex scenes from her Regency porn novella flashed before her eyes. She had been amazed, re-reading that, how explicit she had been; she had completely let her imagination run riot, without a shred of embarrassment about the perversity of the entire story.

It was as if, when she began to write, she stepped into a parallel universe, where she was no longer boring old Caroline with her boring old job and her boring old life, but someone who was able to take a huge step into a world where she could write anything she wanted, creating characters who had everything she didn't: titles, fabulous costumes, amazing bodies, a stately home to play in, a total lack of inhibition, the bravery to live out their fantasies rather than just type them onto a screen.

Like Lexy. Lexy, who seemed to have done almost everything sexually possible, and was utterly unembarrassed telling Caroline about it. That sample of Regency porn had given Lexy the assurance that Caroline would not only be utterly unshocked by anything Lexy could recount, but that she would be able to depict it sexily on the page; not having realized how many tales of her exploits Lexy had been planning to unload on her expectant readers, Caroline had not realized how important her erotica had been.

And now Caroline had not only captured Lexy's voice, but was telling her story, gaining confidence with every sex scene she wrote, trying to emulate her, to become more sure of her own body and her own attraction, to turn herself into the kind of woman who would attract a man like Frank –

Frank. Caroline was coming again, and it was all she could do not to moan his name. Even as she spasmed over Riz's fingers, it was Frank she pictured behind her, his cock inside her. Frank had replaced Jim in her fantasies, the sexy muscled blacksmith of her Regency erotica: how often had Caroline masturbated to the image of Jim hammering away at her, while she had morphed into the lovely Lady Maria, slender as a wand with thighs like steel from riding her wild Arab stallion, blonde hair tumbling over her perfect body?

Nothing was too decadent, too perverse, for the spoilt and beautiful Lady Maria, who had, together with her brother the Marquis, been orphaned very young, and grown up experimenting with him, a pair of youthful libertines in an atmosphere of absolute freedom . . . And now the two fantasies merged. Caroline was Lady Maria, the wet hair slicked to her back no longer light brown and poker-straight, but champagne blonde tresses, her body magically reed-slim; but it was still Frank behind her, a flood of dirty words pouring from his mouth as he pulled out and, bending her down into the sink, her breasts pressed uncomfortably into the cold ceramic surface, shot all over her back.

The sensation of her big boobs squashing into the sink bowl snapped Caroline into real life. Lady Maria's tiny breasts would have merely grazed it delicately, while Caroline's were spilling into the small sink, practically filling it. Meanwhile, Riz was panting like a steam train from his efforts, while Frank or Jim, both prime physical specimens, would definitely not sound like they were about to have an asthma attack just from a ten-minute fuck.

She might not be Lady Maria, Caroline told herself, her

forehead pressed uncomfortably against the back of the sink, but her life had been transformed in the last month. She had regular, very good sex; she had lost half a stone; her skin, after two electro-current treatments and the daily vitamins and omegas she took religiously morning and night, was visibly smoother and less prone to redness; and the book was going so well that she truly thought she might be able to finish the contract and call herself a writer.

Slightly nervous at how racy the memoir was proving to be, she had sent a couple of the sex scenes off to Gareth a few days ago. To Caroline's great relief, he had responded that very same day to say he was loving it, and not to hold back. If the book ended up being a romp through Lexy's entire sex life, he had emailed, why not? It would be a totally fresh take on the celebrity memoir-slash-novel, and it was always easier to tone down sexy bits than to spice them up.

Also, he had started the email with 'Hello my lovely!' and ended it with 'Big hugs!!' which had made Caroline feel very happy indeed. Clearly Gareth felt confident enough in her work to be his jolly self with her, rather than holding her at a coolly professional arm's distance.

'God, that was fantastic,' Riz said, reaching for some loo paper and wiping down her back. Caroline was unable to help observing how scratchy and coarse it felt. Whoever had been on loo-paper-buying rota had clearly bought it from the pound shop on the high street; it had been a false economy, so thin and unabsorbent that Riz needed three fistfuls to clean Caroline up completely. The toilet roll in Lexy and Frank's mansion, by contrast, was quilted and velvet-soft, four-ply, more than up to the TV-ad challenge of being tugged at and unwound by the needle-sharp teeth of a cute Labrador puppy, or wiping a load of semen off someone with the greatest comfort possible.

'Shall we have a bath together?' Riz suggested rather bashfully, chucking the paper in the loo and flushing it. 'Might be nice to have a bit of a soak, eh? I bought a couple of Lush bath bombs on the way home from work. And I was thinking – I've got a game to go to tomorrow, but maybe we could grab a bite to eat on Sunday? There's a new Italian place on the high street. It's got a wood-fired oven and apparently the cooks used to work at Jamie's Italian, so it should be really authentic . . .'

Oh, wow, Caroline thought as she extracted her upper body from the sink. *He's asking me out on a dinner date. How do I feel about that?*

Honesty compelled her to admit that a month ago, before the call from Campaspe, she would have been flattered at the revelation that her booty call no longer saw her as a convenient and semi-secret shag, but a woman with whom he was happy to be seen in public. She couldn't help but be pleased. Nor could she blame Riz for being keener on her now that she had lost some weight, toned up a little, gained confidence; those were, after all, attributes anyone would find attractive.

But Riz wasn't what she wanted in a boyfriend. Even putting aside her crazy daydreams about Frank turning to her one night on the sofa of her living room, telling her that he couldn't stand Lexy's selfishness any more and he realized that she, Caroline, was the woman he really wanted to spend his life with – even ignoring those stupid fantasies, couldn't she do better than Riz now? She was no longer the office drudge, stuck writing tedious press releases for journalists on trade magazines to push aside, but a ghostwriter to a major celebrity. Couldn't she look higher than a podgy guy who worked at . . . where did Riz even *work*? She was pretty sure that he was in IT at an energy company, but which one?

The balance had altered. Before, Caroline had always perceived it as tipped in Riz's favour. Riz was male, and in Caroline's experience that meant he automatically had an advantage: so often it was the woman who wanted to get into a serious relationship while the man held back. Also, Caroline had been fatter than him when they were just hooking up – not sexy fat, which would have been a very different story, but dowdy fat – which in her opinion had also meant that she was lower on the scale than he. She had always secretly felt that the way they had kept their sex life on the down-low had been driven more by Riz than by herself. She would have been okay with the other housemates knowing about it, while she'd had the feeling that Riz would not.

Now it was Riz who wanted to go public, and she who was holding back. But that created a dilemma, as she had no wish to give up her regular sex partner. What with Frank's proximity and the racy scenes Caroline was writing for Lexy, she had sex on her mind a great deal of the time, and though she brought her vibrator with her to Sandbanks, by Friday she was eager to return to London simply because she would be able to get a good couple of fucks over the weekend.

I'll have to go along with this to get what I want, she decided. *I'm perfectly happy to go out for dinner with him every so often, and if he tries to have a talk about us, I'll just say that I'm working so hard on the book I can't possibly think about anything else until I've finished. Basically, I'll string him along and use him for his body.*

Which is definitely what Lexy would do!

The offer of a Sunday dinner date was easy to resolve. As Riz reached past her to put in the rubber bath plug and turn on the taps, she said:

'That sounds lovely, but I can't Sunday night. I have to go to a charity awards show with Lexy. She wants me to write about it for the book. I'm really freaked out about what I'm going to wear, actually.'

'That sounds amazing!' Riz said, turning back to give her a hug. 'Why don't you go shopping tomorrow to buy something new? Now that you've lost some weight, your old clothes might not fit. I could come with you, if you'd like.'

Oh goodness, Caroline thought, as he reached up and smoothed back a lock of her hair. *He really does seem into me. Offering to come shopping to help me choose a party dress – aren't men supposed to hate that kind of thing?*

'You should get a nice pair of heels as well, if you don't have them,' Riz added, looking down. 'Your legs look good from all the exercise. What've you been doing?'

'Running on sand,' Caroline said, unable to help feeling very proud of herself. 'Well, running and walking, on and off. It's *so* hard.'

'We could go for a run in the park over the weekend, if you fancy it?' Riz asked. He was a positive suggestion machine this evening.

'I'll see,' Caroline said, deflecting with a smile. 'I might not have the time – I've got to write all weekend. This deadline's mental.'

'It's really cool that you've become a writer,' Riz said shyly. 'Like, following your dreams.'

He picked up the paper bag that contained the bath bombs.

'Would you rather have Big Blue or Sakura?' he asked. 'That's cherry blossom.' He cleared his throat. 'They did have one called Sex Bomb, but I thought that might be a bit much . . .'

One day, it won't be, Caroline thought, even as she told Riz that cherry blossom sounded lovely. *It might seem like a silly, small thing, but one day, men won't buy me anything but Sex Bombs, because I am one! Just as they would for Lexy.*

Caroline wanted Lexy's bathroom, Lexy's confidence, Lexy's sex life, Lexy's husband. She wanted every single thing that Lexy possessed. And that left her with a burning question: what, exactly, would it take to get them?

Chapter Thirteen

'Lexy! Over here!'

'Lexy! Big smile, love!'

'Lexy, show us some leg, babes? Come on now!'

Although the paparazzi were yelling encouragement and demands at Lexy, it was entirely unnecessary. She was turning and posing like the pro she had been for nearly twenty years, showing off the spectacular ombré jewel-toned sequinned mermaid-tailed dress that clung to every single curve of her body. It had a low boatneck at the front, the start of her cleavage just visible, her firm toned shoulders rising from the sapphire sequins at the neckline: behind, it plunged almost to her buttock cleavage in the deepest of Vs, revealing the elaborate tattoos coiling over her back incorporating the names 'Frank', 'Laylah' and 'London', cleverly designed to cover up the previous tattoo of her name wrapped together with Jamal's.

From deep blue, the ombré shaded into purple, fuchsia and burnt orange. This was a very deliberate choice: it meant that the last colour, flowing in a train over the red carpet, actually co-opted the carpet itself into becoming part of her outfit, orange ripening into scarlet. Lexy had planned this effect with the designer. She wanted the photographs to go viral, so that social media, the weekly magazines, the gossip and fashion blogs would anoint her the unquestioned queen of tonight's event. This was an awards ceremony entirely for reality TV shows, which were now enough of an industry to have their own annual awards ceremony. Lexy was presenting one award, and nominated in multiple categories.

No wonder she had spent weeks intensively planning how to dazzle the viewers and outshine every other participant: it had been a campaign conducted with military seriousness. Jay had piled her hair on the crown of her head so that it wouldn't distract from the blinding dress. Extra pieces had been added to its natural abundance, creating a positive tower of elaborate Greek-goddess-style curls. Her make-up was so heavy that Caroline found it positively eerie. Vast amounts of Jane Iredale mineral foundation and powder, layered with hydrating spray, rendered Lexy's skin so even and perfect that she might have been her own waxwork in Madame Tussaud's.

Nathan and Lexy had decided on a faux-natural look, which always required more make-up than a heavily stylized one. Lexy's eyelids were shaded as thoroughly as if she were starring in a silent movie, her cheeks equally contoured. Earlier that day she had visited Skin3 for a top-up CACI treatment, the electric salad forks applied to great effect, and her jawline was taut as a drum, her cheekbones standing out in superb relief.

Caroline, standing in the cordoned-off VIP section at the head of the red carpet, just outside the theatre where the events ceremony was being held, snapped some shots on her mobile to show her friends and housemates. Her contract meant that she wasn't allowed to post anything about Lexy on social media, but she could at least show off in private. Even on the small screen of her phone, Lexy looked phenomenal, the dress outlining her toned hourglass figure. The rainbow sweep of the sequins was unforgettable; Lexy would only be able to wear it once. Naturally, the designer had given her a huge discount in return for the publicity.

Lexy had her hands on her hips now, her weight on her back leg and her torso slightly twisted – the classic model's pose that made her body as slender as possible, slimming her waist for the cameras. Turning, she looked over her shoulder, both giving a spectacular view of her tattooed back and demonstrating that she could not possibly be wearing a bra. The sequins clung pornographically to her high, firm buttocks.

'Fuck me, she's hot!' said a man beside Caroline. 'I like older women, me. They shag like rabbits and they're up for everything. Give me a MILF every time.'

Caroline glanced sideways and almost jumped when she saw who it was: Deacon, one name only needed to identify him, a boy-bander who had recently jumped ship in a spectacularly scandalous fashion, walking out of the Japanese leg of their tour with a stream of tipsy interviews about how singing in harmony with his four bandmates was crippling his artistic integrity. He was supposed to be recording his much-anticipated solo album, but the gossip blogs and tabloids reported that his real current occupation was having sex with glamour models while cramming as many recreational drugs as possible up his nose or down his throat.

It was dark outside, but the Klieg lights illuminating the red carpet and VIP area gave Caroline as good a view of Deacon as if it had been broad daylight. He was even more handsome in real life than in his pictures, but he also looked more trashed. The phenomenally blue eyes had a red tinge to their whites, while his breath smelt of alcohol. His famously shoulder-length hair looked as if it hadn't been washed in a week; he ran his hand through it, staring greedily at Lexy, causing it to stand up in the unmistakeable way that happened when the roots were oily. He was wearing a nylon shirt, unbuttoned to display his narrow pecs, and its collar was distinctly grubby.

Even in this unwashed state, Caroline, like most of the female and quite a proportion of the male population of the country, would have jumped at the chance to have sex with him. But Deacon's attention was focused entirely on Lexy; as she finally started to move up the carpet, approaching the VIP area, she gestured at Caroline, indicating that her ghostwriter should join her at the main doors.

Deacon turned to look at Caroline. As those amazing eyes met hers, she froze, feeling like a rabbit desperate for the snake to eat her up.

'You her assistant?' he asked, and behind him, his publicist glanced over at Caroline in pity, because if Caroline had been slimmer and more glamorously dressed, Deacon would have asked if she were Lexy's publicist instead.

Caroline's dark blue silk dress, trimmed at the neck with silver embroidery surrounding big clear fake stones, had been purchased at Monsoon that morning with Riz's help. It was perfectly suitable for a sidekick to wear to a smart event, as were her three-inch matching heels. However, the publicists were not wearing Monsoon, which probably didn't even make sizes small enough to fit them. They were dressed in black, to differentiate themselves from their flashily clad clients, but they were just as slim and well-groomed. Their little silk frocks were suspended from flimsy chains strung around their necks or shoulders, and under them they wore equally flimsy Cosabella lace thongs, rather than the M&S high-waisted slimming knickers into which Caroline had sweatily wrestled herself a couple of hours ago.

'I'm helping Lexy write her book,' Caroline managed to answer. Deacon's stare was still paralyzing: it was as hard to move her lips as if she'd just been to the dentist and the Novocaine had not worn off yet. 'Helping Lexy write her book' was the agreed-upon answer if anyone asked why Caroline was shadowing Lexy. After all, not even Lexy's most ardent fans and supporters would expect her to write a novel all on her own.

'Oh yeah? Cool,' Deacon said with an utter lack of interest. 'Fuck, she's got a killer pair of tits.'

He followed Caroline out onto the red carpet, not having bothered to walk it himself. In his currently rebellious state, he had declared to his publicist that he was 'over all that cheesy shit'. But now he stood there, ogling Lexy as she swept towards the main doors, looking her up and down as if she were a cow coming to market. Lexy, delighted at having captured the attention of a twenty-four-year-old who was currently considered one of the sexiest young men in the world, added an extra swing of her hips and a slow fluttering wink as she glided up to him.

'*Hi*,' Deacon said, with the air of a man who, for several years, had only had to utter this single word for anyone he wanted to fall at his feet.

'Isn't it past your bedtime?' Lexy responded magnificently, and Caroline, who felt that she would have melted like the Wicked Witch of the West under a bucketful of water if Deacon had unleashed that 'Hi' on her, admired Lexy at that moment more than she could possibly say.

'My bedtime's at dawn,' Deacon retorted. 'After shagging some lucky woman five times in a night. Could be you, if you play your cards right.'

'Mmn, so you're going to wake me up, what, four times just so you can come in ten seconds each go?' Lexy said, her perfectly outlined eyebrows rising as far as they could. 'That sounds like a lot of fun for me, doesn't it?'

Other attendees, hearing this exchange, giggled appreciatively, but Deacon was not a whit deterred. If anything, he looked even keener on getting into Lexy's knickers.

'Wow, you're so sassy! You're like, MILF on fire!' he exclaimed, and instantly looked thoughtful. 'Mmn, that's a song title. I'm going to write a song about you!'

'If you write *anything* about me with MILF in the title,' Lexy said, sweeping past him, 'I'll personally make sure you never have the ability to become a DILF. Think it over very carefully.'

As she walked away, her sequin-covered buttocks twitched as effectively as Marilyn Monroe's black satin ones in *Some Like It Hot*. Legend had it that Monroe had cut a quarter-inch off one heel of her shoes in order to perfect that sexy, slightly uneven sway; whether that were true or not, Lexy had no need for any help to shimmy as effectively as a Vegas showgirl.

'*Wow,*' Deacon said devoutly to no one in particular. 'D'you think she'd mind me calling her a cougar in a song?'

'Um, could I get a selfie?' Caroline asked, her heart in her mouth as she produced her phone. But when might she get this amazing opportunity again? No way was she going back home tonight saying she'd met Deacon without having proof!

'Yeahsure,' Deacon said automatically, leaning his head into hers and flashing a grin with the speed of a man who has done this millions of times. Caroline principally noticed how dirty his hair smelt, but in the photographs he looked sexy and dishevelled, his smile full of naughtiness. Caroline was the rabbit again, now in the headlights of the flash: her eyes were wide in shock, her jaw sagging unflatteringly, her head at a weird angle.

Still, I have photos of me with Deacon! And I can filter them a bit so I look better . . .

She pulled a small notebook out of the cross-body bag slung across her chest. Again, this was a fashion no-no; the publicists were carrying clutches or tiny Chanel bags on chain straps, not sensible leather mini-satchels. But Caroline had to bring her notebook everywhere when she was with Lexy, as her employer was liable at any time to come out with quick-witted banter and killer putdowns.

Swiftly, she scribbled down the exchange between Deacon and Lexy. Then she scrambled to follow Lexy, who was being escorted up the curving staircase to the Grand Circle bar, the designated VIP area; on a lanyard around Caroline's neck was a coveted Access All Areas pass, so that she could shadow Lexy wherever she went. Fans who were hanging around in the corridor, desperately craning their necks to see their idols inside the bar, shot Caroline jealous looks as a bouncer glanced at her pass and stood aside to let her in.

Her first impression of the *crème de la crème* of current reality show cast members gathered together was not, as she had anticipated, of sparkling, shiny glamour, but of the almost overwhelming amounts of naked flesh everywhere she looked. It could almost have been a pool party in Marbella. Lexy's bare back was one of the most restrained displays of skin on show.

There were women with dresses cut down to their navels in the front and their buttock cleavage in the back, and others in two-piece outfits that stopped just below their breasts and started again just above where their pubic hair would have been, if they had any. There were skintight jumpsuits with cut-out panels in areas so explicit, Caroline couldn't imagine how they could maintain any privacy at all; miniskirts so short that it was equally impossible to picture the wearer sitting down; and skirts slit literally up to the mons veneris. Most of the fabrics were just as shiny and metallic as she had expected, but the bare skin itself, moisturized with gold-flecked oil, gleamed even more.

And of all the flesh, it was the breasts that shone the most. Most were big, round and self-supporting, obviously fake; but a minority of the women – mainly the slim, posh girls – had opted either for what were known by plastic surgeons as 'mini boob jobs' – small teardrop-shaped implants under the pectoral muscle – or fat injections to plump them from an A to a B cup. There were multifarious ways to show off the results of the surgeries: cleavage, side boobs, even under-boobs in tops with sheer fabric just below the nipple, so that the whole lower swell of the breast was clearly visible.

Caroline quite literally did not know where to look. There were tits everywhere she turned. With considerable relief she noticed a woman wearing a tailored red trouser suit, but a few seconds later she realized there was nothing under the jacket but a gold body chain that seemed, from the way it was hanging, to be threaded through a pair of pierced nipples down to the pierced navel before wrapping back around the woman's waist. And when the suit-wearer turned to take a fresh glass of champagne from a waiter, Caroline saw that there was no back to the jacket – just a lattice of more gold chain. Porn stars probably dressed more discreetly at their awards shows.

The sprinkling of male guests present were either gay men enjoying the show, or straight men *really* enjoying the show. Hard-partying casts from Essex and Liverpool mingled with footballers' wives from Cheshire and posh girls from Chelsea. As with their smaller breasts, the last category preferred a more natural look, but all that meant was that they were wearing less obvious make-up, their hair was more subtly streaked, their boob jobs the mini ones: their heels were just as high, their clothes just as revealing as those of their fellow reality stars.

There was a definite hierarchy at this gathering. If you had your own show, you took precedence over people who were just cast members without their name forming part of the title. And if you were Lexy, with the highest-rated solo show in the UK, you were Head Bitch In Charge, to quote a slogan on one of her favourite T-shirts. As she stood in the glassed-off balcony overlooking the Haymarket below, a champagne glass in her hand, her glorious eyes flashing with triumph, she was surrounded by sycophants hoping for a guest appearance on her show and the daytime television present-ers and game-show hosts who were giving out the awards.

Just as Caroline reached the margins of the group around Lexy, she was pushed to one side so abruptly that she stum-bled into a judge on a dance show. He whipped his glass away from her before she knocked into it, *tsk*ing loudly at her clumsiness.

'Really, I didn't expect people to be falling-down drunk *already* –' he started with great disapproval, before drawing in his breath theatrically as he stared over Caroline's head. 'Oh my *God*, look who it is!'

As Caroline recovered her balance, she realized that a massive body in a black suit was blocking her view, clearly the person who had shoved her out of the way. His shaved head and visible earpiece proclaimed him to be either a bouncer or a bodyguard. More men dressed like him were crowding into the bar, clearing a thoroughfare through the centre, quite oblivious to the feet they were treading on and the guests they were strong-arming into each other. There were some protests, but they were drowned out by the gasps as the C-listers present registered the completely unexpected arrival of the most famous A-list reality personality in the world. Precipitated to fame by an infamous sex tape, Silantra was now the star of the hugely popular TV show *Sugar Girls*, which purported to be an accurate representation of her life and that of her two sisters, Shanté and Summer.

'It's *Silantra!*' the dance-show judge wheezed, almost unable to speak from excitement. 'Oh my *God*, and she's wearing Vivienne Winter's pearl choker!'

This was the legendary piece of jewellery – a pearl and ruby choker with an enormous pear-shaped gem hanging from the centre – known as the Medici Pearl. It had been worn by both Catherine de' Medici and Mary Stuart before eventually being gifted to the film star Vivienne Winter by her lover, Randon Cliffe. Silantra and her husband, the rapper Lil' Biscuit, had purchased the choker, along with two tiaras and many other pieces, in a private sale before the auction of Vivienne's extensive jewellery collection on New Year's Eve last year. The total raised by private sales and the auction itself had been three hundred million dollars, Caroline remembered, and Lil' Biscuit and Silantra's purchases had made up a sizeable proportion of that sum.

No wonder she's surrounded by bodyguards! she thought, squeezing sideways as best she could to sneak a glimpse of the notorious reality star. *Just that pearl alone must be worth an absolute fortune!*

Silantra was proceeding down the passage her bodyguards had cleared for her as if she were a queen, nodding from side to side at the enthralled onlookers, a faint smile on her face, as if she did this every night of the week and was frankly rather bored by it. This was the simple truth. It had been years since she had bothered to work a crowd: she was so famous by now that all she needed to do was show up. She had also popped a couple of Xanax, which contributed to the slightly glazed expression in her eyes. This was her trick for maintaining the serene, angelic expression which was necessary to balance out the slutty style in which she usually dressed.

This evening, however, her beaded minidress was much more demure than usual. It was not just a transparent net dress onto which a handful of beads had been sewn in clusters, but positively opaque, made of red silk that clung to the curving contours of not only her breasts but her stomach. Silantra and Lil' Biscuit had announced their pregnancy, as they had put it, a month ago; she was four months along now, and clearly blooming.

'I had no *idea* she was coming!' the dance-show judge breathed worshipfully. '*Such* a coup!'

Silantra's hair, which was done in a dramatic arrangement of fine braids woven around each other into wider plaits, some piled on top of her head, some cascading down her back, was currently blonde, her contact lenses emerald green. Her eyes were, as always, fringed with fake lashes made from mink fur, lashes which fluttered charmingly as she acknowledged a comment her escort made to her. This was Darrell Rose, the one-time presenter of *Who's My Date?*, the show on which Lexy had shot to fame, whom she had seduced as one of her strategies to keep her name in the news.

That had been nearly twenty years ago. Darrell was fifty now, a very well-preserved fifty, with thick pepper-and-salt hair and a body toned by endless rounds of golf with TV executives. His suit was impeccable, but he wore no tie, his shirt collar a little open to show off his smooth youthful neck: he had recently had a discreet tuck and jowl lift, and wanted to show off the results.

'Silantra, Empress of Reality TV – meet your leading British subject, Lexy O'Brien!' Darrell announced in his famous hail-fellow-well-met tenor, deliberately pitched to carry over the hubbub that was accompanying Silantra's entrance.

The group around Lexy had fallen back to gawp at Silantra: Lexy, revealed in her ombré sequins, glittered gloriously. Behind her, the dark London night with its streetlights and stars was the perfect background to set off her rainbow dress.

'Thanks, Darrell,' she said sweetly, quite understanding the dig that her ex-boyfriend had taken time to hone. 'That makes you the butler, does it?'

Caroline, who had managed to shove her way through the crowd by ruthless force combined with urgent mutterings that she worked for Lexy and needed to join her, had a very good view of the frown that crossed Darrell's handsome face at this retort. Lexy was already edging him aside as she took Silantra's hands and dropped a pair of perfectly-judged air kisses just above Silantra's cheeks; no contact, naturally, as they wouldn't dream of smudging lipstick or powder.

'It's cool to meet you,' Silantra said, which for her was the height of enthusiasm. She looked Lexy up and down, her smile widening, and Lexy, like many unsuspecting women before her, suddenly realized that Silantra was conveying not just approval of her appearance, but a distinct interest in seeing what Lexy looked like without her dress.

'You too!' Lexy said, nothing of this revelation showing on her face. 'And what an amazing surprise – I don't think anyone knew you were coming to the awards ceremony, right?'

She looked around her at the awestruck faces, utterly taken aback by the arrival of this über-celebrity, and had her response. Any pretence of coolness had been abandoned; the clicking of phone cameras was as loud as crickets on a summer evening in Tuscany.

'And congratulations!' Lexy continued, glancing at Silantra's small bump. 'You must be over the moon!'

Lil' Biscuit and Silantra structured their entire lives around the constant requirement to provide content for their fans and the media. Having decided it was time for them to have a baby – rumours were spreading about their sexual orientations, rumours which happened to be absolutely true – Biscuit and Silantra had had research conducted which revealed that their fans would prefer a female baby to a male. Silantra had been delighted by this, picturing herself dressing a little girl in specially made outfits that were miniature versions of her own.

So gender selection had been duly performed. Biscuit and Silantra were having a daughter.

'Yeah,' Silantra said rather flatly, even as she cupped her belly in the traditional proud-mother pose. 'It's very cool.'

Having seen Silantra on screen, lively and animated, Lexy was taken aback at her lack of affect. She did not yet know that Silantra only came fully to life in a few specific situations: on camera, planning scenes for her show, promoting her financial interests and having sex. Nonetheless, Lexy continued, with the graciousness of a queen welcoming a foreign dignitary on a state visit:

'It's fantastic to have you here! Are you presenting an award?'

'Yeah, I think,' Silantra said, glancing at Darrell. 'I came in on Thursday to film the *Graham Norton Show*, and then I've been doing, like, personal appearances and promoting my shoe line and my maternity wear drops next month – this is, like, a sample –' she looked down at her dress – 'so they asked me to come along tonight and I hadn't got this dress on camera yet, so it seemed like a good idea. We've been tracking pre-orders and they're, like, through the roof already.'

Lexy blinked not only at this frankness, but at the fact that Silantra had suddenly blossomed into full animation at the mention of the money she would be making from her maternity line.

'That dress looks amazing with your choker,' she observed.

'Yeah, I had it made to go with it,' Silantra said casually. 'I love your dress! I bet it photographs *amazingly*.'

'It was especially designed to work on the red carpet,' Lexy said.

'Very cool,' Silantra said. 'I saw some episodes of your show on the plane. It was fun.'

'Oh thank you! I love yours too!' Lexy said, as a waiter sidled up to Silantra proffering a champagne glass.

'It's non-alcoholic, madam,' he said deferentially.

'Shit,' Silantra said gloomily, taking the glass. 'I hate not being able to drink.'

'I had a glass of wine every other day when I was pregnant with Laylah and London,' Lexy said. 'I talked about it a lot in interviews. It's different in Europe – we're okay with pregnant mums having a bit of wine every now and them. Some people didn't like it but I had a great hashtag – #mumsneedwine – and it was really popular.'

'You're so lucky,' Silantra sighed. 'I like totally cannot be seen to have any alcohol at *all*. I'd lose half my sponsors, plus the TV advertisers.'

'I need to whisk Silantra away now,' interrupted Darrell, who had been visibly fretting at the bond that had swiftly formed between his charge and his ex-girlfriend; he had hoped for instant rivalry instead. 'We're taking her to the Royal Box and doing a big reveal after my opening monologue.'

'Ooh, *opening monologue*,' Lexy echoed mockingly. 'I didn't realize this was the UK equivalent of the Oscars! It's a fucking reality show awards ceremony, Darrell. There's a Best Bum on TV award, for Christ's sake. And one for Most Drunken Fall.'

Silantra sniggered.

'That's funny,' she said. 'You're funny. Will they, like, show the drunken fall clips? I love that kinda stuff on YouTube.'

Darrell, puffed up like a turkeycock with rage, put his hand on Silantra's back to guide her away.

'I'm having a little afterparty afterwards at my hotel,' Silantra said directly to Lexy over her shoulder. 'The St Pancras Grand. You wanna join?'

'I'd *love* to,' Lexy said with great enthusiasm; she'd promised Frank that she would come straight home after the awards ceremony, but surely he would understand that this networking opportunity could not be turned down.

'My team'll talk you through it,' Silantra said, as her

bodyguards once more parted the Red Sea of the bar crowd to shepherd her through.

'Huh,' Lexy muttered to Caroline, who had managed to make it to her side as the VIPs flooded away from her to get a look at Silantra. 'That sounds weird, right? Why not just "My team'll tell you where it is?"'

'I don't know,' Caroline said, still goggling after Silantra. 'But you were *brilliant*.'

'Thanks!' Lexy grinned at her, then bent over to whisper in Caroline's ear: 'And guess what? I'm pretty sure she wants to fuck me!'

Caroline nearly dropped her champagne glass. She was by now almost as familiar with Lexy's sex life as Lexy herself, and no same-sex encounters had featured in the extremely lengthy litany of Lexy's paramours.

'You're not going to – I mean –' she stammered, her brain racing. Was Lexy hinting that she might be about to cheat on Frank?

''Course not!' Lexy said cheerfully.

But the night was young still, and it turned out that she had spoken far too soon.

Chapter Fourteen

Lexy was quite right. Silantra definitely did want to fuck her. But instead of the time-honoured methods for signalling this – asking her to stay behind in her suite as all the other guests were ushered out of the party and then making a pass at her on the sofa, or going into the bedroom and calling Lexy through in sultry tones, only for her to find her hostess lying on the bed entirely naked – it had been handled much more formally. Silantra had described it exactly when she had told Lexy that her team would talk Lexy through it. On her arrival at the party, Silantra's PA had taken Lexy into the meeting room of the lavish suite, where Silantra's manager was waiting; sitting Lexy down, they had produced a contract for her to sign.

'This is longer than the contract for my TV show!' Lexy said, looking at the thick wodge of paper.

'American lawyers,' said the manager laconically. 'Charge a lot, put out a ton of paperwork to justify it. This is all pretty standard – total confidentiality, in perpetuity. Which means if you ever talk about anything that happens between you and Silantra, even in forty years' time, we come and we take your kids, your house, your savings accounts, your implants, your veneers . . .'

Lexy raised her eyebrows.

'That's pretty comprehensive,' she said drily.

'We hafta be,' he said, spreading his hands wide. 'You're in the biz – you get it, right? Public face, private fun. Oh, and there's a clause in there that says we can search you for video recording devices, just FYI. We had an . . . issue a year ago re that, sad to say. Some people are totally unscrupulous.'

'I'm not carrying hidden camera pens,' Lexy said. 'I didn't have time to nip to the spy shop.'

She riffled, fascinated, through the pages of the contract, her brain racing. When she had told Caroline that Silantra wanted to fuck her, she hadn't remotely imagined herself taking up the offer. She had never had sex with a woman before, and, unlike many who regretted not having had a lesbian encounter before settling down with a man, it had not been on Lexy's radar. Frankly, with all the men coming at her in waves, as it were, she hadn't even had time to consider another option.

Of course, she should reject this proposition out of hand. She was only stalling, she told herself, because this process was so fascinating, and she wanted to find out all the details of how the real A-list ran its private life. And yet . . .

Lexy dearly loved a negotiation, and her financial success was a clear demonstration of how well she conducted them. It was impossible to resist exploring what concessions she could extract in return, how she could use this as the biggest career boost imaginable.

'So what would I get out of signing something saying you

can come and take my implants in forty years?' she asked, setting down the contract. 'You give something to get something, right?'

'You want to negotiate a fee? Not a problem,' the manager said, as if this were a perfectly normal request. 'Want to suggest a ballpark figure?'

Lexy's jaw dropped at the revelation that a fund existed for precisely this kind of situation. She supposed that she could understand it. Anyone banned from ever talking about something as juicy as sex with Silantra would have the same question that Lexy had just posed: *what do I get in return for signing the kind of legal document that would financially eviscerate me if I break its terms by indulging in the juicy gossip I'm dying to share?*

'No,' she said, thinking fast. 'I'd love her to make an appearance on my show. We're filming the next season now – could we set up something in the next few days, while she's in London? My crew would definitely scramble to make that happen.'

'Huh,' the manager said. 'She *does* have a day off tomorrow, as it happens. She was going to hit the boutiques, do some shopping. And she's not scheduled to fly back till Wednesday, so we have some flexibility with the timeframe . . .'

He drummed his fingertips lightly on the wenge wood of the table top.

'You guys wait here while I go have a word with her and see what she says, okay? She might actually go for it – she's pretty spontaneous.'

He stood up. It was the make or break moment. Up till now, Lexy had been able to tell herself she had just been playing along with the situation, seeing how far she could push it. But if she let him leave the room, she was practically committed to doing this, cheating on Frank. It was something she had never done, never thought she would ever do. She loved her husband, was entirely committed to him. Although she certainly wouldn't have ruled out getting married purely for the publicity and the photo rights – half the reality stars she knew had done it – her marriage to Frank was entirely authentic, and she had meant every word of her vows.

Yet . . . this was the most famous reality star in the world, someone companies practically begged to pay huge sums for an endorsement of their products! An appearance by Silantra on Lexy's show would take Lexy to a whole different level of fame, maybe even help her crack the US, something she had always dreamed of achieving. And Silantra was absolutely gorgeous; it would be very easy to get naked with her.

Was it really cheating if it was with a woman? Frank wouldn't like it – well, that wasn't putting it strongly enough. He would absolutely hate it. But he would never know! The beauty of the confidentiality agreement was that it protected Lexy as well as Silantra; since every single member of Silantra's entourage would certainly have signed it, there was no way word could possibly get out . . .

She hesitated, visibly torn, taken aback to realize how powerfully she was tempted by the dizzying prospect of having Silantra on her show. If Lexy had been asked, before this moment, what she needed to take her career to the next level, she would have unquestionably put filming with Silantra at the top of the list. And now it was within her grasp, as if a fairy godmother had waved a magic wand and granted her a wish. Only, instead of leaving the ball before midnight, Lexy was specifically required to stay on. And she had always loved a good afterparty.

Lexy opened her mouth to tell the manager not to confer with Silantra. That she had been just playing around, that she had no intention of cheating on her husband. That he would be wasting his time.

But the words simply would not come out.

The cliché about big stars having lawyers on speed dial turned out to be entirely accurate. After a brief discussion with Silantra, who proclaimed herself more than happy to film with Lexy the next day, within a mere half an hour a one-page amendment to the confidentiality contract had been faxed through from Lil' Biscuit and Silantra's lawyers in LA, and duly signed by both the manager and Silantra herself. Lexy had signed the confidentiality contract then immediately rung her producer to scramble up her crew. The producer, near-sobbing with happiness on hearing that Lexy had snagged Silantra for her show, had immediately started tweeting the fantastic news.

'Hey, let's film us going shopping,' Silantra suggested to Lexy as she lounged on the huge bed of the master bedroom. 'My fans love the shopping scenes, plus I get shitloads of free stuff, too. What about my team ringing the PR of Harrods? We could do, like, an episode where you show me London. Remember what that jerk Darrell said? The queen of American TV visits the queen of British TV. You take me to Harrods, we shop for shoes and stuff, and then we have tea, but you have some champagne and we have that conversation about wine and being pregnant that we did in the theatre bar. You know, I say I hate not drinking and you talk about your wine hashtag and how things are different in Europe. Then I can say how I hate putting on weight being pregnant and we can talk about that and how you got the weight off. Then you can offer me, like, a cream puff, or whatever you eat over here for tea, and we can laugh about how many calories it has.'

Lexy stared at her, dumbstruck. Not only was this by far the longest speech she had heard Silantra make, but Lexy had completely failed to grasp how very well attuned Silantra was to anything that might work for her TV show. Lexy had thought they were just making casual conversation in the theatre bar; Silantra, however, had been processing every word through an automatic filter, deciding what was show-worthy and what was not.

'You could get us approval to film at Harrods tomorrow, just like that?' Lexy asked, when she had got her breath back. 'Because that's really hard to—'

'I can get anywhere, pretty much,' Silantra said casually. 'Do you know how many followers I have on Instagram? Seventy *million*. Twitter? Fifty *million*. I'm top ten in the world on both.'

'Fuck, I thought I was doing pretty well,' Lexy said wryly. 'Don't ask me how many I have, okay?'

'You'll have tons more already,' Silantra said matter-of-factly, 'now that we tweeted a pic of us together backstage at the awards ceremony. Check your phone.'

'I can't!' Lexy said, grinning. 'They took it away from me and pretty much strip-searched me for hidden cameras.'

'Yeah, sorry about that,' Silantra said, looking entirely

unapologetic. 'This total bitch filmed me and her having sex last year and then made us pay a fortune to buy the footage. It was really good quality – like, not just a cell phone. Our security said she must've used a professional spy cam. So now we have to be super careful. She was an amazing fuck,' she added wistfully. 'I really miss her! She could just've asked and I'd've put her on salary as a stylist or something, you know?'

She sighed.

'Oh well. So yeah, now everyone I hook up with gets searched. And my staff has my phone, too. Just in case you sneakily take photos of us on it and send 'em to yourself.'

'That's shitty,' Lexy said. 'You getting set up like that, I mean.'

Silantra shrugged phlegmatically. 'Yeah, it sucked, but what can you do? I wouldn't want to be her if Biscuit ever tracks her down, though. He was royally pissed. Forget suing her – he'd go hardcore on her ass.'

Lexy refilled her glass with champagne from the bottle standing beside her in a silver cooler. It had been considerately placed near her armchair by Silantra's PA. Once the little party had run its course, the other guests, including Caroline, had been gently ushered out with the excuse that Silantra had decided to film with Lexy the next day and the two women needed to discuss what scenes they would shoot.

Silantra had promptly retired to the bedroom, followed by Lexy: once the PA had made sure they had everything they needed, they had been left alone. Now, Silantra uncoiled from the bed, moving with impressive grace and ease for a woman who was four months pregnant. Gliding over to the wet bar, she took a flute from the stack of glasses on its marble surface.

'Hit me up,' she said, perching on the wide arm of Lexy's armchair, holding out her glass.

'So you're okay drinking a little in private?' Lexy said, filling the glass.

'A little? Watch me!'

Lifting the glass to her glossy lips, Silantra drank its entire contents down in one gulp and then held the glass out to Lexy once more.

'Hit me again, babe,' she said, her eyes now glinting with mischief.

'Fuck,' Lexy said, frowning. 'I'm all for taking the edge off, but that's too much. They say you can have a glass a day, tops, when you're knocked up. You've got to think of the baby.'

Silantra took the bottle herself and refilled her glass, manoeuvring her long fingernails with the expertise of a woman who has been sporting them ever since the age of fourteen. Then she leaned over, put one hand behind Lexy's head and kissed her, long and hard. It was an excellent kiss, full of passion and technique, again with the expertise of a woman who had been pimped out by her mother since the age of fifteen. Before marrying Lil' Biscuit, Silantra had regularly been required to make trips to Dubai which were billed as shopping expeditions, but were actually to rendezvous with billionaire Saudis prepared to pay seven-figure fees to spend the night with her.

'You ever fucked a girl?' she asked when she released Lexy.

'Kissed a few, fingered each other a bit,' Lexy said frankly. 'But just at school. Once I got on a dick I never looked back.'

'Don't worry, I'll be gentle,' Silantra said, standing up. She downed another half a glass of champagne, set down her glass and then reached round to unzip her dress. 'And you don't have to do anything you don't want. But I *would* really like to fuck you. I have this great strap-on – it really hits the G-spot. Wherever yours is, I'll find it!'

Lexy blinked. It wasn't a surprise to her that Silantra had a strap-on; everyone who had watched her infamous sex tape knew that she liked to dish it out as well as take it. But the nonchalant way she talked about it was almost . . . professional.

Silantra's dress was dropping to the floor, and Lexy did a double take at the sight of what Silantra was wearing beneath it. She had assumed that Silantra would be in shapewear: all of them wore it. Awards ceremonies and red carpet events weren't about being comfortable, they were about looking fabulous, and that meant being as streamlined as possible, no bulges or lumps for the media to mock.

Lexy was well aware of the existence of maternity shapewear: she had relied on it during both of her pregnancies. But the beige bodysuit that Silantra was wearing looked very different from what Lexy had worn back then. Its texture was weirdly foam-like, as if it were moulded onto her body, bulking it out, the opposite of stretch fabric intended to hold her in . . .

Silantra's hands were still behind her, unfastening something else. Bra? Corset? Velcro ripped open, a wide strap came loose, then another . . . and then Silantra widened her grip. Her hands came into view, and she lifted the whole front of her body up and away from her, swollen breasts, pregnant stomach and all.

'No *way*,' Lexy said slowly. 'You're not knocked up after all!'

Chapter Fifteen

The moulded foam prosthetic dropped to the floor next to the discarded dress. Underneath it, Silantra was clad in just a glossy little thong. One did not need to be a connoisseur of fake breasts to find hers superb: big and round and full, but not so out of proportion that they looked entirely artificial. As a woman of colour, she was permitted by the media to be fuller-figured than a white star, and her curves were famously voluptuous – apart, of course, from her stomach, on which not even non-white women were granted an exemption. That always had to be flat, and Silantra's, after multiple liposuctions, was perfectly so.

'Ugh,' she said, rubbing her breasts and stomach with complete nonchalance at her near-nakedness. 'It gets so damn sweaty under there. I hate wearing that thing for more than a couple hours. And I gotta keep going for five more months, and upgrade to bigger and bigger ones too! Nightmare!'

She took up her champagne glass again and finished off the contents, her breasts bouncing fractionally with the movement.

'Still,' she said, shrugging, 'it's better than the other thing, right? This way I can shoot a DVD on getting my figure back real soon after the birth and make a mint.'

'Wow,' Lexy said, working hard to keep her cool. 'I did *not* see that coming.'

'Right? This thing is awesome,' Silantra said, kicking it away as she moved towards Lexy. 'Made especially for me. The tummy part's totally firm, so it doesn't bend in the middle when you sit down and give you away, which is what happened to—'

She mentioned the name of a very famous female actress who had been caught out like that when faking her pregnancy; she had been filmed in a live interview from the side, taking a seat in a TV studio, her stomach creasing in a way that one with a baby inside it could never have done.

'But why . . .' Lexy began.

'I wanna keep my figure perfect,' Silantra said simply. 'I don't want those hormones fucking with me and making me pile on the weight, giving me stretch marks and shit. I'm gonna have cortisone shots in the last month – they puff you up, make you swell round the face and neck so I look realistic. We've put an egg of mine, fertilized with Biscuit's jizz, in a nice Guatemalan lady who barely speaks English, and when she gives birth it'll be in a big suite in an LA hospital, totally sealed off to the media. Major security, which we can spin as needing to protect my and the baby's privacy.'

She looked thoughtful.

'It's kinda crazy, the whole surrogate setup. We control how she gives birth, did you know that? If the doc says she needs a caesarean, she doesn't get to say no. All signed and sealed, contract's tighter than a nun's snatch.'

She was standing in front of Lexy now, and she tilted her glass up to trickle the remains of her champagne over her nipples, which grew instantly erect at the sensation of the cool liquid.

'Wanna lick it off?' she asked. 'And then we need to get you outta that dress. I wanna see your titties. They're not real, right?'

'No,' Lexy said, leaning forward obediently.

'Oh good. I like fake ones. Real ones are so, like, *droopy*.'

As instructed, Lexy started to lick the champagne from Silantra's nipples. Silantra clearly wanted to be in charge, and for Lexy, who was used to being the boss of her empire, this was a delightful change of pace. Eventually she removed her dress, peeled off her own bra and Spanx, and lay back as Silantra climbed onto her lap and played with her tits while kissing her as deeply and deliciously as before. After popping off her fake nails and dumping them in a little sparkling pile on the side table, Silantra's hand went between Lexy's legs, which were already splayed for her.

Lexy started to come very soon. Silantra knew exactly what she was doing, pressing over her, bouncing one pair of surgically enhanced breasts against the other in a way that was completely porny but turned Lexy on to a surprising degree. As Silantra pulled her up, told her to bend over the bed and went to get her strap-on, the entire experience was already feeing quite unreal to Lexy, like a dream in which she had been dropped onto a porn set and told she was one of the lead actors.

It only added to the illusion that Silantra fucked like the professional she had been before her marriage. The Saudis had paid a million dollars for a night with her to recreate the most famous scene from her sex tape: their fantasy was for her to strap on one of her several dildos and give it to them just as she had given it to the guy in the video. She knew how to work a prostate, make her clients scream; by the time they'd shot their load, they always felt the extortionate price they had paid had been more than worth it.

Lexy was dripping wet, more than ready, and the fake cock slid into her with ease. Just as she had promised, Silantra was feeling for Lexy's G-spot, that particularly sensitive area which was engorged, ribbed, with arousal. Once she located it, she worked it so expertly that Lexy's eyes rolled right up into her head with the stimulation. Over her increasingly loud moans of pleasure, she heard Silantra giggling in satisfaction at the sounds she was drawing from Lexy. Lexy had never pictured herself reaching a vaginal orgasm to the backing track of a woman's giggles, but that was exactly what happened, and as she came she felt a flood release inside her, washing over the dildo.

For a moment she was terrified that she had accidentally wet herself. Then she realized that the G-spot orgasm had made her ejaculate; she knew that happened to some women. It felt extraordinary, a physical release that was very different from the clitoral one, leaving her as limp as a man after he had shot his load.

As Silantra pulled out, the rush of liquid followed, streaming out onto the carpet.

'Wow, you come a *lot*,' Silantra drawled. 'I shoulda put down a towel.'

'I didn't know,' Lexy mumbled into the coverlet, completely drained. 'First time it's happened.'

'Cool! I love being the first one to take a chick's G-spot virginity and make her squirt!' Silantra said complacently. 'I must've racked up over a hundred by now. It really turns me on. You shoulda told me.'

'I didn't even know you liked girls,' Lexy managed to say.

'Chicks for fun, guys for work,' Silantra said. 'Not Biscuit though. He's gay. Like, gold-standard. He could *so* not do chicks for work, if you get me.'

Lexy's body had stopped spasming: she seemed to have finished ejaculating, but she still couldn't move a muscle. For the first time, she understood why men collapsed as if they were boneless after they came.

'You're all knocked out, aren't you?' Silantra said, and Lexy heard her unfastening the harness. 'Great, isn't it? You wanna try it on me later? No pressure. But it's a rush if you're into that kinda thing.'

'Sure,' Lexy said to the coverlet. 'Why not?'

Silantra took the dildo to the bathroom to wipe clean, and after they had finished the bottle of champagne while watching an episode of *Real Housewives of Beverly Hills* on catchup, Silantra regaling Lexy with salacious gossip on many of the participants, and raided the kitchen for cheese puffs, canapés of air-dried beef on rye bread with horseradish, and a varietal of white strawberry which tasted eerily like pink champagne truffles, Lexy strapped on the harness. It was immediately obvious why Silantra said it was a rush. As Silantra, a pillow shoved under her hips, told Lexy where to direct the dildo, letting her know when she had hit the spot by starting to scream her head off, her braids whipping back and forth as she tossed her head in pleasure, Lexy felt ten feet tall.

I wonder if Frank would let me do this to him? she wondered as she altered her rhythm, acutely aware of how she hated men just to pound away, fucking Silantra the way she herself liked it best. *He does love a finger up his arse. I could ask him to let me try as a one-off, see if he goes for it . . .*

As Silantra bucked against the dildo, the base of it, in the harness, rubbed against Lexy's clit with increasing pressure. Lexy closed her eyes, riding the dildo even as she rode Silantra, starting to come again, clitorally this time, her thrusts rougher as she focused on her own pleasure; Silantra, knowing what was happening, bucked even harder, pushing back, sending Lexy over the edge and following her just a minute later. Her own orgasm spurted out, trickling down the sides of the dildo, onto the towel that they had sensibly placed under Silantra's hips. Lexy just had the energy to pull out and collapse on the bed beside Silantra, flipping herself awkwardly onto her back to accommodate the big dick strapped between her legs.

'Wow,' she said.

'Yeah.'

Silantra turned on her side, a leisurely movement, and leaned over to kiss Lexy.

'It's just so hot, fucking someone,' she said drowsily, falling back onto the bedspread. 'Why should the guys have all the fun? I'd totally have a dick too if I could. Tits, dick, cunt, everything. I really get why some guys like chicks with dicks.'

She yawned deeply.

'Okay, I'm crashing,' she said. 'You wanna stay over? We could fuck again in the morning. It's the best thing for filming – your skin looks really great afterwards.'

'Oh well,' Lexy said, shifting sideways so that she could unstrap the complicated harness. 'If it's good for filming, we should definitely do it, right? We're professionals – we have to think of what's best for the show.'

Silantra giggled sleepily, reaching down to mop herself with the towel.

'You're funny!' she said. 'I like that.'

She smiled at Lexy with real affection.

'Know why I wanted to hook up tonight, enough to do your show?' she asked. 'I mean, you're hot, but there are hot chicks everywhere. I wanted to hang out with you too. You can't buy funny.'

'Guess what?' Lexy said, deadpan, putting the dildo on the bedside table. 'That's exactly what you just did.'

Greatly to her credit, Silantra thought this was the funniest quip of the entire evening.

Chapter Sixteen

Caroline couldn't sleep. She had been home for an hour and she was pacing her room, unable to calm down. A mug of camomile tea stood on her bedside table. She made herself walk over, blow on it, try to take a sip: it was coming up to two a.m., and if she didn't get to sleep, she would be in no state for the considerable amount of writing she needed to get done the next day.

The discovery she had made back at the St Pancras Grand, however, was so enormous that she was having serious trouble processing its implications. She had walked out of the hotel in an absolute trance. Seeing the line of black cabs on the curving forecourt, she had found herself nodding at the doorman when he asked if she wanted one, getting inside without even thinking about how much it would cost.

The awards show had finished at eleven, the after-party had run past one in the morning; there was no way she could get home at that time on public transport without a night tube journey to Seven Sisters and then a night bus. The journey itself was fairly speedy; it was the company of the drunks on tube and bus, plus the distinctly insalubrious atmosphere of the bus stop at which she would have to wait, and the walk down Edmonton Green at that hour of night, that she dreaded. Especially because she was conspicuously dressed in party clothes: in her experience that always made women more of a target.

Climbing into the cab, she decided to expense it to Bailey and Hart. If they objected, Caroline would have Lexy intercede; Caroline now had a very powerful weapon, if she used it carefully. From this moment on, if she wanted legitimate extra expenses, for instance, all she had to do was joke about how Lexy had told her that Silantra wanted to have sex with her, or ask casually what time Lexy had made it back to the Chelsea flat after her post-party meeting with Silantra.

Lexy couldn't possibly know that Caroline was aware of the true reason she had stayed on at the hotel, but she would be desperate to shut down any speculation on the subject in case she was thought to have violated that terrifying confidentiality agreement. Lexy would be horrified if she knew that Caroline was even aware of the agreement's existence.

Caroline's antennae had registered something unusual about the way the PA had bustled Lexy away as they arrived at the party, murmuring that they wanted to get her contact details so they could discuss possible future projects. Why wouldn't Silantra's team just give Lexy a card, or ping over their contact details and ask her manager to get in touch in due course, which was what had happened every other time someone wanted to work with Lexy?

No one else noticed but Caroline. The other guests were too busy vying for Silantra's attention, taking selfies with her: this was the opportunity of a lifetime to raise their profile by association. Darrell Rose, who, to Lexy's annoyance, had been invited back to the St Pancras Grand, was particularly egregious, his veneered, megawatt smile flashing repeatedly as he held his phone above himself and Silantra, snapping away.

Caroline was the only person who sat quietly to one side. And when plenty of time had elapsed, more than enough to provide an email address and phone number, Caroline slipped unnoticed from the living room. She was nothing and nobody, the least important guest of all. It would have more impact on the party if one of the waiters disappeared.

The meeting room was private, with no floor-to-ceiling glass panel which would allow anyone passing to see inside, as Lexy could not possibly be spotted at a table reading a thick contract. But Caroline could hear a murmur of voices inside, and besides, there was nowhere else they could be. The doors of the other rooms down that corridor – a second bedroom, a kitchen, a staff room with ironing and laundry facilities – were all ajar.

The bedroom adjoined the meeting room; Caroline darted inside. As she had hoped, the rooms were connected by an internal door, but Caroline did not dare to try to edge it open, even fractionally. Instead, using a technique she had seen on an old daytime TV show, she snatched a water glass from the shelf over the minibar and placed the rim of it to the door, pressing her ear against the base.

To her great surprise, it worked.

'This is longer than the contract for my TV show!' Lexy was saying.

Caroline could just make out the sound of tightly bound pages flicking heavily as Lexy leafed through them. Caroline was absolutely agog. It didn't take her long to grasp what was happening. She scrambled to her unfashionable little satchel for her phone, silencing it, turning it on to record and pressing it to a chink between the door and the jamb, just in case; it was very disappointing to find out later that all it had captured was the fuzziest murmur of voices, sounding as if they were twenty feet down a well. But Caroline had heard everything.

When the meeting ended, she quickly transcribed the conversation she had overheard, then slipped back into the living room as unobtrusively as she had left it. Lexy and Silantra were standing together, the mobile phones of everyone present trained on them: clearly, the announcement that Silantra would be filming with Lexy the next day for Lexy's show had just been made.

Silantra, her arm wrapped round Lexy's sequinned waist, was smiling like the cat that had got the cream. Exactly the same smile Caroline saw her give later, when the manager and PA started to bustle the other guests out, saying that Lexy and Silantra needed to discuss their filming schedule for the next day . . .

The camomile tea had cooled down. As Caroline sipped it, she found herself picturing Silantra and Lexy's naked bodies entwined around each other. It didn't take much imagination. Both women had posed naked or barely clothed so often that some of their fans must know the voluptuous curves of their bodies better than their own.

I can't believe this is the first time Lexy's cheated on Frank, Caroline thought. *She agreed so easily! She barely paused for a moment before she went right into negotiating what she could get from it! She's a total whore. She's married to the most wonderful, kind, thoughtful man, a man who's far too good for her, and instead of going home to him she's spreading her legs for another whore who sold a video of herself having sex to kickstart her career.*

She's disgusting. And she doesn't deserve Frank, not for a moment. I can't believe he doesn't know what's going on. I can't believe he doesn't see what she's really like.

Someone should tell him.

Someone should be there to love him and look after him and his kids the way they deserve.

Caroline looked up and met her own eyes in the wall-mounted full-length mirror that hung beside the bed. Setting down her half-drunk mug of tea, she stood up and, very deliberately, peeled off the loose nightdress she was wearing. Standing naked in front of a mirror was something she never did; she had included herself in the observation that many of Lexy and Silantra's fans knew their idols' bodies better than their own.

The excess weight wasn't pleasant for her to look at, but she had a reasonably good shape underneath it. She wasn't pear-shaped; she knew from women's magazine articles that the only solution for that was liposuction for the saddlebags. Her breasts were big and firm, her hair was thick and her skin had been very much improved by the vitamins and omega-plus supplements, the products and treatments Lexy had bought her. After a month of slogging Tuesday to Friday over the damp sands of Studland beach, then limping back to the gym to do a series of situps and press-ups recommended to her by Frank, while sticking to the calorie-counted meals from Lexy's cook, Caroline had quite clearly toned up and lost weight.

Until now, Caroline had been maintaining the exercise and diet regime on the weekdays, letting herself off a morning run on Monday because that was when she travelled down to Bournemouth, giving herself licence to eat and drink what she wanted at the weekends. But now, she realized, the game had changed. The slow, gradual weight loss she had been achieving was no longer enough.

I need to work out and watch what I eat every day, she resolved. *I'll live off slices of chicken and salad, no dressing. I'll cut out booze completely – Frank's always telling Lexy that even if you drink vodka and soda, which has no calories, it breaks down your inhibitions so when you get pissed you either raid the fridge or go for the fags, like Lexy does.*

I need to lose a lot of weight. I need to get a spray tan. I need to wear more make-up, get eyelash extensions, hair extensions, tighter clothes.

I need to look as like Lexy as I possibly can, as fast as I can.

Because I want to take her husband away from her.

Lexy's nickname for Caroline had been biting into her like caustic acid for weeks now. But, making her resolution, seeing her jaw tighten as she pressed her lips together in determination, she realized that she could use the rage it provoked and turn it to her benefit.

Because Lexy would never see Ghost Mouse coming.

The woman was running as if she were being chased by the hounds of hell. She had wrenched off her sandals with such force that she had torn a nail on one of the straps, and she didn't even realize; the only thing of any importance was to move as fast as possible. She tore through the crowded restaurant, dodging waiters, skirting tables; she caught a tray being carried by a waiter with her elbow and it went flying, glass crashing to the tiled floor, and she didn't even break stride.

Heads turned, restaurant patrons exclaimed in surprise, speculation, disapproval. Practically no one had seen the 'cause of the woman's frantic dash, the emergency to which she was responding.

She was turning into the corridor now, swivelling so fast she nearly hit a wall and had to slap her palm against it to right herself. There were hotel guests coming towards her, dressed in bright, flowing clothes suitable for the sultry tropical weather, clearly heading for the restaurant; she yelled 'MOVE, MOVE, MOVE!' at them without slowing down. They stumbled into each other, their expressions shocked and angry; they burst into loud complaints as she sped past, her bare feet pounding the mosaic floor, her long muscled legs moving like a sprint-

er's, her arms pumping the air. In one hand she was gripping a key card, grabbed from the dinner table as she jumped to her feet.

She was counting rooms frantically, making sure she didn't overshoot. She had to get to her suite, grab what she needed, turn round and run right back again, and she needed to do all that in under a couple of minutes. How long had it been? How long had it taken her to drag off those sandals, stand up, start running?

Her breath was coming in quick, sharp huffs. A door started to open in her face, someone coming out of their suite, and she reached out and shoved it back so she could shoot past, hearing a shriek of surprise from the person behind it.

It didn't matter. Even if she'd bumped them, even if they'd tripped, it was nothing in comparison to the emergency to which she was responding. She had spotted it almost immediately; she knew exactly how life-threatening it could be. As she skidded to a halt in front of her door, fumbling the key card into the slot with hands that shook despite her best efforts to keep herself controlled and focused, she was counting the seconds in her head, feeling time ticking inexorably away, beating down the panic that was rising in her chest.

Because this was quite literally a matter of life or death. If she couldn't find what she needed and get it back to that restaurant in the next sixty seconds, a child was almost certainly going to die.

PART TWO

Chapter Seventeen

Two months later

Baby London was glued to my right boob, feeding away, greedy little sod. He just wouldn't wait till the photoshoot was over. I know it's not exactly usual to have wedding photos with one boob hoicked out of your dress, but you could barely see it and who cares anyway! I mean, you see more of my tits in any of my calendars! Wow! *magazine put it on its cover – bit controversial, and we got loads of publicity, which was excellent. They asked me on* This Morning *and* Loose Women *to talk about breastfeeding mums' rights and all that stuff.*

I really love that photo, actually. Laylah's even looking like she's happy to see her baby brother, which is funny as she pretty much tried to kill him loads of times when he was little. God, she was a jealous little mare. Frank had to bribe her with sweeties to get her to smile at me and the baby for the camera.

Oh well, at least she was doing her job for a change, being a good girl, and she really did look lovely in her flower girl dress. As London fed, I took a deep breath and thought about how much I'd achieved, all the boxes I'd ticked. Handsome, loving, minted husband: check. Two gorgeous kids: check. Lavish home: check. The top-rated reality show on UK TV: check. My own column in Lovely! *magazine: check. Endorsements, super-market clothing lines, my own-brand hair products and extensions, accessories, fake nails, with more rolling out every year: check, check, check, check.*

It'd been a non-stop ride since I went on Who's My Date?, *and trust me, it wasn't just in the upward direction! More like a roller coaster – big ups, big downs. But I always held on tight, kept a smile on my face, no matter what was happening, and my fans loved me for that, bless them.*

I glanced down at the ring Frank had slid onto my finger just an hour ago, nestled next to the humongous diamond that had made me burst into tears of happiness when he got down on one knee and asked me to marry him.

Caroline paused. She had no idea whether Lexy had cried when Frank proposed, but she had swiftly learned that Lexy didn't care about strict accuracy. After the first few times Caroline had pestered Lexy with follow-up questions after a recorded session, Lexy had told her ghostwriter not to bother her with this kind of thing, to just go ahead and make it up.

'You'll do a better job like that anyway,' she had said non-chalantly. 'I mean, we're selling what readers want to buy, right? Tell 'em what they want to hear!'

So Caroline simply sent each chapter to Lexy for her approval as soon as it was written. Lexy changed very little, limiting herself to tweaking her own dialogue. As long as Caroline made Lexy seem sympathetic and relatable, Lexy didn't care; and since writing went much faster if Caroline didn't keep checking with Lexy, 'Ghost Mouse' had no com-plaints either.

After all those years of unreliable men, ones who'd cheated on me, lied to me, tried to control me – fuck, the one who was into wearing my knickers and stretching them out, which was bloody annoying considering how much they cost – the dickhead and arsehole parade was over. I felt incredibly lucky to have my lovely loyal Frank.

Caroline stared at the last line. Typing it had made her feel queasy. There was no question that it described Frank correctly. But a loyal man would never leave his wife for her ghostwriter . . .

Ah, she told herself swiftly, *but he would when he found out that she had cheated on him!* He would have to, for the sake of the children, who couldn't be brought up in an atmosphere of betrayal and deceit! When Frank had taken his wedding vows, he had thought he was making promises to a woman who was as sincere as he was, who had the same qualities that he did.

While actually, Lexy was a liar and a cheat, who had no right to be in a relationship with a man like Frank at all, let alone be married to him.

Caroline took a deep breath and typed:

Today was the first day of the rest of my life. There'd be more ups and downs, no doubt about that, new worlds to conquer.

And I'm still on that roller coaster! You lot have been with me from the beginning! I hope you'll stick with me for the rest of the ride. I promise, there'll be plenty of thrills and spills!

Watch this space!

Was this a good enough ending? It *sounded* catchy. And Caroline wanted to suggest that there might well be further memoirs from Lexy, or maybe even novels written under her name – by Caroline, of course. But 'watch this space' – didn't that also sound a bit cheesy? More appropriate for a column in a magazine than a proper book?

The answers, she had the gloomy feeling, were 'no' and 'yes' respectively. But Caroline was totally burnt out. For the last eight weeks, all she had been doing was writing, sleeping, exercising and starving herself, and she could barely muster energy enough to type 'The End' and haul herself from her desk to her bed.

Flopping down, kicking off her slippers, she lay on the coverlet, staring at the ceiling. She wasn't sleepy, but she was incredibly tired – no, she corrected herself. Not tired. The experience of writing a book in such a tearing hurry had trained her to seek at great speed the exact word for what she was describing. She had made her brain into a highly efficient machine, and she couldn't simply press a switch to turn it off. The word, it told her, was drained, completely and utterly drained.

Unbelievably, she had had to finish it even faster than originally agreed. On finishing the first five chapters, Caroline had sent them, as promised, to Gareth and Miranda. Gareth had promptly organized a conference call to tell Caroline how delighted he was with them; so delighted, in fact, that he wanted to get the book finished and into proof as soon as humanly possible so that they could send it out to press and bloggers to get a real buzz building for publication.

This meant, he said blithely, trying to get a first draft done even faster, ideally, than the contract specified. If Caroline could deliver the manuscript in eight weeks, Gareth offered temptingly, Bailey and Hart would authorize another grand to be paid to her on delivery – subject, of course, to the same conditions as her contractual payment, i.e. she couldn't rush so much that the draft was unreadable.

Even though she was Lexy's agent, not Caroline's, Miranda, stepping in, had nudged the 'speed bonus' up to fifteen hundred. And then Miranda had dropped a side email to Caroline, saying that she'd love to have a meeting with her after the book was finished to discuss possible future projects. It was exactly what Caroline had hoped for, and it made her more determined than ever to complete the book to the new deadline.

In order to achieve it, Caroline had initiated a new schedule. She had suggested to Lexy that she travel down to Sandbanks on Sunday night and stay until Saturday morning, as she unquestionably got more writing done in the cocooned surroundings of the guest suite. She didn't even have a desk to work at in her cramped London bedroom; she had to sit on her bed with her laptop on her thighs, a padded computer rest beneath it to stop it burning her up.

Lexy and Frank had been more than happy with Caroline's suggestion. Lexy had joked that she'd slice a bit off Caroline's advance for room and board, to which Frank had retorted that with the amount of childcare Caroline seemed to be doing, they should probably pay her for it. Lina had given notice several weeks ago, London having bitten her one too many times, and in the interim period before the agency could find a nanny who was long-suffering, physically unattractive and willing to be repeatedly bitten, Caroline had stepped up to help.

Caroline wasn't a natural with children. She'd never been one of those people who could instinctively talk to kids on their level, mesmerizing them like the Pied Piper so that the kids would follow them round for hours afterwards, wide-eyed and tugging on their sleeves. But she remembered very well how her mother had kept her large brood in order with a judicious blend of discipline and promises of treats to come.

And she had an advantage that none of the previous nannies had possessed: hardcore motivation to charm Laylah and London, as the children were an essential part of her strategy to win over Frank. A less intelligent woman might have targeted him directly, but to Caroline it was obvious that his family was the key to his heart. Caroline was very aware by now of his wish to have more children, a wish his wife was refusing to grant. Caroline, twenty-seven to Lexy's thirty-seven, was statistically able to have more children than a woman ten years older than her, and her goal was to position herself as the person who was able to give him what Lexy would or could not.

Getting the kids to like her had been surprisingly easy. It had quickly become clear that their rotating corps of nannies had never really spent time getting to know them. Laylah and London had so many toys, so many games, so many gadgets, plus of course their swimming pool and lavish gardens, that all the nannies had needed to do was to supervise them as they ran from one activity to another, make sure they didn't injure themselves, tidy up after them, make sure they ate and went to bed on time, before retreating to their own very cosy room with its high-definition television.

But no one supervised the nannies in their turn. Lexy didn't care what went on as long as the children didn't bother her, and Frank assumed, with typical male naivete, that the nannies knew their jobs already. Much as he loved his children, he had the traditional male attitude that raising children was women's work; when they squabbled and fought, his first instinct was generally to yell for the nanny to come and sort them out.

So the children had had very little quality time with adults, which explained their near-feral behaviour. Caroline started by simply sitting down with them on the floor of their playroom and asking them what they wanted to do. London begged her to set up the £500 Scalextric track that was still sitting in its box, and organize endless car races; Laylah chose to model outfits she had styled from her capacious wardrobe, with Caroline as her audience.

And both of them, more than anything, craved one-to-one chats with an adult who actually listened to what they said.

Caroline did all of that and more. She played hide and seek with them, got into the swimming pool with them – rather than sitting on the side fully clothed, scrolling through her phone, which had been the modus operandi of all the nannies in the past – or took them into the garden and set up obstacle courses, tiring them out so that they would behave better. It worked out very well for her: she ran first thing in the morning, then wrote for most of the day before she picked up the kids from their daycare and school, spending the late afternoon and early evening with them before returning to her suite to read and edit what she had written earlier that day. The break to play with the children wiped her brain clear, leaving her fresh for the editing session, and the extra activity meant that she was burning even more calories.

Lexy, of course, barely noticed any of this. When she saw Caroline and the kids coming up in the lift, wet-haired, wrapped in pool towels and giggling, or noticed Laylah and London running across the lawn, shrieking in excitement as they tried to jump in the right order into a series of hula hoops Caroline had placed on the grass, her only comment was that they were making a lot of noise.

But of course, all this was not being done for Lexy's benefit. When Frank expressed amazement at how much better behaved the kids seemed to be nowadays, how they were laughing instead of screaming at each other, Caroline would modestly say that she was only using the techniques her mother had perfected bringing up six kids close in age: first tire them out, then make sure they ate healthy food and got lots of love.

'They already get great food,' Caroline had said innocently, 'and so much love from you and Lexy! So all I'm doing is playing with them and giving them lots of exercise.'

'Oh,' Frank had said, as Caroline knew he would, 'you're doing yourself down there. Laylah and London really care about you. Look how much they love hanging out with you!'

And since at that point, Laylah had run up to Caroline, grabbed her hand, shrieking: 'London and me want to do a hopping race in the swimming pool, come on, come on, *come on*!' and dragged her off with the ruthlessness of a nine-year-old who knows that an adult will obey her commands, all Caroline had had to do was to shrug, smile apologetically at Frank and let herself be led away to emphasize the point that he had been making.

After a couple of weeks a new nanny was hired – another unhappy Eastern European called Gabriela, who would have much preferred to be in London, where she already had friends and a social life: but word had got round Bournemouth and Poole about Lexy's out-of-control children, and no local girls would take the job, not after several had tried and retreated with bite marks. Gabriela was openly sullen and unmotivated, quite unimpressed by Lexy's fame. Like the other nannies, she did the minimum possible, picking the children up from school, bringing them home and then leaving them to their own devices, which meant that Caroline could work for longer during the day while still maintaining her hold on the children's affections.

She had even managed to cure London of biting people. He wasn't a budding sociopath, just an intelligent, spoilt kid who was perpetually angry, chafing at the dominance of his equally intelligent and extremely bossy older sister. Too scared to bite Laylah, who would without question have bitten him back harder, he took it out on the Montessori providers and nannies who he knew weren't allowed to do anything but complain to his parents.

Caroline had dealt with it the way she remembered her mother handling her little brother when he went through an ankle-biting stage. When London, in a fit of pique, lunged towards her, teeth bared, she let him dig them in and then put her hand on the back of his head, forcing his open jaw right into her arm. Almost immediately, he started choking, and Caroline gave it a count of five before she let him go.

'That *hurt*!' he yelled angrily at her, big brown eyes wide with indignation.

'If you want to act like a dog, you get treated like a dog,' she said firmly. 'That's what you do when a dog bites you, if you can – you shove whatever it's biting even further into its mouth, so it chokes and lets you go.'

'Really?' London stared at her incredulously.

'I dunno if it actually works,' she admitted, 'but that's what my mum used to say. And it's what she did to my brother when he bit her. He only did it once, and that was it.'

'Your mummy was mean,' London said.

'*Biting's* mean,' Caroline retorted, showing him the dents his teeth had made in her arm. 'That really hurt. If you want to be a naughty dog in future, why don't you bark or something instead of biting?'

At this, London had giggled, dropped to all fours and started barking; Caroline threw a ball for him, telling him to fetch it in his teeth, and he scampered around the playroom blissfully for a good twenty minutes before tiring of the game. She had been planning to drop the news to Frank casually that evening that she was channelling his son away from biting people; Lexy was filming at a modelling and fashion show in Birmingham and would be away for two or three days, so the timing was perfect.

But as it turned out, London did it for her.

'Daddy!' he said, running towards Frank when he got back from his radio show that afternoon. 'Daddy, Caroline told me that only naughty dogs bite, and I'm going to be a naughty dog but not like that any more, and when a dog bites you, you should push its head to make it bite you harder so it stops . . .'

'Whoah, whoah, tiger, slow down!'

Frank caught his son and swung him in the air.

'I'm not a *tiger*!' London yelled. 'I'm a naughty dog!'

Laughing, Frank looked over London's head at Caroline, who was coming down the stairs; she had been waiting eagerly to welcome him home, something Lexy never did. In anticipation, she had donned her new slim-cut jeans and a loose silky top that showed a hint of cleavage and spent time she couldn't really afford to take off work doing her make-up and hair very carefully.

'Caroline! What's all this, then?' Frank asked her. 'I can't make head nor tail of what he's going on about!'

'Oh, we're working on London's little biting problem,' she said, looking modest. 'Not a big deal, but I thought I'd try to get him to stop.'

'Caroline, you do too much for us, you really do,' Frank said, looking guilty. 'You're not even his nanny. Where *is* Gabriela, anyway?'

'Laylah's got a friend here for a playdate, and Gabriela's watching them in the swimming pool,' Caroline said, choosing her words carefully.

Frank picked up exactly what she had intended to convey by this seemingly neutral statement.

'Yeah, she's watching them, but you'd be in the pool with them if you were down there,' he observed. 'What *are* we going to do without you, Caroline?'

Caroline drooped her head sadly.

'I know!' she said. 'I'll have finished the book in another two weeks if I keep going at this pace, and then I'll be gone, I suppose. It's silly of me, but I'm going to miss the kids so much!'

This went down perfectly. Frank's expression softened even more as he gazed at her, giving her his entire attention. London, sensing that his father's focus was elsewhere, started to wriggle, and Frank set London down, still, however, looking at Caroline.

And to Caroline's delight, London put the cherry on top of the cake. As soon as his feet touched the ground, he dashed over to Caroline, hugging her legs and wailing:

'No, no, Caroline don't go, don't go, Caroline don't *goooo . . .*'

Lying on her bed now, that memory brought a very satisfied smile to Caroline's face. She lifted her hands to her breasts. Three months ago, they had been two cup sizes bigger, spilling over her chest; now she could pretty much encompass them in her palms. Riz had commented wistfully about her boobs shrinking as she lost the weight, and received the snappy response that it was only the Lexys of this world, who had money for plastic surgery, who had unfeasibly large boobs on a slim frame.

Maybe, when I'm at my target weight, I should have plastic surgery too, Caroline thought. *I won't be a DD cup naturally – no one has that at a size 10, which is what I'm going for. If I want to be as like Lexy as possible so Frank fancies me, I should have a boob job . . . you can get financing for them, I've seen the ads . . .*

Her hands slid down to her ribcage, to the waist that was now defined, the stomach that was unquestionably flatter, the hips that were two inches narrower than they had been when she started working out, the thighs with their strong quad muscles developed from near-daily jogging.

Frank noticed my leg muscles when he came down to the pool the other day, she remembered proudly. The swimsuit she had brought with her, a drab high-necked Speedo style, had long been discarded as too droopy and big for her slimmer figure; she had splurged last month – over a hundred pounds! – for a mauve and white polkadot Miracle Suit at Debenhams. It was low-cut to show off her breasts, gathered and draped tactfully over her tummy, the legs cut in a boxershort style to help conceal the cellulite on her bottom.

She had been standing in the shallow end with the kids, throwing a ball back and forth, and had gradually sensed that there was someone else in the pool room; turning her head, she had seen Frank standing in the doorway, clearly having been there for a little while. Her eyes met his, and he raised his hand in greeting.

'Uh, your quads are looking good,' he said. 'Nice definition.'

It was the kind of comment that, as her unofficial fitness coach, was not inappropriate; but there was something in his tone of voice, something in the way he was keeping his gaze very carefully on her face, that gave Caroline the wonderful sensation that finally, after all this hard work, Frank was seeing her not merely as the dowdy ghostwriter and amateur nanny, but a woman who could actually be considered attractive . . .

The memory of the way he had looked at her was bringing a warm flush to the entire front of her body, a tingling that built as she closed her eyes and called up Frank's face, Frank's body in his tight Under Armour workout clothes. She imagined him sweaty after a gym session, walking into her bedroom and peeling off that T-shirt, hands going to his waist to hook his thumbs in the waistband of his shorts and drag them down . . .

She should lock the door to be safe, but it was early afternoon, with London and Laylah still at school. No one was around. Her vibrator was safely stored on the top shelf of her wardrobe where the kids couldn't reach it – Laylah in particular was very nosy – but Caroline's need was suddenly so pressing that she had to satisfy it immediately, without taking the time to retrieve her Rabbit. Flipping the coverlet over her, she wriggled her sweatpants and knickers down to her knees, slid her hand between her legs and started to stroke herself.

In her fantasy, Frank's shorts and briefs were catching on the tentpole of his cock, and he had to pull them out to make space for it, a big, fat, pink-flushed prong that made Caroline's mouth water as she stared at it. She rose from the bed, instantly slimmer, clad now in the kind of silky negligee Lexy wore around the house, her skin moisturized and perfumed, her hair cascading to her shoulders in freshly tonged curls. As Frank shoved his shorts down to his ankles, she dropped to her knees in front of him, her hands closing around his tight firm sweaty buttocks, her mouth wide to take in his moist, sticky cock.

Caroline couldn't see Frank in his workout gear without wanting to intercept him at the end of a session and do exactly this, lick off his sweat, shove her nose into his most intimate area, showing him that she wanted to know everything about him, how he tasted, how he smelt. He would groan above her, his hands wrapping into her hair, beginning to pump into her mouth; and she would work his cock with everything she had, her lips, her tongue, wanting this to be the best blow job he'd ever had, hearing him yell her name as he shot down the back of her throat and felt her swallow him down, not wasting a drop . . .

Caroline was coming fast and hard, bucking against her hand, the picture in her mind so vivid that she almost believed it was happening. Frank's golden, glowing skin, the salt of his sweat, the almond taste of his come, the scent of his body and his soap in her nostrils, the tight curly black hair at the base of his cock . . . she was coming again and again, her hips pumping the mattress, her fingers damp and viscous with her own moisture. Her lips parted. Over and over, she whispered: *Frank, Frank, Frank, Frank . . .*

She wasn't even aware that she was doing it. It was an incantation, a witch's prayer, a subconscious attempt to summon him, as if by repeating his name she could somehow reach Frank as he worked out in the basement gym, bring him upstairs, into her suite, not even knowing why he suddenly felt drawn there; first startled by seeing her like this, then stripping off his clothes and joining her, his fingers replacing hers between her legs, then his tongue . . .

The two sets of fantasies overlapped, overwhelmed her; she strummed so frantically that the edge of her middle fingernail started to scratch her with the sheer force of her movements. Only then did she reluctantly stop, and realized that her hand was cramping, her chest heaving almost as hard as if she had just slowed to a cool-down walk after a run on Studland beach.

Wow, she thought, her body damp with perspiration. *I really needed that! What a celebration for finishing the book!*

As soon as she could muster up the energy to heave herself off the bed, she'd need another shower to freshen up. The coverlet was clammy. She'd open the window, drape the bedspread over it to get some fresh air and dry it out in the sunshine. And then she'd start thinking about what she was going to do with the rest of her life.

Five and a half thousand pounds would be paid to her as soon as she sent off the book, which, because it chronicled Lexy's wild party years, was to be called *Lexy on the Loose*. Four thousand for the rest of her advance, plus the grand and a half extra for the speed bonus. It sounded like a lot if you thought of it as a lump sum, but it really wasn't. The rent for Caroline's room in Edmonton was four hundred and eighty a month before she paid her share of the utilities. Since starting the book, all her travel had been paid by the publisher and her meals had been almost entirely prepared by The Gables's cook; but she had still had to dip into her bank balance to keep paying the rent.

So a good portion of that five grand was already spent, the thousand she had been paid as the signature advance long gone. She needed a new book contract straight away, and hopefully one that would pay a larger advance.

I bet Sophie Kinsella or Lee Child or J. K. Rowling get to finish a book and then take a lovely holiday, Caroline thought gloomily. *In a really posh spa by the seaside, like that amazing one in Crete I saw on Facebook yesterday – three outdoor pools, one saltwalter, exercise classes every day and lovely-looking diet food all included in the price . . . but with their money they probably go to the Maldives to recharge their batteries . . .*

That image made her picture herself as a car, its driver vainly turning the key to bring the engine to life, but hearing only sputtering sounds under the bonnet as it failed to catch and fell back to nothing.

Out of petrol, out of charge. I'm running on empty.

She took a long, deep breath, kicked off her knickers and sweatpants, rolled off the bed and padded over to the ensuite bathroom to wash off her sex sweat. Lexy was downstairs conferring with her publicity team, who had travelled down from London for the day to brainstorm ideas for the simultaneous launch of the new season of her show and *Lexy on the Loose*. Caroline wanted to sit in on part of the meeting, and if she showered and changed quickly, she could manage that. She'd grab lunch, come back to her room, read over the last chapters again, and see if Lexy wanted to glance at them before Caroline sent them off.

And then she would start thinking up book ideas of her own, maybe even something that she could write under her own name. Turning on the shower, she allowed herself to picture a book jacket with *Caroline Macintosh* below the title; the image made her shiver from head to toe with excitement.

But even as she indulged herself with this fantasy, she had to deal with the fact that she had taken, as it were, two steps forward and one step back. Finishing *Lexy on the Loose* meant leaving The Gables, giving up the rapport she had built with Frank and the children. Even if she were commissioned to write another book for Lexy, Caroline would not be back here for a while, maybe months; that was too long to wait. Out of sight, out of mind.

She needed to come up with a solution to stay on in Sandbanks, keep the momentum going, while simultaneously finding a way to nudge Frank into turning towards her, away from his wife. As she stepped under the running water, her fertile brain turned this question over and over, treating it like a puzzle which must have a satisfactory answer, if she could only find it . . .

Chapter Eighteen

Lexy's meeting was in full swing. They had run through the list of media coverage the PR team had already secured: pieces in weekly and monthly magazines, TV and blogger interviews, a ten-city book tour, a coveted guest slot on *Loose Women*, even a surprise appearance co-presenting a Saturday night dating show. This was a real coup. Lexy was expressing her excitement about presenting on live TV, something she had never done, when Emily, the head of the agency, looked around at the rest of the group enquiringly, clearly asking an unspoken question.

A series of nods greeted her. They were seated in the huge living room that ran the whole length of the back of the mansion, the sunlight so bright as it danced on the sea that the grey and white striped blinds were partially lowered to avoid dazzling the assembled group. The housekeeper had manoeuvred the grey suede sofas and armchairs into a capacious seating arrangement round the central glass coffee table, and was currently setting up in the dining room for the buffet lunch the chef was preparing for the visitors. This was scheduled for two p.m., as a break after the main points had been discussed, leaving time for a further meeting afterwards to summarize their decisions before the publicists left to catch their train back to London.

The subject Emily was about to raise had been extensively discussed throughout the agency. It was controversial, but there was certainly a precedent for it: Lexy herself, when single, had often pulled this kind of stunt to get her name in the papers. Now that she was married, however, the circumstances had altered considerably, as the stakes were much higher. Emily was genuinely unsure how her client would react to the suggestion. But since her job was to garner Lexy the maximum publicity possible, the entire agency had agreed that they would be remiss if they didn't at least propose the idea.

As Lexy wound down, Emily took a long sip of her lime-infused San Pellegrino.

'Lexy,' she said, clearing her throat.

'Ooh-err!' Lexy said irrepressibly. 'Something's coming! I know that tone of voice! Am I going to have to take my clothes off on live TV?'

Emily favoured this with a small smile.

'No, you're a mum now,' she said. 'No nudity for mums.'

She took another sip of water.

'It's actually about Frank,' she said.

'You want him to go full-frontal?' Lexy asked. 'He's already got his bum out a couple of times for charity calendars, you know.'

'No, Lexy,' Emily said, and now her voice had a slight edge of impatience. 'We want him to have an affair.'

Caroline had just entered the living room by the far door, about to take a seat on a sofa next to the central grouping.

This statement from Emily, however, stopped her in her tracks. It was so eerily close to the fantasy Caroline had just been entertaining that for a long moment she expected everyone's head to turn to her accusingly. She felt herself going red, that familiar tingling sensation in her cheeks.

But the attention of the room was entirely on Lexy, whose wonderfully thick dark brows were drawing together in confusion as she stared blankly at Emily. Emily, who had repped Lexy for the last eight years and knew her very well indeed, huffed out a short laugh at Lexy's reaction.

'It's a compliment to me that I can still surprise you with a publicity idea, Lexy!' she said. 'We're not actually saying that Frank should have a real affair, of course. Just that we'll stage the appearance of one to coincide with the book and series coming out.'

Lexy's big blue eyes widened so much she was positively goggling.

'And you think this will *sell* me?' she exclaimed in disbelief. 'It'd make me look like a pathetic loser!'

'We disagree, actually,' said Annika, Emily's second-in-command, leaning forward and pushing her glasses further up her nose. 'In our opinion, it would make you look very relatable and sympathetic. More like an Everywoman. Right now, you have everything, and our perception is that it's starting to alienate your core fans. I mean, look around you!'

She gestured at the beautiful room, the terrace outside with its matching furniture, the perfectly landscaped lawn sloping gently down to the expanse of sea beyond.

'We've seen this room plenty of times in magazines,' she continued. 'The kids running over the lawn, Frank looking gorgeous as he plays with them, you with your perfect figure after two kids – yes, we know about the surgeries, you're very open about that, but a lot of people can't afford to get tummy tucks and lipo from the best doctors. We're concerned that you may not seem vulnerable enough any more for you to be—'

'Relatable,' Lexy said flatly.

It was the word that had been her touchstone ever since she had appeared on *Who's My Date?*, the word advertisers and TV executives and marketing gurus had continued to use about her ever since, the key to her success. Her fans could identify with her; she was like them, only better. She had the prettiness of a girl next door, not the otherworldly, ethereal beauty of a film star. Her swift and cutting wit did not rely on obscure references or clever wordplay. Her confidence came from her faith in her own abilities, not a privileged background. In short, she was a working-class girl made good: that was the crucial factor that kept her fans tuning in to her shows and buying the products to which she put her name.

Losing her relatability would, quite simply, be the beginning of the end of Lexy's career.

'You have it all,' Emily pronounced. 'For the first time ever. Up till now, that's never been an issue – your life's always had built-in drama that we could work with. Even after you met Frank and your romantic life settled down, we had the pregnancy, London's birth, organizing the wedding, plus the battle with Jamal about Frank adopting Laylah. Good job on spinning that out for the show, by the way!'

'I had to keep changing lawyers every time it looked like

we were getting close to an agreement,' Lexy said. 'Cost me a fortune. It was worth it, though, for all the headlines.'

Emily smiled nostalgically. 'My favourite stunt was when you were clever enough to refuse to marry Frank straight away when you got pregnant, so your fans were worried that he wasn't going to propose and you'd be left stranded with yet another guy who knocked you up but wouldn't marry you . . .'

'Frank *hated* that!' Lexy said complacently. 'Of course he proposed as soon as I told him I was in the family way! He's so old-fashioned, he really wanted London to be born *in wedlock*.' She rolled her eyes as she said the last two words. 'It took me ages to talk him round and explain that we'd get much more publicity if we did it my way. I mean, how many cover stories did you lot manage on if and when he was going to pop the question? "Will Lexy Ever Get Her Dream Wedding?"'

'I can't even count them,' Annika said, her eyes dreamy as she relived the happy memories. 'That was a really great six months. We literally got you a cover every other week.'

'But now that's all resolved, sadly,' Emily said. 'We're gearing up to the first season of your show where everything in the garden's rosy. There's no conflict. You've even got a book out with a happy-ever-after ending!'

The PR team were looking very grave at this grim summary.

'So this all puts you in a position where you could potentially be perceived as smug,' Emily concluded. 'Up on a pedestal, looking down on everyone who isn't as successful as you.'

'I'd *never*—' Lexy began, but Emily held up her hand and, to Caroline's amazement, Lexy actually stopped talking.

Emily started to lay out her idea, but Caroline wasn't listening: she was too caught up in fuming on Frank's behalf. How dare Lexy be so cavalier about his reputation, playing fast and loose with the truth just to get magazine covers for herself? He was a good man who had wanted to do the right thing. What was so funny about a man wanting his child to be born to married parents? What gave Lexy the right to mock him for that? She should be – the phrase that popped into Caroline's mind was one her mother had often used – she should be getting down on her knees and thanking God that she had finally found a man who would put up with her shenanigans and was prepared not only to be a father to the child he had made with her, but adopt her little hellion of a daughter.

And now they were actually daring to suggest that poor Frank, who had already put up with so much – who had allowed Lexy to drag his name through the mud by making it seem as if he were reluctant to take on his responsibility as a father – should fake an affair to get press for Lexy's latest show? It was outrageous!

But just then, a thrilling thought occurred to Caroline.

What if they want to say it's me he's having it with? Here I am in the house, under his nose . . . it would get tons of sympathy for Lexy, just like it did for Gwen Stefani and Jennifer Garner when their husbands shagged their nannies . . . Oh my God – what if they staged that, but then Frank realized he really was in love with me? It would be like those romance novels where the heroine's hired to pretend to be the girlfriend

of the billionaire and they gradually realize that they have
feelings for each other . . .

Caroline was quite lost in the fantasy of Frank turning to
her, blurting out that what had started out as a stupid stunt
had unexpectedly turned very real. She would confess in
turn that she had loved him all along, and they would fall
into each other's arms like a final scene from a romantic
comedy.

'. . . So we've just taken on Josie Santana as a client – she'd
be perfect for this!' Emily was saying, and the name bounced
Caroline back to cold, hard reality.

Of course they'd never think of Ghost Mouse as someone
who might possibly have an affair with Frank! she thought
bitterly. *I'm such an idiot! Josie Santana's everything I'm not*
– beautiful, sexy, with a big fanbase of her own . . .

'She's going solo, as you probably know,' Emily continued.
'Taking a hiatus from the band. And she needs something to
get her talked about. Quite frankly, Josie's not the best singer
out there. I'm not saying she's the Victoria Beckham of the
group – they don't have to turn her mike off, she's not *that*
bad – but she was picked because they needed tits and ass,
not because she could stand in for Adele in an emergency,
know what I mean? She's dying to go on *Celebrity Big*
Brother, and she needs a scandal for that. She's totally up for
this. Don't worry –'

She twiddled her fingers at Lexy, who had started to
object.

'– it's all been strictly secret so far. We haven't named any
names to her. But she's completely willing to play the bad-
girl homewrecker. Josie's only twenty-three, she's got plenty

of time to behave badly in the eyes of the public and then do the whole repentance journey later. She reminds me a bit of you, actually, Lexy, back in the day. Young, hungry, willing to do whatever she needs to get herself in the papers.'

'Hmm, I'm not sure I want a mini-me around my husband!' Lexy said wryly. 'Is she okay with saying afterwards that she did all the running? I don't want people saying that Frank chased her.'

'Naturally,' Annika said, leaning forward once more. 'No one wants to tar and feather Frank. The setup would be that she threw herself at him while you were neglecting him and the kids a bit with all the focus on your show, and writing the book –'

She glanced over at Caroline, sitting quietly further down the room.

'– which of course you *did*,' she continued, fixing Caroline with a look that required Caroline to nod in confirmation.

'We don't want to use that as an excuse for Frank straying, though,' contributed Brandon, the only man on the team. 'It won't go down well if we fall into the trap of blaming Lexy for being a working mother.'

'Agree one hundred per cent,' Emily said. 'It won't be an excuse, but a sort of explanation. Frank's lonely, Josie targets him with her tits and arse hanging out, he has a moment of weakness – maybe not even an actual affair, okay?' she added, reading her client's body language. 'It could be a snog, some fumbling around – then Frank comes to his senses, realizes he can't cheat on you, but Josie sells the story and he's too honourable to deny it.'

Lexy's shoulders visibly relaxed.

'Yeah, that's more like it,' she said. 'I couldn't get Frank to go for the full affair story, and honestly I wouldn't want to. I don't want anyone thinking that some little tart can get into my husband's jeans that easily. I'm being really honest here – I'm *not* okay with people thinking I'm married to a cheater. I've got rivalries going with all those basic bitch reality sluts who want my career, you know? I don't want them gloating in their crappy columns for the rest of my fucking life because my hubby went outside his marriage for some slap and tickle.'

'Okay, we hear that, Lexy,' Emily said, nodding. 'Josie and Frank meet up a couple of times for drinks, let's say. All above board, if not great judgement, but then she convinces him to come back to hers when he's tipsy and not thinking straight – the media'll want at least one *illicit rendezvous* . . .'

She made quote signs as she spoke the last two words, indicating that she was speaking tabloidese.

'She's the temptress, he's weak,' she continued. 'We open up a great conversation about working women and having it all without blaming you, like Brandon said.' She nodded at the young man. 'Our line has always been that though Frank has pots of money, you're determined to have your own career, Lexy, because you've come from nothing and had to battle Jamal for support for Laylah. You're a modern woman, a plucky survivor—'

'This *really* builds the plucky survivor part of the brand,' Brandon chimed in, emboldened by praise to speak up once more. 'Her fans respond brilliantly whenever we push that button.'

'We'll break the story a couple of weeks before the series

and book launch,' Emily said. Her tone, which had been very measured up till now, was becoming increasingly enthusiastic as it became clear that Lexy was on board with the idea. 'Initially, we'll make it sound as if Frank *did* actually cheat, which'll get us the most amount of press possible. We run that as long as we possibly can – get Josie to tease that she and Frank shagged without ever actually saying it. Finally, she confesses. She's always had a huge crush on Frank, she took advantage of you not being around, she snogged him but then he came to his senses and left. She stirred things up in the hope that you'd dump him, Lexy, but now she feels she has to tell the truth.'

'What about Frank?' Lexy asked warily. 'He'd die rather than talk about this kind of thing.'

'Oh, he never has to say a word,' Emily assured her. 'We put out a statement after Josie comes clean, saying that he had a momentary lapse in judgement, you've understood and forgiven him, you're getting some marriage counselling. And maybe you renew your vows next year? That gives us a whole story arc for the next season as well!'

'Yeah, I love that!' Lexy sat up straighter, eyes bright. 'I've been worrying about this too, you know? I mean, how much tension can I get from "is my book jacket design on brand enough" or "am I going to make top ten on the *Sunday Times* bestseller list"? But if I'm having to do signings with a brave smile while my fans ask me if everything's okay with Frank, and maybe once I break down and have a bit of a cry, or run off, and then get myself together and come back because I don't want to disappoint them – that'd be *brilliant*!'

She considered something.

'Bugger it, Frank'll never let us film with a marriage counsellor,' she said gloomily. 'He'd kill himself first.'

'What are you cooking up here, you lot? Why am I killing myself?'

Everyone turned to look at Frank, standing in the doorway. He was fresh from the gym, a towel around his neck, his skin glowing from his recent exercise. There was a tangible increase in energy from the assembled group, the women unconsciously grooming themselves in the presence of a very attractive man, pushing back their hair and smiling at him. It was an instinctive response not just to his handsome face, but the amount of Frank's flesh that was on display. As a professional athlete, he was so accustomed to walking around in a tight T-shirt and shorts that he was sweetly naive about the effect his rock-hard body had on women and gay men.

'Hey!'

Lexy jumped up from the sofa and dashed across the room to kiss him, something that Caroline had never seen her do before.

'Emily and everyone's come up with this amazing idea for getting a ton of publicity for the next season of the show, plus my book publication,' she said, fluttering her eyelashes. 'Want to hear it?'

'Uh-oh,' Frank said cautiously, taking her shoulders and holding her off a little. 'Actually getting off your arse and running over to kiss me? Doing your sweet as sugar, I-want-something tone of voice? Bitter experience tells me that means something I'm definitely not going to like . . .'

Chapter Nineteen

'What? *Fuck*, no way! *What?* Tell me you're fucking joking!'

'Frank, lots of people are doing it,' Emily, no coward, said loudly to cut through Frank's torrent of resistance. She named a very famous reality star who had staged an affair between her boyfriend and her best friend, all elaborately planned; the two women had feuded bitterly all over the tabloids, with the friend having been paid a substantial sum to play the villainess. In a few years' time, they would reconcile; the boyfriend, meanwhile, had expressed extreme contrition and agreed to extensive counselling for sex addiction. He had been photographed for six months attending the offices of a therapist who had agreed to let him hang out there for an hour, streaming shows on his iPad.

After that, he had declared his 'addiction' under control and proposed to his girlfriend. The wedding was the story-line for the next season of her show. Viewers always, always loved a wedding.

'Emily, I don't fucking care if half the world is doing it!' Frank almost yodelled, such was the level of his distress. 'This is my *wife* we're talking about! I don't want people thinking I'd cheat on her with some little tart – I mean, no offence to this Josie girl, though fuck knows why she'd want to be known as someone who'd go after a married man! And what about the kids? How're they going to cope with all this?'

'Oh, they'll be fine,' Lexy said breezily.

Too breezily: this, for Frank, was the straw that broke the camel's back.

'*Fine?*' he yelled. '*Fine*, with paps staking out their schools every morning and afternoon, yelling stuff at them about their daddy not loving their mummy to make them cry? You know how many times my mates've told me about the shit that's been shouted at their kids? I always told 'em that it was their bloody fault for not keeping their dick zipped up round the slappers at the clubs. They have their fun, but it's the wives and kids that pay the price. And you know what – they respected me because I keep it in my pants myself! They'd listen to me and hopefully sort their shit out a bit for the sake of their kids! So how the *fuck* do you expect me to go along with exactly the kind of behaviour I've been lecturing the guys about for nearly twenty fucking years now?'

His hands were in fists on his hips, his eyes blazing, his jaw thrust out furiously. He looked magnificent, a warrior ready for battle. Not just Caroline, but most of the PR team were ogling him in blatant admiration.

'It's really *for* the kids, if you look at it the right way!' Lexy said in a last attempt to convince him. 'We're not going to be raking it in forever – no one's going to want to watch me getting a bum wax when I'm sixty, are they? We have to coin it now so that—'

'Oh, bollocks, Lexy! That's just bollocks!' her husband

yelled. 'This isn't about Laylah and London getting big trust funds! It's about you being fucking addicted to publicity! We all know that – everyone here knows that! Don't piss on my head and tell me it's raining!'

Frank's trainers squeaked on the marble hallway floor as he turned and strode off, his powerful hamstrings flexing, his calf muscles bulging. Reaching the central staircase, he took the treads two at a time in his haste to get away from his wife.

'Well, *that*'s a washout,' Lexy said gloomily, sagging back in the armchair and pulling up her knees to wrap her arms around them. 'Honestly, this is my *job*, you know? You'd think he'd see it like that, wouldn't you?'

'Well, it was worth a try!' Emily said, shrugging. 'So on to Plan B. Annika, you want to take this pitch?'

Caroline did not wait to hear Plan B. She was on her feet, slipping from the room as discreetly as she had entered it, taking the side staircase up to the first floor, which actually brought her out closer to Frank and Lexy's master suite than the main one. The speed with which she was able to dash up the steps took her by surprise; she arrived at the top as if she had been shot out of a cannon, with no shortness of breath. The regular beach running and her weight loss had all kinds of extra benefits.

She intercepted Frank just as he came marching down the corridor, his tread heavy, his head hanging low. He looked completely taken aback at the sight of Caroline popping like a Jack-in-the-box out of the stairwell; having been designed for staff access, it was cramped and narrow and rarely used.

'Uh, Caroline,' he said, barely breaking stride, 'I can't talk right now—'

'I know what happened,' she said quickly. 'I was downstairs in the meeting. I just came up to say how sorry I was you got upset. I'm sure she didn't really mean it . . .'

Frank stopped dead and flopped down into the window seat beside him as if someone had just cut his leg tendons with a straight razor.

'She *did* mean it,' he said simply, sinking his face into his hands. 'You know she did, and so do I.'

'Oh, Frank . . . I'm so sorry . . .'

It took all the courage Caroline had to take the few steps needed to cross the width of the corridor, and then, heart in her throat, sit down next to Frank on the padded cushion made especially for the bow window embrasure. It was capacious enough for there to be plenty of space between their bodies, but Caroline's pulse was racing now in a way it had not when she sprinted across the hall and up the side staircase.

She folded her hands in her lap so that she couldn't be tempted to reach out and touch him. His thigh was so close, his skin so glossy, his scent so intense . . . and then her senses were completely overwhelmed, because, quite unexpectedly, Frank reached out and put his arm around her shoulders, a solid, heavy weight, thick with muscle. Caroline had a sudden, vivid image of his arm as a python that had draped itself over her, sexual and dangerous, pulsing with life. There was a sudden lump in her throat, and the only way to get rid of it was to swallow it down; she almost choked herself in the process.

Fortunately for her, Frank was oblivious to anything but his own pain. His hug was entirely comradely, the kind of embrace he might have given to console a teammate who had scored an own goal or fumbled a crucial pass.

'I can't believe she'd even *ask* me that!' he said, his voice sounding as if it were being dragged out of the pit of his stomach. 'She knows what I think about guys who put it around! She's heard me bang on about it often enough!'

'She wasn't thinking,' Caroline said softly.

'Well, you got that half-right,' Frank said bitterly. 'She wasn't thinking about anyone but herself. We both know that the kids getting stick for a story about me playing away never even crossed her mind!'

Caroline heaved a sigh.

'I'd hate Laylah and London to be pestered by paps shouting horrible things,' she agreed. 'They're such great kids. I really care about them.'

This was rewarded by Frank's arm tightening around her, his hand on her shoulder pulling her closer.

'They *are* great kids,' he said. 'Laylah's like my own, you know that. She's never had any dad but me. The two happiest days of my life were when the adoption came through for her and when London was born. Could have done without them both being filmed, of course, but that's Lexy for you. Only thinks it's real when it's on camera.'

This was an opportunity to make trouble, and Caroline grabbed it with both hands.

'It must have been really hard for you and Laylah with the legal delays,' she said sympathetically. 'I know Lexy needed to spin the adoption process out as long as possible for the

TV show – I mean, that's her job. But still, when it's a little girl in the middle of endless back and forths with lawyers, it had to be very painful for you to wait it out until the series had finished shooting—'

'*What?*'

Frank spun round to face her, gripping her arm.

'What are you talking about?' he demanded, his breath hot on her face.

Caroline was genuinely frightened, her heart battering at her ribcage so violently that the pulse was visible at her throat. Had she miscalculated? What if Frank stormed away and took this information straight to Lexy?

'I thought you knew!' she whimpered. 'I really did! I didn't think that could have happened without you knowing! I'm so sorry, Frank –'

She allowed herself to say his name again: it always gave her such a secret, blissful, erotic thrill.

'Lexy was talking about it in the meeting, really openly,' she continued. 'I didn't have any idea you didn't know what she was doing with the lawyers . . .'

'The lawyers? What are you *talking* about?'

Frank almost shook Caroline in his impatience to find out what she knew. Lowering her eyes, unable to look directly at him, Caroline explained in stumbling, disconnected sentences what she had just heard: that Lexy had artificially drawn out the process of Frank formally adopting Laylah, had fomented trouble between herself and Jamal, even changing legal teams to make sure that as much drama as possible could be extracted from the adoption process before the triumphant ending of the series.

The colour drained from Frank's handsome face.

'I want to say I don't fucking believe it,' he said slowly, and to Caroline's deep disappointment, his hand dropped from her arm. Once again, he covered his face with his palms.

'But I do,' he said into them. 'Of course I do. It's exactly the kind of shit she'd pull. All those months, I was so fucking furious with Jamal! I kept telling Lexy I was ready to get on a plane, fly over to the US and knock his head against a wall to get it sorted out, make him sign the papers – no *wonder* she looked so worried every time I said it! Now it turns out it wasn't Jamal putting a spanner in the works after all!'

'I'm so sorry, Frank,' Caroline repeated, her voice still frightened. If he stormed downstairs to Lexy and confronted her with this, Caroline's goose would be not just cooked, but burnt to a crisp. 'Please, *please* don't tell Lexy you heard it from me!'

Frank rubbed his face as vigorously as if he were trying to exfoliate it. And then he reached out and rested his left palm on top of Caroline's folded hands. A thrill ran through her, a stab to her ribcage that pierced straight down to the centre of her pelvis.

'You've done so much for us, Caroline,' he said heavily. 'I know you're getting paid bugger all to write Lexy's book, and you've not only never complained, you were a godsend helping out with the kids when we were between nannies. Even now, you're brilliant with them. I'd never dump you in the shit. Don't worry about that.'

Relief flooded through Caroline. Although she was sitting still, she felt as battered by emotions as if she were tied to one of the worn wooden posts that marked out the sea lanes for the ferries that plied between Poole Harbour and the Channel Islands; waves crashing over her, the wake of the ferries slapping as they passed. Fear, excitement, love, lust, hope, reassurance . . . after this, she was definitely going to need to lie down on her bed to recover from the intensity of the moment when Frank had put his hand on hers and told her how much he valued her.

'Thanks,' she said softly. 'That means a lot.'

'*You* mean a lot,' Frank said, but rather more absently than she would have liked. 'God, what a fucking mess. What am I going to do? How'm I going to tell Lex that I can't stand it any more? I can't take it being all about her show all the time. Me and the kids are just actors in it. They actually call us cast members, did you know that? And that's how she treats us.'

Caroline made a sympathetic *mmn* of agreement, but Frank, deep in misery about his wife's behaviour, was barely aware of her any more. Patting her hand, he stood up, rolling his shoulders back as painfully as if he had been carrying a heavy load of boulders up a steep hill.

'Sorry,' he said, turning away to the door that led to the master suite. 'I just need to . . .' He let out a long sigh, and, without finishing the sentence, walked slowly down the corridor.

Caroline watched him go, her body motionless, her brain racing. She was processing everything that had just happened, the sheer rush and sweep of it. Frank had reached out to her physically, not once but twice; the memory of his arm around her, his hand on hers, was so powerful that she didn't want to move from the window seat. As long as she sat here, she could close her eyes and remember what it had felt like to pretend in those moments that she was his wife, that they were sitting together, sharing a break in their day, catching up with what had happened to each of them . . . after all, what she had just told Frank had felt a little like that, a confidence that the two of them now shared . . .

Caroline clung on to that image for as long as she could. But gradually, the creeping awareness that she was crushing on a married man, her boss's husband, whose arm around her shoulders was just a crumb falling from his and Lexy's banquet table, forced her to open her eyes again.

She looked down at herself, at the breasts that were no longer so prominent that they obscured her view of her lap, at the flatter stomach and the thinner legs, clad in size 12 jeans that weren't even digging into her waist. The jeans were baggy boyfriend cut, however, and her narrower, more sculpted torso was concealed under a loose sweater. These were very strategic clothing decisions. No one at Sandbanks had noticed the extent of her weight loss. She was Ghost Mouse to Lexy, and in a way she was still Ghost Mouse to everyone here. Frank had reacted to her just now as a friend, not a woman to whom he could be sexually attracted.

And that's how it should stay for a while, she thought. *I have to keep my head down if I want to stay in Frank and Lexy's lives. Lexy may not notice that I've lost a stone and a half, but she will as soon as I start wearing clothes more like hers. And she didn't hire a sexy Lexy lookalike – she hired dowdy, plump Ghost Mouse. I need her to see me like that for as long as possible.*

While she was showering, Caroline had realized that the

manuscript of *Lexy on the Loose* would surely require edits which would need to be turned around in lightning-quick time. So could she manoeuvre to come back to Sandbanks during that process? The excuse of needing to be close to Lexy for research would barely apply, but Caroline had done everything she could to insert herself into the daily life of the house, become as familiar a face to Lexy and Frank as the housekeeper, the chef or the nanny; her fingers were very tightly crossed that, once Gareth had read through the draft and given her his edits, she would be able to return to the guest suite, her morning beach runs, her free diet food, her daily contact with Frank . . .

Her stomach grumbled, and Caroline realized that she was starving. She was hungry most of the time, of course, having taught herself to welcome it as a sign that she was losing weight. Glancing at her watch, however, she realized that it was past two. She'd grab some food and have a much-needed post-lunch nap before reading over what she had written that morning and deciding whether it was ready to be sent off to Gareth.

Lexy and the PR team were already in the dining room, tucking into the lavish lunch buffet provided by the chef. The drinks fridge was stocked with bottles of white wine, lagers and an extensive selection of vitamin waters and non-alcoholic mixers; Emily, chatting away to Lexy, was clasping a large glass of Pinot Grigio, signalling to her team that it was fine for them to follow suit.

Recovering from the drama of the scene with Frank, permitted the release of a couple of drinks, the young staffers were buzzed already, and the lunch gathering was in full swing. As per her status as Ghost Mouse, Caroline was barely noticed as she entered the room, merely garnering a few friendly nods of acknowledgement as she picked up a plate and served herself with two big spoonfuls of shrimp and salad leaves. Eschewing the tempting rose-pink of the cocktail sauce in a silver gravy boat on the side of the platter, she limited herself to squeezing half a lemon and a twist of black pepper over the contents of her plate.

Caroline had been abstemious since embarking upon her hardcore diet, but the sight of everyone with a glass in their hand was hugely tempting: and besides, that morning she had not only finished the first book she had ever written, but earned five thousand pounds. If there was ever a time to celebrate, it was now.

So she poured a wine glass a third full with Pinot Grigio, topped it up with soda, and took a seat at the far side of the table. Most of the PRs were around her age, but their London hipster style – girls in crop tops with their heads shaved on one side, boys with ironic facial hair and elaborate jewellery – was a world away from Caroline's boring pony-tail and comparatively loose clothes. Edmonton wasn't that far from Hoxton as the crow flew, but it might have been separated by an ocean as far as their relative styles were concerned.

And Caroline didn't aspire to Hoxton, not at all. She had no desire to live in a trendy shared loft, throwing dusk-to-dawn parties while doing the latest drugs and having sex with boys so skinny she couldn't get into their jeans; she'd never seen being a writer as a career that came with a wild lifestyle. She wanted what Lexy had: a solid bourgeois, middle-class life, a home, a husband, kids. Friendly as the PR team was, she couldn't see herself having much in common with them.

So she sat quietly, sipping her spritzer as she cut the shrimp into small pieces to make it seem a larger portion than it was, chewing and swallowing each one as slowly as she could, all part of her new diet regime.

'Hey, Ghost Mouse! Drinking at lunchtime? Thought you were on a whole health kick!'

Strolling over, perching her tight little bottom on the edge of the dining table, Lexy flicked a shellacked nail against Caroline's wine glass.

'Emily's asking about an ETA on the book,' she said. 'She wants to get proofs out to journos as soon as we can. No offence, but should you be boozing it up this time of day with the kind of psycho deadline you've got?'

It was a fair question, but it still made Caroline bristle. Especially as, from the pitch of Lexy's voice, Caroline could diagnose her employer as having already drunk one full glass of Pinot with lemon; the one she was currently holding must be her second. There was an extra fizz and vivacity to Lexy's affect when she was at this stage of wine consumption, and by now Caroline could recognize it very well indeed.

'I finished the book this morning,' Caroline said, as coolly as she could. 'So I'm celebrating. It's just a spritzer,' she added, and then mentally kicked herself for even saying that; she didn't owe Lexy an explanation of what was in her wine glass. 'I still have stuff to go over, but I wrote "The End".'

'Wow, get you!' Lexy said, clinking her glass with Caroline's.

'I'm not sure about the ending, though,' Caroline admitted. 'I was thinking I should get you to have a look at it before I send it off?'

'Honestly, Ghost Mouse, just bung it over to Gareth and see what he thinks,' Lexy said. 'I'm no editor, you know that. Let him have a look at it first. I can't be arsed checking something if he's just going to want to change it anyway, and I've been fine with everything you're written so far, haven't I? And he wants it as soon as poss.'

'Okay,' Caroline agreed. 'I genuinely can't believe it's done!'

When do I get paid? it occurred to her to wonder. *Probably only when I've finished the edits, which means a few weeks yet . . .*

'Yay! Then you should go home, crash for a few days,' Lexy said cheerfully. 'Or get one of those cheapo last-minute holiday deals somewhere with a bit of your bonus – Fuertaventura, Mallorca, something like that. Grab a bit of sunshine while you can. 'Cause you'll have to have another go at it once Gareth's done his editing job, won't you?'

Caroline nodded, but she was bristling again at Lexy bracketing her into a cheap and cheerful downmarket destination, somewhere people went to get sunburnt and tipsy.

'I was actually looking at weekend package getaways to Venice,' she said, her tone defensive.

'Ooh, get you!' Lexy said, laughing and drinking some more Pinot and lemon. 'Very posh! Or is it a romantic thing? You seeing someone, Ghost Mouse?'

Caroline had been working for Lexy for months, and this was the first time Lexy had asked her that question.

'There's a guy in London,' Caroline said. 'But it's not that serious. More a sex thing.'

'Good for you!' Lexy said with a salacious wink. 'I should've known – you're a dark horse, aren't you? Like your writing. All quiet and butter-wouldn't-melt on the outside, but dirty porn on the inside. Come on, let's toast! To finishing the book, plus you getting your leg over in Venice! Nice one! I've always wanted to do it in a gondola, but they're just too wobbly.'

Caroline raised her glass to Lexy's, not letting her seething resentment show on her face. Caroline had spent months slaving away, for very little pay, on a book that required her to get to know Lexy in forensic detail, while Lexy didn't even know whether Caroline was dating, or that she would prefer Venice to a sun and beach getaway if given the choice.

'You heard all the kerfuffle with Frank, yeah?' Lexy said, clearly in a chatty mood. 'I got carried away with the pitch, but I should have known he'd react like that. He's all "my kids are so precious and any dad who cheats on the mother of his children should be flogged in the middle of Trafalgar Square", blah blah blah. I suppose I'll have to apologize to him on my knees to make up, if you know what I mean.'

She flicked Caroline a wink, her mascaraed lashes fluttering theatrically up and down. Caroline, who had devoted two pages to Lexy's vivid description of her blowjob technique, did indeed know exactly what her boss meant, and she felt a vivid, burning resentment at the image of Lexy with Frank's cock in her mouth.

'So what *are* you going to do for an extra publicity push when the book and the series come out?' Caroline asked, dragging her brain back to the subject under discussion. 'What was the Plan B?'

Caroline had a very keen interest in *Lexy on the Loose* becoming a runaway bestseller. Although she was not in line to earn royalties, if the book hit the *Sunday Times* top ten it would be a strong negotiating point for Caroline as she tried to get a book contract of her own, or to ghost another book for Lexy for a higher rate of pay.

'Ah, not much,' Lexy said gloomily. 'Stage a feud with that Josie slag. Say that she was coming on to Frank and I had to drag her off – you know, keep any idea that Frank was flirting with her out of it, just make it about me being jealous. But I was like, why should I give *her* any publicity? The whole catfight thing's so been there, done that. Half the stupid cows who've got columns in the weeklies just make 'em up if they're running short of stuff to say – Michelle thinks Katie's new hair extensions are ugly, so Katie slaps back next week saying that Michelle still hasn't got the baby weight off – I mean, the fans aren't morons, they just flick past it. Besides, Josie's fifteen years younger than me. I'd look like an insecure older bitch worrying about the younger slags on the scene.'

Caroline had to admit that Lexy's instincts were spot on. As good as Lexy looked at thirty-seven, Josie Santana was not only stunning but had the full freshness of youth, possessing not only a pneumatic figure and a naturally good head of hair, but the impressive flexibility of someone who had been taking dance classes since she was five. She was a very average singer, but her signature move, which was to touch her toes with one hand while holding the microphone in the other, still singing while she wiggled her bottom in the air, never failed to draw attention.

'That's the thing about PRs,' Lexy continued, barely bothering to lower her voice, even though the room was filled with them. 'They never work for just one client, you know? Unless you're, like, Tom Cruise. So they're never thinking of only your interests. This Josie shit's very typical – Emily represents her as well, so for them it's easier to tie us together, get two campaigns for the price of one. But to quote Marilyn Monroe, there's always one person who gets the fuzzy end of the lollipop, and that's not going to be me. They've had loads more of my money over the years than they've had from Josie Santana, for fuck's sake!'

And this was simply the perfect opportunity served up to Caroline on a shining silver platter.

'If there's going to be an age difference, shouldn't it be a younger guy chasing *you*?' Caroline suggested as casually as she could manage. 'Everyone would believe it. Look how Deacon came on to you at the awards ceremony! I haven't shown you that bit, but I put it in the second to last chapter of the book – all the back and forth banter and the "MILF on Fire" stuff. It came out really well. He was totally into you.'

She stood up.

'I should get back to work,' she said. 'I can't believe I'm actually sending the book off today!'

But Lexy's hand closed around her forearm, guiding Caroline back down to the dining chair.

'Hang on,' she said. '*What* did you just say?'

Chapter Twenty

'Well, look who it is! My favourite cougar!' Deacon crowed happily as he embraced Lexy.

Deacon was in better shape tonight – at the launch party to celebrate the new, limited-edition flavour of a famous vodka brand – than he had been at the awards ceremony. He looked as if he had slept in the last few days, taken a long shower, used products to wash his hair rather than relying on the traditional hippie wisdom that the natural oils on his scalp were all it needed.

His curly locks were pulled back in a man bun, and the style threw his sharp cheekbones into devastating relief, making his eyes look even larger. His beauty was tradition-ally feminine, which was one of the reasons he had so many tween and teenage female fans. They were the age group that, not yet ready to engage with the full hairy horror of masculinity, preferred to swoon over relatively unthreaten-ing, slim-hipped, smooth-skinned, pretty-featured young men.

'What the fuck's that on your head?' Lexy countered as she stared at the bun. 'Looks like you've got a dead rat up there.'

Deacon promptly reached up, pulled out the elastic and shook his hair free. As it cascaded around his face, sighs of appreciation could be heard from the party guests. Even Lexy had to dig her nails into her palms to stop a gasp issuing from her lips. The cliché of the boss only realizing the beauty of his secretary when she removed her glasses and took down her hair was so powerful because it was so effective: Deacon was just as handsome with his hair pulled back, but the cascade of curls tumbling down was very intimate. It was as if the scene had instantly shifted from public to private, bar to bedroom, evoking a sexual atmosphere, suggesting that the next thing he would do would be to unbutton his shirt even further.

'That better?' he purred.

Lexy swallowed hard.

'Well, at least it doesn't look like something died on your head any more,' she managed to say.

'You tell me to shave my head, I'll do it,' Deacon said recklessly, at which his long-suffering manager squealed in horror.

'He does *not* mean that,' the manager said firmly, as Josie Santana, her lavish curves poured into a canary-yellow catsuit cut practically to her navel, her torrent of hair tumbling around her shoulders, slinked up beside Deacon and wrapped her arm through his.

'*I'd* never ask you to shave your head, sexy!' she said, reaching up to stroke his hair.

The response to this was, for a woman as experienced as Lexy, a simple matter. Lexy ignored Josie completely, shot Deacon a fleeting, but dazzling smile, and turned her back on him to talk to the PR whose drink account was organizing this launch party. Screens around the room flashed the name of the flavour, Cloudberry, together with striking nature photos of the bright orange-yellow berry, shaped like a stunted raspberry, and of the golden-tinted bottle.

'So we're supposed to drink this stuff to cheer us up as we watch all the gloomy TV series about Swedish paedos?' she said, pitching her voice loudly enough to reach Deacon's ears.

The PR for Clearly, the vodka brand, tittered nervously.

'Um, let's not use the "p" word?' he said. 'But yeah, it's definitely like a marketing awareness that everything Nordic is super-hot right now. Or cool!'

He laughed immoderately at his own joke.

'Do you like the flavour?' he asked. 'It's a little tart, but in tastings we found that—'

'Yeah, it is a bit. But I put lemon in my white wine, so I don't mind that,' Lexy said, finishing off her shot and setting the empty glass back on the tray a waiter was proffering. She took another one, and tilted the miniature glass to look at the way its base was gold-tinged to reinforce the branding.

'These're nice,' she said. 'Can I get a set?'

'That shouldn't be a problem,' the PR started, 'if you could—'

'Oh yeah, I'll tweet and Instagram away, no worries,' Lexy said, flicking her fingers to summon Brandon, who had been assigned to social media duties that evening. 'And I'll put it in my column,' she added. 'With a pic of me at home drinking it from my new glasses, okay? I actually like this stuff, so I'm cool with that.'

She finished off the second shot of cloudberry vodka and took a third from the tray.

'It's very rich in vitamin C,' the PR assured her.

'Oh great, I'll make sure to finish the bottle then,' she said drily.

As she had known he would, Deacon appeared beside her, having succeeded in detaching Josie.

'Hey,' he said in her ear. 'I told her they were doing free STD tests over by the bar and she shot off. Must be in need of one.'

Lexy snorted an unsisterly laugh.

'*You're* the one that probably needs a test,' she said.

'Will you fuck me if I show you my latest results?' Deacon said. 'Go on, say yes! I'm a really good shag and clean as a whistle.'

Lexy couldn't help giggling.

'You are *blatant*,' she said, as Brandon held a thumb up to indicate that he was ready to take a series of photos which he would then tweet and Instagram from Lexy's account.

Watch and learn, Lexy thought smugly, noticing Josie Santana sulking across the room. *You may be able to get away with a catsuit that looks like someone spraypainted it onto you, but your social media's really basic and your flirting skills are as obvious as a kick in the teeth. Watch and learn, little wannabe.*

Expertly, she tore through a series of poses, nailing each one, the Cloudberry screen logo in the background, over one shoulder, visible throughout: she held up a bottle and a shot glass, looking excited, intrigued, and then saucy. She smiled next to the PR, making sure the bottle she was holding was front-faced to the camera, then brought in Deacon to take the vodka and pour her a glassful. She clinked shot glasses with the others, then posed with Deacon, natural-looking pictures of the two of them 'sharing a laugh', as society magazines used to caption party photos.

And then, knowing exactly what she was doing, she touched the tip of her tongue to the rim of her glass, winking at Deacon: he eagerly followed suit, licking his own glass as Brandon delightedly snapped away, their glasses so close that their tongues were nearly touching. The next thing she knew, the shot glass was whipped from her hand, a few drops of cloudberry vodka trickled over her dress, and Deacon's mouth was on hers, his tongue now in her mouth, tasting so deliciously of the tart spirit that her instinct was to suck it hard, suck it like a lollipop and relish every sweet, sharp drop of juice . . .

Grabbing his shoulders, she pushed him away, managing to close her mouth to avoid being photographed with her mouth gaping open like a blow-up sex doll.

'You are so fucking naughty!' she complained, dabbing at her bosom. 'Is this shit going to stain? This is a Hervé Léger dress!'

'Buy you a new one if it does,' Deacon said, grinning widely as he set down the two empty shot glasses: he knew perfectly well how much she had enjoyed the brief kiss.

'*Honestly*, what are you like?' Lexy said, tossing back her hair. 'I'm going to have to wipe this down. Thank God it's mostly black.'

'Can we not use any shots of her with the product on her dress?' the PR said hastily to Brandon, who rushed to assure him that no one had any intention of tweeting a photo of Lexy with a Clearly Cloudberry damp patch on her chest.

The bandage dress was vintage, an 80s style that was now back in fashion for those who had the curves to carry it off. Black, with red trim around the vestigial cap sleeves and low-cut bodice, it pushed Lexy's boobs up and out, nipping in her waist with the clever design of the wide strapping which narrowed to a V over her belly button and then clung to her hips, giving her the perfect hourglass silhouette. There was a reason that all the supermodels in that decade had been curvaceous Amazons. The clothes of that period were designed to be worn by statuesque women, rather than the heroin-chic waifs of the 90s who had been the next incarnation of the ideal female figure.

Lexy had no intention of dabbing herself to dry the damp spot in public; people would snap photos, put them online with all sorts of snarky hashtags. She could just imagine the things they'd say – God knew, if it had happened to someone else, she'd have been sniggering about how she could wring plenty of innuendo from the words 'Deacon', 'shot' and 'dress' herself.

Wiggling across the room, the only way one could move in a bandage dress and five-inch Gina heels, she made her way to the ladies' loos. The launch party for Clearly Cloudberry was being held on the big second-floor room of the Camden Club, a private members' club to which Lexy had never been before. So she had no idea what was going on when she pushed open the toilet door and was greeted by the sound of a man's voice saying:

'It was the White Rabbit, trotting slowly back again, and

*looking anxiously about as it went, as if it had lost something;
and she heard it muttering to itself: "The Duchess! The Duchess! Oh my dear paws! Oh my fur and whiskers! She'll get me
executed, as sure as ferrets are ferrets!"'*

'What the *fuck!*' Lexy exclaimed loudly as the voice continued:

*"Where CAN I have dropped them, I wonder?" Alice
guessed in a moment that it was looking for the fan and the
pair of white kid gloves, and she very good-naturedly began
hunting about for them, but they were nowhere to be seen –
everything seemed to have changed since her swim in the pool,
and the great hall, with the glass table and the little door, had
vanished completely.'*

'It's a recording of *Alice in Wonderland*,' a woman said,
emerging from one of the only two cubicles; the other was
empty. Lexy hadn't heard a toilet flush, so she was unsurprised that instead of washing her hands, the woman was
sliding a small packet of something back into her clutch bag
and zipping it up. 'It plays in a loop. We've got used to it by
now, but non-members are always freaking out.'

'Well, yeah!' Lexy said, as the voice continued to narrate
the book. 'Especially having a man's voice, you know? It
makes you think there's a perv in here trying to watch you
take a pee.'

'I *know*,' the woman said, staring at herself narrowly in a
mirror and checking the underside of her nostrils. 'Believe
me, we've all complained but they just won't change it. Love
your dress, by the way.'

'Oh, thanks,' Lexy said as the woman smiled and clicked
out of the bathroom. Lexy leaned across the long copper

sink, designed for some reason to look like a farm trough, and turned on the closest tap, collecting drops on her fingertips to dilute the vodka that had splashed on her; since her artificially enhanced bosom protruded like a shelf just below her collarbones, it had landed there, the stain visible on the red trim of the dress, so that when the main door swung open again she was standing with her hands on her breasts, wiping them down.

'Fuck me, that's sexy,' Deacon said, leering at her as the door swung shut behind him. 'Look at you, holding your tits like you're in a porno!'

Lexy had a few seconds to decide how best to handle this. The idea was to whip up a smallish, manageable scandal; that was the whole point of her being at this launch, which Deacon, she had ascertained from Emily's team, would also be attending. Photos of Deacon snogging her unexpectedly as the two of them posed with vodka shots would not be shocking enough to capture much attention, as the public was very used to Deacon being his usual flirtatious, outrageous self. The shots would do for a *Daily Mail* sidebar, complete with some catty comments from the writer about the difference between her age and his, but no more than that. Deacon had dated women fifteen years older than him plenty of times before and would be out at another launch kissing another woman tomorrow night, chronicled by a new sidebar, his photos with Lexy forgotten.

No, Lexy needed more – but not *too* much more. This was a dance for her to choreograph carefully. Enough of a story to get the press attention she needed to kickstart the book and the launch of the new series, yet not so outrageous that Frank went ballistic. She hadn't warned her husband what she was up to tonight; hopefully she would be able to convince him that it had been quite by accident that she had ended up causing exactly the kind of headline-grabbing scandal which Emily and her team had recommended by way of publicity. Lexy knew perfectly well that Frank would hate this almost as much as the idea of him faking an indiscretion with Josie Santana.

Only Frank wouldn't let Josie anywhere near him in real life, she thought now as Deacon stepped towards her. *He's a good guy. While if I'm being honest, if I wasn't married, I'd throw Deacon on a bed and climb all over him like he was my personal jungle gym . . .*

Her hands were still on her breasts. She dropped them to her hips and cocked one hip bone towards Deacon, an aggressive stance that had held off more men than she had had hot dinners.

'I don't know what you think you're doing in here—' she started, playing for time as she worked out a strategy.

And then her words turned into a squeal worthy of one of his teenage fans as he completely overrode her forbidding body language and lunged towards her. His mouth still tasted deliciously of vodka, sweet and tart, his hands cupped the back of her head as he kissed her, ridiculously expert for a twenty-four-year-old, and into her forward-tilted hips he pressed his crotch, his cock fully hard already and so big that the squeal turned into a full-throated moan of excitement.

'Yeah, that's what I've got for you,' he muttered against her lips. 'You like it, right? Fuck, you get me going, babe!'

248

Lexy had instinctively reached back and grabbed the copper trough behind her for balance as he grabbed her, making her totter on her precariously high heels. Much as she wanted to clamp her hands around his buttocks, grind that big cock even closer into her, she didn't dare do anything that Deacon might take as encouragement. He was already turbo-charged. How could she have known he'd be this aggressive?

She'd thought of him as a puppy whose tummy she could tickle. Instead, it was like having a tiger by the tail.

'Wait—' she started, but then his tongue was in her mouth again, and she found herself helpless to do anything but respond. It was all she could do to keep her hands on the sink edge instead of running them all over him as he was doing with her, tracing every curve through her body-clinging dress, making her shiver from head to toe.

Lexy had been with Frank for six years, married to him for nearly three of those and faithful to him all that time – if you didn't count the recent encounter with Silantra, which Lexy was definitely not doing. Her husband was one of the best lovers she'd ever had, always up for it. She could roll home drunk and horny, climb into bed with him, straddle his sleeping body and know that he would wake up nothing but hard and happy at this unexpected early morning bonus treat, holding out as long as he could while his wife rode herself to one drunken orgasm after another.

But this – a sexy stranger ambushing her in the loos, pushing her up against a sink, snogging her as frantically as if the world were about to blow up in five minutes and he needed to drive himself inside her and explode as the whole planet combusted in flames – this knee-trembling, frantic-ally urgent passion that only a man under thirty could summon, as if he would literally die if he couldn't fuck her this second – *this* was the kind of encounter it was simply impossible to have with your husband.

You could sneak off for a quickie, say, in a broom cupboard at a restaurant, suppressing your giggles as you fumbled around to manage a consummation as diners clinked cutlery and waiters bustled back and forth so close to you. Frank and Lexy had done that at Nobu years ago, and it had been great fun to exit with smug smiles and twin glows of satisfaction on their cheeks, Lexy's knickers plugged with a wodge of paper hand towel ripped from one of the huge industrial rolls that had lined the shelf she had clung to, arse in the air, while Frank gave it to her from behind.

Delightful though it had been, however, it could not com-pare to this. There was something about the intensity and heat of a young man entirely driven by his erection, his full straining balls, that you would never find in a forty-year-old like Frank. Young men genuinely thought they would die if they couldn't have you: they begged and pleaded as if their very lives would be forfeit if they weren't granted the satis-faction of ramming their cocks into you with an energy and desperation that no older man could reproduce.

Deacon's hands were dragging at the tight elasticated bodice of her dress, pulling the cap sleeves down to bare her shoulders. The Léger was so snugly fitted that this had the unintended effect of binding her upper arms to her sides. Her hands flew up to stop him, grabbing at his shirt, but with only her forearms able to move, they flapped like a penguin's flippers, so awkwardly that her fingers caught on its buttons and pulled it open even more, baring his chest.

It was so smooth, so hairless, so *young* that it made Lexy's breath catch in her chest. She stared at it, hypnotized, wanting to see even more, to pull the shirt right off him. And then her gaze dropped down to his concave stomach, the belly-button a neat little shallow swirl like a whipped white chocolate bite, the faint, almost invisible trail of pale brown hairs starting below it, the most delicate of pencilled lines leading down to the big insistent cock that was pressing even harder between her legs. Deacon groaned and shoved his hands under the edge of her dress, cupping her breasts around the silky bra cups, squeezing them together, his tongue delving into the even deeper cleavage he had created, dipping wet and hot into the cleft.

Her eyes rolled back in her head. She tottered back, half-supported by her bottom catching on the ridge of the copper sink trough, half by Deacon's crotch holding her in place. Still licking her breasts, his hands stroked down her hips to the hem of her skirt, tugging it up, wrestling against the tight elastic of the fabric; just like a bandage, it rolled up tightly, hobbling her legs together, making it even harder for Deacon to get his hand up her skirt.

'What the *fuck*?' he groaned into her breasts. 'This is like you're wearing a suit of armour!'

And then his fingers hit an even more impenetrable barrier, because beneath the bandage dress, Lexy was wearing Spanx, a high-waisted style that reached right up to her bra. It was a garment she would never have dreamed of putting on if she had planned to give someone access to her crotch that evening.

'This is going to slice my dick off if I try to fuck you!' Deacon complained vividly, trying to pull the gusset to the side, defeated by the expensively heavy fabric. 'How the fuck do I get it off?'

He managed to get a couple of fingers into the small space he had created, tickling her as expertly as he was kissing her now, tongue in her mouth, fingers parting her, sliding inside her, finding her wet and ready in both places.

'I'm going to come in my jeans if I don't fuck you!' he panted. 'Take this thing off, come on, let me, you want it just as much as I do –'

In retrospect, it was extraordinary that no one had come into the women's toilets before now. Lexy had been so caught up in the rush of lust that she hadn't even considered the fact that they weren't in a private space. Besides, her plan had been to garner attention, to create headlines about herself and Deacon. A passionate embrace in a bathroom, with them both fully clothed, was about right for the level of publicity she wanted. That would definitely crank the lever several turns on the gossip mill, get her name plastered for weeks over gossip blogs and magazines, keep her in the *Daily Mail* sidebar on a daily basis as their paps followed her and Frank around.

And yes, the kids too, she'd admitted to herself, *but Frank worries about that way too much. They're much too young to realize what's going on – we'll just tell them we're playacting for the new show. God knows, Laylah loves having her photo taken, the little minx! That one takes after me – I'll have to watch her like a hawk when she gets into her teens . . .*

This would be a fantastically juicy story. Fans and foes alike would reach eagerly for Lexy's novel and TV show, wanting to see if they could detect cracks in the happy facade of her marriage.

And this way, she'd reflected, *I don't come off like some stupid wife who nearly got cheated on, but a sex bomb who can pull the guy that half the world wants to shag! God knows why Emily even suggested it the other way round – thank goodness Ghost Mouse came up with the idea to flip it! Come to think of it, Ghost Mouse's been more use to me than the PR agency I pay a fortune to every year . . .*

Deacon couldn't know, however, that Lexy's intentions towards him were strictly limited. Which was why he had stopped the woman who had been powdering her nose in the toilet as she emerged from the ladies' loos, asked her whether there was anyone else in there but Lexy, and on receiving an answer in the negative, had stationed his manager outside the door of the loos with strict instructions not to let anyone else in.

The manager had, for some minutes, been directing women to the disabled toilet just down the hall with an excuse that these ones were out of order. But that had only worked for so long. Eventually, while her back was turned as she shooed one woman away from the door, two other tipsy partygoers slipped inside and promptly froze at the sight of Lexy O'Brien, her dress pushed down at the top and rolled up at the bottom, her head thrown back in ecstasy as Deacon's fingers drilled between her legs.

Oblivious to the fact that he now had witnesses, Deacon hooked his fingers and pulled them out slowly, hitting the exact point to send Lexy, stimulated as she already was, into an instant orgasm. Overwhelmed, she toppled against the sink. Her hips thudded against Deacon's hand, her mouth opened in an O of pleasure, and the sight of her coming so fast and hard was way too much for Deacon, already on the road of no return.

Just as he had said would happen, his balls tightened fatally as his cock strained against the fly of his jeans. If these had been looser, he might just have managed to exert some control. But the jeans were so fashionably skintight that they had already ripped at both knees, and the insistent pressure of the fly against his swollen cock head was the last straw. A sound that was half a grunt, half a yell of surprise issued from his lips; he slammed against Lexy, and a rush of hot come started to spread over the front of his jeans. The expression on his face, simultaneously horrified and blissful, was superb, and it lasted long enough for both of the partygoers to whip their phones out from their bags and start snapping away.

There was plenty to capture. The women might not be sober, but neither were they drunk enough for their photos to come out blurred and unusable. As Deacon crashed into Lexy, he tipped her back into the copper trough, legs in the air on either side of his waist, her head smashing into the mirror behind it. Still coming, Deacon's fingers between her legs, she yelped in shock and pain; by this time, one of the spectators had been quick-reflexed enough to switch from photo to video mode, and the moment that Lexy's head hit was captured live.

'Shit!' Deacon said when he could, reaching out for her. 'You okay? Sorry, babe, I shot my load, but give me ten minutes and I'll be good to go again—'

It was then, in the mirror, that he saw the women with their cameraphones.

'*Fuck!*' he yelled, jumping back instinctively from the image in front of him. Unfortunately, this put him closer to them, and now that the front of his body wasn't pressed against Lexy, the cameras captured, both in video and in slow-motion stills, the come stain as it widened over his crotch. It was bad luck for Deacon that his jeans were not a dark colour that would have helped conceal it, but a virulent shade of chartreuse which the fashion magazines were declaring the colour of the season. It was light enough to show every drop of come, and, Deacon being young and virile, there were copious amounts.

'Can you stop, *please*?' he pleaded, as Lexy started hoicking herself out of the sink.

Such was Deacon's charm that the women, dazzled by his smile, did in fact lower their phones, which meant that at least Lexy's inelegant descent, skirt hoicked high, one hand pressed to the back of her head, was not recorded on camera. She staggered as her high heels made contact once more with the black-tiled floor, catching onto the edge of the trough to steady herself, the cap sleeves still wedged down her shoulders; she shrugged them up again, but the process was horrifically inelegant, and one of the women, unable to resist the temptation, started surreptitiously taking pictures again with her phone at waist level.

'Deacon, management's telling me I have to let people in!' his manager called urgently, cracking the door open a foot or so, for discretion. 'Are you guys done, or at least –'

She stuck her head into the room and gasped at the sight

255

of the two women, who, as soon as the door had opened, had shoved their phones into their bags and, their need to use the toilet subsumed under the much more urgent priority of getting their photographs out of the club, shoved past her and shot out down the corridor. In members-only clubs, taking photographs – unless you were in a private room having a launch – was strictly forbidden. That was the whole point of these clubs. Celebrities could relax and let their hair down, knowing that photographs of them drunk and chatting up people they weren't married to would never hit the papers.

If Deacon or Lexy had alerted the management, they might have managed to stop the women, confiscate their phones, delete the photographs they had taken. But to Deacon, being caught *in flagrante delicto* was no big deal. People expected him to be a bad boy. And Lexy, after all, had wanted this, or something very like this, to happen . . .

'Oh, *no*,' Deacon's manager said, in the infinitely weary tone of a woman who has spent the last year following around a priapic ex-boybander, trying to encourage him to write and record the occasional song in between his endless escapades. She sounded like the owner of an enthusiastic puppy that was not only addicted to dragging toilet paper rolls all round the house, but left messes everywhere for her to clear up. 'Deacon, your *jeans*!'

She stared at his crotch, her shoulders sagging as she asked a question to which she already knew the answer.

'Please,' she said faintly, '*please* tell me that's just water on them?'

Deacon's sheepish expression was both endearing and

comical. In the silence that fell as the manager heaved a sigh and Lexy rubbed the back of her head, grimacing in pain, a man's voice made itself heard once more:

'The Caterpillar said: *"So you think you're changed, do you?"*

"I'm afraid I am, sir," said Alice; *"I can't remember things as I used – and I don't keep the same size for ten minutes together!"'*

Deacon burst out laughing, looking ruefully down at his crotch, his cock detumescing inside his tight jeans.

'Fuck me,' he said, shaking his head. 'I know *exactly* how she feels!'

Chapter Twenty-One

Lexy made the biggest mistake of her life that night, but it wasn't the fumble with Deacon in the toilets of the Camden Club. It was how she acted directly afterwards.

In her defence, she had hit her head fairly hard against that mirror. While not concussed, she was genuinely dizzy and sore from the impact. So, making her way out of the toilets, she was in no condition to summon her driver and be taken back to Sandbanks. Although her head was spinning with the blow it had taken, she was also buzzed on vodka and dizzy from the high of her amazing encounter with Deacon. She could still feel his fingers between her legs, remember vividly the intoxicating sensation of coming all over them.

So she was physically and mentally dazed, and quite unable to make good decisions. If she had managed to calm herself down, she would have known that it was essential that she go home straight away and break the news to Frank before the papers could get hold of it. That way they could wake up the next morning and present a united front to the journalists who would be camping outside the house.

In her dizzy, over-stimulated state, however, there was no

way that Lexy could contemplate docilely climbing into a car and being driven home so early in the night. It was barely eight-thirty, and she simply wasn't ready for a two-hour drive home. Of course it would look terrible if she went back to the launch. She definitely needed to avoid Deacon, so that she could spin the story of their encounter as a one-off moment of madness. So while Deacon was cursing, splashing water all over his crotch, and speculating loudly about whether he could go back to the party without his trousers on, Lexy, with Brandon by her side, had taken the lift upstairs to the roof terrace, where she planned to have another drink or two to calm herself down and get a grip on her roiling emotions before she headed home.

Even if she drove back to Sandbanks straight away, she reasoned, Frank would be tucked up in bed and snoozing when she got home; he liked to be asleep by ten at the latest. So what was the point in rushing to give him the bad news? Couldn't she get home at midnight, say, climb into bed next to her sleeping husband and let him have a good night's sleep so he was nice and fresh tomorrow morning to deal with the mess she'd created?

The plan had been to find a quiet corner on the sprawling terrace, curl up there with Brandon and go over the plan for how they would spin the scandal. But that idea had been scuppered when Lexy was spotted by a couple of her frenemies on a girls' night out, women she posed with regularly on red carpets and at parties, gossiped about behind their backs, sniped at in her column and feuded with on Twitter. They might have been part of the cast of a larger reality show, generating endless reams of press to keep them all in the news.

Sam, a TV presenter who specialized in bubbly commentary on recap shows, diving into a studio audience to giggle and flirt with them while coaxing saucy observations from them about the people they'd just seen compete, and Michelle, a reality star who was not as quick-witted or charming as Lexy, but had worked her way up the greasy pole from cast member to household name partly by having sex with her fiancé live on camera, were in a corner banquette, a champagne cooler set up beside them. Their seating choice was highly strategic: everyone could see them, but no one was close enough to hear what they were saying, so that they could let their hair down in privacy, chattering about topics that would never, ever, make their way into the press.

The sexy pink lighting, palm trees and black-upholstered banquettes of the terrace were more Miami Beach than NW1. Candles glimmered on the low glass tables, uplighting below the trees cast dramatic shadows: the entire atmosphere was of a wonderful, enticing party, and Lexy was delighted to see Sam and Michelle, at one of the best tables, beckoning her to come over and join them. She was promptly ensconced between them, giggling about how naughty she had just been, teasing them with the prospect of gossip to come and telling Brandon to order more champagne.

No matter how much they begged, she wouldn't tell them what had just happened. She didn't trust them for a second, knew that they'd be sneaking out to try to ring up gossip bloggers. They wouldn't make any money from the tip-off, but they'd earn themselves credit for future positive mentions and definitely some plugs for whatever brand they were pushing that month.

Sam and Michelle had planned the evening well ahead, ordering in some extra goodies to make the evening go with a bang. Ten minutes in, one of them was palming Lexy a wrap of cocaine under the table. Ten minutes after that, the pain from her head had magically disappeared; and after that, the hours positively flew by.

Lexy was, after all, celebrating. Things with Deacon had certainly gone much faster, and much more crudely, than she had planned. She had intended to be photographed kissing him in infinitely chicer surroundings than a women's toilet. A secluded corner up here on the roof terrace would have been perfect, the two of them half-concealed behind one of the palm trees, fronds throwing dramatic shadows over the picture. But at least in the mobile phone photographs snapped in the loos, her body had been concealed behind Deacon; she was comfortable that nothing too incriminating could make it to press.

Lexy had no idea, of course, about the second set of photographs, the very explicit ones of Deacon in his stained jeans, of her on the sink with her legs in the air, then staggering down again with her skirt hoicked up high on her thighs. If she had known about them, her reaction would have been very different indeed.

So Lexy was under the mistaken impression that she had got exactly what she wanted. A scandal that would hit the papers and be kept there by her PR team spinning it out; stories about her making heartfelt apologies to Frank; photos of her dressing as demurely as a nun on day release from the convent as she picked up her kids from school and daycare; her and Frank photographed looking tense, heading out for a meal in a staged photo opportunity that would be labelled 'Crunch Time' or 'Crisis Talks'; 'sources close to the couple revealing' that Lexy and Frank were close to divorce; Lexy visiting a counsellor, perhaps, since Frank was very unlikely to agree to fake visits to Relate with her; then a visit for the whole family to a theme park, the nanny staying well out of shot, which would be the first hint that the couple might be reconciling and putting the past behind them . . .

It was straight out of any reality TV star's basic playbook. Emily's firm would know how to handle it for maximum effect. Ideally, if Frank could bear it, a story about the two of them spicing up their sex life would run in the week that the series and the book both launched. That would chime in with the narrative that they were pushing: that after a child together and a few years of marriage, Frank and Lexy had made the all-too-common mistake of taking each other for granted. Their different tastes had led to largely separate social lives, their once-passionate sexual connection had grown stale; they needed a shake-up.

The classic next move was to sell the exclusive rights to an article covering a romantic weekend getaway, comped by an upmarket resort, at which Lexy would pose in a series of outfits currently available from her supermarket line. The kids would be looked after by Frank's mother back home as the couple reconnected with each other in a swimming pool, over cocktails, on a beach at sunset; at the end of the piece they would hint coyly at the possibility of a vow renewal, whose organization would occupy a large part of the next season of Lexy's show . . .

But Lexy couldn't be sure Frank would go for all this.

Much as she loved him, sometimes she regretted not having married a partner who was as committed as she was to the process of moulding their lives into a narrative that would keep readers and viewers hooked. And, tipsy and coked up, she found herself spilling some of this frustration to Sam and Michelle. The latter was engaged to another reality star with whom she had very little in common apart from their active sex lives and their ambition. However, since Michelle and her fiancé Jake spent their entire time either shagging or planning out new stunts to get them into the papers, the couple that worked together seemed, so far, to be staying together.

'I really should be doing pieces about mine and Frank's sex life, like you and Jake do!' Lexy slurred enviously to Michelle. 'You're so lucky that he doesn't mind that!'

'Oh, Jakey's a total slag,' Michelle said, hoisting the empty bottle of champagne out of the ice bucket and waving it to signify to the waiter that they needed another one. 'Likes it every way to Sunday and doesn't mind me spilling all the deets! The only thing I can't talk about is the threesomes, for obvious reasons –'

She grinned at Lexy, waving her hands as if conducting an orchestra as the two of them chorused together that refrain repeatedly nagged into them by their publicists: '*Not family friendly!*'

'We'd lose every single endorsement overnight, can you imagine?' Michelle said, as the waiter came over. 'I don't even want to *think* about what that'd cost us!'

Her pretty face, plump with fillers, contorted as she squinched up her eyes, trying to calculate how much she earned from her eyebrow kits, being the face of a suntan line, and endorsing diet supplements, then adding on Jake's protein powder, fitness equipment and men's underwear deals.

'Err . . . basically *so* much dosh,' she eventually concluded. 'But we worked out a good way to hide it. Everyone knows what a fitness freak Jakey is, so people take it for granted that we'll always have a personal trainer around. Even on holiday. So we can travel with whoever it is we're playing with.'

She winked at Sam.

'Or, when Sam was having it off with us, we said that she was lonely 'cause she just got dumped and that's why we took her to Marbs on holiday. Got some nice pieces out of it too – Jakey got a few articles about him being grumpy that he wasn't getting enough alone time with me because I was having cocktails with Sam, and I got three weeks' worth of columns about how friendship's so important because men can come and go, even the best ones, but friends are forever—'

'That was a good week!' Sam said nostalgically. 'And I got loads of publicity off it too – honestly, I don't think I'd've got *Strictly Come Dancing* without it. They were really keen on me being single so they could run stories about me getting off with my dancing partner – as if, he was a total gayer – and all the wives worrying about me being a danger to their marriages because of the *Strictly* break-up curse. All bollocks, of course. You know me – I never want just a guy in bed.'

'Yeah, poor Jakey!' Michelle said, grinning. 'In Marbs he

was all, like, *I wanna just fuck Sam this afternoon one-on-one* and she'd be, *Yeah not feeling that so much, Michelle needs to sit on my face while you do it, okay?*'

She hiccupped as the waiter came back with the new bottle of champagne.

'Need the loo again,' she said significantly, picking up her bag and heaving herself to her feet. 'You wanna come, Lex?'

'Just one more time,' Lexy said, a statement she had made several times already that night. 'Then I've really got to get going – where's Brandon, I need him to sort my car out . . .'

'You told him to piss off a couple of hours ago!' Sam said, giggling. 'What are you, mental? Don't you remember? You said he was doing your head in, hovering around telling you that you ought to get going!'

'Oh! Did I?'

Lexy had no idea how much she had drunk by now. They had been joined for a while by the Clearly Cloudberry PR, who had made a big deal of ordering rounds of shots for the table, cleverly extending the promotional evening to the club terrace. Lexy had been entirely genuine when she said she liked the cloudberry flavour, and had put away more shots than anyone. She had a legendarily hard head, but everyone had their limits, and the amount she had drunk meant she needed to do more lines so that she didn't fall over, and then the lines made her want to drink more to balance herself out. It was what she had once heard Sam call a viscous circle.

'I need to get a car,' she heard herself say, and realized that she was starting to slur. 'Got to get home to Frank.'

'He's in London?' Sam looked surprised. 'I thought he never stayed up here.'

'No no, Shandbanksh,' Lexy said. '*Sandbanks.*'

'Lex –' Michelle plopped back onto the banquette again. 'No way can you get back there tonight! You'll puke all over the fucking car and then pass out in the mess!'

This frank assessment was so accurate that both Lexy and Sam erupted into laughter.

'Okay, when you're right you're right,' Lexy admitted. 'I'll crash at the flat tonight and then go back at the crack of dawn tomorrow morning . . . come on, then, Mish, just one more trip to the ladies, then I'll head off . . .'

Chapter Twenty-Two

Of course, it wasn't just one more trip. They didn't leave until the club closed at three a.m., and even then Lexy was reluctant to move from the cosy banquette, the salacious gossip, the champagne and the charlie. The manager had to usher them out tactfully, instructing the bouncer downstairs to make sure that all three of the very coked-up and drunk women were safely seen into black cabs. Lexy was so out of it that she had no memory of the last hour she had spent in the Camden Club, of her journey home, or the tumble she had taken getting out of the lift, fumbling for her door key in her bag. One of her heels had caught on the edge of the carpet, and, her hands occupied, she couldn't save herself: she had crashed heavily down on her knees, her bag flying across the corridor.

Luckily she hadn't woken up the neighbours as she kicked off her shoes, scrabbled to retrieve the bag, hoisted herself to her feet and drunkenly tried three keys in the lock before finding the right one. Once inside the flat, she had been unable to wriggle out of her dress, due to its extreme tightness and her extreme inebriation. She had managed to remove most of her hairgrips, but that was the extent of her efforts.

Having fallen into bed, snoring heavily, with all her clothes and make-up on, she had slowly, painfully awoken to a pillowcase smeared with mascara, lipstick and, gruesomely, a drop or two of blood from her nostril: the coke she had taken had irritated the lining of her nose. Her eyes closed, she was still half-dreaming, and the image she was seeing was a nun standing in a tower, pulling on a bell rope, tolling it over and over again. On the roof below was a woman's body, spread-eagled, a blonde woman in a grey skirt suit who had fallen from the tower . . . the bell kept ringing, the nun kept tugging that bell rope like an automaton, on and on and on . . .

Lexy managed to pry her eyes open, a sticky procedure because of the mascara and fake eyelashes she was still wearing. She hadn't closed the curtains the night before, and the daylight was so piercingly bright that she had a sudden, vivid flash of sympathy for vampires. She turned her head sideways into the pillow, squinting, getting accustomed to the light. Gradually, she realized that she had been seeing the last few frames of the Hitchcock film *Vertigo*. And the reason her brain had summoned up the image of the nun in the belltower above Kim Novak's corpse was that a bell was indeed ringing insistently.

It was the landline. That was why Lexy had taken so long to recognize it: she was much more used to the ringtone of her mobile. She sat up, groaning as the movement caused pain to stab through her head, and promptly fought an urge to retch, sitting still till the nausea passed. After a while, she noticed a pattern. The phone rang seven times, stopped, then started up again almost immediately, as the caller got the answering machine, hung up, and then redialled the number straight away.

As her eyes focused, she caught sight of herself in the floor-to-ceiling mirrored fitted wardrobes opposite. Lexy had, ironically, loved this feature when they bought the flat. So much time, money and hard work had gone into her appearance that she relished the sight of the fruits of her labour. Today, however, the woman in the mirror was not a lithe, big-boobed sex symbol but an extra from the *Rocky Horror Show*. She moaned aloud. Her bra was digging into her, and her Spanx were so tight she had probably got a yeast infection from wearing them for so long.

She swung her legs over the side of the bed and yelped at the sight of her right knee. On it was a weal the size of a two-pound coin, red and puffy. A flash of memory snapped across her brain, like a near-subliminal cut in a film: the carpeted floor of the corridor hallway, seen in a very tight close-up, so close that she must have been on hands and knees looking down at it . . . It hurt to put weight on that leg. She might have twisted the knee a little when she landed on it. Nothing major, but she would definitely need to stay off high heels for a while.

Everywhere in this flat were reflective surfaces. It was a new-build, its interior design all glass and chrome or mirrored walls. As Lexy limped into the ensuite bathroom, she had to direct her gaze to the floor in order to avoid catching a glimpse of her smeared, grotesque face. She turned away from the mirror over the sink, peeling off the Hervé Léger dress; the wriggling, writhing movements required to drag it down to her ankles made her feel off-balance and nauseated.

It was just as painful wrenching off the Spanx. She pulled off her fake lashes, started the shower running, smeared her face in make-up remover and stepped under the rainforest shower head, turning the temperature down as cold as she could bear to help with her screaming headache.

Black trails poured down her face as her make-up washed off, the chilly jet on her scalp at first agony but then slowly doing its work, waking her up and cooling her down, helping to diminish the effects of the hangover. She managed to stay under it for a good five minutes before she finally stepped out and wrapped a towel around her, brave enough now to look at herself in the mirror. It wasn't a pretty sight. The whites of her eyes were bloodshot, the eyes themselves seeming to have receded in her face, small and piggy, her skin blotched.

If she had been able to, she would have rung up Skin3 right away, begged for an emergency appointment and gone in for a full restorative face mask. The staff were very used to her staggering in, hungover and in need of TLC: first, Eva would mix her a restorative potion of cucumber water in which she had dissolved glutamine powder, an amino acid that she swore acted as a conditioner for the stomach, soothing a tummy sore from a heavy drinking session. Then she whisked Lexy into a mercifully dark treatment room where the vitamins and collagen she so sorely needed would be worked deep into her epidermis as soothing music played. Lexy always emerged a different woman after one of these emergency sessions, ready to face whatever the day threw at her.

But, she told herself wistfully, she had to get back to Sandbanks as soon as possible. The phone was still ringing;

whoever was calling her would not give up until she answered. She patted in her serum and eye cream and vitamin oil, dusted herself with a layer of mineral powder, then spritzed her face with hydrating spray, more powder, even more hydrating spray, till at last she could bear the sight of her reflection. Padding back into the bedroom, Lexy took a deep breath, sat down on the bed and, finally, raised the receiver.

'Hello? *Hello?* Lexy, is that you? *Hello?*'

It was Brandon, sounding fairly deranged at the surprise of hearing something else but the expected seven rings and then the answering machine clicking in. Lexy opened her mouth to say 'Hello' back, but it came out like the croak of a dying raven. She cleared her throat, hawked up a large gob of phlegm, and tried again.

'Hello? Brandon?' she managed hoarsely.

'Lexy!' he squealed. 'Oh my God, what a relief to hear your voice! Emily was saying we should call the management of your building and try to get in so we could see if you were there and doing okay – you *are* okay, aren't you?'

Lexy winced at the stream of words, holding the handset further from her ear.

'Yeah, I'm okay. But I have a monster hangover,' she said.

'Have you gone online? The photos are all over everywhere, *everywhere*! It's bad, Lexy. You look like you were having sex with him. *Were* you having sex with him?'

No one could have seen that Deacon had fingered her, Lexy was sure. All that would have been visible was his hand up her skirt, and though that wasn't great, it certainly didn't translate to looking as if she was having sex with Deacon . . .

'No, I wasn't,' she said firmly.

'Lexy?' the head of the agency interrupted. 'It's Emily. Brandon's been ringing you over and over for *hours*. What the *fuck* were you thinking? Frank's furious and I don't blame him! You've gone way too far!'

'I really didn't . . .' Lexy said feebly. 'I didn't have sex with him, I really didn't . . .'

'I'm booking a car for you right now,' Emily said crisply. 'It'll be twenty minutes, tops. Clean yourself up, get dressed in your most covered-up, repentant outfit. Flat shoes. No ripped jeans. Nothing tight. No leather, apart from your shoes. Make-up minimal – it has to look like you're not wearing any at all. Hair back, so everyone can see you looking sad. Dark colours only, no jewellery, but make sure they can see your wedding ring. Do the walk of shame through the paps. No sunglasses. Rub your eyes in the car as you get there so it looks like you've been crying. Got all that? Do I need to come round and check you over?'

'No, I've got it,' Lexy said feebly, overwhelmed by the barrage of instructions.

'Remember, it's a *total* walk of shame,' Emily said. 'You're humbling yourself, showing everyone how terrible you feel. Get home and do whatever you need to do to calm Frank down. Charge your phone in the car – it's out of juice. If you spend the time looking at the press, trust me, you won't even need to rub your eyes. This is *not* the kind of thing we were after! You know better than this, Lexy! Thank God we've got months before the series and the book come out to fix this fucking disaster!'

Ensconced in the car, her phone charging, Lexy Google-searched herself. She was dressed exactly as per Emily's instructions, in navy jeans, a long, bottom-skimming, high-necked grey sweater, and a demure knee-length navy coat, ballet flats on her feet. Her hair was brushed back into a ponytail, her only make-up a single layer of mascara. It would have taken an observer quite a while to recognize the woman in the back of the car as the one in the photographs, with the latter's piled-up hair, fake eyelashes and smeared lipstick, her disproportionately large boobs spilling over the tight bodice of the dress, her skirt high enough to look as if she wasn't wearing any underwear at all . . .

Photographs of her with her bottom in the sink and her legs splayed in the air on either side of Deacon. Photos of her staggering back down again, heel tipping underneath her, her skirt caught up almost to her crotch, but not high enough to show the Spanx that would to some degree acquit her of having just had penetrative sex. Photos of Deacon turning away towards the woman, looking dazed and shocked, the stain on his trousers visible.

Okay, at least those last ones proved that he hadn't got his cock out – but still, they looked awful, because the clear inference was that he and Lexy had been so hot and heavy that they would have done it if they hadn't been interrupted. And since that was probably no more than the truth, Lexy's emotions as she stared at those pictures were cripplingly painful.

She could have sworn that the cameraphones had been put away after Deacon had pleaded with the women to stop; she hadn't been drunk then, and she had fairly clear memories of the whole time in the bathroom. One or both of them must have kept taking surreptitious photos.

It was clear from the angle that they were being shot upwards – *thanks for that chin bulge, by the way!* she thought ruefully. *I always say never let anyone photograph you from below!* There was a whole series of the come stain on Deacon's jeans spreading, from a tiny patch to the sodden crotch a couple of minutes later. Some of the more satirical gossip sites had done a slide show of the process, with amusing captions.

And then there was the video. Oh God, the video, the most incriminating thing of all. Deacon humping away, moaning, coming, telling Lexy that he was sorry he'd shot his load but he'd get hard again in ten minutes . . .

She dropped the phone onto the seat beside her, staring ahead blankly. The only way she could describe her situation was, given the circumstances, deeply ironic. She was totally fucked.

Chapter Twenty-Three

Lexy had always been indomitable, priding herself on her ability to face whatever life threw her way. Barely eighteen when she shot to fame on *Who's My Date?*, she had had to navigate her way through the shark-infested seas of producers, agents, presenters, many of them wanting something in return for promoting her career. She had dodged and ducked as much as she could, smiling as she slipped out of this one's grip, that one's attempt to kiss her; but she hadn't always been able to get away scot-free, not from a few very important men who had made it clear that this was not a negotiation but an ultimatum.

She had chosen her career, every single time. She had gone along with what she couldn't decline without losing a crucial work opportunity, and done her best to scrub her mind of the memory directly afterwards. Her mantra had been to always look forwards: to keep herself motivated, she had pictured herself as Dorothy on the Yellow Brick Road, a smile on her face and a spring in her step. Her fans wanted a Lexy who was upbeat, funny, positive, a fighter and a survivor, an ideal version of themselves. To use another very useful American expression, she had always made lemonade out of lemons.

But this situation with Deacon was so serious that she could see no possibility of spinning it successfully. Lexy's mouth tasted as acid and bitter as if someone had squeezed one of those lemons directly onto her tongue.

Her usual bravery had completely deserted her. She couldn't summon the strength to pick up her phone and dial either the home number at Sandbanks or Frank's mobile; it would be better to wait until she could see him in person. Lexy had always been able to rely on her beauty, her charm, her quick wits, to talk her out of trouble. She was almost sure that when she saw Frank, if she cried profusely and begged him to believe she was telling the truth, he would eventually forgive her.

She had been rehearsing her version of events all during the drive. She had been in the women's toilets: Deacon had followed her in there of his own accord. She had had a few drinks, Deacon had thrown himself on her, she'd got carried away for a moment or two, he'd taken advantage of her, she'd been so guilty she couldn't bear to tell Frank what had happened, so she had skulked back to Chelsea Harbour, taken a sleeping pill, cried herself to sleep . . .

The car was heading down Banks Road, the only way to reach the small peninsula. The road looped to the left, a short turnoff running down to the chain ferry, which was currently docked, a couple of cars and a bus driving slowly off it; the car swooped around the wide curve which became Panorama Road, and Lexy braced herself. She knew what was coming in three . . . two . . . one . . .

And there they were, the paparazzi. Massed outside the gates of her house, sipping coffee out of takeaway cups, chatting desultorily to each other, checking their phones for updates, waiting for her to come home. How often had she returned home to precisely this sight? How often had her heart raced with excitement at the proof that she was important enough to generate this level of interest? Whether the story they were waiting to report was real, fake or wildly exaggerated, never before had Lexy been anything but delighted as her car slowed down, as the paps realized that their target was inside and sprang to attention, cameras raised, video equipment hoisted to their shoulders, the pack forming around the car as it turned into the driveway, coming to a halt by the big wooden gates . . .

'*Lexy!*' they screamed as one.

Faces pressed eagerly into the windows of the car, cameras snapped away.

'Lexy! Where've you been? Why didn't you come home last night? Were you with Deacon? What does Frank think? Have you talked to him yet? Lexy, Lexy, *Lexy . . .*'

Normally she would have rung the house to buzz open the gates so that she didn't have to get out of the car. But Emily had told her to do the walk of shame, and Emily was right.

'I'm getting out to unlock the gates,' she said to the driver, who stared at her in disbelief in the rear-view mirror, shocked that she was going to walk the gauntlet. Taking a deep breath, Lexy reached out and opened the car door.

There was a brief resistance: the bodies thronging around the car were tighly packed. However, as soon as they realized what was going on, the paparazzi closest to the door backed away, yelling:

'She's getting out! Back off! She's getting out!'

Every moment of Lexy's exit from the car was captured. They gave her just enough room to walk over to the electronic panel set into one of the stone gateposts, but they were screaming questions the entire time. It was hell. Her head was ducked, but they still got a good view of her face, pale and drawn, her lips pressed tightly together, her shoulders hunched.

There were only four numbers to enter, a simple sequence, yet when she inputted the code there was no responsive click from the lock, no whirring of machinery as the mechanism of the gate opener started up. She tried it again, thinking that her nerves were to blame, realizing for the first time that she had had nothing to eat since a couple of canapés at the Cloudberry launch party; after that, the cocaine had kicked in, obliterating any appetite she might have had.

Her hand was shaking. Shockingly, the second try was no more successful than the first. She dragged her phone out of the pocket of her coat, frantically searching for the fake contact entry under which she had stored the codes: no, she hadn't made a mistake. Those were the right numbers, and yet they weren't working . . .

'What's up, Lexy? Locked out?' yelled a voice in her ear. There were cameras on either side of her face, pressing in, everyone now taking up the cry: had Frank locked her out? What was going on? *Tell us, Lexy, turn round, give us a statement* –

Her whole body was trembling now. It was hard to get control of her fingers as she tapped in the door code for the third time, desperately hoping that the gate mechanism was just having a glitch, that she would be able to take refuge in the safety of her home . . .

But no reassuring click followed, no familiar buzz to indicate the gates were opening. Nothing at all.

There was only one conclusion to draw, and the paparazzi had got there much faster than her. Frank had changed the code so she could not get in.

Lexy would genuinely never have thought this possible. Frank, her loving, devoted husband; Frank, who loathed the idea of washing one's dirty laundry in public, who hated any kind of scene; Frank, the man she had always been able to trust implicitly, her rock, her comfort, had stranded her outside her own home, at the mercy of the paps, humiliating her with absolute, deliberate intent.

It was this realization, as much as the fact that her mortification was being captured and transmitted all around the world, live-streamed to gossip sites, that caused the tears to form in her eyes. She turned away from the gatepost. There was an intercom button there, of course, but she was not going to press it, to plead futilely with her husband to let her in for the benefit of all the microphones around her.

How people would love to watch that! No, it was enough for them to see her humbled like this, Lexy who finally, after many ups and downs, had managed to get it all: career, beauty, handsome husband, healthy children, wealth and happiness. How the women who didn't have every one of those things would gloat as they watched the videos, scrolled greedily through the photographs, read the coverage speculating about whether Frank was already meeting divorce lawyers, picking one who handled the big-name celebrity clients and was famous for wringing every last drop out of their spouses . . .

Lexy wasn't even trying to hold back the tears. They were flowing down her face in sheets of salt water. And because she knew that she deserved to cry, deserved to be punished, she didn't even raise a hand to wipe them away. She walked slowly back to the car feeling as if she had just been slapped violently across the face.

The driver was out of the car now, shouting to the paps to fall back, make room for her. It wasn't his job: he wasn't a bodyguard. But the sight of beauty in distress had stirred his protective instincts. Miraculously, the paparazzi actually obeyed him, shuffling to either side, creating a path for Lexy back to the car, another gauntlet to walk. The driver was holding the door open; safety beckoned if she could only make it down the narrow passage whose walls were shifting, pressing bodies, ranks of cameras clicking. For a few seconds, there was silence, almost as if it was a funeral, the journalists paying a kind of instinctive respect to the sight of her tear-streaked face.

It didn't last, of course. Their job was to provoke a reaction, get a killer quote, and after the brief hush of reaction they were feral beasts again, yelling questions at Lexy: what was she going to do? Had Frank been in touch? Was he getting a divorce? Had she been shagging Deacon last night? Had he lasted longer than in the Camden Club toilets? It was a full-on barrage, and she was shaking so badly by the time she reached the car that the driver had to help her step inside.

She literally fell onto the leather seat as the door slammed after her and the driver started up the car.

'Where are we going?' he asked, careful not to meet her eyes in the rear-view mirror, putting the car into reverse and starting to back, gingerly, onto Panorama Road, going as slowly as possible to avoid hitting one of the many paparazzi who were surrounding the car again, taking their last pictures of a white-faced Lexy looking like an aristocrat during the French Revolution being driven to her execution in a tumbril.

Lexy thought suddenly of the Ferry Hotel. Even though she, and many Sandbanks residents, nicknamed it 'Fawlty Towers', it was very close by, just a few minutes' walk away. She could ask the driver to take her there, see if a suite was free, ring Frank and plead with him to let her in . . . and if he agreed, she could wait it out until the paparazzi packed up and left, then slip back to her home . . . and if Frank didn't answer, she could still go back to the house, lean on the bell, beg him, sobbing, with everything she had in her, to please, *please* let her come home . . .

Chapter Twenty-Four

'I can't believe I did that,' Frank said, his voice cracking as he turned away from the window embrasure of the first-floor study, concealed from view by the heavy velvet curtain. The sound of the paparazzi screeching Lexy's name had carried across the courtyard into the house, but Frank had in any case been keeping an eye out for his wife, sure that she would be coming back some time today. He could barely see her over the gates, but from the shouts of the journalists, the way they were clustering around the gatepost, the car pulling away again as the paparazzi crowded around it to get the shots of Lexy leaving, it was clear what had happened.

'I know it must have been really hard,' Caroline said softly. 'I'm so sorry you're going through this, Frank.'

Frank's complexion was ashen. He shook his head slowly as if trying to deny what had just happened: his wife, in tears, being turned away from the house they shared together.

'I'm so glad you're here, Caroline,' he said, slumping down onto the sofa on which she was sitting. Much as she had wanted to watch Lexy trying and failing to gain access to the house, Caroline had refrained; it wouldn't look right for her to have her face pressed against the glass next to Frank's.

'Oh, I couldn't have stayed away!' she said in the same soft tone. 'Not if you and the kids needed me.'

That morning, seeing the story breaking online, Caroline had tried to ring the house but failed to get through, as it was already under siege. Having delivered *Lexy on the Loose* a couple of days ago, she had reluctantly returned to London the next day.

With the house phone going straight to answering machine, she had texted Frank, wondering if she dared just to pack a bag and get on the next train to Bournemouth. But to her great relief, a mere few minutes later Frank had rung her, sounding terrible. This had emboldened her to offer to come to Sandbanks and help look after Laylah and London. Frank had almost sobbed with relief, confessing that he had been hoping she would suggest it but that he hadn't dared to ask her himself, as it seemed like such a huge imposition . . .

The paparazzi had beaten Caroline to it, of course: the mansion was staked out by the time she arrived. But it had been easy enough to make her way through the crowd, mumbling about being a friend of the family. It had been scary, but exciting, to have that quantity of attention briefly directed her way as they realized she was entering the house to which they all wanted access. The questions rat-tat-tatted out like machine-gun fire: was Lexy leaving Frank for Deacon? Was she with Deacon right now? How was Frank coping? Did the kids know what their mum was up to? It gave Caroline a vivid sense of what it was like to be Lexy, to have people surrounding you, literally begging you just to give them a quote.

Many people would have disliked being pestered like this. And a few months ago, Caroline would have been one of them. But not now. Now, she liked it quite a lot.

The kids had not gone to school or Montessori that day, of course. They were out on the back lawn, which was entirely sheltered even from long-distance photo lenses: it was a major reason Lexy and Frank had bought the house, the privacy it gave them from press intrusion. The house's two wings curved around the lawn and gardens below, while thick trees lined the fences on either side. The next-door neighbours' houses were as impregnable as their own. The richer people were, the more privacy they could purchase.

Leaving Laylah and London in Gabriela's charge, Caroline had slipped away to find Frank, who had told her that Lexy was on her way to Sandbanks. For the last hour, the two of them had sat in the study, both so aware of what would happen when Lexy arrived that they were barely able to say a word. Now that it had happened, however, the floodgates had opened.

'I still don't know if I did the right thing,' Frank said, twisting his hands together in his lap. 'I'm just picturing her face as she typed in that code and realized that I changed it . . .'

'You said you couldn't face seeing her right now,' Caroline prompted, steering him where she needed him to go. 'You said you needed time to get your head straight, and you didn't want a big scene in front of the kids.'

'I don't,' Frank said unhappily.

'And you said that if she just came home as if nothing had happened, without ringing first to try to explain or say sorry, you wouldn't be able to stop yourself from being angry and a scene would be bound to happen,' she went on.

Frank nodded.

'I know it was a shock for her,' Caroline continued. 'But Frank –' she had heard that repeating someone's name was an effective way to make them inclined to do what you wanted – 'it was a shock for *you* to be woken up by a journo ringing you at six in the morning to ask you if you had a comment to make on your wife snogging a boybander in the loos of some club!'

'Yeah,' he said, nodding gloomily. 'Yeah, that's true.'

'And then the photos, and the video!' she continued. 'The impact on the kids! So awful!'

Frank, who was staring at his hands, nodded vigorously at the reminder of his very strong feelings about parents who caused scandals that affected their children.

'That was why you decided to change the codes,' she reiterated. 'You said if she'd come home last night and talked about it then you wouldn't have been as angry. Where *was* she, anyway?'

'Emily says she was out with Sam Hope and Michelle McCrain,' Frank said flatly. 'On the lash. They stayed out till three a.m., apparently. Sam was tweeting about it this morning.'

Caroline pulled her phone out and quickly went onto Twitter, searching for Sam's account.

'Up till 3 w @michelleeeeMc & @sexylexyoriginal, ow, head hurts can I go back to slp now??'

'Just seeing fotos @sexylexyoriginal you are SO SO SO naughty OMG.'

'WOW @sexylexyoriginal said last nite big goss today no kidding! #juicy #naughty #noway #scandal @yeahimDeacon I mean you!'

Caroline read the tweets aloud, assuming a sombre tone which contrasted with the frivolity of the words. Frank was shaking his head in disbelief.

'This is awful, Frank,' she said, putting the phone down. 'I can't believe she told her friends that there was juicy gossip coming! That's *so* disrespectful.'

'They're not her friends,' Frank said flatly. 'They're – partners in crime. They all set each other off, especially when they're coked up. Lexy thinks I don't know she gets caned sometimes, but of course I bloody do. No way are any of them up till three a.m. without taking charlie, not with the amount of drink they all put away.'

'Oh,' Caroline said, rather shocked. 'I didn't know that. She doesn't talk about it in the book.'

'She wouldn't, would she?' Frank said almost sharply. He caught himself at once. 'I'm sorry, Caroline,' he said contritely. 'I'm really wound up, I didn't mean to snap. I'm just . . . she copped off with Deacon, then went and found Sam and Michelle and did a ton of charlie instead of coming back home to her family. And the reason she's getting back so late is because she woke up with a massive hangover. It's just all so bloody irresponsible! She's a wife and a mother. She shouldn't be giving a guy enough encouragement that he thinks he can follow her into the loos and start trying to give her one!'

Nodding in agreement, Caroline reached out a hand to him, and to her great relief, he took it. His fingers were dry, warm, enveloping hers, and he did not let go, but rested their clasped hands on the sofa between them.

'You're such a comfort, Caroline,' he said, heaving a long sigh.

Caroline hoped that he would notice how perfect her French manicure was – she had done it on the train, not caring about the irritated stares of the other passengers at the smell of nail polish – how smooth and moisturized her skin. She was dressed in an outfit which was part of an entire wardrobe she had bought for her newly slim figure; she would have loved to be able to wear really skinny jeans like Lexy's, but the constant running on the sandy beach of Studland had given Caroline too much calf and thigh muscle for those. The jeans were close-fitting, though, showing off her newly slim legs, and over them she wore a V-necked T-shirt and loose sweater, both from Joseph on sale, the quality much better than anything she had previously owned.

The bonus money had not yet hit her account, but Gareth had emailed to say how pleased he was with her for finishing before her deadline, and that, based on the quality of the previous sections of the book she had sent him, he was authorizing the payment with the accounts division of Bailey and Hart. On that assurance, and the knowledge that Lexy was planning to stir something up with Deacon in the next couple of days, Caroline had gone shopping very strategically for a new, fitted, elegant wardrobe that would hopefully see her through a stay at Sandbanks in Lexy's absence.

Caroline leaned forward, putting a little cleavage on display. That was the reason behind the V-neck T-shirts. She had learned from Lexy that when you were amply endowed, a V-neck was the best cut. It showed off your breasts by highlighting the cleavage, while the downwards point of the V gave the illusion that your waist was smaller than it was.

Frank's gaze could not help but flicker over the swell of Caroline's breasts.

'You look nice,' he said naively, not realizing why that statement had popped out of his mouth. 'Still working out? Did you find a gym in London, or are you doing park running, like I suggested?'

'I joined a gym,' Caroline said. 'There's a chain near me that's really cheap, just twenty pounds a month and no contract. But it's weird running on a treadmill – it feels so easy after doing it on the beach.'

'That's why I said park running,' Frank said. 'If there's a grass track you can get to, that's the closest to what you've been doing.'

'There *is* a park not that far away,' Caroline said. 'I just haven't had time to go over there and have a look yet – I only finished the book a few days ago, so . . .'

She bit her tongue. Mentioning the book had been a mistake; it had brought Frank's thoughts back from the delightful topic of how good she looked onto the much gloomier one of what his wife had been prepared to do in order to garner publicity for herself.

'I just don't know how she could do this,' he said so poignantly that Caroline felt a lump in her throat. 'No matter how much Emily tells me that it's all for publicity, that he jumped Lex in the loos and she only kissed him back because she remembered what they were talking about in the meeting and thought it would work – how is that supposed to make me feel better? It's obvious that she's kissing him back! You can see that! And how come those women were in there photographing it? It looks like a setup to me!'

'Did you see the video?' Caroline asked quietly, and Frank's hand tightened on hers, squeezing it almost painfully.

'No,' he muttered. 'No, I couldn't. Is it – is it bad?'

Caroline lowered her eyes and fell silent, as if she couldn't bear to say the words of confirmation.

Across the room, on the desk, Frank's mobile buzzed with a text coming in. This was nothing new; friends and family had been trying to get in touch all morning. But given the timing, and the fact that Lexy had not been in touch all day, Frank jumped to his feet, his hand dropping Caroline's as he hurried over to the desk and grabbed his phone.

'She's at the Ferry Hotel,' he said, looking down at the screen.

'That's unusual,' Caroline couldn't help saying. 'She's always so snarky about that place.'

Frank gave a half-smile.

'She's saying she'll wait till the paps clear out, and then can she come over and talk?' he said, still reading. 'She says she's really sorry, it's not what it looks like . . .'

His voice trailed off, and Caroline remained silent once more, again seeming like a loyal employee who, unable to come up with anything in her boss's defence, preferred not to say anything at all.

'But it is, isn't it?' Frank said, not really as a question. 'I haven't even watched the video, but from what the media's saying about it –'

He looked at Caroline, who squinched her brows together and drew her lips back in an expression that conveyed, very clearly, that she did not want to describe what happened in the video to Lexy's husband.

'I really hope the kids never see it,' she murmured, knowing this would trigger Frank. 'I mean, just those photos of his jeans . . .'

'Yes!' Frank agreed furiously at this successful attempt at adding fuel to the flames. 'He came in his trousers! He came in his fucking trousers while his hand was up my wife's skirt! The little bastard – if I ever come across him he'd better run. Otherwise I'll wring his fucking neck!'

He stared down at the phone in his hand.

'She must think I'm the biggest mug in the world,' he said. 'A total fucking mug. How can it not be what it looks like? They were humping away and then that skinny little dipshit came in his fucking jeans – what's she going to tell me to explain *that* away?'

But Caroline had the feeling that Lexy would think of something. She was so quick-witted, so clever, so able to wrap Frank round her little finger. Caroline had watched Lexy get away with neglecting her children, running roughshod over Frank's wants and needs, but then, just as Frank's resentment reached boiling point, turning on her dazzling charm and heading any trouble off at the pass with a display of perfect wife and mother virtues that lasted just long enough to settle Frank down and allow Lexy to resume her selfish behaviour as before.

If Lexy gained access to Frank now, she might well be able to talk him into forgiving her, letting her come home. And that would fatally scupper Caroline's chances with him, which couldn't be allowed to happen.

Caroline found herself remembering a historical novel she had read recently about the six wives of Henry VIII. When the fifth one, young, pretty Katherine Howard, had been accused of adultery, she had screamed and pleaded, trying to get to his rooms and beg him for mercy. But Henry's advisers had not allowed Katherine to see the king; she was so charming that they were afraid that, given access to him, she would use her wiles to convince him not to have her executed.

Caroline needed to apply the same principle with Lexy. There was a wedge between Frank and his wife now, but this was only the start. If Caroline couldn't drive the wedge in deeper, she would lose all the advantage she had gained.

'But Frank, how could she explain the photos of Deacon's jeans to the *children*?' Caroline asked, looking up at Frank with big doe eyes. 'That's the worst part! They'll see them sooner or later – no matter what we do, some kid at school will show them the pictures – maybe even the *video* – kids can be so cruel! I don't even want to *imagine* how that'll make them feel.'

Frank dropped the phone to the desk and knuckled his eyes hard.

'Oh God,' he said. 'I can't think about that! I've always said to guys on the team who're playing away that they're scum for not thinking about the effect on their kids, and here's my own wife doing exactly that . . .'

The phone buzzed again. Frank gulped out a hopeless sob.

'If it's her, I *can't* see her right now . . . Caroline, I *can't* . . .'

Caroline got up and walked across to the desk, picking up Frank's iPhone. Sure enough, the screen was showing another text from Lexy: 'Frank pls pls ring me, pls, Im crying my face off, Im crying & so guilty, pls answer, need 2 talk to u NOW pls.'

'I'm not sure if you should even look at these,' she said, sounding sad. 'There's no explanation or anything for what she did—'

'Like there's any she could give!' Frank said, his voice thick with tears.

'She wants to talk to you, but—'

'I *can't*,' Frank said again, to Caroline's great relief.

'I'll just delete them and turn off your phone,' Caroline said, pitching her tone between a question and a statement, so that later she could always say that she had thought it was what Frank wanted.

Frank said nothing, which she took as consent. Swiftly, Caroline deleted the messages from Lexy. And then, her heart racing, she went to the Favourites list in his iPhone contacts. Pulling up Lexy's number, she blocked it, doing it so fast that she didn't give herself time to think about what she was doing. Lexy could text and ring as much as she wanted, to no avail: Frank would think that, discouraged and guilty, she had stopped trying to get into contact with him. The home phone was going straight to the answering machine, but that, Caroline knew, was already full from the sheer volume of calls that morning. Lexy would not be able to leave a message there.

Had Caroline gone too far? Maybe. But Frank's phone was always lying around. If she lost her nerve, she could easily unblock Lexy's number.

There and then, however, Caroline had no regrets. Turning the iPhone off, she set it down on the desk and pushed it away a little, symbolically creating a distance between Frank and his conduit to the world outside. She glanced over at the desktop computer and thought that later on, when Frank was safely out of the way for twenty minutes or so, she would log on and block Lexy's email address too. In for a penny, in for a pound.

'I'm so sorry this is happening to you and the kids, Frank,' she said sadly. 'I'd do anything to make the pain go away.'

She was standing in front of him, looking up at him, her eyes wide. Tentatively, she reached out and touched his arm.

'I could do with a hug,' she said in the same small voice she had been using all through this talk. 'Would that be all right? I know I'm not going through what you are, but I'm feeling pretty upset. I really thought she was a better person than this.'

Wordlessly, Frank dropped his hands from his face. His handsome features were distorted by grief, his eyes red. Slowly he opened his arms, and equally slowly Caroline stepped into the space he had created, so close to him that she could feel the heat from his body. Tentatively, she wrapped her arms around his wide, solid chest, her heart racing faster than she could ever remember it doing in her life.

The weight of his arms pulled her even closer, until the whole front of her body was pressed against his. It was the first time in her adult life that she had ever felt comfortable with a man's body fully against hers, because it was the first time that she'd felt in reasonable shape. Her breasts, in a T-shirt bra that shaped them and pushed them up, were large and firm, and below them she no longer had a roll of fat. Her stomach was not flat, and never would be unless she got lipo, but she was seriously considering that option. Now that she had started to change her body, she never wanted to stop.

Her bra straps weren't digging into her, nor was the waistband of her jeans. If Frank should one day not only hug her like this, but run his hands up and down her back like a lover, it would feel relatively smooth. She wouldn't need to flinch away with embarrassment for fear of him feeling how tightly cinched in she was, or dread red welt marks forming as soon as she took her clothes off.

His scent was all around her. She pressed her cheek against his chest, settling there, breathing him in, and with exhilaration she felt his head lower, his jaw resting against her forehead, his breath warm on her hair. Tears started to form in her eyes. She was in Frank's arms, exactly where she had wanted to be from the moment she had seen him. In the days to come, they would hug more frequently, comforting each other. And one day, when she felt his body language responding to her as a woman, not just a friend, Caroline would pull back, just a little, and tilt her head to look up at Frank, her lips parted.

And he would bend down and kiss her. She knew it. She

could tell by the way he was holding her, the way their bodies were relaxing against each other. When you had this kind of full-body contact, your reactions could not be faked. Frank liked holding her, liked being close to her, not just intellectually but physically. Look how long he was maintaining the embrace, much longer than a simple hug for reassurance and comfort. She could feel his heartbeat against her cheek, and she heard herself sigh as she relaxed even further against him.

'You're crying,' he said into her hair, and she shivered at the sensation of his lips so close to her, the light, sensual tickle of his breath on her scalp.

'I'm sorry,' she mumbled. 'I'm getting your T-shirt wet.'

Frank slid his hands up her back to her shoulders, almost as she had fantasized about him doing. Looking down at her with concern, he thumbed the tears from her eyes. The intimacy made her tremble with excitement.

'I hate that you're caught up in all of this, Caroline,' he said. 'I'm really sorry you've got sucked into our mess.'

'It's okay, Frank,' she said. Every time he said her name, it was a secret thrill; every time she said his, she felt it was as if she were casting a spell, drawing him into an increasingly intimate relationship.

'Honestly, it's all about the kids as far as I'm concerned,' she continued. 'I'm not even thinking about myself. I just want to make sure they get through this as best they possibly can.'

Frank's smile was all the reward she needed.

'I was thinking – why don't we try to take Laylah and London out for the afternoon?' she suggested. 'They'd love to spend some quality time with you, and I honestly think it would do you the world of good as well. You know what it's like when you're spending time with small kids – you can't think about anything but them and all the questions they're firing at you.'

Frank pulled a face.

'I'd love to,' he said, 'but where are we going to go? There'll be paps hanging round the house for days, and they'll follow us as soon as they see us going out—'

'I thought we – I mean, you – could take the boat out?' Caroline said. 'I'll happily come to make sure the kids don't fall overboard! We could pack a picnic, have lunch and snacks if the weather keeps nice . . .'

Frank's expression cleared like the sky after a summer rain.

'That would be great!' he enthused. 'It's why I got the boat, to have family days out on the water. But Lex never wanted to come – she was always fussing about getting splashed or rained on and messing up her hair, or she was shooting off to London and couldn't spare the time.'

Caroline knew this perfectly well; she had heard Frank offer several times to take the family out on the power boat, only for Lexy to come up with one excuse after the other. The kids were too lively to be left to run around on the large boat without being constantly supervised, even with life-jackets on, so Frank couldn't take them out alone; and besides, as he had plaintively repeated to Lexy, the whole point was for the four of them to be together.

Frankly, Caroline wasn't looking forward to it. She couldn't swim very well, and although the power boat was generously sized, with a big covered indoor cabin and wide back deck, she knew that even in a lifejacket she would be nervous the entire time. But she would do much more for Frank than get on a boat for the afternoon and put a smile on her face as she handed sandwiches out to the kids and dried them down after they had taken a dip in the sea.

'I'll go down to the kitchen and get a picnic together, shall I?' she said. 'You go tell them what we're planning? I can't wait to see the excitement on their faces!'

But frankly, the expression on their father's face was all that she needed to make her wild with happiness.

Chapter Twenty-Five

Decades later, Lexy was still unable to look back on the day when she had been locked out of her own home without shivering with embarrassment and shame. She had sat on the balcony of her suite at the Ferry Hotel for hours, bawling her head off, a box of tissues next to her, blowing phlegm out of her nose, wiping her eyes repeatedly so that she could clear the tears away enough to check her phone for messages from Frank.

Unfortunately, the hotel balconies were not only small but linked together. Lexy had had to fend off concerned fellow guests, naturally worried about the continual, heartfelt sobbing, calling over to ask her very politely whether she was all right, or if there was anything they could do. Lexy had managed to snivel a 'No, thanks' while waving a hand in a gesture that asked them to leave her alone, but she could hear them still talking in hushed tones, speculating about what on earth could have happened to make her cry like that.

At least they didn't know who she was. Lexy always carried a baseball cap in her bag, together with a featherweight viscose scarf, so light that it took up very little space. The cap was pulled down tightly on her head, sunglasses covering her eyes, and the scarf wound around her neck, up to her chin, leaving as little of her face visible as possible. She looked eccentric but unrecognizable. Just a crazy woman going through heartbreak, ruining the lovely sunny afternoon for everyone else.

Still, even with her mumbled reassurances that she was okay, that no one was hurting her, eventually Lexy had retreated inside. It was too much not only to field the questions, but to hear the comments as another hotel guest returned to their room, slid open the glass door to the terrace and, shortly after, said in a horrified tone to their companion that it sounded as if someone had just heard that there was a death in the family.

Unfortunately, the decor of the suite was so appallingly depressing that when she compared it with her lovely sea view living room just a short distance away, it made her cry even harder. She joked that the hotel's rooms looked like a Travelodge, but that would have been cosier; there weren't even any loose cushions on the sofa. She ended up hugging a bed pillow, crying, waiting, crying, waiting, as texts and calls flooded in. It was like water torture, a near-constant drip, drip, drip of text alerts and buzzing rings, giving her hope every time which was never satisfied: because in all that time, there was not a single message from Frank.

The glorious view of the sea – the waves glittering in the sunshine, the expanse of the Studland peninsula stretching out on the far side of the channel, yachts slipping by, sails beating in the wind – was no consolation. Instead, it was a relentless stream of salt into her wound, because she could be watching the same view from her own terrace, curled up in Frank's arms, still crying, but knowing that her apologies were being forgiven, that her tears were serving a purpose, helping to expiate her sins.

Lexy was completely lost and lonely. She had no real women friends to lean on for support. Although Sam and Michelle were texting and calling, along with many other female acquaintances, there wasn't one of them she could trust enough to confide in. If she spilled her guts to them, as she would dearly love to, she knew perfectly well that they would turn around and sell the story to the press. Frank had been quite right to say that Sam and Michelle were best classified as partners in crime.

Having shot to fame at eighteen, Lexy had left everyone she had grown up with very far in her wake. She saw her family at the holidays, of course, had them to stay for the occasional visit, but she was the lone girl, the youngest to boot, and her mother was very disapproving of Lexy's lifestyle, the sexy photographs, the multiple partners, the babies out of wedlock.

Frank had been, quite literally, the answer to her mother's prayers: a good, steady man ready to be a father to Laylah, to settle down with Lexy and hopefully keep her at home at least a few evenings a week. So there was no way that Lexy could ring her parents now and expect to hear anything but complete support for her husband and a lecture about how he was a much better parent to their children than Lexy. Even Lexy's doting father, who found it almost impossible to admit that his baby girl could do any wrong, would have no choice but to take Frank's side in this situation.

Eventually, as the sun started to set, Lexy had to make a decision. Did she stay here overnight, hoping against hope for Frank to finally ring? Call her manager and ask someone to head over to the Chelsea flat, bundle her up some clothes and toiletries, and bring them down to Sandbanks? Or was she going to give up the wait and go back to Chelsea herself?

For the last hour she had been slumped on the uncomfortable sofa, the bedpillow wedged against her chest, tearstained and smeared with the remnants of her mascara and her tinted BB cream. Looking down at it, the sight made her queasy. She still hadn't eaten anything; when she had checked in, she had asked for some sandwiches to be brought up to the room, but she had not been able to face them. The tray sat on the small dining table, the edges of the bread curling up now as, like her tear ducts, they slowly dried out.

There was, unbelievably, no minibar in the suite. She had searched everywhere some hours ago, desperate for a drink, but eventually had to concede defeat. How could a four-star hotel not have a minibar? Did they not *want* to make money? She was in no state to ring down for room service. No disguise would conceal her identity, because she had had to check in under her real name. The waiter would know who she was and immediately try to sell a story to the papers about drunken Lexy, out on a much-publicized binge the night before, now ordering wine in her hotel suite . . .

Not only did Lexy crave a drink: she realized that she genuinely felt as if she needed one. If she stayed here, she would not get through the long dreary evening without ringing down to room service and ordering a bottle or two of Pinot. And knowing her capacity, she would certainly end up finishing one and starting on the second.

It was that flash of awareness that forced her to pick up her phone and call her manager, then ring down to the front desk to request that they get her bill ready. After that, she stood up, dropping the stained pillow onto the sofa, and walked into the bathroom. Washing her face in cold water, she wetted down a hand towel and pressed it against her eyes to take some of the swelling down. As well as the baseball cap and scarf, Lexy never went anywhere without a full make-up kit: carefully, she worked layers of foundation and powder onto her face so that, for the sake of her pride, not a trace of redness from her crying jag could be seen when she checked out.

The drive back to London was even worse than the one coming down to Bournemouth. Lexy was forced to realize that things were much worse than she had imagined. Googling her name and checking her Twitter feed brought home to her just how poorly her actions of the night before were being seen by not only the general public, but even her hardcore fans. Her decision to stay out late after the bathroom tussle with Deacon, rather than rush home, had clearly been the tipping point. Lexy couldn't blame Sam and Michelle for that, however. They hadn't tied her down and poured champagne down her throat before squirting coke up her nose: she had chosen to do that all by herself.

Emily and Jason, her manager, would be waiting for her in the Chelsea Harbour flat. Doubtless they would already have brainstormed an idea of how to spin this disaster, redeeming her image in the media. But in the time Lexy had been waiting for her car, and on this ride back to London, she had finally done something sensible, even wise, and come up with a completely unexpected proposal of her own.

* * *

'You want to do *what*?' Jason said, staring at her blankly.

'Brilliant!' Emily exclaimed, her publicist's brain working faster than Jason's managerial one to grasp the PR advantages of Lexy's suggestion. 'I love it! That'll solve everything in one go! You can hole up in my country house in France for a month – it's in the Auvergne, very quiet, practically no British tourists. If you stay in the house most of the time and just pop to the village when you need to get supplies – no make-up, not calling attention to yourself – no one'll spot you and blow your cover.'

She considered for a moment.

'We'll pick you up some outfits from Boden and the White Company,' she said thoughtfully. 'Make sure to buy a straw hat at the airport. That way you'll look like a typical upper-middle Brit on holiday – no one'll give you a second glance. Seriously, only tourists ever wear those.'

'Emily, you don't understand,' Lexy said patiently. 'I'm not suggesting this as a PR exercise. I actually *want* to go to rehab.'

Both Emily and Jason stared at her as if she had taken leave of her senses.

'I don't get it,' Jason said, frowning. 'Why put yourself through that if you don't have to? We don't need to brief the press on exactly where you are, just that you've realized you have a problem with alcohol and you're taking care of it so that you'll be a better wife and mother, blah blah blah . . .'

Emily cracked a smile at the world-weary tone. Anyone used to managing celebs was all too familiar with the wording of the press statement in which a client's latest scandal was attributed to their addiction to booze, drugs, casual sex or all three. Whether the therapy was real or – as in the case of the husband of the reality star who had staged an affair with her friend for publicity – faked for media coverage, it still counted as a Get Out of Jail Free card which, unlike its use in the Monopoly game, could be played again and again.

'But I *do* have to,' Lexy assured her team. 'I need to stop drinking, or at least cut way down. If I hadn't been drinking, I wouldn't have gone that far with Deacon. It would just have been a snog, and then I would have headed back home with everything done and dusted. I'd have got a great story for publicity, but not so terrible that Frank would have gone ballistic. If I hadn't had a few shots before Deacon followed me into the loos, I'd never have let it go that far. And if I hadn't wanted to get my drink on afterwards, I'd have gone home and everything would have been okay, instead of turning into . . .'

She tailed off, but Jason was more than ready to fill in.

'A total fucking shit storm!' he summarized. 'We *have* to get Frank back on side. Without him, you're just a single mother slutting about town, and at your age the fans aren't going to be as okay with that as they were when you broke up with Jamal.'

'Yeah, what if you break up with Frank, get knocked up by someone else and then you're a three-by-three?' Emily said brutally. 'That's *not* the way to sell products and get endorsements.'

Lexy shuddered at the term.

'Do you really think you actually *need* to go to rehab, Lex?' Jason asked. 'Frankly, clients tend to come back incredibly po-faced after they've done a stint there – they can be really hard to work with for ages afterwards . . .'

'I don't know,' Lexy said honestly. 'I'm not an expert or anything. But I left that hotel today partly because I knew that if I stayed on there, I'd sink at least a bottle of wine this evening. Maybe two.'

'You *did* just have a fucking bad day,' Jason pointed out.

'Yeah, but at the least I need to cut down,' Lexy said firmly. 'Not rely on it. I drink a *lot*, you know. I drink every day.'

Emily sniffed.

'So what?' she said. 'So do I – it's pretty much part of the job.'

'You should at least take a couple of days off a week,' Jason said, directing this to both of them. 'Give your liver a fighting chance.'

Lexy nodded.

'And Frank hates me drinking,' she said. 'It'll make him much happier if I do a detox.'

'Okay, that settles it. If Frank wants it, we'll do it,' Emily said, as if the decision were hers and not her client's. 'And yeah, let's call it a detox, not rehab. It sounds a bit less extreme. I don't want you at the Priory, though. That's a cliché now. I think people hear "she's going to the Priory" and roll their eyes, you know? As if it's more for PR than anything else, or you're just going to hang out with other celebs and have a bit of a holiday.'

'I was thinking not even in this country,' Lexy said. 'Somewhere that I don't know anyone. Like a fresh start.'

Jason nodded.

'I like this, actually,' he said, warming to the idea. 'What about going to America? I know a couple of people who've raved about this amazing rehab in Cascabel – that's in California – Peaches Gold went there and she's only had one relapse since—'

Lexy shook her head.

'No,' she said firmly. 'Not California. Nowhere that it sounds as if I'm getting a tan or having fun. It should be really serious. Like . . .'

She tried to think of the most serious place in the world.

'. . . *Germany*,' she finished.

'Eww.' Jason flinched. 'I'm picturing somewhere really strict where the Fräuleins and Herr Doktors hose you down every morning and give you compulsory enemas before you go on a ten-mile run.'

'That'd probably do me a lot of good,' Lexy admitted.

'Fuck me, you are *not* yourself,' Jason said, pulling a face.

'Honestly, I think I need to stop being myself for a bit,' Lexy said. 'Look what trouble it's got me into.'

'Switzerland!'

Emily, who had been staring into space for a little while, wrestling with the question of where Lexy should go to detox, finally came up with the solution.

'The Swiss Alps! Perfect!' she said, relaxing back on the sofa for the first time during the fraught conversation. 'Clean air, detox, early mornings, early nights, lots of exercise, no booze – no one associates booze and Switzerland – totally not the kind of lifestyle that a party girl likes – you're suffering, you're atoning – let's have you come back with not much make-up so we can see how much better you look – actually, let's get photos of you leaving looking like a total mess so we can do a nice contrast . . . stay for a month, that looks serious, and still gives us nearly three months after that till the book and series come out . . .'

Jason was nodding so rhythmically he could have been a woodpecker drilling into a tree.

'Love it,' he said when Emily ran out of breath. 'Love it. Love it. Ticks every box. It'll be bloody boring for you, Lexy, a month of no booze and cold showers. Probably enemas in Switzerland, too.'

'You still don't get it,' Lexy said, leaning forward. 'I'm not joking around. I'm not doing this so Frank agrees to finally answer the phone. I need to see if I can cope with not drinking for a month.'

'Hey,' Emily said, shrugging, 'it's a whole new story to sell. And now you have kids, it totally works for your audience. I don't have a problem with this.'

'Phew, *that's* a relief,' Lexy said with a degree of satire that quite escaped her manager and her publicist.

The intercom buzzed, the doorman saying that the Thai food they had ordered for dinner had arrived. Fishing some change from her wallet for the tip, Lexy opened the door of her apartment and waited for the lift. The enormous Deliveroo box, black and turquoise, was the first thing to emerge as the doors opened, only the legs of the delivery guy visible beneath it; advancing on Lexy, rather than following her back into the apartment, he set the box down on the hall carpet with an audible clatter of plastic containers.

'Hey, careful!' she said, reaching out to steady it. 'There's soup in there!'

Then she yelped as the delivery man straightened up, and

she realized that he was not wearing the uniform black and turquoise jacket, but a dilapidated-looking hoodie and, underneath it, the ironic yellow and red DHL T-shirt, made by a company called Vetements, costing two hundred pounds, which was the latest hot menswear must-have that season. He was so slender that Lexy was amazed he had managed to lug the box this far: no wonder he had almost dropped it.

'Surprise!' Deacon carolled gleefully, his eyes bright as he lunged eagerly around the gigantic box. 'I brought your dinner! Let's work up an appetite and eat the whole thing afterwards!'

Lexy's survival instincts told her to duck back inside the apartment straight away. If any of her neighbours heard Deacon's very recognizable voice, cracked their door and took photos of the two of them together in her building, Frank would probably file for divorce the moment he saw them. Deacon, misunderstanding the reason for her swift retreat, followed her inside the hallway, leaving the delivery box in the corridor.

'Didn't see that coming, did you?' he said gleefully. 'I'm a genius! I dropped round earlier and waited for you, but you weren't around, so I thought I'd come back, but the bloody doorman wouldn't let me in – but then I saw the delivery guy and I bribed him to let me bring in the food so I could get into the building. And then it turned out to be for you! Meant to be, right?'

Lexy could have pushed him out of the door, but then, she knew, he would make a scene in the corridor. Furious, she reached round him and closed it, leaving the food box outside, and as he tried to grab her waist she elbowed him off with a sharp jab to his ribcage, winding him briefly.

'The reason the doorman wouldn't let you in,' she hissed, 'was that you made a total nuisance of yourself hanging out earlier in the lobby! Thank God the press don't seem to have got hold of it! I can't be seen with you after last night – don't you get that?'

'No problem!' Deacon said when he got his breath back. 'I'm here now, no one saw me, I can nip out of the deliveries entrance tomorrow morning . . . *Oh.*'

Emily and Jason, hearing the commotion, had by this time emerged from the living room and were standing in the doorway, their expressions identically horrified.

'Hey, no need to look at me like I've got horns and a tail,' Deacon said rather sulkily. 'I don't suppose you'd piss off and leave me and Lexy to catch up?'

'You little shit, sneaking in here like this when you know you're banned from the building!' Jason said furiously. 'Haven't you done enough damage?'

'Hang on!' Deacon said, outraged now. 'She gave me a massive come-on at that launch party, plus she kissed me back like a total sexaholic! I don't go after women who don't want me – I don't bloody have to! Ask her – she was totally into it!'

He looked at Lexy.

'I'm not going to embarrass you in front of your friends—'

'They're my manager and my PR,' Lexy snapped.

'Oh right, they're your bosses!' Deacon said irrepressibly. 'Come to tell you what a naughty girl you've been! They don't know all of it, do they?'

'Shut *up*!' Lexy said, practically stamping her foot, feeling her face turn red with embarrassment, knowing that he was referring to having made her come.

'Her husband won't let her in the bloody house to see her kids!' Jason said.

'That's *real*?'

Deacon looked back at Lexy, his jaw dropping, suddenly looking very young as the cockiness faded away to be replaced by genuine concern.

'I thought him locking you out and all that was just a publicity stunt!' he said. 'You know, getting as much press as you could out of it, yeah? I didn't think it was actually –' he searched for the right word – '*real.*'

Emily snorted.

'Well,' she said. 'Under the circumstances, isn't *that* fucking ironic!'

Chapter Twenty-Six

Three weeks later

'Finally fast asleep, both of them,' Frank said, walking into the kitchen. 'London's kicked the duvet off as usual and he's snoring like a little pig, and Laylah's got her nose buried in Dolly's hair. God knows why she does that, but she's never happier than when she's sniffing that doll's hair.'

'Ugh, it's getting really manky now,' Caroline said. 'I tried to wash it the other day but Laylah screamed like a dolphin and wouldn't let me near Dolly.'

She had been sitting at the kitchen table, scrolling through gossip sites on her tablet, but she laid it down on seeing Frank.

'She likes the dreads!' Frank said, grinning. 'Gets that from my side! Mind you, those are the rattiest dreads I've ever seen. Pongy, too.'

Laylah's doll – to which she had given the very creative name Dolly years ago – was her fetish object. Dolly's blonde hair was by now completely clumped into dreadlocks and, as Frank had said, smelt very musty.

'She and Carmen have that in common,' Caroline said. 'They're both obsessed with hair. Did you know that Carmen's mother knits stuff out of her and Carmen's hair?

Carmen has a kind of head wrap she wears in the winter. Laylah was actually trying it on the other day.'

Frank shuddered.

'There's something very wrong with that kid,' he said cheerfully. 'Hey, did you just say she screamed like a dolphin? That's bang on. You should be a writer or something.'

Caroline smiled up at him.

'Funny you should say that,' she said, standing up and going over to the built-in drinks fridge. 'Because the book's officially finished! I got an email from Gareth this afternoon. He loves the edits and he says he's telling accounts to pay me my bonus!'

'Fantastic news!' Frank said, as Caroline bent over and pulled out a bottle of Veuve Cliquot from the fridge. 'I still feel crap that you won't take a penny for everything you're doing for the kids. Honestly, you spend more time with them than Gabriela does.'

'Oh, I couldn't take money for that!' Caroline said, sounding horrified. 'I love spending time with them! It's silly, but I've come to think of them as family just a little bit . . .'

She set the bottle on the table.

'I bought this today when I went with Gabriela to pick the kids up from school,' she said, getting two flutes out of the glass-fronted cupboard. 'I wanted to get something to celebrate delivering the book. That's what it's called – funny, isn't it? As if you just gave birth.'

'*Caroline*,' Frank said, shaking his head in disbelief. 'You went out and bought your own champagne? What were you *thinking*? We've got cases of it here!'

'Well, I'm living in your house for free, not paying bills,

eating and drinking,' she said humbly. 'I didn't want you to think I was taking advantage—'

'Oh, for God's sake,' Frank objected, 'stop sounding like Cinderella! You barely eat anything anyway!'

Frank strode around the table, took the bottle from her masterfully and started to peel off the foil.

'I'm so excited! I couldn't wait to tell you,' Caroline gushed. 'This means so much to me – actually finishing my first ever book! I know it's not under my name, but still, Gareth thinks it's great, and so does Miranda. It's always been my dream.'

'You'll get your own name on a book soon,' Frank assured her as he started to untwist the wire. 'It'll happen. You're really good at what you do.'

Caroline giggled.

'You don't know that,' she said with a flirtatious edge now. 'You haven't read a word of what I've written.'

'Hey, I can't!' Frank said. 'You know that! It's all about Lexy – it would be much too weird.'

Caroline had known that Lexy would come up sooner or later; it was inevitable, with the book under discussion. Her strategy, on hearing her rival's name, was to smile her way past it, make as light of it as possible. She had been monitoring Frank's phone over the last few weeks, which was easy enough, as he regularly left it around the house. It had only taken a few attempts to find out that his password, annoyingly enough, was *lexy*. The block on Lexy's calls and texts was still in place, as was the one on her emails.

A few days after Lexy had been turned away from Sandbanks, a letter had arrived from her for Frank: it had been very easy to spot, as the address was handwritten. A week and a half later, another hand-addressed letter had come, this one doubly easy to identify, as it bore a Swiss postmark; it was followed by another, about a week after that.

Naturally, they knew that Lexy was in Switzerland. Jason had rung Frank the day after the meltdown, saying that he understood that Frank was currently so angry with his wife that he did not want to speak to her, but assuring him that Lexy was heading to a very reputable and serious detox centre high in the Swiss Alps, and that, since Frank wasn't taking her calls, she had asked Jason to tell Frank that she was going there to deal with her issue with alcohol.

To Caroline's great irritation, Frank had been impressed and elated by this news. She had countered it, however, by saying, wide-eyed: 'Oh! Not actual *rehab*? I thought detox was more about losing weight,' and watched his face fall.

Frank had never realized that Caroline had blocked Lexy's number on his mobile, and until Caroline knew that Lexy was in Switzerland she had been monitoring the home phone very carefully. She had checked with Jason after his phone call to ask whether Lexy was able to make calls from the clinic; on hearing that she couldn't, Caroline had removed the block and relaxed her vigilance on the landline.

So all she needed to do was monitor incoming letters, and that was easy enough. The post was brought in by Carmen every morning and stacked on the front hall table. Frank, who was very uninterested in paperwork, often left it there for days before going through the accumulated pile; it hadn't occurred to him that Lexy might write to him. It could not have been simpler for Caroline to check through the stack every morning as soon as the coast was clear. She could have shredded Lexy's letters, but she had preferred to burn them in the bathroom sink, fan on, window open. There was a drama in that gesture which she thoroughly enjoyed.

That'll teach you to call me Ghost Mouse, she had thought, looking into her own eyes in the mirror as the acrid black smoke rose around her as if she were casting a spell. *You treated me as if I was invisible most of the time. You never saw me as a rival, or important in any way. Even now that I'm stealing your life, you don't even realize what's happening. Even if you knew I was living in your house, you wouldn't think for a moment that I might be after your husband, or that he might look at me with interest . . .*

And you would be very, very wrong.

Frank was popping the champagne cork, starting to fill the glasses. Caroline exclaimed, as if an idea had just occurred to her:

'Oh! This is probably going to sound mad, but – no, forget I said anything . . .'

Of course, Frank responded by telling her to keep going, as anyone would.

'I want to toast to finishing my first book in the Jacuzzi!' she admitted shyly. 'Drinking bubbles in bubbles! Is that stupid? It'd make me feel really glamorous – like I was Jackie Collins for an hour, you know?'

Frank, holding the bottle, paused momentarily as he was about to fill the second glass.

'Never mind!' Caroline said quickly. 'It was silly of me – we can toast here and then I'll go to bed—'

'Nah, you were right the first time,' Frank said. 'Why not?

It'll be a laugh. We don't use that Jacuzzi enough. And we could both do with some R&R, couldn't we? I've been non-stop today, and you did your run, finished your editing, picked up the kids and gave them dinner . . .'

'Oh yay!'

Caroline clapped her hands girlishly, then decided that this was a gesture too far and dropped them to her side.

'I'll go and change,' she said. 'I won't be long. See you down there? Will you take the drinks – do you mind?'

Frank, she knew, kept his swim gear in the pool changing room; he could simply head down in the lift. Whereas she needed to run upstairs, strip her clothes off and don the very expensive bikini that she had bought two weeks ago in anticipation of this evening.

She had planned this meticulously, even to the extent of wearing loose clothes today that wouldn't leave any red marks on her skin, a trick she had picked up from Lexy's stylists. Her bra was a soft sports one with wide straps, her leggings had an equally wide elasticated band at the waist so it didn't dig in. She had been into Poole that morning for a spray tan at a beauty salon, the fourth in a package for which she had signed up the day after Lexy was locked out. The salon had also applied discreet fake eyelashes, which they swore would be waterproof, and dyed her lashes and eyebrows several shades darker. Her nails were newly varnished, of course: a shellacked French manicure on her hands, a light shade of rose on her toenails, pretty and elegant.

That afternoon she had straightened her hair, and after stripping off her clothes, she piled it on top of her head in a style she had practised several times, a seemingly careless knot that gave her extra height and made her cheekbones seem more prominent. She fastened it with plenty of pins, fixed it with hairspray, and applied a coat of long-lasting rose lipgloss. There was no point applying perfume or body lotion, as the water of the pool was chlorinated. The last thing was the bikini, and her hands were shaking as she pulled it out of the drawer.

It had cost nearly two hundred and fifty pounds, and she had spent one whole agonizing afternoon on Oxford Street tracking it down. Caroline would never feel comfortable in those tiny triangles, more strap than fabric, which naturally slender women could wear; this was much more structured, but cleverly cut not to show how hard it was working. The cups were underlined, lifting and separating her breasts, a halter neckline that was very flattering to the full-bosomed. The bottoms were high-cut, with plenty of coverage, but trimmed on each side with sexy large gold rings that were echoed on the halter straps.

And the colour was the bravest thing of all. White, clear pure white. Hence the regular spray tans. Caroline would have liked to have gone even darker, but if she stripped down to reveal a tan that looked as if she'd come back from a week in Ibiza, it would have looked as if she were trying much too hard.

She couldn't look at herself in the mirror. The contrast between her still imperfect figure and her memory of Lexy's high, artificially symmetrical boobs and flat stomach would have scared her too much. Pulling on a towelling robe and slippers, Caroline took a deep breath.

Asking herself the question 'what would Lexy do?' in

these circumstances might be the height of irony, but it definitely gave the right answer. If Lexy were about to try to seduce a married man in his own spa, she would sashay to the lift with total confidence.

Frank was ensconced in the bubbling Jacuzzi, which was set in a raised aquamarine and emerald tiled cylinder at the far side of the swimming pool, positioned to give a view out over the lawns that sloped down to the sea. He had placed the bottle of Veuve on the tiled surround, which had cobalt tempered glass panels sunk into it for holding drinks, and was sipping from his flute, gazing out through the huge glass doors at the distant view of tiny twinkling lights of the boats moored in the Poole Harbour marina, the nightlife of Poole town curving away behind it.

As Caroline came in, he turned to look at her. This was the ultimate *what would Lexy do?* moment, the defining point of transformation, everything for which she had been working out and starving herself over the past few months. If she behaved like herself, like Caroline, she would shuffle across the pool surround like a granny in her robe and slippers, slip them off at the last second and then duck into the warm bubbling water with the furtiveness of someone profoundly ashamed of her own body.

But no one would be attracted to a woman who behaved like that, especially not a man who had chosen to marry a sexpot like Lexy O'Brien . . .

Taking that robe off by the door was like shedding the old Caroline, a snake transforming itself by sloughing off its skin. She knew what she needed to do, had rehearsed it many times over the last few days: as Frank smiled at her, raising his glass in a friendly greeting, she kicked off the slippers, met his eyes and, holding his gaze, dropped her hands to the belt of the robe and unfastened the loose knot, pulling the robe open.

She saw the exact split-second that Frank's expression changed, his eyes widening, his jaw sagging open, his entire body rigid as he took in the sight of Caroline in her bikini. Ideally, she would have dropped the robe behind her to the floor, but that would have looked suspiciously seductive. So, sucking in her stomach with everything she had, she swivelled to hang the robe on one of the pegs by the door; she was delighted, on turning back, to see Frank still gawping at her, struck dumb by the curves on display.

Now came the worst part. Walking towards him in the bikini, feeling like a contestant in a low-grade seaside beauty competition; sure that her stomach was wobbling, feeling her thighs slide against each other with every step, her bare feet slapping like flatfish on a fishmonger's slab as they landed on the tiles, her breasts bouncing; hoping that, as a boob man, he would be so mesmerized by those that he wouldn't notice all her other flaws . . .

As she got closer, however, she could no longer hear the sound of her feet over the rumble of the Jacuzzi. It was the longest walk of her life, and climbing up the steps to the side of the Jacuzzi, her hand slipping on the rail, her thighs and stomach briefly at eye level with Frank, plopping her bottom awkwardly down to the edge and then sliding in, water displacing with her entrance, she felt as big as a manatee, acutely conscious of absolutely everything that was unattractive and heavy about her.

Thank God for champagne! Frank was shifting on his side of the built-in seat, turning to face her, but clearly still in shock. His mouth was open, his eyes dropping to her cleavage, then up to look at her face again; he hadn't made a move to hand her the glass that was waiting for her. She reached out to take it herself, feeling much more confident now. The parts of her body she didn't like were hidden underwater, and on display was the face that was so carefully adorned with fake lashes and subtle make-up, her firm arms, round shoulders and large plump breasts. Below the bubbling water, she squished her breasts together with her elbows, deepening her cleavage as she raised the flute.

'To finishing my book!' she said, flashing a sweet smile, and Frank gathered himself with a visible effort, shook his head as if he were trying to get rid of a fly buzzing round him and reached out to chink his glass with hers. Caroline, pretending that she couldn't quite reach, moved closer to him along the tiled seat, tilting her breasts enticingly towards him.

She saw him look down at them and keep looking this time, and the sight of him unable to tear his glance away from her bosom made her whole body fizz.

'Cheers!' she said, and watched him almost miss his mouth with the glass before he dragged his gaze up again.

'*Men are incredibly basic,*' Lexy, via Caroline, had written in her upcoming book.

'*If they like you, trust me, you'll know. And if they don't like you, who gives a fuck? Move on to someone who does! The trick is to like men who like you back. You can't get all huffy if you're into a man who likes tall black girls and you're short and white, you know what I mean?*

I'm always seeing covers of women's mags that tell you ten or twenty or fifty ways to snag a man, and most of it's bollocks. I mean, if you're reading this, you know what I'm like, right? I'm hardcore. I go in for full-on teasing when I'm flirting. I like to mess with their heads and get them going so they don't know which end's up.

But if I were going to write one of those articles, here's what I'd say: men are basic, so keep it simple. If he's a boob guy, get your tits out. Boob guys are the easiest, by the way. It's like they literally get hypnotized by them. If he's a leg guy, wear a short skirt. If he fancies you, he'll come after you and all you need to do is laugh at his jokes and play with your hair and tell him he's being naughty, even if he isn't. Guys really love it when you say the word 'naughty'. Pathetic, I know, but it works.

Basically, you'll know if he likes you, and not just by spotting his stiffie. He'll ask you questions and actually sound interested in the answers – which, honestly, you should enjoy while you get it, because it never bloody lasts! And he'll give you really clumsy compliments, which'll probably sound cheesy. But don't be sarky about it, just say 'Thank you!' really sweetly, like he quoted Shakespeare or something.

So just keep staring into his eyes and smiling at him and playing with your hair and every so often touch your tongue to your lips, if you can manage that without looking like a complete fuckwit. And when you want him to kiss you, lean in, make your eyes go really big and take a deep breath so your boobs look great. That always works, and believe me, I've probably snogged more men than you've had hot dinners . . .'

Caroline drank half of the champagne in one go, and noticed that, very unusually for the mostly abstemious Frank, he had followed suit.

'Can I get a top-up?' she said, holding out the glass. Anything to keep leaning forward, showing off her boobs. Besides, if he filled her glass up, he would probably refill his, and it would be very beneficial if Frank had several glasses of champagne.

'You look in really good shape,' he said as he picked up the bottle. 'I didn't realize you'd been working out so much. Uh, of course I did, because you've been going running! I just meant . . . you're in really good shape . . . I didn't realize . . .'

'Thank you!' Caroline cooed.

It was extraordinary how accurate Lexy had been in her guide to flirting with a man, or rather letting a man flirt with you. There was the awkward compliment, just as Lexy had predicted, and clearly 'Thank you' was all Frank needed to hear to feel acknowledged.

'I've been watching my diet too, of course,' she said, drinking the champagne and blocking out her new knowledge of how many calories it contained. 'That's really helped.'

'Oh yeah,' Frank agreed automatically. 'Diet's just as important as exercise.'

Since Caroline had her hair up, she couldn't play with it; she compromised by putting one hand up to pat it as if concerned that it might be coming down. This worked perfectly; Frank's gaze followed her as if he had been hypnotized.

'You look so different,' he blurted out. 'Did you change your hair or something?'

Caroline smiled sweetly.

'I've put it up because I didn't want to get it wet,' she said.

'It suits you,' Frank said, drinking some more champagne. 'It really does suit you like that.'

'Maybe I'll wear it like this more,' she said, feeling as if the words they spoke were becoming increasingly less important. She was daring, now, to look at him for increasing lengths of time, having kept her gaze away from him at first because the sight of his bare torso was so overwhelming.

She had seen it before, of course, in the pool and on the boat, his strong, muscled body, diving from the deck, frolicking with London and Laylah, following them up the steps as they climbed out again, water dripping down his torso, both hands rising to shake water out of his tight dark curly hair, the declivities of his armpits, the blatant sexuality of the dark hair trailing down his belly to the low waistband of his swim trunks. She had never been so close, though.

His nipples were dark little bullets from which the water streamed constantly as it bubbled around them; pert and thrusting, set into the breastplate of his torso, which glowed light bronze, golden pecan. The silky dark body hair made him seem infinitely more sexual to Caroline than a waxed male model. You thought straight away of the hair at his crotch, the cock nestling in it, rising up so smooth and sculpted, such a contrast to the thick mass of black curls . . .

Poor Riz, back in London, had been completely sidelined

in the last few weeks. From the day Frank had been convinced, subtly, imperceptibly, by Caroline to change the gate code on Lexy, sure that it had been his idea all along, Caroline had not had sex with Riz. It would have felt wrong, a distraction. Like a footballer told to abstain until the tournament was over, all her energy had been concentrated into the ultimate goal of bagging Frank.

Riz had been surprisingly upset when Caroline had told him that she just didn't have time for a relationship while she was trying so hard to build her career as a writer. It was the best excuse she could think of. His reaction when she said she wanted to go back to just being housemates for the moment had been extensive and messy; certainly, moving temporarily back to Sandbanks had made that situation much less awkward. Yet another reason she was hoping to stay on now the book was delivered.

'Ooh!' she said, giggling girlishly as the bubbling water splashed her glass. 'This is so much fun! I've barely been in the Jacuzzi, because I'm always down here hanging out with the kids, and they aren't allowed to get in until they're older.'

'Yeah, it's too hot for them,' Frank said automatically, finishing his champagne, watching the bubbles wobble the upper curves of Caroline's breasts up and down in continual motion.

Caroline, noticing his empty glass, climbed over to pull the bottle of Veuve Cliquot out of the cooler, kneeling up on the tiled seat close to Frank. Her heart was pounding. She felt it was time to take the biggest risk of all. If she left it too long, the sexual charge would fizzle; Frank might sober up and decide to go to bed, and if that happened, she sensed that the window of opportunity would be forever bolted shut. Having teetered on the edge of temptation, but pulled back, he would be extra careful not to put himself in the same position again.

No, it was now or never. And however much Frank was staring at her breasts, she knew that, as a married man, he would never make the first move. It had to be her who initiated it, and it had to happen in a way that seemed accidental, serendipitous. Lexy would be coming back to London in a few days, her month in Switzerland completed: Caroline was on a deadline even tighter than the one she had been given to write *Lexy on the Loose*.

'Here you go!' she said, turning to him, bending over him, filling up his glass, her knees pressed against his thighs now. 'Oh, this is so much fun! If this were my house I'd be in here every night, winding down to get lovely and relaxed before bed.'

She knew, of course, how Frank complained about Lexy being out so much, partying in London instead of spending quality time with him. Sliding the now-empty bottle back into the cooler, she plopped herself down next to Frank, smiling at him, her thigh brushing his. She was sitting in the curve of his arm, which was stretched out along the Jacuzzi surround. It was time. Greatly daring, she did as Lexy had suggested and touched the tip of her tongue to her parted lips.

Frank's pupils dilated. Even though his irises were dark, she was close to him, she could see it happen, the blackness spreading in his eyes as his body reacted to hers.

'*Lean in, make your eyes go really big and take a deep breath so your boobs look great . . .*'

Trembling with fear of failure, of being rejected, Caroline did exactly that. Frank's gaze dropped to her breasts, rose again to her mouth; feeling ridiculous, Caroline licked her lower lip, just fractionally.

He groaned. She leaned in still more, her heart now pounding so hard and fast that it was physically painful, as if it were bruising the inside of her ribcage. Lexy had given no further instructions, but it felt as if Frank needed just one more thing to tip him over the edge.

'Frank . . .' she breathed softly.

Saying his name, it turned out, was all it took. The arm behind her closed around her shoulders, pulling her towards him; his mouth came down on hers. Tears of relief budded up as she threw her arms around his neck and kissed him back with everything she had.

It was wonderful. It was everything. It was overwhelming. Caroline genuinely thought that she was going to pass out, collapsing in his arms like some fainting Victorian maiden. The heat, the alcohol, the sensation of Frank's body against her, hot and wet, his lips tasting of champagne, were all so dizzying that she clung to him helplessly, going limp, her breasts pressing into his chest. It was the best thing she could possibly have done. Frank, so used to his tough, sexually aggressive wife, had his protective instincts stirred by Caroline clinging to him like ivy round an oak; he tightened his arms around her and drove his tongue possessively into her mouth, pulling her onto his lap.

Under the water, Caroline felt lighter, less insecure about

Frank taking her full weight on his thighs. She curled herself around him, feeling his cock fully hard against her bottom, moaning as she rubbed against its length.

'Caroline . . . bloody hell . . .' Frank groaned, and she got up the courage to reach back for his hands, pull them to her breasts, her fingers over his, showing him that she wanted him to squeeze them, push them together, exaggerate her already bountiful cleavage.

His head ducked, dropping to her breasts, licking them, pulling away the bikini fabric, exposing her nipples; she pulled a leg free, clambering awkwardly, clumsily over his lap so that she could straddle him. She was terrified that this was going too far, but as she settled on his lap again, his cock pushed up right between her legs and they both groaned again in sheer delight as it almost stabbed into her, only the fabric of their swimming costumes stopping it from going further.

Frank's hands were so tight on her breasts now that they were almost hurting her, and she loved it. She ran her hands over his chest, relishing in finally being able to do what she had wanted to do from the first moment she saw him: bending over him, kissing his shoulders, his upper arms, his neck, her face pressed into his neck, kissing him frantically, holding on to his shoulders for leverage so she could raise and lower her bottom again and again against his hard, bobbing cock, finding the tip and working it, feeling it butt into her just that little bit every single time, her entire body craving the rest of it, unable to hold back.

'Please, please, *please* –' she heard herself beg. 'Please, Frank, I want it so badly, I need it . . . just once, just one time – please, Frank, *please*—'

'God, Caroline,' he moaned against her breasts, his fingers still clamped around them, his thumbs teasing her nipples. 'This isn't right – we shouldn't—'

'Please! Just once, *please* . . . I need it so badly, let me have it . . .'

Desperately, she reached down, found the waistband of his trunks, stretched them out and closed her hand around his cock. His body sagged against hers as if her touch had released something inside him, given him permission to let loose; before he could make any more objections, she squirmed her other hand between her legs, and, not caring if she ripped her very expensive bikini bottoms, dragged them aside and directed the tip of his cock up into her bared flesh.

It hurt, even though she managed to lower herself on him as slowly as she could. Sex in water takes away the lubrication, and she felt dry and rough inside, had to bite her lip to stop any sounds of pain coming out as his whole length entered her. But he was gasping, crying out in pleasure, and those sounds were all she needed to hear; even if his cock had felt like Brillo inside her, she would have kept pumping up and down on top of it.

And it got better. The sheer thrill of having Frank's cock in her was stimulation in itself, even though it was mental rather than physical. She heard herself starting to wail: they were cries of sheer triumph, calling his name over and over again as his hands slid to her bottom, pulling her even closer, his cock going wild, thrusting up as his lips moved frantically from one nipple to the other, sucking, pulling, kissing.

She buried her hands into his tight curls for the first time ever; how often she had dreamed about doing that, feeling the short ringlets twist around her fingers, his head at her breast, her crotch pounding against his! His cock bounced inside her so deeply that she shrieked aloud, mainly in pain; but he didn't realize that, and the sound of what he thought was her extreme enjoyment was his cue to lift her up, push her off him, his face agonized, his lips pulled back over his teeth as he dragged himself up, fisting his cock in his hand, trying frantically to direct the fountain of sperm out of the Jacuzzi water. There was a towel folded on the tiled surround, and he grabbed it, shoving it towards his cock, catching in it what he could, on his feet now, leaning against the edge of the Jacuzzi, panting as frenziedly as if he had just sprinted for a mile.

Caroline grabbed at the edge of the Jacuzzi just in time to avoid smashing her knees painfully against the seat. She too was breathing heavily, and swept with disappointment. She had wanted him to come inside her; how perfect it would be if she got pregnant! She wasn't broody – in fact, spending time with Laylah and London had made it even less likely that she would want kids in the near future – but *Frank's* baby . . . a kid to bind him to her forever, to help break up Lexy and Frank's marriage – *that* would be a miracle.

Chapter Twenty-Seven

Caroline reached out and stroked his flank, feeling like a character in a historical romance novel trying to gentle a wild horse. Frank shook his head slowly as he cleaned himself off with the towel, still with his back to her, his naked buttocks and legs, the intricate muscles of his back such a beautiful sight that in other circumstances she could have stared at him for hours. What if he climbed out of the Jacuzzi and walked away?

But Caroline refused to panic. Pleading with him – being as vulnerable as his wife was insulated and tough – had got her what she wanted before. Why shouldn't it work again?

'Please, Frank,' she said softly, 'can you sit down next to me for a little while? I feel really funny.'

With a deep sigh, he turned around. His face was smoothed clean with physical release: he looked ten years younger for a little while, before his forehead started to crease with worry and guilt about what they had just done.

'Please, Frank,' Caroline repeated, and, with another sigh, he sat down on the edge of the Jacuzzi, slid his legs into the water and dropped back into the foaming bubbles. She nestled against him and his arm came around her, which emboldened her to rest her head onto his shoulder.

'That was amazing,' she said softly. 'I know we shouldn't have done it, but it was amazing.'

'Jesus, Caroline,' he said, shaking his head. 'I can't believe that just happened.'

'I know, me neither!' she lied. 'But it was wonderful.'

There was no answer, but his arm tightened a little around her. They sat there for a while in silence, and though Caroline was burning up with eagerness to say more, she managed to control herself, knowing that she must not rush him.

'This is a mess,' he said finally. 'A real mess.'

She turned her face into his shoulder.

'I'm so sorry,' she said. 'This is all my fault. I begged you – I wanted you to . . . I should never have done that, but I wanted you so much . . .'

When this didn't immediately provoke a response, she pulled back, covered her face with her hands and pretended to cry into them. There was so much water around them that he couldn't possibly tell that she was faking, not if she gave her eyes a good rub to redden them a bit.

'Caroline, don't cry!' he said, as she had known he would. He wrapped her in a hug; resting her head gratefully on his chest, she kept pretending to sob.

'I just feel so bad!' she mumbled. 'I care about you so much, and it was so wonderful, so amazing . . . it hurts to think it didn't mean anything to you . . .'

'I didn't say that!' he assured her immediately. 'I never said it didn't mean anything to me! It was great, really great.'

'Being so close to you just felt so right,' she tried, pushing things further, and for response she got another sigh and a slightly tighter hug, which she took, at least, not as a denial.

'You're really sweet, Caroline,' he said after a while. 'A really sweet girl.'

Pulling back, he looked down at her, gently pushing some loose strands of hair back from her face. Then he reached down and took the edges of her bikini top, lifting it up, covering her breasts once again. Caroline didn't know whether to see this gesture as an ending, a definitive line drawn under what had happened between them, or him taking care of her, wanting to preserve her dignity.

'Thank you,' she said, deciding to take in the best possible way everything he did that could be interpreted ambiguously. 'I probably shouldn't say this –' she ducked her head shyly – 'but I'm so happy. I shouldn't be, but I am.'

'Oh, Caroline,' he said almost tenderly. There was a long pause, and she waited eagerly for what he would say next.

'We should get going,' he said eventually. 'It's late. Time to go to bed.'

She nodded as he reached over to turn off the Jacuzzi.

'Can you help me out?' she said in a small voice. 'I feel really wobbly.'

'You should drink some water,' he said, concerned, starting to climb up the moulded steps, holding out his hand to her. 'Let's get you hydrated, okay?'

Once she was out of the Jacuzzi, he told her to wait there while he got her robe and slippers and a cup of water from the gym area. She thanked him, looking up under the fake lashes, letting him help her with her robe, watching him stare involuntarily at her breasts again as she drew out the process of slipping it on; once he had donned his own robe and flip-flops, she asked if she could hold his arm as they went, because she was still feeling dizzy. Frank turned the lights off on the main panel; they stepped into the lift, and she half-collapsed against him, apologizing for her weakness, so that his arm came round her, holding her up.

When the lift stopped on the first floor, and they both stepped out, the master suite was immediately to the left, with Caroline's guest suite all the way down the other end of the corridor to the right. She felt Frank hesitate, his arm not immediately leaving her; within its curve, she turned and looked up at him, her eyes as wide as she could make them.

'Please, just stay with me for a little!' she pleaded under her breath. 'I don't want to be alone tonight . . . I still feel dizzy . . .'

The kids and nanny's bedrooms were all on the third floor. No one could possibly overhear her and Frank; this conversation was entirely safe.

'Oh, Caroline,' Frank said, looking down at her, his fore-head creasing, but his eyes soft, as conflicted as he had been ever since they had had sex. 'I really shouldn't . . .'

'Please, Frank, please! Just till I go to sleep!'

She managed to get a little sob into her voice.

'I don't want to be alone – it'd feel so sad, after being so close to you . . .'

He pulled her close, hugging her, for a moment. Then he turned in the direction of her room, taking her hand, mum-bling:

'Just for a short time, okay?'

Curled up in bed, Frank's arm over her waist as he spooned her, both of them naked, Caroline's heart was still racing so fast that she felt as if she had taken amphetamines. Even with him in her bed, she was in disbelief that she had pulled off her plan so successfully. She didn't care how much she had had to beg or plead with him; in fact, every time she had done so, she had felt a strange sense of power. Making herself vulnerable, oddly, had also made her strong, because it had caused Frank to behave in a way he knew that he shouldn't; her will had overpowered his many times that evening, and he still didn't realize it. Ironically, he thought he was taking care of her.

She snuggled against him, but didn't say a word. Having lured him back with her, she had seen, as they were towelling off in her bathroom, how nervous he was: the whites round his eyes were showing, his movements were jerky and nervous. He was like an animal she was convincing, slowly, tentatively, to trust her.

What he did not realize was that she had a secret weapon. She was particularly well-informed on everything that he liked the best.

Frank loves naked spooning! Lexy had said, in one of the many stream-of-consciousness monologues recorded for the book, open confessionals that she had made with Caroline's Dictaphone running. Caroline had listened to it live, and then again as she transcribed the tapes. *He'd do it all night*, Lexy had continued. *I get too hot and I have to wiggle away after a couple of minutes, and he gets so whiny when I do . . .*

Caroline remembered those confessionals very, very well indeed.

'I didn't want to be alone either,' Frank eventually said against her shoulder.

She had thought he was falling asleep, hadn't expected him to say a word. She whispered back: 'I was scared you wouldn't stay with me. I'm so glad you're here.'

'It's been so tough,' he mumbled into the pitch dark, where he was finally safe enough to confess to a sympathetic listener how isolated and sad he had been feeling these last few weeks. 'With her never getting in touch, literally as if the kids and I didn't exist any more. Not a word from her. Nothing. I've been so lonely.'

Caroline reached around to touch the hand that was lying on her hip, and stroked it comfortingly. Frank's fingers twined around hers, holding hands with her, and she felt his lips touching her shoulder in a light kiss.

'I didn't realize how lonely I was,' he said. 'Touching you, holding you . . . it's what I want. Someone to hold at night, every night. I've been missing that so badly.'

Caroline's hand, clasped in his, pulled his up to her lips so that she could kiss his fingers.

'I keep thinking, what if she doesn't come back?' he said, the words sounding as if they were being dragged out of him. 'What if the only thing I hear from her is a letter from her lawyers? And if she hasn't been bothered enough to get in touch by now, do I even *want* her back?'

Caroline smiled into the darkness. She was picturing Frank's iPhone, his Gmail, the messages and emails that must have pinged so frequently against the blocks she had set up before Lexy went to Switzerland, the letters she had removed from the hall table and burned, ritually, in her bathroom. It was a delicious pleasure to be able to smirk with triumph as Lexy's husband lay beside her, telling her he wasn't sure about the state of his marriage.

Lexy, who had nicknamed her Ghost Mouse. Lexy, who had everything Caroline wanted. Lexy, whose husband's hand Caroline was holding as she lay beside him naked.

Without saying a word in response, Caroline lowered their linked hands until Frank's palm was resting on her breast. Their hips were not touching, but soon, very soon, she knew his body was stirring, could feel his breathing get faster, shallower, his heartbeat speeding up. He shifted, and the head of his cock butted against her buttocks; she let out a moan and edged herself backwards, just fractionally, pressing into it.

Frank becoming excited again so fast was no surprise to Caroline, one of the reasons she had pushed so hard to have Frank come back to her bedroom was because Lexy had frequently boasted to Caroline about Frank's sexual prowess.

He wants it all the time, she'd said. *It's like being married to a horny teenager. I'm not complaining, don't get me wrong – I'm really horny too. We're at it like rabbits! But Frank uses sex like a tranquilizer. He doesn't drink, he doesn't smoke, he doesn't gamble. Working out and sex are his two big things. He's got to do both on a regular basis or he gets a bit mental.*

It hadn't remotely occurred to Lexy that her ghostwriter was not just listening, but internalizing every single word she said, bitterly resenting Lexy for not just her great good luck but her willingness to show off about it. Caroline didn't need this level of detail for the book. Frank had stipulated from the start that details of their private life were off limits;

he would appear on the show with good humour, be filmed in family scenes, but absolutely not shoot anything intimate between him and Lexy. Other reality shows put the stars' sex lives very much on display, filmed scenes with them naked in bubble baths, making out; the wife surprising the husband in sexy lingerie, the husband, oiled up, doing a stripper routine for the wife clad in just a skimpy thong.

Lexy would have done all of this and more for ratings, but Frank was the sticking point. Their sex life was not put on television, and it would not feature in the book either. So there had been no need at all for Lexy to overwhelm Caroline with unnecessary details about her wonderful husband with his big cock and strong sex drive, to make poor, single Ghost Mouse listen to this torrent of bragging. Caroline had sat there silently, burning up with envy, imagining herself married to Frank, having sex with him all the time, anywhere, everywhere; sucking his cock with the technique Lexy described for the book; letting him do anything he wanted to her, anything at all.

Did Lexy know, when she told Caroline all these details, that Caroline was in lust with her husband? Often, Caroline had thought that Lexy did. It would have been different, maybe, if Lexy were warning Caroline off because she considered Caroline a rival. That would have been flattering, in a backhanded kind of way.

No, it had been much worse, Caroline decided. Lexy had been absolutely oblivious to Caroline's feelings, incapable of imagining that drab little Ghost Mouse was capable of attracting Frank for a moment; she had been showing off gleefully to someone she felt was beneath her in every way.

It had been obnoxious, insufferable. She deserved to be punished for it. She deserved to have her silent, intent listener take everything she had been told and use it to seduce Lexy's husband.

After all those confessional tapes of Lexy's, Caroline knew, better than Frank could possibly imagine, what he wanted. She took his hands and pressed them once more to her full, bare breasts.

'Please,' she sighed. 'Hold them, hold them tight . . . God, I love it, I love to feel you squeezing them like that!'

Frank would seriously just walk around the house holding my boobs if he could, Lexy had said. *I wake up and he's got his hands round them. I go to sleep and he wants to hold on to them till he passes out. And when we shag, he's always at my tits – fucking them, motorboating me, everything you can think of. Just can't leave them alone.*

Frank let out a deep grunt as he grasped her breasts, started to knead them, play with her nipples.

'I love having my boobs played with,' Caroline said, wriggling her buttocks even closer against his cock. 'Oh my God, yes, like that . . . oh Frank, you're so big . . .'

He shifted down the bed, climbing over her, his lips finding her nipples again, licking them, mouthing them, as Caroline's hips started to buck.

'Oh yeah,' she moaned, 'I love it when you kiss my tits like that!'

Tell guys how much you love what they're doing, Lexy said. *They can't get enough of that, trust me. Then you can ask 'em to do what you want much more easily, because they think everything you're saying is totally positive.*

Frank was kissing down her stomach now, his hands firmly clasped around her breasts. His knees planted themselves between her legs, pushing them wide, and she moaned louder when she realized what was going to happen. She was clean and fresh from the Jacuzzi; she had no embarrassment about him going down on her, not since she had broken through her previous limits, learned how to ask Riz for what she wanted. She spread her legs and tilted up her hips and as his mouth closed around her she pumped against it and thrashed her head and let the sensations build as she closed her hands over Frank's, squeezing her breasts still more, delighting in the fact that she knew that her crotch was exactly how Frank liked it: neatly trimmed, but not shaved.

Frank doesn't like a woman to be hairless, Lexy had said. *He's always says how creepy that is – only a perv would fancy that, he says. I had to grow my pubes out for him. Tidied up, but a natural shape, you know? Not a landing strip or anything too fake-looking.*

And certainly, the way he was eating her out could not have been more enthusiastic.

'Just this once more,' Frank groaned after she had come again and again, kissing his way back up her belly, reaching down to his straining cock, guiding it between her legs as she gasped eagerly. 'God, you're so wet . . . just this once more . . . I'll pull out in plenty of time, I promise – I just need to fuck you once more . . .'

'I can suck your cock,' she moaned. 'I want to suck your cock . . .'

'I need to fuck you now,' he said with great conviction, and she switched gear immediately.

'Yes, Frank, please, please, do it!' she sobbed. 'Please, fuck me, please, I want it so bad!'

She had realized already that a shift had happened. She was still pleading for her needs, but now he was vocalizing his too.

'Just once more,' he said, hissing between his teeth, lifting her, pushing her back so she was half-sitting up against the pillows; this way he could hold her breasts as his cock slid into her, starting to pump away. 'Oh, fuck, yes, I need this, I need this, just once more . . . I need to be inside you . . .'

Caroline wrapped her hands around his muscled, hairy forearms, more glad than she could say that it was too dark for him to see the swell of her stomach in this position. She was as limp as a rag, drunk on happiness, as she held on to him, as he worked up a rhythm, pounding away at her; she had come so much already that just lying here was more than enough for her. Frank's scent was all around her, his hands heavy on her breasts, his knees holding her legs wide as his cock thrust inside her.

If I can just keep this going, she thought, *if I can just keep giving him what he wants . . . a wife with big tits who'll fuck him twice a day . . . please, please, let me be clever enough and quick-witted enough to keep this going, so that when Lexy comes back he'll be conflicted about who he should be with . . .*

As Frank pulled out, threw himself onto his back beside her, groaning as he came again, his sperm running down his six-pack, Caroline ran through a to-do list in her head:

Buy a really slutty push-up bra

Buy condoms
Poke holes in them
And, after a moment's consideration:
Ring Lexy's pap agency.

Chapter Twenty-Eight

A few days later

'He's shagging her. I don't believe it. He's bloody shagging my ghostwriter!'

Lexy stared with utter disbelief at the photos on the gossip website. The headline was 'Playing at Home?' and the accompanying text read:

While Lexy's in detox, is Frank getting friendly with a younger woman? Pretty Caroline Macintosh is apparently a family friend who moved into Lexy and Frank's £8 million Sandbanks mansion the day that the explosive story of Lexy snogging Deacon broke . . . Careful, Lexy, while the cat's away detoxing, the mouse might be playing a game of his own!

The photos told their own narrative, beginning with Frank and Caroline picking up London at daycare, then Laylah at school, all long-lens paparazzi shots. The two adults were casually dressed and doing nothing as overt as holding hands, but as Lexy scrolled through the series of pictures, she decoded every single signifier one by one, picking them apart until the entire situation was horribly clear to her.

Firstly, the paparazzi had clearly been tipped off. There was no way that they simply happened to find themselves in

Poole, outside first one location and then the other, set up in advance at the ideal angles to capture every interaction between Frank, Caroline and the children. And the tip-off could only have come from one individual. Frank would never have rung the paps in a million years, and neither would Lexy's PRs: this was the worst possible publicity for her imaginable, another woman by her husband's side, hugging her children as they ran towards her. Sometimes the tips came from someone in the household, looking to make some quick dirty money, but Carmen, the housekeeper, had always been entirely trustworthy, and the latest nanny – if there even *was* a nanny now, with Caroline seeming to have taken over – would be yet another newly arrived Eastern European with not the faintest idea that pap agencies existed, let alone how to call them.

No, it could only have been Caroline who made the phone calls, and the reason was immediately obvious. Each photo had a caption beneath it, commenting slyly on the way Frank jumped down from the Range Rover first and went round the vehicle to open the door chivalrously for Caroline, the smiles between them as Frank hoisted London onto his shoulders, the way their hands touched as they strapped the kids into their car seats. Their body language was that of a couple, relaxed, a team, moving easily into each other's personal space. They looked like a couple too, well-matched physically, both in great shape, wearing near-identical outfits, jeans and navy sweaters . . .

'What the *fuck* happened to Ghost Mouse?' Lexy said slowly as she took in all the details of Caroline's appearance.

Lexy had been aware, of course, that Caroline had been

exercising and dieting ever since she came to Sandbanks. In the beginning, the ghostwriter had asked Lexy for a detailed breakdown of her own regime, and Lexy had answered all her questions very frankly, listing her tricks, her tips, her cheats, what worked and what didn't, how she wanted to quit smoking but was scared she'd pile on the pounds, the lipo that she'd had after London's birth, everything she could think of.

Of course, Lexy had thought all the questions, all the scrutiny, were for the book. She'd had no idea that Ghost Mouse had been studying her, not just so that she could successfully capture her thoughts and voice and character on the page, but so that she could wait for the right opportunity to steal her life.

How much weight had Ghost Mouse lost? How could Lexy not have noticed her slimming down and toning up to this extent? Looking back, Lexy could only ever remember Caroline in the same capacious, unflattering clothes that she had worn that first time she had come to Sandbanks for her interview: big sweaters, baggy skirts, so you couldn't quite tell what the body underneath was like, but assumed it was as bulky as the layers indicated.

Caroline must surely have lost a couple of stone, Lexy realized. She must be a size ten or twelve now, everywhere apart from her boobs, which she had sensibly dressed down in her school pick-up outfit, knowing that any hint of cleavage would have her instantly targeted as a homewrecker. Her clothes were perfectly chosen for the occasion: slim-cut jeans skimming her thighs, ankle boots with a small heel to lengthen her legs, a V-neck sweater with a white T-shirt visible underneath it, the neckline of the sweater the most flattering style for a top-heavy woman . . .

She'd learned all this from Lexy, her victim realized, looking back with a burst of delayed shock at the dawning awareness of the blueprints to her life that she had given Caroline. Dieting. Fashion advice. Exercise that worked for her physical shape. Make-up tips. Sex tips. *Sex tips* . . .

'My God,' Lexy blurted out. '*Frank*. I talked about sex with Frank, what he likes . . . I spilled my guts to her, I told her everything, *everything!*'

And Ghost Mouse had taken full advantage, ably using so much that Lexy had told her, even how to tip off the paps and dress for a staged photo session that should seem entirely spontaneous. Caroline's hair looked as if it were newly, subtly streaked. She had either had a professional blow-dry that afternoon or learned how to do an expert job herself, rollers and all; the thick, sleek, volumized mane fell around her face in a girlish style that made her look innocent and youthful. Her skin was so preternaturally smooth that Lexy suspected Caroline of having gone into her dressing room and used her BB cream and powder. It looked as if she had done some clever, subtle contouring with blush and shader, and was wearing fake eyelashes too.

Although Lexy could see all the tricks Caroline had used, the overall effect was demure and unshowy, perfectly calculated for picking up someone else's children from school in the company of their father. For signalling, in short, that she would make a far better mother than their real one, who was currently off on a Swiss mountain, doing some sort of detox diet, apparently quite happy to have caused a major scandal with the hottest ex-boybander of the moment, and then fled the country without even seeing her children first . . .

'Well played, Ghost Mouse. And fuck you,' Lexy muttered as she scrolled down the long page of photos, so many that it took forever for the screen to load.

Because after picking up the kids, Caroline and Frank had taken Laylah and London to the local park. Sitting on a bench, Caroline had produced bottles of water, apple slices and healthy snacks, including what looked, according to the caption, like home-made mini pitta sandwiches from her Cambridge Satchel leather backpack – a bag with which Lexy would not have been seen dead, because it signified a no-frills, solid, maternal respectability which was a million miles away from her own style.

She and Frank pushed London and Laylah on the swings, supervised them on the big roundabout, laughed at London's attempts to run up the slide. Caroline even joined the kids in the huge round rope-woven swing, big enough for all three of them to lie there, clinging to each other, heads thrown back, as Frank swung them back and forth.

It was surreal for Lexy to watch this, as if she had been in the photographs herself, only to have been Photoshopped out and Caroline's image substituted instead. But if she were honest with herself, she had to acknowledge the impossibility of that happening. Lexy had never taken the kids to the park; she considered it was the nanny's job to tire them out after school and bring them home with that burst of after-school energy thoroughly worked off.

'Fuck you, Ghost Mouse,' Lexy said again, the full significance of the nickname that she had given Caroline months ago slowly sinking in. Her target was beginning to understand that Caroline had not only noticed everything Lexy did successfully, but what she had failed to do. Ghost Mouse had identified every single one of Lexy's weaknesses so that she could slip in a wedge and work it deeper.

And the perfect place for the tip of that wedge had been the attraction between Lexy and Deacon. Ghost Mouse had observed that spark as they flirted at the reality TV awards show, been clever enough to remember it and suggest Deacon as a possible fake love interest for Lexy, flipping the suggestion made by Lexy's PR team that it should be Frank to be tempted outside their marriage. How very astute of Ghost Mouse! She had moved impressively fast, hearing that idea in the meeting and using it almost straight afterwards at the lunch. It had been so well done that Lexy had practically thought she had come up with the idea herself.

Lexy had said, she recalled, that Frank probably wouldn't mind too much about a few blurry photos of her with Deacon. Caroline had agreed, pointing out that Lexy had done all sorts of wild things for the show, and by her own account, though Frank had been angry with her from time to time for crossing the line, his bad mood had never lasted that long. This, she had said blithely, would be just another one of those times, a few awkward days to live through; but Frank would understand, of course, that Lexy hadn't really been attracted to Deacon, was just following the template laid out by Emily and her team . . .

While of course, Ghost Mouse must have been calculating that once Lexy had a few drinks in her, and started flirting with Deacon, his insatiable libido would take things much further than she had planned.

'I really played into your hands, didn't I, Ghost Mouse?' Lexy said aloud.

She was staring at the last photos, the images of healthy, wholesome Caroline lying on the big rope swing with Laylah and London climbing over her. Caroline's hair was hanging down in a long, silky sweep over the edge of the swing, and London was encircled in one of her arms, being held safely even as he crawled over her, telegraphing that Caroline was showing appropriate maternal concern.

It was very easy to behave perfectly when you knew cameras were on you, very easy to keep a smile on your face, never look impatient or weary or frustrated. Lexy should know. She'd pulled that trick herself many times, and now it had been played on her.

She put down her phone and walked across the room to stare out of the window. It was a view with which she was now very familiar: the majestic panorama of Alpine mountains whose slopes were snow-covered all year round, the light so clear and white that it felt as if it was meditation just to gaze at it. Sliding open the balcony door, she stepped outside, shivering in the cool air, breathing it in to calm herself down. The cold in her lungs focused her on her body, helping to balance the turmoil in her mind. It was a technique they taught here at Schloss Hafendammer, and Lexy found it surprisingly helpful, though she had told her doctor sarcastically that it wasn't really something she could recreate at home without installing a gigantic walk-in freezer, or the kind of snow room it was now fashionable to find in spas.

She should have known better. Doktor Weinstein had told her to step into a cold shower and stay there as long as necessary. Jason's speculation about a German detox centre hosing her down and giving her enemas had turned out to be a fairly accurate picture of Swiss ones as well. Her regime had included colonics, purges, fast days, specially prepared herbal teas and sessions where she sat with an 'eating coach' and chewed every bite of food twenty times, counted out loud by the coach, before she swallowed it. The tedium had been unbearable, but she had understood and expected it, unlike many of the complaining clients, who had gone there for weight loss but bitterly resented the deprivation they had to endure in pursuit of their goal. Lexy, at least, was used to keeping her weight down.

She craved a cigarette, but she knew that desire was psychological, not physical. It had been explained to her that nicotine addiction left your body after forty-eight hours, and after that the work was purely mental. She had quit smoking when, analyzing with Doktor Weinstein when she was most likely to drink, she had realized that one of the primary triggers was having a cigarette in her hand. Going back home an ex-smoker and maybe even an ex-drinker would surely impress Frank, and she had known anyway that she needed to kick the habit: not one facial analysis at Skin3 had failed to mention the damage done to her epidermis by smoking.

With the cigarettes, Lexy had chosen her figure over her health for years, and now she was reversing that hierarchy. Yes, it was at least partly out of vanity; but she could tell Frank that she was setting a good example to the kids, and certainly it would be true, if not the whole truth . . .

Lexy had been thinking non-stop about Frank and the kids: what changes she needed to make on her return, how much humble pie she'd need to eat. It was hard to believe that Frank had not responded to one of her pleading emails and texts, let alone the letter she had sent from London, followed up by two from Switzerland. Those had been very hard to write, not only because she hadn't actually handwritten anything but her own flashy signature in so long that it had taken her several goes to be able to manage readable cursive script, but because she had known they had to be considered, come from the heart. Lexy had been living so superficially for so long that simply sitting down and being honest about her feelings, with no attempt to charm her way out of trouble, had been truly hard for her to do.

Doktor Weinstein had helped with that. Some shrinkage, as Lexy had called it, had definitely taken place. She had needed to work out why she'd kept drinking and smoking and partying instead of spending more time with her kids; a spoilt little girl who'd become a spoilt young woman and reality star, she hadn't been ready to change gear and finally put herself second.

Well, she was prepared to do that now. Despite Frank having locked her out of Sandbanks, despite him not having responded to her efforts to contact him, she had never had any doubt that he would be willing to reconcile when she returned to the UK. They had two children together. She hadn't cheated, she had just been stupid and got carried away for a moment. She had done serious, substantive work on her problems. And most importantly, they still loved each other.

In her letters, she had explained to Frank that she was unable to contact him any other way. She had asked him to write back, or at least send a card from him and the kids. Every time she had returned to her room hoping to find an envelope that had been slid under the door, and every time she had been disappointed.

Bitter as it had been, she had understood the message. Frank was punishing her for her sins, and it was no more than she deserved. When her plane landed at Heathrow tomorrow, her plan had been to drive straight to Sandbanks, sit outside London's Montessori daycare until picking-up time, walk over to Laylah's school with her son and whoever had turned up to collect the children, and then take her kids back home. Start as she meant to go on, be a mother instead of a selfish, Pinot-sodden bitch.

But *now* what did she do? The only reason she had been allowed her phone was because Jason had rung the Schloss urgently, saying that it was an emergency and that Lexy needed to see something online; she had assumed it was more pictures or video of her and Deacon, but how much worse could those be? How could she have expected *this*?

Lexy couldn't blame herself. No one could have expected this, not even Frank. Caroline had played her hand superbly. She must have had her eye on him ever since she came to The Gables, gradually working out the best way to his heart. Lexy remembered Caroline's lack of interest in the kids when she first visited the house; she hadn't been bothered with them at all apart from making sure she got their names and dates of birth right for the book. It was only later that she had evolved into bloody Mary Poppins, chucking a ball around in the pool with them, rating Laylah's endless outfits at the little girl's request, talking to London's teddy bear as if it had opinions of its own – Lexy's heart clenched as she thought of London and his precious Brown Bear, of Laylah trying on one tutu after another and demanding to know whether the blue went better with her top than the silver. Jealousy flooded through her at the realization that Caroline was in her house, looking after her children, taking her place in bed with her husband. Lexy had never wanted her family life so much as now, when it looked as if it might be slipping away from her.

Because that danger was real. Lexy knew Frank: he wouldn't be doing this if he didn't have feelings for Caroline. He had never been a man who indulged in casual sex, as the groupies who always hung around footballers had discovered to their great disappointment. Lexy had been genuinely appalled on their first meeting that, although he saw her home, he did not take up her enthusiastic invitation to come inside, in all senses; instead, he asked her out to dinner the next evening. When, after three dates, they did eventually go to bed and she realized how high his sex drive was, she had expressed surprise that he had held out so long. Frank had just smiled and said that he'd always been good at waiting for the right person to come along.

Lexy had never thought he would cheat on her, and she was sure that until now he never had. But did he even consider this cheating? Did he think that what Lexy had done with Deacon meant their marriage was over, that they were headed for divorce, with Ghost Mouse lined up to take Lexy's place? Ghost Mouse, who had wormed her way into

Lexy's home without Lexy even noticing. Ghost Mouse, who had learned from Lexy exactly what Frank liked in bed. Ghost Mouse, who had seen from Lexy's behaviour what Frank was missing in a wife, and had set out to provide it . . .

There was no doubt in Lexy's mind that her husband and Caroline were having an affair. She could see the tenderness in his eyes as he looked at Caroline, the care with which he handed her down from the Range Rover, his smile of contentment as he took the Tupperware box she was handing him with the children's snacks inside it. Was he in love, or just happy to have found a woman with big tits – oh yes, Caroline was lucky she had those! – who wanted to spend time with his children, have sex with him twice a day, stay in with him in the evenings instead of going out most nights to parties and launches?

Whether it was love or just convenience, Frank's affair with her ghostwriter was, Lexy thought with great bitterness at the irony, a fantastically strong storyline for a whole new season of the show, plus a sequel to *Lexy on the Loose*.

Only Caroline would scarcely be commissioned to write it.

Chapter Twenty-Nine

The next day

'Twist in the Tale: Frank's new love wrote Lexy's book!'

'The Write Stuff – Lexy's ghostwriter steals her hubby!'

'Why it matters that Lexy didn't write her own memoir: we want our idols to tell us the truth'

'Who is Caroline Macintosh – the girl who's told Lexy's story and taken her man?'

'What am I going to do?' Caroline sobbed, turning away from the computer screen. 'I signed a confidentiality agreement! No one was supposed to find out that I wrote Lexy's book! I'm going to be in such trouble with Bailey and Hart!'

Frank, who was sitting next to her on the sofa, enfolded her in a comforting embrace.

'It's going to be all right,' he said, cuddling her, spouting the standard words that men used to calm down crying women.

'How *can* it be all right?' she wailed. 'What's going to happen? What am I going to do?'

'I don't know,' he said honestly. 'You'll just have to wait and see what Lexy's editor says. When is he ringing?'

'Twenty minutes,' Caroline said into his shoulder. 'With her agent. It's a conference call.'

'It's going to be all right,' Frank repeated. 'Look, you haven't done anything wrong. You worked so hard to get that book written, and they love it! Everyone loves it! Didn't he tell you everyone at the publisher really enjoyed it? And the agent did too?'

Caroline nodded against him. His hand cradled her head, stroking her hair.

'This isn't anything to do with you,' he said soothingly. 'You just got caught in the crossfire. How did people even find out it was you? I thought no one was ever supposed to know!'

'They weren't,' Caroline said, pulling back and wiping her eyes. 'I mean, everyone who thought about it would assume Lexy'd have some help writing a book, but you never actually admit there was a ghostwriter. There was a pop star who said she wrote a book last year, and it turned out that someone else got paid to write it. It sold tons, and I don't think her fans really cared at all.'

'And how did people find out she hadn't written it herself?' Frank asked again, a question upon which Caroline wished he wouldn't focus quite so hard.

'I don't know,' she said. 'I think she thanked her ghostwriter in the acknowledgements and people recognized the name, because the ghost had written books of her own.'

'But that wouldn't happen with you,' Frank said naively.

'Yes, I haven't had anything published under my own name,' Caroline said, rather irritated that he had needed to make that comment. 'And *Lexy on the Loose* isn't even out yet. When J. K. Rowling did a crime novel under a pseudonym, there was a weird tweet that hinted at it from someone who knew her lawyers, and people put the pieces together from that. It was a really odd situation.'

Frank was frowning.

'I can see why someone would want to break that story,' he said slowly. 'I mean, the crime books would sell much more if they realize that it's her who wrote them. But this is different. I don't get why anyone would want to make it public. It doesn't help anyone at the publisher, does it?'

'No, of course not! Quite the opposite!' Caroline agreed quickly. 'Especially with you and me being in the press – those pictures of us picking up the kids –'

Frank heaved a deep sigh.

'Look, Caroline,' he said, taking her hand. 'I'm really confused, and I've made no secret of that. I have a wife, and I said vows to her, and I meant every word. But after what she's done . . . when it came out that guy visited her at our London flat before she went off to Switzerland, and she hasn't bothered to text me once, not even to ask how the kids are!'

It had been a great stroke of luck for Caroline that Deacon's first visit to the Chelsea flat had been documented by a lurking paparazzo. The later one, where he had bribed the Deliveroo driver and obscured his features with the big food box, had gone unnoticed, but the photographer had sold to a tabloid the pictures of Deacon entering the building and talking to the doorman; the paper had used them to imply that Deacon had been given access to Lexy's apartment. It had been an extra nail in Lexy's coffin as far as Frank was concerned, bolstering his conviction that she was having a full-blown affair with Deacon.

'I should go back to London,' Caroline said, squeezing his hand and then letting it go. 'I'll start packing this afternoon. My being here's just making things worse for everyone.'

'It isn't, though,' Frank said, leaning forward, propping his hands on his knees. 'We've talked about this already. You make me feel better. I'd be so lonely without you. The kids are really happy you're here – they think you're family by now. And Lexy's abandoned us, hasn't she? So why should you go?'

Caroline looked at him, wondering if he had any idea how he truly felt about her. She doubted it. He had just said how confused he was, and yet when she gave him the opportunity to ask her to leave, he had turned it down, just as she had hoped. She was giving him what he had always wanted: the wife at home, doing her own work but still an essential part of the family, not just someone who came and went in a cloud of perfume and glamour and film crews.

'I'm not asking for anything,' she said gently. 'I think we just need to live day to day and see how things go. And I don't want to leave, I honestly don't. But I also don't want to put you in a difficult position. I mean, Lexy's due back the day after tomorrow!'

Frank lifted his shoulders and let them fall as heavily as if he were carrying weights strapped to his back.

'That's what Jason says. I wouldn't bloody know. Haven't heard a word from her, have I?'

'What will you do if Lexy gets in touch?' she asked. 'I mean, not "if" – she will, of course, one way or the other . . .'

'I don't know,' he said. 'I really don't.'

The landline rang, and they both jumped, as if it were

Lexy calling, as if they'd summoned her by speaking her name. Frank answered it.

'It's for you,' he said to Caroline. 'That call you were expecting.'

She noticed that his expression, on realizing it was not his wife on the other end of the line, was a complicated mixture of relief and sadness.

'I'll leave you to it,' he said, giving Caroline the handset. 'I'm going to work out. Come down to the gym afterwards and join me?'

'I'd love to,' she said, flashing him a smile and switching the handset to speakerphone as she sat down at the desk.

'Caroline? It's Gareth,' her editor said grimly. 'Miranda's here too.'

'Hi, Caroline,' Miranda said, sounding no more cheerful than Gareth. 'Well, this is a total bloody shitstorm, isn't it?'

'I'm so sorry,' Caroline said. 'What do you want me to do?'

Gareth heaved a deep sigh.

'Nothing,' he said. 'Not a thing. We're drafting a press release as I speak, saying that naturally Lexy, as a novice, needed some practical help putting a book together and that she asked you, as a blogger she admired, to work with her collating dates, organizing the book structure, etc. It turns out it was a very good thing you hadn't written a book before, eh? We might be able to get away with it by highlighting your lack of experience, making you look like just an assistant.'

'So, are you and Frank an actual couple, Caroline?' Miranda asked bluntly.

'It's much too early to say anything like that,' Caroline said, managing not to let any anger show in her voice at the 'assistant' comment. 'I'm just helping out with the kids and seeing how things go.'

'I *can't even* with this,' Gareth said, and from the squeak of leather shifting it sounded as if he was slumping in his chair. 'We have a book coming out about Lexy settling down after a wild ride, and her ghost is fucking her husband! The publicists are going mental! Why didn't we just do a bloody novel instead?'

It was Miranda's turn to heave a huge sigh.

'I know,' she said, sounding weary. 'Do you mind if I vape in here, Gareth? I really need a smoke. There's just been so much crap with celebs not writing their own novels recently and getting bad press for it – or they actually try to write them, God help us, and of course they're always terrible . . .'

'Tell me about it,' Gareth said ruefully.

'So we thought a memoir would be safer,' she continued, 'and God knows Lexy's got enough stories to tell! It wasn't like Caroline even needed to pad it out.'

'The bloody ironic thing is, it's a great read!' Gareth said in a very annoyed tone, and although she had already been told this, Caroline beamed with pleasure. Authors, it turned out, could not hear too much praise of their work.

'I mean, this whole thing's so messed up!' Gareth moaned. 'We both had huge doubts about you, Caroline – that's not a secret, we were very open about it at the time. Lexy insisted, which is *also* bloody ironic, but she was right. You've turned out something that's honestly much better than I thought it was going to be, and on deadline to boot.

You did a really good job, and now you've gone and fucked up your own bloody work! It was going to be hard enough pushing a book about Lexy finding true love with you living with her husband. But now we've got to deal with the media screaming about her not even writing the book, and here's your name coming up all over again! How the fuck did that even *happen*?'

'Do we know who leaked it to the media?' Miranda asked.

'NFI,' Gareth said. 'But it wasn't anyone at Bailey and Hart, I can tell you that. We've done tons of ghostwritten books and no one's ever breathed a word. They know better than that. Apart from anything else, it almost always fucks with the sales figures. It's not in our interest to tank a book, is it?'

'Same with us,' Miranda agreed. 'No one at my agency would say a thing.'

Gareth drew in a deep breath.

'Look, Caroline, the main reason for this call is to say that we had you under option to write a follow-up book for Lexy,' he said, 'and obviously that's not going to happen. We'll send you an official letter to that effect. But that doesn't mean the confidentiality clause isn't still in effect. You know that, right? You can't say a word about this to anyone, or even drop the smallest hint on social media. You keep your mouth shut and let us push the official line, that you helped her out a bit with structure and research, blah blah. I'll email the press release over to you now so you can see exactly what we're saying.'

'Of *course*,' Caroline said, sounding as heartfelt as possible. 'I won't say a word about it.'

'Not on your blog either,' Gareth warned, his tone almost threatening.

'I haven't said anything!' she protested. 'You can check it out right now! I haven't updated it for a while. And you can check my Facebook and Twitter too!'

'Oh, we have, believe me,' Miranda said. 'I got Campaspe to go over everything with a fine-toothed comb first thing this morning. You're clean as a whistle.'

Of course I am! Caroline thought. *I'm not stupid! I called the pap agency on Gabriela's mobile and put on an Eastern European-sounding accent so if anyone ever tried to track down the number, it would look like she did it . . .*

She didn't truly think anyone would go that far; it wasn't exactly a matter of national security. But she read enough crime novels to know how easy it was to trace calls, or to pay someone at a phone company to look up the name in which a number was registered.

'So how do *you* think the press got this info, Caroline?' Miranda asked, with a certain edge to her voice that Caroline couldn't quite interpret. It might have been accusatory, or it might have been something else entirely.

'The only thing I can think of is phone tapping,' Caroline answered, delighted to be able to give the answer that she had formulated in case anyone asked this very question. 'I was here the day Frank locked Lexy out, and all the paps saw me come in. If one of them wondered who I was and managed to find out, they could have been tapping my phone for the last month. And we've been back and forth a lot about the edits, haven't we?'

'Hmn. Well, it's a theory,' Gareth said.

'Look, it is what it is,' Miranda chimed in. 'Lexy's coming in to Bailey and Hart as soon as her plane lands tomorrow, and we'll see what damage control we can do on all of this. Caroline's assured us she isn't in breach of the confidentiality clause, and you've told her she obviously won't be writing any more books for Lexy – as if it needed saying. We're done here. I'm going out for a real fag, okay?'

'You wound me,' Gareth said. 'I thought I was real fag enough for you, darling!'

Miranda snorted. The leather chair squeaked again, presumably as Gareth leaned forward to terminate the call.

'Okay, Caroline. Good work on the book,' he said. 'Excellent work, actually. Oh, the *irony*! Bye.'

He hung up before Caroline could say 'Goodbye' in turn, but she couldn't really blame him. Her relationship with Frank alone was enough to make Lexy's editor irritated beyond all measure.

There was a hollow feeling in Caroline's stomach. She had, however, been hoping – stupidly, she could see that now – that Gareth might have added that, if she had any ideas for books of her own, he'd be very interested in hearing about them. But clearly that had never been even the remotest of possibilities.

In the pocket of her jeans, her mobile started to vibrate. She pulled it out and saw, with a surge of mingled surprise, excitement and terror, that Miranda was calling her. Had Lexy's agent guessed that it had been Caroline who had told the press about having written Lexy's book? But why wouldn't she have accused her of it five minutes ago, if that was the case?

'Caroline? Hi. I'm outside now, there's no one around,' Miranda said, audibly taking a drag on her cigarette. 'So, look. I've got a pretty good idea of what's been going on, okay? No need to confirm things one way or the other. But what I'm seeing here is an author who's very much in the public eye at the moment, who's got a lot of self-promotional skills – which, believe me, is key in publishing nowadays – and who can turn a book around really fast.'

'I'm sorry?' Caroline said, confused, thinking that Miranda, standing outside the offices of Bailey and Hart, was looking at a writer she knew.

'I mean *you*, for fuck's sake!' Miranda said impatiently. 'Can you write another book as quickly as possible? Ideally a novel with a thinly disguised Lexy character in it – think *The Devil Wears Prada*. Your character is the innocent hero-ine, she's the crazy bitch. You couldn't be her ghost, of course. Maybe you're the nanny. Or a secretary.'

'Oh, wow,' Caroline breathed. 'You think I could—'

'You'd have to get it right,' Miranda said. 'But the tone could be very like the book you've done already.'

Another drag on the cigarette.

'I couldn't rep you myself, of course,' she said, to Caroline's great disappointment. 'Or give you to someone else in the agency. That'd be too messy, and Gareth would never forgive me. But there's someone I used to work with who'd be perfect for this, really commercial, and I owe her a massive favour. No one needs to know I connected you two.'

'That would be amazing—'

'Have a think about it, sit down, see if you can knock out a chapter or two ASAP. And an outline. Publishers'll want to see that much before they'll give you a contract. But this'd come with a whole raft of built-in publicity, and they always love that in a proposal. You'd have to do a lot of interviews to promote the book, so you'd have to be okay with all of that . . . think it over, I need to go for a meeting with another editor here in a few minutes, so I need to go—'

'I want to do it,' Caroline said breathlessly. 'I want to be a full-time writer. That's always been my dream.'

'Easier said than done! But you'll make more money from this than you did for Lexy's book, that's for sure,' Miranda said. 'Her name's Naomi, the agent I know. I'll give her your info. And if you want this, I'd get going right away. Sit down and start it now. Today. Ideally, the book'll come out while the scandal's still fresh in everyone's minds.'

'I will! Thanks! Thanks so much!' Caroline babbled, before realizing that she was talking to a dial tone. Miranda had hung up.

Caroline put the phone slowly down on the desk, her gaze moving gradually around this room, which had become her cosy nest. Frank's office was furnished with capacious chestnut leather sofas, a coffee table made from a gilded antique door mounted under a sheet of glass, a huge flat-screen television on the wall, and framed photographs of Frank playing for Kensington and for England, holding high the FA cup, rendered in tasteful black and white, hanging on the walls. The interior designer had made it as much den as office, much cosier than the sprawling living room downstairs, and it was one of his favourite places in the house.

With the children tucked up in bed and the door locked,

Caroline and Frank had had sex on one of the sofas last night, taking it as slow as they could, Caroline straddling him, working away with her newly strong, muscled thighs, Frank's fingers between her legs making her come over and over again as he watched her face contort in pleasure, his dark eyes huge. Just the memory of his hands on her, his soft gaze delighting in the pleasure he was giving her, his cock inside her, hard as a pole, refusing to quit, holding out as long as it could, made her legs twitch together, her centre start to dissolve to a liquid thick and rich as honey. And after they were done, they had walked slowly up to bed together, holding hands, and cuddled in Caroline's bedroom, spooning for a few hours, until Frank slipped away, as he always did, so that Laylah and London would find him in the master bedroom if they got up early and came to look for their dad.

The sex with Frank was the best Caroline had ever had in her life, as was the relationship she had with him. But if she wrote the book Miranda had proposed, Caroline would sacrifice all of that in one stroke. Frank would never stay with a woman who had published a tell-all about the mother of his children, dragging them even deeper into the tabloid mud.

However, if she didn't, it was by no means guaranteed that she would eventually find an agent for any other books she might write, let alone get them published. This was her big chance to get her name out there, to write a novel that would reach as many people as possible, show readers that Caroline Macintosh's name on a book meant a really good read.

And wasn't this where Caroline had been heading all

along? Why else had she tipped off the paparazzi agency that she would be picking the kids up with Frank, and told the media that she was the ghostwriter for Lexy's book? Caroline had pushed hard to get herself into the news; Miranda hadn't needed to tell her that publishers loved a book proposal that came with built-in publicity.

In one of the framed photographs of Frank playing football that hung on the wall opposite her, Caroline made out her own reflection, the shape of her head and torso floating, superimposed, over the silhouette of one of Frank's teammates. Her physical transformation had happened so fast that sometimes she barely recognized herself in the mirror. This was one of those times; the slim-cheeked young woman in a V-necked blouse with smooth straight hair falling around her face looked enviably poised and composed, very different from how Caroline was currently feeling.

She was hugely conflicted. After all, she had been secretly trying to get pregnant during the last few weeks; but looking back, hadn't that been completely insane of her? She had got wildly carried away, so excited that Frank wanted her that she had jumped right into the fantasy with both feet, seeing herself as the mother of his kids, living here with him, having Lexy's life. It was the dream she had been incubating ever since she'd visited The Gables for the first time.

Caroline watched as her reflection pursed its lips together, thinking hard. Ever since that first meeting with Lexy, Caroline had been calculating odds and options, working out potential moves far in advance. She hadn't even known that she was capable of this kind of planning; but then again, wasn't it very similar to writing a book, plotting it out in advance, like the outline for the novel that Miranda had suggested she write? Ideas for the story were already burgeoning in her mind, seeds germinating in fertile dark soil; she could feel them twist and turn and grow.

Caroline was realizing that having Lexy's life was actually a twofold proposition. The husband, the home and the family were half the balance, but the other half was her thriving career, which had required Lexy to put so much of her private life on public display. Frank would certainly not want to replace Lexy with a woman who had the same need for publicity as his wife did.

The trouble was that, now she felt relatively attractive, Caroline *did* have the same need for publicity. Every time she saw her name in print or online, she felt as excited as if she'd taken drugs. Her heart raced, her head span, she felt light and dizzy, and she wanted more. Since the paparazzi photos had broken, she had set up a Google alert for her name and had been glued to her phone. She didn't care, it turned out, about the snarky journalese pointing out that she was less attractive than Lexy, the comments that called her a homewrecker and a slut.

They knew her name. They were talking about her. That was all that was important. She, who had been nothing, a dowdy, plump drudge picked out by Lexy partly because she was no competition, nicknamed Ghost Mouse for a good reason, was now, in a way, Lexy's equal!

Caroline knew she wasn't a great beauty, but she looked pretty enough in the photographs, a woman who it was plausible for Frank to be dating, her hair done, her skin clear. Lexy had forgotten to cancel her offer of her credit card to Caroline for her beauty treatments, and Caroline had happily continued with them at her ex-boss's expense; after all, Lexy had allowed Caroline to be paid a very meagre sum for working all hours on the book to which Lexy was going to affix her own name.

On meeting Lexy, Caroline had craved what she had: fame, fortune and Frank, the three Fs. But not even Lexy, Caroline was beginning to realize, had managed to hold on to all of those things.

So if Caroline couldn't have all of them, she wondered, which would she be prepared to sacrifice?

Chapter Thirty

'What are we going to do?'

Frank stared hopelessly at his wife. They were sitting on sofas in the Chelsea Harbour flat, face to face across the coffee table, an oddly formal way for a married couple to talk to each other. His back was to the big windows that looked over the water below, the boats moored in the shelter of the small marina, and the clear daylight meant that he could see Lexy's face very clearly. She was make-up free, her hair pulled back, modestly dressed, very much as she had been the day when she had come down to Sandbanks only to find herself surrounded by paparazzi, locked out of her own house.

'You look pale,' he found himself saying when she didn't immediately answer his question.

'Yeah,' Lexy said, managing to sketch a smile at her own expense. 'No sunbeds or spray tans at Schloss Hafendammer! No drink either. And I've kicked the fags, you'll be happy to hear.'

'That's *great*,' Frank said with huge relief. 'I always wanted you to do that.'

'It wasn't that hard,' Lexy admitted. 'No one there smoked,

so it wasn't like you saw someone at it and got a craving. Same with the drink. After a while I stopped even thinking about fags and booze. It was herbal teas and filtered water from morning to night. Honestly, not having coffee was the worst thing of all.'

She managed a grin.

'I'm really going to watch the drinking now I'm back, I promise. Did you see I lost weight? That's from not having wine for a month.'

Frank nodded, and a memory of Caroline gently dismissing Lexy's detox by calling it a diet retreat couldn't help but pop into his head.

'It's like a miracle! No one ever loses weight giving up fags, do they?' Lexy said lightly. 'I got bloody lucky, eh? I'll be sending everyone I know who wants to quit to Switzerland for a month! You can't nip out to the shops for extra snacks when you get the munchies – you're stuck up this mountain with them feeding you vegetable soups and tiny little portions of poached fish and making you chew every bite twenty times.'

'Doesn't sound much fun,' Frank said.

'It's not supposed to be *fun*,' Lexy said. A slight edge came into her voice. 'I wasn't at a spa in the Maldives getting massages every day, Frank.'

'I didn't think you were,' Frank muttered.

Silence fell, and not for the first time. Frank stared down through the glass coffee table at the rug below, a black and white swirling design that he had never much liked. Lexy's gaze, however, was fixed on him as she tried desperately to read his mind, to work out what he wanted. It was the day after her return from Switzerland, and she had asked him to come up and see her in London: she was unable to bear the idea of asking to come to Sandbanks, only to have him tell her that she wasn't wanted there because Caroline was in residence.

Frank, however, had taken the request that he come to London as just another sign that Lexy wasn't committed to their marriage or their children. She had asked after Laylah and London, of course, as soon as he arrived, and said how much she had missed them; but how much did that actually mean?

A very straightforward man, he had never been more conflicted in his life. Although he had resisted the awful, sick temptation to watch the video of Lexy and Deacon getting hot and heavy, the photographs of them together were etched into his memory. What if those images never left him? How was he supposed to deal with that?

He didn't know how to tell Lexy about these doubts. They were too scary for him to articulate; it was as if speaking them aloud would make them concrete. So he stayed quiet, waiting to hear what she had to say.

'Look, Frank, I'm not going to make any excuses. I really fucked up. I'm sorry,' Lexy said, leaning forward, trying to meet his eyes. 'I wanted to get publicity, like Emily suggested. That's why I went along with it and didn't push Deacon off me straight away. But that's not an excuse, I promise. It's an explanation. I was a bit pissed, and I got carried away, and I should have come home straight afterwards. I did everything wrong, okay?'

Frank nodded slowly, still staring at the carpet.

'And I tried to say sorry,' she went on. 'I came to the house to apologize. I rang and rang you from that shitty hotel to beg you to let me in, so I could see you all and say how sorry I was. Sat on the balcony and cried my head off. I get why you locked me out – I might have done the same thing under the circumstances, I suppose. But you could at least have rung me back.'

Lexy had no idea, of course, that Frank had never heard any of her messages or read any of her plaintive emails or letters beyond that first text. She blamed Caroline for a great deal of the extent to which this situation had escalated, but she had not yet reached the point where she realized the degree to which Caroline had actively tried to break up her marriage.

'I wouldn't've known what to say, Lex,' Frank said quietly. 'To be honest, I still don't know what to say to you.'

Lexy took a deep breath.

'I want to stay married, Frank,' she said: she was determined to avoid saying the word *divorce*. 'I fucked up, I went too far, but I'm really trying to fix things. I know you always thought I drank too much. And, like I said, I've given up the fags.'

'It's almost too good to be true, isn't it?' Frank said, raising his head to look at her. 'Like you waved a magic wand and turned into someone else.'

Lexy felt strangely light, as if the ground had dropped away from her. Not in a good way: not like the thrill of a roller-coaster ride, but the experience, in an unfamiliar swimming pool, of stepping into what you think is shallow water and finding yourself floundering in the deep end instead. She had not expected this reaction. She had assumed, naturally enough, that Frank would be overjoyed at hearing how she had cleaned up her act.

'I mean,' he said, not realizing the extent to which he was parroting words Caroline had drip-fed into his mind for precisely this eventuality, 'it's not just that you went too far. You got caught out, and now you're saying everything I want to hear so you get back in my good books again.'

'Not just *saying*,' Lexy protested. 'I'm *doing* it! I really have stopped smoking – and honestly, I'm not going to drink half as much now as I used to do—'

'What about the blow?' he said, inexorable. 'You still planning to go on caning it with the girls?'

'No. I promise,' she said firmly. 'I'd do some lines when I'd had a few drinks and someone had it, or ordered it in, and I'd get carried away. But I'm not going to be drinking like that any more, so I won't make bad decisions. I'll be coming home earlier. It just won't be an issue.'

Frank stood up, and Lexy hoped that he was coming to sit next to her, maybe even hold her hand. Instead, however, he barely glanced at her as he walked round the sofa, turning his back to her, looking down at the marina several stories below.

'Frank?' she said nervously. 'I'm getting really freaked out. I don't know what to say. I thought you'd be happy about all of this—'

'It's just,' he said to the window, 'I already said it sounds too good to be true, didn't I? You've done something that you know's the biggest no-no for me in the world – you've dragged our kids through the mud – and so you try to fix it by fucking off to some luxury spa and coming back telling me you've somehow magically changed into everything I wanted you to be! It sounds too easy, doesn't it?'

'Frank!' she protested, panic rising now. 'Please, you have to believe me that it wasn't easy, and it wasn't a luxury spa! I've been working so hard – talking to Doktor Weinstein about my drinking and smoking, what triggered them, how to make sure I don't fall back into bad habits. I promise, this is me realizing that I need to sort my life out. I'm getting too old to piss around, I need to—'

'Lex!'

Frank swung around, and even with the light behind him, Lexy could see how contorted his face was.

'Do you know how many times you've said "I, I, I"?' he burst out. 'It's not just about you, that's my point! Or if it is, it shouldn't be!'

Lexy's breath caught in her throat. There was no arguing with this. Frank was right. For all her newfound virtue, for all the quasi-therapy sessions she had had with Doktor Weinstein, working out why she reached for her Pinot with lemon slice, and then another and another, she hadn't made a connection beyond that to her responsibilities as a wife and mother.

She had made it all about her; her need to get back Frank and the happy life she had had with him and the kids. She had thought that if she fixed what Frank didn't like about her, what had caused her to behave so recklessly, then she could return to it very easily, as if it were just an upgrade to an operating programme. Lexy 2.0, now with improved communication skills, less alcoholic intake and a nicotine patch firmly applied . . .

'I wrote letters to you and the kids,' she said weakly. 'From the detox centre. I asked you guys just to drop me a line, or send me a card . . .'

'*Lex*,' Frank sighed wearily. 'Come on, don't lie to me. This is why I'm so worried. You dropped us like a stone for a month, and now you want to walk back in as if nothing has happened – no, actually, even more than that, you want me to give you some kind of credit for having cleaned yourself up! It was so hard for us with you suddenly gone, and head-lines screaming about you having run off with *Deacon*, of all people . . . I mean, Laylah actually knows who he is! She and her friends listen to his band! Please don't try to tell me that the Swiss post just managed to fuck up sending multiple let-ters to us! Have some respect for my intelligence, eh?'

Lexy's eyebrows shot so high up her forehead that she could feel the muscles, weakened from her regular Botox injections, struggling feebly to do what was suddenly being asked of them. She realized in that moment how much had been going on in her home while she had been away. There was absolutely no way that all her letters had failed to reach Frank.

She thought of the phone messages, both to the landline and the mobile, the stream of texts she had sent him. She remembered sitting on that balcony at the Ferry Hotel, curled up on the horrible sofa, crying and waiting, unable to believe that Frank would not even pick up the phone and ring her. And she understood, with the slow, calm sensation of a loser in a chess game working out how her opponent had constructed their winning strategy to surround and conquer her troops, that none of her attempts at communi-cation had ever reached Frank.

Lexy opened her mouth to speak, and then stopped. She had seen the positioning of the final chess piece, and she had realized that it would be counter-productive to tell Frank the truth. He would not, her instincts were screaming, believe a word she said about Caroline having intercepted every attempt Lexy had made to contact her family.

And if she persisted, Lexy would simply sound paranoid and turn Frank against her. Frank would perceive her as lashing out against a sweet, innocent young woman who had helped him look after the children when Lexy had walked out on them, who had consoled him when he was lonely and certainly never rolled home drunk and randy on a regular basis after having downed a vat of Pinot Grigio with her girlfriends . . .

You're not going to beat Caroline in an argument with Frank, some small, cold part of her brain told Lexy. *She's covered her back against any direct attack. After all, who's he going to believe? You're the drunk. You're the one who went on a coke binge after you snogged the face off a boybander. While she's been swanning around your house making big eyes at Frank and pretending she enjoys plaiting Laylah's hair for hours as Laylah bangs on about whether* Barbie, Island Princess *is better than* Barbie and the Three Musketeers . . .

So, knowing all that, who's he going to believe?

Not you.

'Okay, you're right,' she said, and a sense of calm wrapped itself round her as she spoke those words, as cool and clear as the Swiss mountain air. 'You're right about everything. I *have* made it all about me. I've been doing that my entire life – just ask my mum, it's the first thing she'd say if you asked her what I was like! So yeah, it's not just stopping smoking, cutting down on drinking, is it?'

Frank, his muscular bulk silhouetted against the sky and sea behind him, shook his head slowly.

'I need to prove myself,' Lexy continued, thinking fast. 'I get that. I'd feel the same if it had been you behaving like I did. I wouldn't just let you walk back in as if nothing had happened.'

Frank rewarded this with a single nod.

'So,' Lexy said, feeling increasingly sure that she was saying exactly the right thing, making exactly the right decision. 'Here's how I should do it. I should move back to Sandbanks –'

She saw Frank flinch, but she dug her nails into her palms and carried on bravely.

'– and look after the kids myself,' she said. 'I'll sack the nanny – they're all useless anyway. I'll hole up there and spend my time being a proper mum. Cook their breakfasts and dinners, take them back and forth from school every day, the whole works.'

'But –' Frank shuffled his feet awkwardly.

'And you can move in here – with Caroline if you want,' she said, managing, through a heroic effort, to pronounce her rival's name without venom dripping from each syllable. 'I mean, I know what's been going on. I could see from the photos that you two're . . .'

She considered how to phrase this without either sounding like a raging bunny boiler or giving him and Caroline legitimacy by calling them a couple.

'. . . having sex,' she finally continued. 'I'm not stupid. I've known you for a long time, Frank. I know you two are . . . I know you two got together while I was away. I hate it, of course! Don't get me wrong. I absolutely bloody hate it.'

She held her breath, hoping that he would tell her that Caroline meant nothing to him, that he wanted to work on his marriage, that he'd never see Caroline again.

But he didn't.

'I was so lonely,' Frank mumbled to his feet. 'I don't feel okay about cheating – don't get me wrong. I broke my own rule and I'm not proud of it. It just – happened.'

Lexy dug her nails into her palms once more to stop her saying the words that were trembling on her tongue, desperate to be spoken.

Just happened, my arse, she thought bitterly. *That may be what you think, but I'm willing to bet Caroline planned the whole thing, softened you up, and picked just the right time to go in for the kill.*

Normally, Lexy would have blamed the cheating husband. He was the one who had made the vows, not his affair partner. She'd always railed against the term 'homewrecker' in her column, complaining that there were much worse words for the woman involved with a married man than for the man himself, who was the cheater in the situation; she'd often added that it was interesting that when the genders were reversed, and it was a man having an affair with a married woman, there were no offensive terms for him. 'Homewrecker' didn't sound quite right applied to a man, somehow.

But in this case, considering Lexy's own bad behaviour,

she couldn't blame Frank for falling for someone who must have waged a very clever and careful campaign to get him into bed. He had been completely destabilized, believing that Lexy had barely tried to get in touch with him, a sitting target for a woman prepared to present herself as everything Lexy was not, clever enough to have twisted him round her finger to the point that he could not bring himself to tell his wife that he would give her up.

Lexy had already forgiven Frank. She wanted him back. She wanted her life back. And if she had to let him move in here with Caroline, have them occupy the marital bed in both damn houses until she worked out how to make a brilliant counter-move, that was exactly what she'd do.

Frank had slumped back onto the sofa now, his head in his hands; she couldn't see his face, couldn't read any sense of how he was feeling. Knowing him, however, his wife was sure that the predominant sensation was guilt. This was the type of behaviour he had always vehemently opposed, and even though the circumstances were very unusual, it was the first time ever in their marriage that Frank had not occupied the moral high ground.

That bitch Caroline, Lexy thought viciously. *Look at the state of Frank! She's really done a number on him! I'm going to play her at her own game – fuck her over, just like she's done to me!*

And it wouldn't be enough revenge, Lexy realized vindictively, just to get her husband back. She wanted more. She wanted to destroy Caroline, grind her underfoot, see her reduced to nothing, sobbing in misery. A famous quote from *Conan the Barbarian* popped into her mind, Conan responding to the question: 'What is best in life?' with the answer: 'To crush your enemies, see them driven before you, and to hear the lamentation of their women.'

Lexy set her teeth. She was ready to go full Conan. She wanted Caroline crushed, driven, lamenting, a public laughing stock.

And when I get Frank back, the first thing I'm going to do is drag outside, with my bare hands, the mattresses the two of them had sex on, pour a can of petrol on each one and watch the bloody things burn to ashes.

Chapter Thirty-One

A few weeks later

'Caroline! Who are you wearing?'

'Caroline, can you give Sam a hug?'

'Caroline, are you writing another book for Lexy?'

As she answered 'Stella McCartney,' slid her arm around Sam's waist to pose with her, and smiled through the last question without responding to it, Caroline realized that she was actually getting used to this. Sam grinned at her as if they were old friends, mugging for the camera as they stood on the strip of red carpet in front of the 'step and repeat wall', a vinyl banner, tacked to a foam background, which bore the brand logos of the event and its sponsors. This afternoon, these were an obscure company promoting a new eyebrow product and a low-calorie sparkling wine launched by a terrifyingly thin American Real Housewife.

It wasn't exactly Dior or Dom Perignon at the Savoy, but for Caroline it was a tremendous step forward into the glamorous life that Lexy led on a daily basis. As soon as Caroline had come back to London, this kind of low-level, C-list invitation had rolled in, courtesy of the PR agency to which she was paying a large proportion of the advance she had got for her new novel. Publishers, it turned out, didn't do publicity for you until the book was about to come out, so, it had been gently made clear to her, if she wanted to raise her profile, she had to invest in it herself. And the more she did, they had intimated, the more her book would sell.

Naomi, her agent, had recommended a PR who worked with a lot of the rent-a-celebs who were here today. Reality stars, low-grade TV presenters, soap starlets, the troupe who could be relied on to don full make-up, new extensions, bandage dresses and five-inch Kandee heels to turn up to the opening of a crisp packet. But even with the PR working on her behalf, as a mere author Caroline would never have been invited to this kind of thing. Even if she had slipped in, there would have been zero interest in taking a single shot of her.

No, she owed her status entirely to the scandal trailing her, the fact that she was Lexy's one-time ghostwriter and now her love rival. No one knew yet that Caroline was busy writing a novel that would be a *Devil Wears Prada*-style tell-all about Lexy, certainly not Frank; her editor was pushing her to make it as scurrilous as possible, while disguising Lexy's identity just enough to make sure that she couldn't sue for libel. From the reaction of Lexy's so-called friends to Caroline, it was clear that they would lap up every last saucy detail with absolute relish.

'You look great!' Sam said to Caroline, kissing her cheek for the cameras, but careful not to actually touch her skin and risk smearing her brightly glossed fuchsia lipstick. 'How's Frank?'

'Great!' Caroline said with a big smile to show off her newly whitened teeth. 'Really good!'

Next year, will they be asking me about Frank? she wondered. *Will I be able to hang on to him if I've ripped his ex-wife to shreds in print?*

Almost certainly not, she thought ruefully. *But I got a six-figure advance for two books, and I'll get a ton of publicity for the first one. That'll be out in five months, as they're going to turn it around super fast. Plus I'm selling my Regency porn novella really successfully on Amazon already! I realized when I signed the contract that I was choosing my career over Frank, so there's no point second-guessing that choice now . . .*

'I loved your column in *Sizzle* this week!' she said brightly to Sam as they turned to walk into the cocktail bar which was hosting the launch.

Caroline was getting used to the eccentric setup of these events. They were almost always held in the late afternoon so that the venue could reopen to paying punters by six or so, not losing too much custom. The attendees spent hours dressing up to the nines, looking as if they were going to a gala dinner, putting on shoes in the taxi in which they could barely stand, let alone walk; they tottered up the strip of tatty red carpet to the step and repeat, hoping that the photographers would know who they were and want to take their picture.

After that, the job was done. You didn't even need to go into the venue. You had fulfilled the conditions of the invitation, got your face into the papers and promoted the brand that was looking for publicity by association. Many of the celebs who were most in demand did precisely this; on busy nights, they cabbed from one launch to another, collecting goodie bags as they went, then headed on to a club that would let them into the VIP area and comp them drinks in return for the draw of their presence.

Caroline was by no means at this level. She was grateful for anything offered, and had been delighted, as she got out of her taxi, to see Sam standing at the edge of the red carpet, checking her make-up in a compact mirror. Caroline had bumped into Sam at a few of these occasions before and found her surprisingly friendly, considering that she was supposed to be a friend of Lexy's.

It had been a slow process of realization that friendship, in these circles, meant mutual association for mutual benefits, rather than anything involving loyalty or trust. Right now, Lexy's frenemies were very much enjoying being seen out with Caroline, as it emphasized Lexy's fall from the pinnacle she had occupied for so long.

Caroline had waved at Sam and was promptly beckoned to her side for photos, just as she had hoped. She intended to network as much as she could at the launch, and then, ideally, attach herself to Sam's group and continue the party elsewhere. Since Sam was one of the leading lights of this social circle, allying with her and Michelle gave Caroline entrée to an extensive posse comprising a surprisingly large number of reality stars, soap actresses and footballers' wives who were ecstatic to finally sink their claws into Lexy and draw some blood.

'Hah!' Sam said, giggling as they accepted glasses of the low-calorie sparkling wine from the waiter stationed just inside the door. 'I *bet* you liked my column, eh? You owe me, girl – I made you look fantastic!'

'*Lovely hanging out with Caroline Macintosh at Mahiki last week!'* Sam had 'written'. *'Frank's new girl is a total stunner and a brainiac to boot – never thought I'd be mates with a real author! Guess what – Caroline's clever enough to write her own books, ahem ahem! Can't wait to read her novel, she says it's going to be well saucy and I believe it!'*

'I did!' Caroline said. 'I'd buy you a drink to say thanks, but oopsie, they're all free!'

She took a sip of her drink.

'Wow,' she observed, her mouth puckering up. 'It's way too sweet at first and then it goes sour afterwards. Like one of those new double-flavour Tic-Tacs.'

Sam giggled again.

'You're so funny,' she said. 'Oh look, there's Michelle, she said she'd be coming along . . .'

Michelle, new hair extensions hanging down to her waist, her heels so high they forced her bottom into a back-arching tilt upwards to enable her to maintain her balance, made her way carefully across the polished floor towards them.

'Hey!' she said, eyes artificially bright, her speech pouring out very quickly. 'Anyone know what the fuck this one's for? It's my third tonight and I've got no fucking idea what the product is!'

'This wine, and the eyebrow stuff,' Caroline said. 'It's supposed to fill in the gaps and stay on for ages. That's what it said on the invite, anyway.'

'Ooh, that sounds good,' Michelle said. 'Bagsie a goodie bag! Thanks, Writer Girl. Trust you to actually read the crap they send us. How're you doing?'

'Brilliant!' Caroline said, faux-kissing her cheek.

'How's Frank?' Michelle gushed. 'God, he's a hottie, lucky you! Lexy must be going mad stuck down in the sticks with the kids while you get to shag Frank's brains out and go out on the town!'

Caroline flashed a huge and entirely genuine smile; this statement summed up exactly how she felt about the situation.

'He's great,' she said. 'Just not much of a partygoer.'

'No, he never was,' Sam said wistfully. 'Not like my Ryan, the fucker. Out on the lash all the time and up to all sorts of crap. I'm just like, make sure they're over eighteen, for fuck's sake, you know? And not so pissed they start snoring while you're doing them, either, and then say they didn't know what they were doing when they went back to your hotel room, the slags. Because they're really strict about that nowadays, aren't they? And I don't fancy having to dress up like a fucking schoolteacher with a *Daily Mail* sadface for your trial, know what I mean?'

Sam had very recently started seeing Ryan Banks, the goalie for Kensington, who was famously promiscuous and undiscriminating. She was right to be worried on both counts. The relationship was something of a convenient arrangement, as Ryan wanted a girlfriend to improve his playboy reputation, but had barely slowed down the pace with which he tore through girls he met clubbing.

'I mean, it's not like we're married and I can divorce him for a ton of dosh if he gets done for letting some fifteen-year-old tart suck him off, is it?' Sam continued in the characteristically loud and unselfconscious tone of a woman who has already snorted half a gram of coke that evening.

'Hey, you'd get a nice juicy wodge for standing by him,' Michelle pointed out. She lowered her voice. 'Chantelle got half a mil last year for that, did you know? She played it really well – banged on about being really upset and embarrassed and everything when her Darrell got arrested for grooming, said she was going to leave him. His lawyers went ballistic and said it'd look terrible in the media if she did that. So she cried a lot and then said oh no, I couldn't possibly, and finally he went okay, what's it worth to you? She turned up every day, all classy looking, hair done like she was going to church, and he still got four years for sexual activity with a minor. Paid that half a mil for nothing.'

Caroline was greedily absorbing all these juicy details for a future novel. Michelle, who, for all her laboriously cultivated ditzy blonde appearance, was sharp as a whip, tittered: 'Ooh, look at Writer Girl, Sam! Careful, that'll all end up in one of her books!'

'Just as long as you change the details,' Sam said, winking.

'Actually, Darrell was up on more charges, wasn't he?' Caroline said, remembering the much-publicized case. 'I think he got let off some of them. So maybe it was worth the money after all . . .'

'Ladies, hi!' said a very glossy young man, approaching their gossip huddle with a big smile. 'Have any of you tried Browfinity yet? Or Browtastic? We have a beauty station all set up in the back and we'd *love* one of our fantastic technicians to give you all totally complimentary eyebrow makeovers – or, as we like to call it, Browkover!'

'Yeah, let me stop you there, mate,' said the uninhibited

Sam. 'That is *never* going to catch on. Sounds like you just threw up over yourself, dunnit?'

'The thing is,' Michelle confided in Caroline several hours later, sitting at the very same rooftop table in the Camden Club that she, Lexy and Sam had occupied several weeks ago, 'no one likes Lexy. She acts like she's better than everyone else.'

Um, she sort of is, Caroline thought, even as Sam nodded in agreement with Michelle, the carefully sculpted curls of her weave bouncing on her shoulders. *Lexy's got the top reality show in the country, she makes way more money than any of you from her products and endorsements, and now I'm dating her husband she's all set with a great storyline for the next season of the show.*

It was ironic that she, Lexy's greatest enemy, was able to acknowledge Lexy's superiority, while Michelle and Sam could not.

'I bet she was a nightmare when you were writing her book,' Sam said.

'Ahem, I could confirm that, but then I'd have to kill you!' Caroline said, grinning. 'Officially, I was helping her do her research, get her dates right, that sort of thing.'

She executed a large comedy wink.

'But yeah, safe to say that during that process it could not have been more about her all the time,' she went on. 'And it wasn't just me who feels like that. Lexy's the big bright shining sun and Frank, the kids, the staff – we're all just little planets circling in her orbit.'

'Get you, Writer Girl!' Michelle said admiringly. 'I'm not actually going to read Lexy's book that you didn't write –'

She did a wink back at Caroline.

'–'cause I don't have the time to read books, what with being really busy doing, um, stuff. But I bet it's well classy from the way you talk.'

The description of Lexy as a sun with strong gravitational pull was a line Caroline had come up with just that morning, as she knocked out her daily five thousand words of her novel. It was to be called *Bad Girl*: her editor had said that anything with 'Girl' in the title was bound to sell well.

'You must be really disciplined,' Sam said admiringly. 'I don't know how writers do it. Where do you get your ideas from?'

'I don't get paid if I don't deliver my book,' Caroline said, unaware that she was answering questions that writers have been asked since the dawn of time. 'And the ideas thing – I don't know, really. Things just pop into my head. I read a ton of magazines and gossip sites, and the way people act in real life is crazier than anything you could put in a novel.'

This was quite true. Outlining her first novel, Caroline had realized that she could not put in many stories which, as they said in the reruns of *Law and Order* she watched on breaks from writing, were 'ripped from the headlines': her book would have careened from one exaggerated setup to the next. Her editor had made the point that the Lexy character, for instance, could not be an out-and-out villain with no redeeming qualities at all – that would look too crude and cartoonish. She had at least to be as talented, quick-witted and charming as her real-life inspiration, capable of attracting the legions of fans that Lexy had, or it simply wouldn't be plausible.

'I'm not supposed to tell anyone, so don't pass it on,' Caroline continued, a phrase that had Sam and Michelle leaning in to listen with avid attention, 'but the book's about Lexy. Like a tell-all, but a novel, so—'

'So she can't sue you!' Michelle said quickly. 'Ooh, what fun!'

'I heard that *The Devil Wears Prada* was supposed to be a memoir originally,' Caroline said, 'but then they told her to write it as fiction.'

'OMG, I can't *wait* for the book to come out! I might even read that one!' Michelle said eagerly. 'I mean, you know, like, *shitloads* of dirt on her!'

She shot a knowing glance at Sam.

'I was wondering if Caroline might like to meet Dorinda,' she said faux-casually. 'What do you think?'

Caroline had apparently gained full access to the most exclusive of inner circles. 'Meeting Dorinda', it turned out, was Sam and Michelle's private code for doing cocaine, based on an obscure character from a childhood cartoon who'd had a habit of rubbing her nose a lot and sniffing. Caroline had barely done coke before; apart from anything else, at seventy-five pounds a gram, she simply couldn't have afforded it. Ecstacy, weed and ketamine were much more within the price range of struggling young professionals crammed into a dilapidated house share in Edmonton.

As it turned out, a liking for coke was something else that Caroline had in common with Lexy, as well as vaulting ambition, a love of the limelight and a strong attraction to Frank. Sam and Michelle were highly amused by how eagerly she took to it, so much so that she even proposed getting another gram in at her own expense. They were dubious at first, because Sam's guy would not deliver to an address in W1 that wasn't a private home, because of the CCTV that was everywhere in the heart of London: but then Michelle spotted a contact across the bar, the tattooed Eastern European boyfriend of a girl she knew, and they were able to do a deal on the smoking terrace of the club, which was notoriously dark and therefore ideal for this kind of thing.

In fact, the presumption among Camden Club members was that the terrace was kept as crepuscular as possible precisely to facilitate exchanges of folded bills in return for small packets. Although there were posted rules in the toilets warning that the club had a zero-tolerance policy for drug-taking, no one even flickered an eyebrow at the sight of two people going into a single cubicle, and the smooth marble covers of the cisterns might have been designed expressly to provide its clientele with an ideal surface for cutting lines.

Just as Lexy had done before her, Caroline found time suddenly compressing, as if it had folded over, jumping three hours ahead in what felt like the span of barely thirty minutes. When the bar manager presented their table with the bill, an apologetic smile on her face as she explained that the club was closing, she was horrified to realize how late it was, and, looking at her phone, she saw, to her panic, several increasingly worried texts from Frank.

'You've got sleeping pills, yeah?' Sam asked Caroline.

On hearing the answer no, Sam looked taken aback and slipped Caroline a Valium.

'Take it now,' Sam said kindly. 'And I'd put a towel on your pillow tonight, yeah? You might bleed just a little bit from your nose.'

Caroline was able to make it back into the apartment, but only because she had changed out of her high heels and into her fold-up ballet flats in the members' club. If she hadn't had the sense to do that, her legs would have buckled underneath her – as Michelle's did spectacularly, tumbling her into the cab over her Kandee spikes. Caroline was wobbly, but still buzzing, when she sneaked back into the Chelsea Harbour flat, and even when the Valium kicked in, it had barely any calming counter-effect after all the coke and the copious espresso martinis she had put away.

Frank stirred in the master bedroom, hearing the front door close.

'Lex?' he called out from the depths of sleep. 'That you?'

Caroline's jaw set in fury.

'Yes!' she whispered back, not wanting him to wake up and realize that his girlfriend was coming back at three a.m. in just the same state, after just the same kind of evening, as his wife had so often done. Hopefully this way he would think it was a dream. 'Be in bed soon!'

She heard a mumble, a grunt, as he turned over and sunk into unconsciousness again. How was she possibly going to join him in bed, though? Her brain was still racing, her teeth chattering, and not with cold. She felt a thousand miles from being able to fall asleep. If only Sam had had a sleeping pill as well!

Wait, thinking about sleeping pills – Lexy was bound to have them, wasn't she? According to Frank she had done this kind of thing very often, come home buzzing and high. Surely Lexy must have a stash?

Sneaking on stockinged feet through the master bedroom into the ensuite, Caroline shut the door before turning on the lights around the sink, in an attempt not to wake Frank again. She checked out the contents of the medicine shelf. What would send her to sleep? She couldn't risk getting it wrong, and she hadn't brought her phone into the bathroom to Google which was which . . .

Eventually she found codeine, and swallowed two with water gulped from the tap. Raising her head again, she saw with horror that a bead of blood was issuing from her nostril, just as Sam had warned her. Her reflection looked mad: wild-eyed, her eye make-up smudged, her pupils visibly dilated. If Frank woke up and came into the bathroom, he would know at once what she had been doing. Frantically, she grabbed a tissue from the Blomus stainless-steel tissue box (which had cost, Lexy had boasted, seventy pounds) and shoved it up her nostril, wadding it up there to hopefully soak up all the blood.

She had wanted this, Caroline thought ruefully. She had wanted exactly this: to be like Lexy, to lead her wild life, to hang out with her glamorous friends, to see people looking over at their table, gossiping about her as she passed on her way to the toilet to do coke with Michelle or Sam, to be namechecked in the gossip magazines and the *Daily Mail* sidebar, people knowing who she was with just a few words to clue them in. 'The one who ghosted the book for Lexy'; 'the one who stole Lexy's husband', 'Frank Callis's new girlfriend' – 'Oh, *that* Caroline!'

Well, 'that Caroline' had a spinning head, a bleeding nose, and was dizzy and weak. She was desperate for sleep that still felt very far away, and she did not feel remotely glamorous. She had spent the evening talking a load of nonsense to two women she didn't even like, who would stab her in the back the instant she turned around if it suited them to do so.

For all she knew, she might have given them plenty of ammunition – or daggers – during those last coke-fuelled hours. Even before that, she had spilled about her novel being a thinly veiled satire of all Lexy's scandalous behaviour! Thank God she hadn't got off her face enough to tell them about the deal Lexy had made with Silantra. She was putting that in the book, of course, but disguising it so thoroughly that Silantra would not be identifiable, as no one wanted to risk her wrath or that of her equally powerful husband.

A wave of exhaustion flooded Caroline, tiredness and nerves. Maybe the codeine and the Valium were interacting, finally balancing out the jitters. She took off her make-up, washed her face, and padded back through the bedroom into the spare room next door, in her hand the darkest towel in the flat, a medium grey one. Placing the towel on the pillow – she didn't trust herself in bed next to Frank right now, not if her nose continued to bleed – she lay down on the bed, staring at the ceiling.

So this was the downside to being Lexy. Caroline's heart was racing crazily, her body twitching, her brain teeming with doubts about what she had confided in Sam and Michelle, what might appear in their columns or be spread on the grapevine. It was the classic three or four a.m. wakeup, when your eyes snap open and you run through, in pitiless detail, all the stupid things you did that evening. But this time, she hadn't even gone to sleep; she'd had no rest at all.

She lay there for an hour or so, the insecurity plus the coke withdrawal becoming ever more difficult to bear. Finally she got up, slipped down the darkened corridor in the kitchen and poured herself a glass of brandy, forcing it down as she stood there in the faint glimmer of moonlight. It was disgusting, but it worked, the alcohol enough to tip her over the edge; she could feel sleep finally reaching out for her with soft, gentle tendrils. Rinsing out the tumbler, she padded back towards the bedroom, and slipped between the sheets with Frank. There had been no blood on the towel; she had checked it carefully. Hopefully she would be fine.

So, would she have to get used to this if she wanted to hang out with Sam, Michelle and their crew again? Yes, was the answer. She'd plan it better, though. Get herself a prescription for Valium, and one for sleeping pills: she could tell the doctor she had travel anxiety, problems with jetlag. Stop doing coke at midnight, rather than right up to the time they had to go, so she started to wind down; leave earlier, so Frank didn't get pissed off at her rolling in at three in the morning.

And with those resolutions running through her mind, quite unaware that Lexy had made both of them before her and completely failed to keep either one, Caroline finally fell asleep.

Chapter Thirty-Two

'Mummy, *no*! You put green beans in my lunchbox *again*! You *know* it's London that likes them and I hate hate hate *hate them*!'

'I can eat them—' London started helpfully.

'*Noo!*' Laylah screamed. 'They've *touched* my pasta now! It's all disgusting and ruined!'

Lexy's head was throbbing. She didn't think she would ever get used to getting up this early. Her natural sleep schedule was bedtime between one and two, rising at ten. With a full-time nanny, she had always been able to maintain that very easily; everyone knew that the children were not to be allowed into Lexy's bedroom before then. Mummy needed her beauty sleep.

Even after a few weeks of taking care of the children on her own, Lexy still hadn't got used to Laylah waking up at the crack of dawn. London slept in longer, clearly taking after Lexy in that respect, but Laylah's eyes snapped open at six a.m. and, little attention-seeker that she was, she required adult company the moment she was awake. When Lexy had realized this, she had very reprehensibly tried keeping Laylah up beyond her bedtime to tire her out. But no amount of watching TV with her mother till late, it turned out, had stopped Laylah from climbing out of bed at six every morning and making her way downstairs to find Lexy. No bribes or pleading could persuade her to stay in her own lavishly appointed bedroom; she was like a battering ram in human form. Nothing could stop her.

The first solution Lexy had tried was to allow Laylah to crawl into Lexy's bed, bringing her tablet with her, and watch episodes of *Dance Moms* with her headphones on in the semi-darkness as Lexy slowly woke up. Gradually, however, it had been impossible for Lexy to remain unconscious with Laylah fidgeting next to her, and the buzz of the music and the screeches of Abby Lee Miller, the near-psychopathic dance coach, had permeated through the ear buds. She had found herself sitting up in bed, pulling off her eye mask, and leaning over to watch what was screening on Laylah's tablet, gradually intrigued by the show, asking why Chloe was crying, if Maddy had ended up kissing Gino, whether poor, put-upon Nia had ever got a solo . . .

Finding a shared interest in the show with her daughter had allowed Lexy to evolve an even better compromise. Laylah agreed to stay in her room until six thirty, giving Lexy a much-needed extra half-hour of sleep. But then she was authorized to patter downstairs and turn on the big TV in Lexy and Frank's bedroom, loading the next episode of *Dance Moms* from the TiVo: there was always a next episode. Lexy had shown Laylah how to look things up on Wikipedia, and the expression of sheer bliss on Laylah's face when she had discovered there were over two hundred episodes had made her mother hoot with laughter.

So the door handle would turn, little feet in Minnie Mouse slippers would patter across the floor, little fingers would turn on the TV and snatch up the remote, and a small warm body would snuggle beneath the duvet, panting comically with excitement at watching her favourite show on the big screen in the company of her mother. Not a bored and yawning nanny who was constantly messaging her boyfriend, not even Caroline, but her actual mother, who was genuinely interested in her favourite show. This was the best part of Laylah's whole day.

Lexy would stir as the familiar intro played, Laylah gleefully chanting the theme, '*Living on the dance FLOOR!*' This was Lexy's cue to prise her eyes open, pushing the pillows up the headboard, sitting up against them, pulling her daughter into her arms as they watched the episode together.

When it finished, Lexy would head for the shower, much as she hated the shock of water hitting her in the early morning. She had quickly learned that if she took the children to London's Montessori and Laylah's private school without being fully groomed, the judgement from her fellow mothers would be unbearable. It was bad enough facing them in the aftermath of the scandal. Lexy had known, of course, that this would be part of her punishment, the Via Dolorosa she would have to walk in order to redeem herself in Frank's eyes, demonstrating how repentant she was.

Even the foreign nannies had known who Lexy was immediately. She was that famous, or possibly notorious. The first morning she appeared around the corner of the street where London's Montessori was situated, holding London and Laylah's hands, the gasps, immediately followed by excited whispering, had been clearly audible. No one had expected to see her, and her appearance instantly gave rise to a stream of speculation and criticism, as she was dressed down in tracksuit bottoms and a loose sweater, her hair pulled back into a straggly, unbrushed ponytail, trainers on her feet.

It could have been even worse. Having often sneered in her column at newspaper reports of women who dropped their kids off at school wearing pyjamas, Lexy had almost, that morning, done exactly that. She had been completely unprepared for what a gruelling effort it was to get Laylah and London clothed and fed, faces washed, teeth brushed, lunchboxes packed: it had been such an excruciating time-suck that she had barely even managed to brush her teeth. She had not realized that she needed to get herself washed, dressed and groomed before she started on the children, and it had only been when she was about to leave the house with them, and the kids had started howling with laughter and pointing at her, that she had realized though they were appropriately clad from head to toe, she was still in her La Perla silk nightshirt and slippers.

'The other mummies are all smarter than you,' Laylah had pointed out devastatingly as they approached the group of exquisitely turned out, extremely wealthy Sandbanks mothers who were clustered in a group by the gates taking prime position, as befitted their status; the nannies were segregated further down the street.

'Just be glad I'm not in my nightie,' Lexy had snapped back, only for her snarky daughter to retort:

'Your nightie's *much* nicer than what you're wearing now,

Mummy! At least it's pretty and silky. And it doesn't have egg on it.'

Lexy would not be making scrambled eggs for breakfast for the kids ever again. They had flatly refused to touch them, and, after having run upstairs to change, she had realized she was starving, and dashed into the kitchen to fork some of the curds into her mouth, desperate to get some protein down her before leaving the house. The trouble with big, high, fake boobs, however, was that they formed a shelf which was perfectly positioned to catch anything that fell from your mouth if you were eating carelessly. She hadn't had time to go upstairs for another top, and thought she'd managed to dab the stain away. Looking down, however, she grimaced. Laylah was right, there was still some yellow egg caught on her right breast.

She flicked it off, but she was sure that some eagle eyes had already spotted it. The stares of the women she was approaching were so greedy for gossip, so ready to tear her down, that she was vividly reminded of the scene in *Game of Thrones* where Queen Cersei was forced to do a walk of shame through King's Landing to atone for having had an affair during her marriage. Lexy wasn't naked or being pelted with filth by the bystanders – *I took care of that myself,* she thought ironically, *threw egg down my own front* – but she was certainly humbled without her usual faceful of make-up, her ears, throat and hands sparkling with showy jewellery, five-inch heels on her feet.

In fact, she realized, looking from one group to the other, she did not resemble a mother at all, but one of the nannies. In an unspoken but very clear job requirement, the employees were required to appear much more dowdy than the lady of the house. The mothers, by contrast, were as chic and sleek as if they were about to head out to lunch at The Cliff, the smartest restaurant in Sandbanks, high on the Canford Cliffs; the village there was stocked with boutiques and cafes for the yummy mummies whose houses in the prized BH13 postcode were worth several million each.

Amusingly, Canford Cliffs was so rich that it had become infamous in 2007 for the decision of its local HSBC branch to offer what it called a 'premium' service only. Although the outside cashpoints were free to use, no clients were allowed to maintain an account there unless they had savings of fifty thousand pounds and a mortgage of two hundred thousand pounds, or alternatively a salary of a hundred thousand and a mortgage of seventy-five. There was an exception; if you were prepared to pay twenty pounds a month for the privilege, you could still bank there.

The vicar, the ex-mayor of Poole and campaigners for the elderly had all protested, to no avail. The richer locals, naturally, had loved the prestige and the publicity: it had been the only Premier branch in the whole of the country, something about which the account holders had boasted incessantly. The branch had closed down in 2015, but the Sandbanks and Canford Cliffs residents could still pride themselves on living in one of the richest areas in the world, where Lamborghinis and Bentleys were as common as Minis and BMWs.

And every single woman in that cluster by the school gates was living proof of their high net worth. Their hair was streaked and blown dry, their faces and nails perfect, their bodies slimmed down through vigorous exercise and meticulous dieting. Many of them had risen at six to work out in their private gyms, shower and do their hair before the school drop-off; every one of them employed a nanny for the grunt work of getting their children up and dressed and fed. They met their offspring at the front door for the first time that morning, ready for the short walk to school where they would socialize with their clique, show off their latest clothes purchases and catch up on gossip.

Lexy's egg-stained arrival was manna from heaven, gossip overload. The mothers cast swift glances at her, taking in every detail of her scruffy, unkempt appearance, their expressions a mixture of pity and contempt; the nannies, further away, stared openly, less constrained by social mores.

'Rigby! Blue!' London dropped his mother's hand, shooting off to join two of his friends, who were swinging from the gates. Deliberately unusual names were par for the course at his daycare: none of the parents seemed to have realized that calling a child John or Susan would, in this social circle, have been refreshingly original.

'Well, that's London dropped off,' Lexy said gamely, looking down at Laylah. 'Shall we go on to your school straight away, or do you two wave each other goodbye or something?'

Laylah snorted.

'As *if*,' she said precociously. 'That's for babies. Let's go, Mummy. But you should try to get that egg stain off your sweater before we get there. Did you bring any water? Those mummies are all staring at your front and it's *really* embarrassing me!'

* * *

Now, a few weeks after that disastrous first morning, Lexy had become an efficient parental machine, groomed to a high enough standard to pass muster with even the sleekest of Sandbanks mothers. If that sounded robotic, it was exactly how she felt. It was a discipline, a routine she had learned to embrace. Once you had worked out, through trial and error, the timetables and structures that allowed you to best manage the children from morning till night, you just had to keep on repeating them. You didn't try to reinvent the wheel. And you kept reminding yourself that it wasn't about you: it was about the children.

The children, who had very differing views on whether green beans were absolutely delicious, or invented by the Devil strictly to torment them . . .

'I don't have time to make more pasta for you, Laylah!' she said now, a headache starting to form behind her eyes. 'You'll have to eat this. I've taken the beans off and put them in your brother's lunchbox instead—'

'No, no, *no!*' Laylah shrieked, and she did something she had not done for years; she actually threw herself to the tiled floor and beat it with her fists, sobbing hysterically. London, sitting at the kitchen table finishing his cereal, giggled in delight.

'She is *cwazy*,' he said gleefully. 'Carmen says she's cwazy and she's right. Carmen's always right.'

'Shut *up!*' Laylah yelled from the floor. 'Shut *up*, I hate you, I *hate* you, it's all your fault because you like stupid nasty beans, if you didn't Mummy wouldn't *make* them, I *hate* you . . .'

These were the moments that made Lexy feel utterly

abandoned and alone. But that had been the deal all along, hadn't it? She was supposed to be a single mother, plunged in at the deep end, learning as she went. Being lonely, struggling with all the multifarious tasks there were to do, many that she hadn't even realized existed before now; not just keeping them fed and clean, but trying to bring them up right, to set them a good example . . .

'Caroline knows I hate green beans!' Laylah was screeching now, upping the stakes into near-hysteria. '*Caroline* never makes me eat things that touched them! *I want Caroline!*'

It wasn't the first time, of course, that Caroline had been mentioned by the children. Frank had clearly been discreet enough for them not to realize that he had been carrying on an affair with her during Lexy's absence, for which Lexy was truly thankful, as it meant that he was not entirely committed to breaking up their marriage, to leaving Lexy for Caroline. Even now, the children had simply been told that Daddy was working in London, and that Caroline had gone back home now that Mummy was here to take care of the children herself. Frankly, Gabriela had made so little an impression that there had been no need to explain why there was no longer a nanny working for the family.

But Caroline was missed. The children asked after her repeatedly: why she had gone, when she was coming back, why Lexy couldn't do things the way Caroline did, play games in the same way Caroline had done . . .

Staring down at Laylah writhing on the kitchen floor, hearing her daughter yell for the woman who was currently sleeping with her husband, Lexy felt the tears welling up in her eyes. There was a lump in her throat as big as a golf ball.

With every scrap of willpower she had, she forced herself to blink hard, to banish any signs of upset at Caroline's name. If Laylah knew that she could use it to manipulate her mother into giving her what she wanted, it would never end. Laylah was as smart as a whip; it was dangerous to give her any advantage at all.

Frustrated at Lexy's lack of response, Laylah, little madam that she was, upped the stakes to the ultimate code red level.

'And I hate *you*, Mummy!' she yelled. 'I hate you for being so mean and nasty! I want you to go away so Caroline comes back and makes my lunch!'

London looked horrified, his eyes going wide, his jaw dropping comically in the way of little children, who will actually open their mouths into an O of shock. He stared down at his sister, exclaiming: '*Naughty* Laylah! Mummy, tell her she's naughty!'

Lexy took a long, deep breath and thought harder, faster, than she ever had in her life. This was an even bigger challenge than those crucial minutes on *Who's My Date?* when she had known that her witty, pert, unscripted responses to the presenter and the suitors on the show were catching fire with the audience, hearing the laughter and applause, using them to power her on to even greater heights, grabbing at a chance at fame and fortune with everything she had. The words currently trembling on her tongue were just as mean and nasty as her daughter had just told her she was; it took everything she had not to scream back at her that at that moment, she hated Laylah too . . .

'You look like you've been crying,' said a quiet voice at Lexy's shoulder as she watched Laylah, who had completely forgotten her earlier temper tantrum, running off into the school grounds with not a glance back at her mother, her blonde curls bouncing on her shoulders, the lunchbox dangling from her hand.

It still contained the pasta that had touched the despised green beans, but also, to Lexy's shame, two Guylian chocolates in the shape of sea shells, which were Laylah's absolutely, entirely preferred treat: for 'shells', she would do almost anything, including eat contaminated pasta. Lexy was trying very hard not to bribe the children, and she also knew that the school forbade chocolates in lunchboxes, but sometimes you had to forget your principles. She had wrapped the chocolates tightly in silver foil and put a pack of tissues into the lunch box, instructing Laylah not to eat them first, not to let anyone see them and to wipe her hands well afterwards. She knew, of course, that Laylah wouldn't obey the first command, but she was crossing her fingers that she'd follow the latter ones.

Surprised, Lexy turned to look at the woman who had spoken to her. She knew her face by now, of course, but she wasn't one of the mothers of children with whom London and Laylah were friends, with whom Lexy regularly organized playdates. These women were without exception distant and polite, maintaining constant small smiles which, Lexy was perfectly aware, were intended to demonstrate that behind them they had nothing but pity and distaste for Lexy's unfortunate marital situation.

This one, however, was not wearing the V-shaped, disapproving smile with which Lexy was so familiar. She looked, as far as Lexy could tell, genuinely sympathetic. And she was not one of the highly groomed mummy clique which took pole position right next to the school gates; the ones who drove black Land Rover Evoques and Porsche Macans with seats so high, they and their children had to clamber up into them as if they were mountaineering, who wore J Brand jeans and Muubaa fitted shearling jackets and carried Celine bags. This one was much more county in her Boden print dress and Monsoon coat, her skin starting to show signs of sun exposure, her blonde hair cut into a sensible layered bob rather than slicked back into a perfect ponytail.

'I'm Sophie,' she said, holding out her hand to Lexy. 'Sophie Billingham-Waites.'

'Lexy O'Brien,' Lexy said in return, shaking her hand, feeling disoriented. After weeks of being snubbed, this was the first time a mother had bothered to approach her and introduce herself, and the posh voice, formal manner and quiet poise of Sophie Double-Barrel were intimidating for a reality TV star who did not, unlike Sophie, sound as if she regularly had tea with the Queen.

'Tough morning with the kids?' Sophie asked, and despite the cut-glass accent, her gaze was so friendly that Lexy heard herself blurt out, the tears welling up again:

'Laylah said she hated me at breakfast.'

'Oh dear,' Sophie Double-Barrel said very sympathetically. 'They all do it, I'm afraid. What did you say back? That's the really important bit.'

'I said I knew she didn't mean it,' Lexy said, swallowing hard. 'And that I loved her very much and she was making me sad.'

'Oh, well done you!' Sophie said with great sincerity. 'Very good job!'

It was like a head girl at school, even the headmistress herself, giving her a nod of approval. Lexy felt suddenly as if she were Laylah's age, a surge of relief rising in her as a person in a position of authority told her that she had done the right thing. It was so unexpectedly powerful that the tears filled her eyes now, blurring her vision.

'Stiff upper lip!' Sophie said briskly, and she took hold of Lexy's upper arm, swivelling her around ninety degrees so that Lexy's back was to the school gates and the gossiping mothers. 'Never let them see you cry! Deep breaths, one – two – three. Good girl. Now fake a sneeze and get those eyes wiped as you do it. Here's a tissue.'

Obediently, Lexy obeyed.

'You know you're a mother when you always have plenty of Kleenex to hand,' Sophie said cheerfully. 'Mummy always did. And one day, after the twins were born, I reached down into my handbag and there was a full pack inside and one already open, and I thought: Oh, here I am! I've turned into Mummy, just like I knew I would!'

'I've got to get more tissues, clearly,' Lexy said, blowing her nose and managing a watery smile.

'Buy 'em in bulk,' Sophie advised. 'Then put a pack into every handbag you have.'

'I will,' Lexy said, crumpling up the damp tissue. 'And thank you. Sorry I went off like that.'

'Oh, it's fine,' Sophie said. 'I could see you were having a moment. I've been watching you these last few weeks, of course, everyone has. I think you've done jolly well, considering. You're always on time for drop-off and pickup, the kids look washed and fed and happy and behave nicely on playdates. Apparently their lunches are home-made and you don't give them fizzy drinks full of additives. You've pulled yourself together and come home to look after them. Good for you.'

Sophie rolled her eyes.

'That little madam who's trying to take your place was working *very* hard on it, you know. Butter wouldn't melt. I didn't like her, I can tell you. I could see she was playing a part. So when I saw you looking very down today, I thought you might need a bit of bucking up.'

Lexy nodded, even as she processed in shock the sheer amount of information that the mothers' network held on its unsuspecting members.

'Yeah,' she said. 'I worked out what she was like eventually – took me ages, though.'

'Better late than never, eh?' Sophie said encouragingly. 'And you're doing *exactly* the right thing now.'

'Thank you,' Lexy managed gruffly, ducking her head, worried that this kindness from a total stranger would set her off all over again.

'I was going to say shall we go for a coffee on Canford Cliffs,' Sophie said, 'but you're in no state for that, are you? Would you like to come back to mine?'

Lexy nodded gratefully. It was a humbling realization, as she followed Sophie around the corner to an old, dented Volvo which spoke as eloquently about her social class as the shiny new Evoques did of the yummie mummies', that she had never really had a female friend who would have her back in a crisis. The Sams and Michelles would never have told Lexy not to cry; instead, they would have gleefully relished the drama, inserted themselves into it by hugging and comforting her to make clear that their role was the confidante, then spread the story to everyone they knew.

This brisk, supportive woman was like nothing Lexy had ever known before. Small, plump and utterly confident, she looked to be in her early thirties, younger than Lexy herself, which was ironic considering her maternal aura.

'So!' Sophie said as she clicked shut her own seatbelt and automatically glanced sideways to make sure Lexy's was fastened too. 'Now you've proved your good-mummy credentials by doing full immersion in the ghastliness of bringing up your own children, I assume you have a plan for getting your husband back?'

'Fuck, you're direct!' Lexy said; she was gradually getting her mojo back after the stress of the morning. 'Are you always like this?'

She wasn't sure how Sophie Double-Barrel would deal with the swear word, but Sophie grinned as she started up the car.

'Always,' she said cheerfully. 'I come from a military family and I married into one. We're all terrifyingly direct and practical. I like fixing things. I'll freely admit I see you as a bit of a project.'

'Plus,' Lexy said, back to normal now that she was in a safe space, a car where even if she started to cry again, no one would see her and judge her, 'I bet you want to piss off those yummy mummies too. They were having such a good time sending me to Coventry, and now you've messed with them by talking to me.'

Sophie's grin deepened.

'There's a bit of that as well,' she said. 'I was getting rather sick of watching you be shut out like that. I wasn't really sure about whether I wanted to get involved, but seeing you today looking like death warmed up made me want to cheer you up a bit.'

'I'm really glad you did,' Lexy said very gratefully. 'And to answer your question, no, I don't have a plan for getting Frank back, not yet. I thought I'd go mental if I tried to think about that straight away. I've been concentrating on teaching myself to cook for the kids, working out, doing my sobriety journal—'

'Good Lord,' Sophie muttered at this.

'But now, I'm ready to go for it,' Lexy continued.

A bus came towards them, heading for the ferry, an advert for an upcoming reality series plastered over its entire side.

'And you know what?' Lexy said slowly, staring at it. 'I just got a really good idea for how to manage that . . .'

Chapter Thirty-Three

A month later

'Hello, contestants! Welcome to *Celebrity Island Survivor!*' Dan, one of the pair of hosts who helmed the show, yodelled in the most cheerful voice possible.

'Blue Team, looking *great* in those bandannas!' chimed in Pip, Dan's brother, who was the other host. '*Love* what you've done with them!'

Dan and Pip, barely in their early thirties, were unquestionably the most successful TV presenters in the country. Non-identical fraternal twins, they had been infant prodigies, doing stand-up comedy as a double act, and now regularly presented two of the country's most famous live TV programmes as well as hosting their own chat show. Dan was straight, and a well-known man about town, while Pip was gay and happily married. They had an answer for everything and had the confidence of siblings who knew each other perfectly: nothing could faze them.

Caroline simply could not believe that she was standing here, in a group of C-list celebrities, taking part in a ritual that she had watched year after year, never missing an episode. The smiling faces of Dan and Pip were so familiar to her that they might have been part of her family. She looked down at herself, wearing the blue T-shirt with the show's logo on it, and shook her head momentarily in disbelief. Since meeting Lexy, her life had progressed in leaps and bounds so dizzying that it was as if she were wearing rocket-propelled shoes; but this was by far the highest jump into the stratosphere, up where the air was rarefied, even more dizzying than seducing Frank.

That, after all, had been a private triumph. This was a public one. And by now, Caroline had learned how much she loved publicity.

The odds of her becoming a cast member had been hugely stacked against her. For the last couple of weeks, she had kept telling herself that it would never happen, in order to protect herself against the sick, crippling disappointment that she knew would overcome her when she sat on her sofa watching the opening credits of *Celebrity Island Survivor*, rather than being in them. It had been down to the wire, almost an overnight decision. When another, much more famous contestant dropped out at the last minute, Caroline had had barely a day's notice that she, one of the backups, was being summoned to take her place.

She had burst into tears when the call had come, sobbed aloud, been unable to utter an actual word for a couple of minutes. Thank God it had not been a producer but her TV agent ringing her with the news, almost as excited as she was, though less teary: he had emphasized from the start that though it was amazing that Caroline was considered newsworthy enough to even be considered as a contestant, nothing was certain, even if she passed the psychological tests.

Those tests! The psychologists had given nothing away, had been friendly but perfectly neutral even when asking the most personal of questions about her family, her upbringing, her ambitions, her sex life. Caroline hadn't even been sure if she was supposed to answer everything they asked. She had begun to wonder whether this itself was a test. Were they checking to see if she would overshare so much that it meant she had no boundaries, did not have enough self-control to stick it out in the stress of the jungle island environment?

So she had started to politely demur at the most invasive questions, saying she preferred not to answer them, and had noticed that they did not press her further. She hadn't been able to tell how well she'd done, but she had trusted her instincts, which, after all, had guided her through her tortuous journey of writing Lexy's book while, at the same time, successfully making herself over and undermining Lexy with her husband.

And clearly, once again, those instincts had served Caroline well. She had been told that she was to keep herself available, making sure she was contactable at all times, her phone charged and accessible. Apparently the majority of the drop-outs happened at the last minute, as the full reality of the deprivation and humiliation for which they had signed up started to dawn on the more pampered and neurotic celebrities.

Ever since her agent had first informed her she was being considered for the show, Caroline had been on the strictest of lockdown diets, just in case. She had dropped several pounds, enabling her to get into a one-piece swimsuit with sexy cutaways and a 50s-style bikini that showcased her breasts very successfully, while the high bottom held in her stomach. No matter how slim she was, she knew that if she did get picked for the show, she would be cast with glamour models and reality stars in string bikinis, whose fake boobs would not shrink as the shortage of rations caused them to lose weight. If she tried to compete with those women in the skimpy clothing stakes, she would look ridiculous. Better to wear flattering outfits, rather than make a laughing stock of herself by looking too overtly sexy.

Which had been harder, Caroline wondered now as she smiled for the cameras, her Team Blue bandanna tying back her hair in a twisted hairband which she had practised endlessly that morning so that she could manage the style without a mirror, as she would have no access to one on Survivor Island. Had it been picking out those swimsuits, knowing that almost the entire nation would see her figure flaws in a matter of days? Or breaking the news to Frank that she was going to compete in a reality show that would bring her exactly the kind of press attention he had so disliked Lexy chasing?

Both had been awful. Shopping for swimwear was bad enough without knowing that you were going to be on national TV wearing it, filmed from all angles. And Frank had been just as upset and distressed as she had anticipated; angry, too, feeling that Caroline had misled him. She had always presented herself as fame-shy, a victim of the paparazzi rather than complicit with them. He felt betrayed, and no matter how much she pleaded that this was a once-in-a-lifetime chance for her to build her writing career, get herself known to the general public, Frank wouldn't see her point of view. He had been through this once already, he said. He didn't know if he could do it again.

Of course, Frank didn't realize that Caroline had known about the possibility for a fortnight, as she had hidden that information from him. If she didn't pass the tests, or if after meeting her, the producers didn't think she was attractive or charismatic or interesting enough for the show, why throw a spanner into the works for nothing? Frank had no idea about the psych tests or the pre-screening process. It was easy for her to pretend that it had all happened in a whirl at the last moment: one swift interview, the approval from on high and the business class, open return ticket booked for Australia, where *Celebrity Island Survivor* was shot. That she had been scrambling to finish *Bad Girl*, working practically non-stop from morning to night, not just because the deadline was so tight, but in case she got the summons that might change her life.

Naturally, her publisher had been ecstatic at the news. This casting had catapulted Caroline to a whole new level of fame, infinitely more than they had anticipated when they signed her up. Her editor had read the book as soon as Caroline had submitted it a few days ago and sent back a list of questions and basic edits; Caroline had spent the twenty-one hours of flight time, plus the stopover in Dubai, working through them and crafting responses. The editor would organize the edits, polish up the text and turn the book around with maximum speed to capitalize on Caroline's newsworthiness at the height of media attention for the show. Ideally, it would hit bookshops as soon as possible after her return from Australia.

I feel as if I'm playing a game of chess with real people and job opportunities, Caroline thought now. *Moving them around, jumping them sideways – or wait, is it more like juggling? People keep throwing me more and more balls to keep up in the air, and I'm desperately trying not to drop any . . .*

'So we're switching things up this year!' Dan carolled cheerfully. 'But that's not a surprise, is it?'

'It would be more of a surprise if we *weren't* surprising you, right?' Pip added, winking. 'We're going to draw mini-teams! You'll be partnered up with one of your teammates for the first three days. Together, you'll have to navigate your way to camp in pairs, complete your assigned tasks, cook, eat, sleep, go to the dunny . . . while you're shackled to each other at the waist!'

As Dan and Pip chortled in delight, the camera crews captured the horrified reaction of the six Blue Team contestants. A runner wheeled forward a trolley on which lay three long chains with padlocks at each end. It was a surreal sight, particularly as they were still in the luxurious, landscaped gardens of the lavish five-star hotel where the show's contestants and team stayed every year, marble steps fringed by palm trees leading down to the sparkling azure waters of the bay below. Across those waters, the contours of the sprawling private island on which the contestants battled it out could be seen in the distance; the setup was ideal.

'Here's the picking bag!' Pip cried, as a runner handed him the familiar linen sack, stamped with the name of the show. 'You all know about the picking bag, contestants! Time to find out who you're going to spend the next three days with at *very* close quarters . . .'

417

Caroline darted glances at the other contestants as Dan and Pip chortled once again; they were all doing it, wondering who they hoped to be chained to and who they were fervently hoping to avoid. Next to Caroline was Veronica Breeze, an older woman, her hair dyed a vivid red, full-figured to the point of verging on obese. She had been a well-known television chef twenty years ago, and was camp enough to still have a small but ardent gay following. Then there was Santino dell'Aquila, also a TV chef, as handsome and fit as Veronica was out of shape; they had clearly been cast as contrasts in the hopes that Veronica, who was notoriously volatile, would lash out at her younger and much more charming rival. Beside him was Debbi Miles, one of the glamour models with whom Caroline had dreaded filming, a bleach-blonde beauty queen with genuinely pretty features so far seemingly unmarred by plastic surgery, though the same could not be said of her breasts.

The last two were St John Devizes, an elderly tennis commentator who had just been censored by the BBC, for which he worked, for making increasingly sexist comments about the appearance of women players; the show was hoping, of course, that he would stir up controversy by making salacious remarks about the pretty female contestants and unflattering ones about the others. And then there was Joe Dale, the male beefcake, a boxer who was better known for his endorsements than his success in the ring, the possessor of a face as angelic as his body was buff.

It was better than a comedy to watch the expressions on everyone's faces as Pip drew the first name from the bag. No one wanted to be shackled to Veronica or St John, so

Caroline, Debbi, Joe and Santino looked distinctly more nervous than those two; they, on the other hand, were fairly complacent, calculating that the odds of their being drawn together were comparatively small.

'Debbi!' Pip said gleefully, waving the tile in the air for a second. 'Who's going to be lucky enough to get gorgeous Debbi?'

'Ooh, I wouldn't say "lucky", exactly!' Debbi said nervously. 'I'm really useless, me!'

Pip was fishing in the bag again.

'It's . . . Veronica!' he exclaimed.

Sneaking a look sideways, Caroline saw that Veronica and Debbi's faces were pictures of distress and frustration. It might be live television, but the giggling of the crew was audible. They were allowed a certain licence; Dan and Pip would banter with them regularly during their pieces to camera, and many of the Australians who worked on the show year after year had become minor characters in their own right.

'Well,' Dan said, barely suppressing his own mirth, 'I can tell that this is going to be a cracker of a year! Shall we shackle 'em up now, Pip, or wait till we've drawn the lot?'

'You will do it,' Veronica said icily, 'at the very last possible moment.'

'Yes, ma'am!' Pip said, for some reason saluting as if she were his commanding officer, which had Dan collapsing with mirth.

'What are you *doing*?' he said to his brother. 'You look like a complete prat!'

Cheated out of being chained to Debbi, St John was now

staring so hopefully at Caroline that she involuntarily leaned back a little. As with so many men who criticized women's appearances, he was no beauty himself. Overweight, with a pot belly that strained at the buttons of his Hawaiian shirt as if he were seven months pregnant, his grey hair was so sparse that it was a miracle of nature that it produced enough dandruff to be visible on his shoulders. His rubicund face, with its gin-blossom cheeks and high colour, was silent testament to the amount of alcohol he consumed on a daily basis, and his full, rubbery mouth never quite seemed to close, his jaw perpetually sagging open to show the shiny underside of his lower lip.

Caroline's arm brushed against Santino's as she shifted under St John's hopeful gaze, his gobstopper eyes bulging as he stared at her. She pulled back, mumbling an apology, but Santino smiled down at her so charmingly that the 'sorry' died on her lips. Calabrian by origin, with his bronzed skin, high flat cheekbones and long narrow dark eyes, he was regularly mistaken for a Native American, a resemblance heightened by the thick straight black hair he wore in a clubbed ponytail. He had moved to the UK twenty years ago, opened a series of successful restaurants and married an Englishwoman with whom he had had three children. On her death a couple of years ago from cancer, he had established a charity in her name to raise money for research, to which he would be donating his appearance fee for this show.

Caroline knew that technically, it was impossible for eyes to be black: they could only be the darkest shade of brown possible. But looking up at Santino, she found that hard to believe. His irises were indistinguishable from his pupils, sparkling like jet, and though his eyes were narrow they were full of amusement and sympathy.

'Joe!' said Pip, and all the contestants turned, instinctively, to look at Joe, who beamed back at them with a sunny smile.

'Is going to be chained to . . . St John!' Pip continued.

One of the reasons that Dan and Pip were such a successful presenting duo was that they never judged, mocked or flirted with the contestants or the interviewees on their chat show. Always friendly and professional, they would never let their own personal reactions show. So it was only the contestants, with the exception of St John, who stared at Joe with tremendous sympathy. Being a very sweet-natured guy, however, Joe received the news that he would be shackled to St John for three days by leaning across to him, shaking his hand, and saying: 'Nice to team up with you, mate! We're going to have a lot of fun together.'

'*Ciao, amica!*' Santino said to Caroline, and the next thing she knew, he had bent down, picked her up by the waist and was swinging her round in a circle, stepping forward adroitly so that her feet didn't kick anyone. 'Together we will be a fantastic couple!'

She heard herself squeal like a little girl as she clung on to his shoulders for dear life, their faces very close to each other. He was laughing at her reaction, his teeth very white, his smile so charming she was dazzled by it.

'Hey, let's chain those two up first!' Dan said happily. 'Looks like they can't *wait* to get started!'

Chapter Thirty-Four

Three days later, as the Blue Team slogged through the thick jungle growth of the island to reach the beach on the far side that would form the main camp, it was one member down. St John had been removed for that all-purpose cover story, 'health issues'. The truth was that he had developed delirium tremens from alcohol withdrawal, something that had never happened in the history of the show. Apparently St John had not been boasting when he claimed on the first day that like Dr Johnson, author of the famous dictionary, 'he could drink three bottles of port wine a night and be no worse for it'. The trouble came when the port was no longer available.

At first when St John casually mentioned that he was hearing voices, his teammates had assumed that he was clowning around for attention. He was such a larger-than-life character that they had swiftly learned to expect pretty much anything to come out of his mouth. But soon afterwards, they started to worry. He began to shake to the point of finding it hard to even do simple tasks, or raise a spoon to his mouth; his irritability went through the roof; he started to hallucinate. After two days, the medical team was called in, and researchers back at the hotel discovered that he had not been charging all his alcohol to the show, but ordering bottles on room service and paying for them with his own credit card to conceal the degree of his addiction.

The consensus between the remaining five Blue Team members once St John had been stretchered away raving about gigantic snakes trying to squeeze him to death – a scene that would definitely not be shown on TV – was that he could not possibly be expected to return. Joe, who had been a fantastic sport and taken very good care of his teammate during the meltdown, was given the reprieve of a day chain-free, which he spent improving his spear-fishing skills for the benefit of the camp, watched admiringly by Debbi and Veronica, who had both formed enormous crushes on him.

At least it meant that the two women rarely fought about where to go in camp. If they weren't eating, sleeping or using the dunny, they were sitting together staring at Joe, engaging in increasingly bawdy talk about his muscles and his physical prowess. And then, when he was chained to the two of them, their delight in being so close to him was even better comic relief.

This left Santino and Caroline entirely to their own devices. They volunteered for the challenge on the second day, which involved racing against two other pairs from the Red and Yellow teams, who were sequestered on different beaches around Survivor Island, to win food for camp. Santino jogged regularly, and Caroline's recent experience with running on sand meant that, to everyone's surprise, they were the victors. It was very obvious that the embrace into which Santino swept Caroline after they crossed the finish line, having dropped the rubber ducks they had been assigned to collect into the big Blue Team paddling pool, was noticeably more passionate even than the normal excitement felt by hungry people who had just won a pack of chocolate digestives for their camp.

Caroline knew very well how this was going to look to the viewers at home. She was burning her bridges with a vengeance. But it didn't even feel like a choice she was consciously making. Now she fully understood what Darrell Rose had meant when he compared Lexy to a tornado, all those years ago: Santino had picked Caroline up just like a twisting cyclone and whirled her away with him.

From the moment they had climbed into their kayak together and started to paddle towards Survivor Island, he had been openly flirting with her. Each shackled couple had pushed their camp beds together so that they could, for instance, turn over as they slept without jerking their partners over with them, but Santino and Caroline were the only ones who slept pressed to each other for warmth in the cool night air. They fed each other, giggled incessantly at each other's jokes, and when they needed to use the dunny, Santino had announced that he would sing opera during the process to cover Caroline's embarrassment, as he knew that British people were shy about that kind of thing. This had quickly progressed to him teaching her some Italian folk songs, including one called 'Bella Ciao', which he told her was very sad: she didn't understand any of it, of course, but there was a repeating line, '*O bella ciao, bella ciao, bella ciao ciao ciao*', which she could belt out with him every verse.

It would have been impossible, Caroline honestly felt, for any woman to resist Santino dell'Aquila when he set his sights on her at such close quarters. Even a married woman would have flirted with him, and Caroline was neither married nor engaged, but having an affair with a man who had a wife from whom he was not even formally separated. Besides, the clock was ticking down to the release of *Bad Girl*, and it would be a miracle if Frank still wanted to be with her after that came out.

Viewed through the lens of cold, hard calculation, this was by far the best resolution to the situation. Caroline had been utterly obsessed with Frank, infatuated with him; if Santino hadn't been in the picture, she still would be. But after all, she knew, she had made her choice when Miranda called her to suggest that she write a tell-all about Lexy. Caroline had already picked her career over Frank. This was just the last nail in the coffin.

Yes, Caroline would look like a slut to the British viewing public, but she had nothing to lose, as frankly that was how they saw her anyway. It was why she had been cast on *Celebrity Island Survivor*: she was the homewrecker who had sneaked into Lexy's home and her marital bed, taking advantage of the moment that Lexy had a slip of judgement.

Besides, engaging in a flirtation, or even an affair, on the show was one of the best ways to get publicity for yourself and keep you on it longer. There was absolutely no way that Caroline could win: not only did she lack a fanbase, but most of the married women in the UK resented her for her affair with Frank. But the prospect of salacious scenes of her and Santino canoodling were almost a guarantee that she wouldn't be voted out immediately. The public would want to see how far the two of them would go.

Santino, after all, was famously single, a widower who had recently declared himself ready to look for love again after the tragic death of his adored wife. This made him an infinitely more appropriate romantic interest for Caroline than Frank was. In her dizziest imaginings, she pictured Santino beside her as she signed copies of *Bad Girl*, staring at her lovingly as the fans thronged to see both of them together in real life, now an established couple.

It was crazy, of course, to think like this when she had barely known Santino for three days. But a reality show was a hothouse of emotions. When a group of people were marooned together for several weeks, hungry and bored, the producers were always hoping for sexual tension to spark into something fiery enough to titillate viewers; cast members, over the years, had done everything from sneaking kisses to stripping off and making out in the sea. It was nothing compared to the antics of the recent *Big Brother*, on which not one, but two couples had actually had sex, barely concealed underneath the sheets; but then, that show was particularly known for casting young, attractive and unstable contestants striving for their one chance at any kind of fame, even if it was infamy.

As much as some of those couples might swear that they had fallen deeply in love, almost all of the pairings had split shortly after the show, when they no longer had the heightened excitement of being isolated from the world while given challenges and pitted against each other. Caroline knew this, of course. She was an intelligent woman. But as she had fallen asleep last night on the uncomfortable canvas camping bed, Santino's arm over her waist, his breath warm on her shoulder, the smell of his body, musky and rich, all around her, it had been frighteningly easy for her to tell herself that three days chained together were equivalent to weeks of dating, that after this was over, they would be sharing a king-size bed in the hotel instead . . .

He wrapped his arm around her waist now, above the chain, and Caroline turned to smile at him even while they trudged along in unison. Ahead of them, Veronica, Debbi and Joe, a cheerful threesome, were giggling together, Joe and Debbi on either side of Veronica as they helped her along the uneven dirt track. They had to pause frequently so Veronica could get her breath, and after twenty minutes or so Veronica, wheezing, declared that she had to sit down for a while and drink some water.

The threesome ensconced themselves on a log she had spotted by the side of the path, and Santino whisked Caroline into the undergrowth, behind a tree, both hands at her waist now, the links of the chain rattling as he smiled down at her. The chain was such a part of their lives now that they barely noticed the noise it made, automatically adjusting it whenever necessary. It was extraordinary how swiftly they had got used to it.

'*Ecco*,' he said. 'We have a moment of peace before we meet everyone and it is crazy.'

There was a lens pointed at them, naturally. Two cameramen had been with them in camp, and had followed them on their cross-island trek; one was capturing the three Team Blue members chatting on the log, while the other, seeing Santino and Caroline slip away, was only a few feet behind, picking his way through the foliage to find the best angle from which to film them. Meanwhile, their body mikes were recording everything they said.

It was a cliché that, as every cast member of a reality show had said in post-show interviews, you quickly became accustomed to the presence of the hovering camera, learned never to look at it directly; the reason clichés become so prevalent, however, is because they are based in truth. Besides, Caroline and Santino had no wish to avoid the camera. They were both perfectly aware of the advantages of creating scenes that would hopefully be selected by the programme's editors as part of that day's show, forming the headlines in tomorrow's red-top papers. A stolen romantic moment would be highly prized.

'I'm not looking forward to getting to a bigger camp, with people we don't really know,' she confessed coyly. 'We've had such a lovely time these last few days, the five of us—'

'The five of us?' Santino feigned distress. 'The *two* of us, *cara mia*!'

Caroline giggled.

'Well, both,' she admitted. 'Who'd have thought you could have so much fun chained to someone?'

'I am going to be sad when they take this off,' Santino said, jingling the chain at his waist.

'Will you still sing to me when I go to the loo?' she asked.

'Of course! And I will sing for you when I go too!' he responded instantly.

'We are so stupid!' she said happily, beaming up at him.

'*Carolina*, I very much like to be stupid with you,' Santino said, and he captured both her hands in his and brought them to his lips.

She knew that she should let Santino make all the moves, that her reputation meant that she needed to be the one seduced, not the seducer; but having her fingertips kissed was so delightful that she couldn't help raising one hand and stroking his cheek, gazing up at him.

'Ah, *Carolina*,' he said, 'when you look at me like that . . .'

She waited breathlessly to see how he was going to finish the sentence, but instead he lowered his head, very slowly, taking all the time in the world. An uncharitable person might have thought that he was ensuring the cameras captured every moment of this first kiss, but Caroline was mesmerized.

His resemblance to a bird of prey, the narrow eyes, the proud beak of the nose, had never been more pronounced, and his lips, chapped by the sun, were dry and hard. But the sensation of his mouth on hers, the tip of his tongue hot and wet, not forcing anything but asking her a question, made her instantly respond to it with an unspoken 'yes', opening her lips, answering with her own tongue, her eyes closing, her body softening against his.

Her arms reached around his neck, his sunwarmed flesh hot against hers. She smelt his sweat, very strong now; it was inevitable in this weather, with just a bar of soap for them to share and no real way yet to wash their clothes. He was heavily stubbled already, of course, and it scraped against her sunburnt skin, rubbing her raw. Despite herself, she flinched, and he pulled back.

'*Cara*, are you all right? I thought you wanted—'

'Yes! Yes, I did! It's just—'

'It's Frank?' he asked, frowning. 'I am confused about how things are with him, with you and me . . . but these last days I have felt there is something with us, something strong . . . I think that to kiss you is okay, that you want it too . . .'

'Yes, I did!' she said quickly. 'I'm confused about Frank, too, of course . . . it's such an odd situation, I don't know what to say . . . but I did want you to kiss me, it was just the stubble! It scratched me . . . I'm a bit sunburnt.'

'You must put more cream on,' he scolded. 'I tell you many times, it's important for the women! For men, it is not manly. But for the women, yes, they need the smooth skin.'

'You're so sexist!' Caroline said happily, even as Veronica's deep voice boomed:

'Santino! Caroline! Where the hell are you two lovebirds?'

They emerged from the forest grinning, hand in hand for the first time.

'Did you snog?' Debbi screeched. 'Oh my God, you did, you snogged, didn't you? You fucking dirty birds!'

'I am chained to a beautiful woman for three days!' Santino said, shrugging. Caroline had learned that a shrug from an Italian was not necessarily dismissive; it could also be used to signal that you were stating the blatantly obvious. 'I need to let her know I find her beautiful, before we are free and she can go to find another man.'

My God, Caroline thought, her head still spinning from

Santino's kiss, the taste of his mouth still on her lips. *Half a year ago I was nothing and no one, dowdy and fat, with nobody but Riz looking at me twice, and that was just as a secret fuckbuddy.*

How far she had come in that short time! She had lost almost three stone. Her skin was clear and glowing, her body slim. She had snagged Frank Callis, and Santino dell'Aquila, Italian heartthrob, had just called her beautiful. Unless he was toying with her horribly, it seemed very clear that he wanted her, not Debbi or the other two glamour models and beauty queens on the show. He could easily have waited until today, when the teams merged and their chains came off, to hit on one of them.

Instead, he had picked Caroline. And his reputation was very far from being a sleazy flirt or fame-whore. Santino and his wife had been childhood sweethearts, and even as his fame built and temptation was increasingly strewn in his path, there was never a shred of gossip about him cheating. He hadn't rushed into another relationship after the tragedy of her premature death; he had taken time to mourn her and devote himself to their sons. Was it possible that now he was ready to contemplate giving them a stepmother?

Caroline had learned from Lexy, her mentor and her target, that each new boyfriend was a way of garnering more publicity for the project she was currently selling. It was vital, as Lexy had explained, that the man have something newsworthy about him. Although ideally you would always move up the ladder – from a C-list footballer to one in the Premier League, say – you could temporarily also settle on a stripper or a male model, as long as he understood that he would be required to take most of his clothes off and pose with you as much as you needed.

Santino was a step downwards in status. Frank Callis, with his vast football fortune and regular TV punditry, was definitely at the top of anyone's ranking. No wonder Lexy had married him. But Caroline's relationship with Frank would tank as soon as her book came out, while it would be an excellent image makeover for her to leave the married man behind and take up instead with a much more suitable candidate, a widower who seemed flatteringly interested in her . . .

After all, Caroline thought as Veronica levered herself to her feet and started to waddle away down the dirt path, supported by Joe – Debbi turning not just to wink at Caroline as they went, but making a lewd gesture which suggested that Caroline and Santino would soon be having sex – *it's not like I don't have experience in pretending to get on with someone's children in order to make them like me!*

Santino was still clasping her hand as they set off slowly behind the unlikely trio, their chain clanking between them. There was a cameraman ahead, filming the group's progress, and one behind. That evening, on the UK daily round-up show, everyone would see them kissing, holding hands, hear Santino saying that he had wanted to mark his interest with her before they were unchained and she could flirt freely with other men.

The die was cast. Anything with Frank was dead in the water from this moment on.

There was no guarantee, of course, that she and Santino would last even the duration of the show. But the camera ahead of them showed Caroline's face glowing, her eyes bright, her lips unable to stop smiling as she kept looking down at her hand clasped in Santino's. For that moment, her sheer elation truly made her what he had just called her: beautiful.

Chapter Thirty-Five

At home in Sandbanks, sprawled on one of the big sofas in the TV room, Lexy watched the latest episode of *Celebrity Island Survivor*. Her normally lively, mobile face, so vivacious and responsive that it had been the making of her career, was unusually inscrutable as the bond between Caroline and Santino became increasingly obvious: the two of them clowned around in the sea together, washed each other down, visited the dunny, Santino's baritone resounding surprisingly well off the wooden structure as he sang snatches of opera.

And Lexy's expression did not even alter as she viewed Caroline and Santino packing up their belongings and leaving camp. As the other three team members set off, Joe and Debbi helping Veronica up the sloping path, Caroline and Santino turned to look back at the beach where they had spent the last three days.

'Goodbye, Blue Camp,' Caroline said, her eyes misty. 'I'm going to miss you! It's really weird to think I'll never come back here again.'

'You never know,' Santino said, his head very close to hers. 'My son Giova watches this show every year and before

I left, he said we just can't tell what's going to happen. Even when the teams come together—'

'Merge,' Caroline said, giggling at the sexual connotations of the phrase he had used. 'Honestly, Tino, you must have heard that word over and over again! Dan and Pip say it every day when they come to visit!'

'I have learned enough English,' Santino said magnificently. 'I have enough English for everything I need. I do not need this "mairge" word too.'

Caroline giggled again, very girlishly. It was, as Lexy had drily observed earlier, the main thing Caroline did on the show: giggle.

'So Giova says . . .' Caroline was prompting Santino.

'Ah, yes!' he said. 'He says that even when the teams mairge, Dan and Pip will play many games with us. They move us – we are separated – we vote for who we want to send away to another camp or to leave. It is not just the public who make all the choices. So maybe we will come back here to Blue Camp, you and I! *Chissà?*'

He accompanied his last word with the characteristic shrug he always gave with it: *Chissà* meant, Caroline had learned by now, 'who knows?'

'I'm sure Giova knows what he's talking about,' Caroline said, smiling. 'He sounds really clever.'

'Ugh! That's how she gets them,' Lexy observed to Sophie, who was sitting on the other side of the huge L-shaped sofa, at a right angle to Lexy, sipping tea. 'Bangs on about how great their kids are. Little slut.'

'People do rather like to hear that, Lexy,' Sophie pointed out.

'James and Libby have the best manners,' Lexy said promptly, winking at Sophie. 'I just wish some of them would rub off on my terrible twosome.'

'Your two *are* getting better,' Sophie said fairly. 'I can hear the pleases and thank yous popping out on a more regular basis now.'

'Thanks,' Lexy said in a genuinely heartfelt tone. 'It's because they're spending time around you. Even Laylah's scared of you, and that little madam doesn't give a shit about anyone! There's something about your accent. It makes me want to tug my forelock and say sorry automatically, just in case I did something wrong.'

'You silly girl,' Sophie said, laughing. 'Oh, look, you're going to have to rewind now . . . we missed a bit . . .'

'Did you ever use to watch this show before you met me, Soph?' Lexy asked, reaching for the remote.

Sophie turned to look her fully in the face.

'My dear girl,' she said. 'Is that a genuine question? But I must say, it certainly has been an education.'

'Wait till they start eating all the nasty stuff!' Lexy said, rewinding. 'Testicles and eyeballs and all sorts!'

'Oh,' Sophie said, with a mischievous smile. 'That really wouldn't be a problem for me. My great-grandfather was a Lieutenant Colonel in Ceylon during the Raj, and his son, my grandfather, used to be quite the explorer. He went all over the Middle East – practically an honorary Bedouin. Lived on camel testicles and eyeballs as a matter of course. And we all have terribly strong stomachs. It's being country folk, you know – big offal eaters. I love sweetbreads and tripe. Very good for you, offal, and very cheap. Such a shame poor people don't know how to cook it any longer.'

Lexy stared at her new friend, her jaw dropped. No matter how much she hung out with Sophie, she could never anticipate the next thing that might come out of her new friend's mouth.

'Um, sweetbreads sound nice?' she said faintly. 'But that's not jam on toast, is it?'

Sophie's smile deepened.

'They're brains,' she said. 'Delicious, very lightly fried. And terribly good for you.'

'I am never, ever coming round to yours for dinner,' Lexy said devoutly. 'Not even if you beg me.'

She clicked the remote, and they both settled back against the pillows once more. Lexy knew that this kind of sofa – sectional, sprawling, overstuffed, with plenty of matching pillows – would never, ever have been allowed into Sophie Double-Barrel's house. She had visited Sophie several times now, and had been fascinated by how different her home was to Lexy's.

Everything at Lexy and Frank's was either new, or maintained in mint condition. If something got scratched, it was replaced immediately. Sophie's home, however, had been furnished entirely with items that had been in her family since at least the grandfather who ate camel eyes with the Bedouins: not only was nothing pristine, it was positively scuffed, knocked about, the kind of 'brown furniture' that auction houses were refusing to take nowadays, as the modern taste was for light pine, white-painted wood, or mirrored furniture, all of which were anathema to posh people.

Sophie was undoubtedly a fish out of water in nouveau-riche Sandbanks. But though she was living here for her husband's job – selling luxury yachts to the millionaires, who were deeply impressed by his upper-class drawl – she and her Freddie had refused to adopt the Sandbanks style. Sophie was much too polite to criticize Lexy's decor, and from the way she settled into Lexy's ridiculously comfortable, oversized sofas with an involuntary sigh of pleasure, Lexy suspected that Sophie secretly preferred them to her own ancient, faded Chesterfields.

But ever since Lexy had caught Sophie wincing at one of Lexy's big 'inspiration' posters – Sophie would never have done that if she had realized that Lexy could see her reflection in one of the many corridor mirrors, of course – Lexy had quietly taken them all down. Gone were *Bitch is the New Black*, *I Need More Shoes* and *More Issues Than Vogue*, all of which Lexy had thought were genuinely witty. Gone also were the gigantic decorative, free-standing, light-up letters spelling out LOVE and HOME which had welcomed visitors on specially built shelves in the entrance foyer. Sophie hadn't given them the side-eye, but she pointedly avoided looking at them directly, which Lexy had taken as a sign that they were not in the best of taste either.

And they had come from the same boutique on Canford Cliffs as the inspiration posters! How was Lexy to know what was right or not? She wasn't going to make over her whole house to meet Sophie's tastes – that would be impossible – but she certainly didn't want to keep anything that made a Double-Barrel cringe. The gigantic letters had been replaced with some very unobjectionable silver vases from the White Company, and Sophie, seeing them for the first time, had promptly commented on what lovely peonies they contained, so Lexy had relaxed with relief in the assumption that the vases had also gained Sophie's approval.

Onscreen – almost lifesize on Lexy's gigantic TV with its surround sound from built-in speakers, so different from Sophie and Freddie's eight-year-old television in the scruffy back living room – Caroline and Santino walked slowly along the island path, brushing palm fronds aside, the chain at their waists clinking between them. Veronica stopped, wheezing, and Santino whisked Caroline into the jungle, behind a tree, giving the viewers the sensation of spying on a thrillingly private encounter, even though the outline of Caroline's mike pack could clearly be seen under her Team Blue T-shirt.

'Here we go,' Lexy said beneath her breath.

Santino kissed Caroline's fingertips. Caroline caressed his cheek. Santino lowered his head, slowly, slowly . . .

'*Yesssss!*'

Sophie, in a very unusual display of emotion, sat up bolt-straight and punched the air as Santino and Caroline started to kiss.

'I don't bloody believe it!' she exclaimed. 'After only three bloody days! My God, this is *wonderful*! That's it, my dear. You have your husband back!'

She turned to Lexy, her eyes bright with satisfaction.

'Little *minx*,' she said. 'Though I could think of *many* worse words! Jumping from one man to another like – like a frog on lily pads!'

Lexy, who had paused *Celebrity Island Survivor* on the kiss, the kiss that was clearly an open-mouthed one with full tongue involved, burst out laughing at the expression Sophie had used. You truly never did know what Sophie would come out with next.

Lexy felt ridiculously lucky to have been taken under Sophie's wing, especially as it was obvious that Sophie had zero interest in profiting from Lexy's fame. She had genuinely never watched Lexy's show or followed her career in any way. Her husband, Freddie, apparently sometimes watched Frank on his Sunday football roundup show and thought he was 'sound', but that was as far as the Double-Barrel family's acquaintance with Lexy and Frank went.

The friendship, therefore, was entirely genuine. Famous since eighteen, sharp as a tack – apart, obviously, from where Caroline had been concerned – Lexy was acutely aware of when people wanted something from her, because they almost always did. Sophie, however, didn't want to take anything. She wanted to give, to organize, to bring order to chaos. In other lives, she would have been a school matron, the head of the Red Cross, an army quartermaster. As it was, she did fundraising for local charities and ran the local cricket club with an iron hand in a fairly iron glove.

'Look, Lexy, I know how good you're being about cutting down on drinking, but shall we have a small liqueur to celebrate?' Sophie suggested, a flush of colour on her cheeks now. 'I couldn't be happier for you if it were the little bitch who tried to steal Freddie getting caught out like this on camera!'

Lexy's jaw dropped. Sophie and Freddie's marriage, in the glimpses Lexy had had of it, seemed enviably happy, running on very smooth wheels. Lexy had had no inkling that it might not be everything it appeared to be.

Sophie waved a hand quickly, indicating she didn't need any sympathy, as Lexy started to respond.

'It's all over now,' she said briskly. 'Let's just say, there'll be no more female doubles partners at tennis for Freddie apart from me, and he knows better now than to complain about my wonky backhand! So, what do you say? Shall we have a toast to Caroline's downfall, or am I being very naughty to suggest it?'

'No, it's a great idea,' Lexy said, standing up and crossing over to the onyx-clad, chrome-backed wet bar built into the corner of the room, a feature that would never appear in any house owned by a Double-Barrel. 'What would you like?'

Clinking their glasses, looking at the freeze-framed screen, Lexy said to her new friend:

'Okay, here's the toast. To Santino!'

'Oh, very good,' Sophie said. 'It would be wonderful if he turned out to be the fickle type and went after one of those women with the gigantic knockers to make the slut look like a complete and utter idiot! But the damage is done now as far as Frank's concerned, which is the important thing.'

Lexy nodded.

'Still,' she said soberly, 'it only gets things halfway. Just because Frank's seen what an opportunist she is, that doesn't mean he'll come back to me.'

Sophie frowned deeply, her sensible features contorting into a positive grimace.

'Nonsense!' she said very firmly. 'You're his wife and the mother of his children! You've apologized for behaving like a silly fool with a younger man, and you're making amends now by looking after the brats all by yourself. You've stopped smoking, you're barely drinking, you've taken a good hard pull at yourself. And frankly, he didn't marry an angel, did he?'

Lexy couldn't help a smile.

'No,' she admitted. 'He definitely didn't.'

'So now you sit and wait,' Sophie instructed. 'And when he comes back to you, you never *ever* mention the slut again.'

'Is that how you handled it with Freddie's tennis doubles partner?' Lexy couldn't help asking.

'Ah,' Sophie said, settling herself comfortably on the arm of the sofa. 'That's a nice little story. It turned out that she had quite a restrictive prenuptial agreement with her husband. Usual drill – second wife, much younger, very decorative. Air stewardess who picked him up in business class. She got bored and started working her way through the men at the tennis club. Little idiot – everyone knows you stick to the tennis pros in this kind of situation! But she was stupid enough to target our husbands. One of the other wives is a partner at the solicitors' office which drew up the prenup, and she checked the terms. Of course, these things are never cast-iron, but judges do take them into consideration, and there was a clause about her not getting a penny if she committed adultery . . .'

Sophie gave a little V-shaped smile and sipped at her brandy.

'I suggested we get up a collection,' she said, 'and I found us a very innocuous-looking middle-aged lady with a very high-quality camera and a very respectable and boring estate car. She followed the trolley dolly around for a week or so. And then the trolley dolly got some incriminating photographs of herself in the post, together with a polite suggestion that she resign from the tennis club immediately.'

She took another sip of brandy.

'Now the dolly is the golf club wives' problem. I've warned a couple of the ladies there I know, of course. And offered them the contact number of the innocuous-looking woman, should they find they need it.'

Lexy chinked her glass with Sophie's.

'I wouldn't like to get on the wrong side of you,' she said frankly.

'Oh, I'm not naturally vindictive,' Sophie said cheerfully. 'You have to do something really quite terrible for me to go to the trouble of applying my special powers.'

'So that's why you befriended me,' Lexy said, the penny slowly dropping. 'You'd been through it, and you wanted to help someone in the same situation.'

Sophie nodded.

'It was certainly a factor,' she said. 'And I truly think this will end as well for you as it did for me.'

'You'll still be my friend if – when – when everything's okay again, won't you?' Lexy blurted out.

Sophie looked taken aback.

'Of course I will! Where did *that* come from?' she asked.

Lexy felt like a kid back in school again, asking someone if they were still best friends. It was a sensation she had not had for thirty years, and she didn't enjoy it one bit. She was remembering a girl at primary school who only stayed friends with someone if they were having problems: divorcing parents, a bullying older sibling, health issues. As soon as the issue was resolved to some extent, the girl would be off to find another tortured soul who she could try to succour. It made her feel superior in some way, gave her a sense of power.

Sophie didn't remind Lexy of that girl, and yet . . .

'Oh no, don't worry!' Sophie said, catching on. 'I don't go around rescuing lame ducks, fixing their wings and then dumping them back in the pond again while I go on my merry way! I very much enjoy your company. It's . . . refreshing.'

'I'll take that as a compliment,' Lexy said wryly.

'Oh!' Sophie looked at the glass in her hand. 'Naughty me, I started drinking and forgot to toast! To Santino!'

Lexy looked once more at the image frozen on the huge screen, Santino's handsome head bending over Caroline's, his lips on hers.

'Oh, definitely! To Santino!' she echoed, raising her glass to him.

Chapter Thirty-Six

'You big slut!' Jamie-Lee shrieked, so loudly they could probably hear her on the mainland. 'You massive whore! You fucking disgusting, dirty slag!'

'Lord,' Veronica commented to Caroline. 'Whoever does the bleeping on this show is going to have a very tired index finger pressing that button constantly, don't you think?'

Caroline giggled.

'I'm just enjoying the entertainment,' she said.

Of course she was already calculating how she could insert herself into this scene, snag some extra camera time. This was why Jamie-Lee was kicking off like this: of all the contestants, she was by far the most expert at drawing attention to herself. In Caroline's opinion, Jamie-Lee had already emerged as one of the front-runners to win.

'You fucking took your *top* off?' Jamie-Lee was shrieking. 'And got Joe to help soap you? You are fucking *rank*!'

Jamie-Lee was on a roll. Wearing a cream crochet bikini that was comprehensively failing to contain her pneumatic curves, her lush dark hair piled on top of her head, her hands planted on her substantial hips, she was confronting Debbi, whose crime was to have lured Joe into the freshwater shower set up in a glade a short walk from the beach camp. This shower had been the source of a considerable amount of gripping footage on *Celebrity Island Survivor* over the years; the female and male contestants who were in optimal physical shape would strip down and wash themselves as seductively as possible in order to ensure plenty of coveted camera time.

Debbi had been very canny with the shower gambit; it had been guaranteed to stir up trouble. From the moment the teams merged, Joe had been thoroughly entranced by Jamie-Lee, who was delighted by this, as couples forming on the show always drew plenty of attention. They flirted, kissed, cuddled; after a couple of days, Joe had pulled their campbeds next to each other, just as Santino and Caroline had done. Jamie was even calling Joe her 'island husband'.

So Debbi asking him to accompany her to the shower to 'help her wash her weave' had been guaranteed to set off a furore when Jamie-Lee found out about it an hour or so later. Debbi's 'accidental' loosening of her bikini top during the weave washing, carefully rehearsed in advance, was definitely the icing on the cake; Joe had not been aware of what she was planning, and his expression as her bosoms popped free had been priceless.

'You're a dirty, dirty slag!' Jamie-Lee continued, pointing accusingly at Debbi, just in case anyone had any doubt to whom she was referring. Her own bosoms, even more lavish than Debbi's, wobbled superbly as she did this, hypnotizing every single one of the male members of camp. Even Caroline couldn't look away. Jamie-Lee was a plus-size model, a term which, when she had introduced herself and explained her profession, had drawn surprised comments from many of the campmates at what counted as large in fashion: although she was built on an Amazonian scale, she was a size fourteen, her curves sculpted and toned.

Debbi and Jamie-Lee had chosen the timing of their confrontation very well. All the contestants were in camp, rather than away doing trials or challenges, and they had been hanging out on their beds and hammocks, which were arranged in a loose semi-circle in a shady area of the beach. This functioned like arena seating, with the curve of the beach serving as the stage: Jamie-Lee had positioned herself centre stage, with Debbi cowering downstage left.

'I didn't mean—' Debbi whined.

'Don't even *start*, Debbi!' Jamie-Lee interrupted. 'Don't even *front* like you're not going after Joe!'

What Debbi had been doing, of course, was trying to ensure that photographs of her half-naked, bosoms blurred, water pouring down her body, would be on the cover of as many red-top papers and weekly gossip magazines as possible, with blaring headlines like *Debbi Does Down Under* or *Soap Me, Joe!* But this fact could never be mentioned. Every contestant had been thoroughly coached before the start of the show, made aware that they were never allowed to look directly at the camera, break the fourth wall, talk about the machinery that drove the show. They were supposed to create drama, but not to say why.

Judging from his panicked expression, however, poor Joe was the only one who did not fully realize that his role was to be the innocent pawn over which Jamie-Lee and Debbi were enthusiastically pretending to fight.

'You *bastard*!' Jamie-Lee yelled, turning her attention to him. 'What the fuck were you *thinking*, going off to the shower with her? You thought I wouldn't find out, didn't you? Well, you're busted! Veronica told me all about what you got up to behind my back!'

Veronica smiled complacently, knowing that this meant her scene with Jamie-Lee fifteen minutes ago was almost guaranteed to be used for that night's show. All eyes were on Joe now as he strode out of the ocean, a couple of gleaming silver fish in the net bag slung over his shoulder, a spear in his hand. He cut a magnificent figure, his muscles honed by the physical labour, his body leaner because of the restricted diet, his skin tanned to a burnished deep gold by the Australian sun.

'Babes,' he said, baffled, 'what's up? I could hear you screaming from underwater! Look, I got two fish for camp, yeah?'

Taking the bag from his shoulder, he held it up in an attempt to pacify Jamie-Lee, which was pretty much his default setting nowadays. Joe was magnetically drawn not only to Jamie-Lee's beauty but to her demanding and possessive nature. Nice, accommodating Debbi, who had been hoping to pair up with him, had been left in the dust – or the sand – as Joe gave all his attention to the fickle goddess who was Jamie-Lee. She accepted his attentions one day and spurned them the next; this capriciousness only made him keener.

'*I don't want bloody fish!*' she screamed, striking the bag from his hand violently.

It flew through the air in Debbi's direction. Debbi, seeing

her cue, screeched theatrically and made a big show of jumping back to avoid being struck.

'*Madonna*, no, not in the *sand*!' Santino protested; in true Italian style, he cared principally about the food. Jumping up, he retrieved the bag and marched swiftly to the sea to wash the fish as thoroughly as possible.

'You could have hit me with that!' Debbi complained, as Joe looked at her and then back to Jamie-Lee again, realization slowly dawning on his handsome face why exactly his paramour was throwing a scene worthy of a drag queen whose rival has sprinkled itching powder on the lining of her wigs.

'Now, babes,' he said warily to Jamie-Lee, 'If this is about this morning, I was just helping Debbi wash her weave . . .'

Jamie-Lee embarked upon a tirade that made everything she had yelled before seem PG-rated.

'That bleeping finger you mentioned's going to get RSI from this,' Caroline commented to Veronica, who smiled at this observation. When even Jamie-Lee's capacious lungs started to run out of breath, Veronica began to applaud, clapping her hands loudly.

'Excellent speech!' she commented loudly. 'Worthy of a Billingsgate fishwife!'

'You can fuck off, you old bag!' Jamie-Lee screeched at her.

Veronica looked complacent, knowing that she had secured a nice little moment on camera. Caroline put her arm supportively round Veronica's wide shoulders – Veronica shooting her a look of frank surprise at the idea that she would need any comforting – and said:

'Come on, Jamie-Lee! Veronica's got a point – you're making a massive scene and it's really unnecessary. Everyone knows Joe can't take his eyes off you.'

'He did it fast enough when that slag asked him to wash her tits in the shower, didn't he?' Jamie-Lee yelled. 'And who the *fuck* do you think you are shoving your nose into my business, you bitch? You're only fucking *here* because you were shagging a married guy whose wife you used to work for! And it wasn't five minutes before you were making googly eyes at Santino!'

Santino, squatting in the waves washing off the fish, caught his name and raised a hand in acknowledgement, calling '*Ciao!*' cheerfully, a moment with which Dan and Pip would have great fun when they did their recap the next day. It would become a regular skit for the duration of the show; one of them would throw a massive strop while the other, in the distance, recreated the friendly '*Ciao!*' and wave.

This was Caroline's cue, of course. Jumping to her feet, fitting her hands to her waist in imitation of Jamie-Lee, she said furiously:

'Stop picking on everyone just because you're pissed off that Joe went to shower with Debbi! Maybe if you were nicer to him he wouldn't have done that!'

Joe writhed in embarrassment at this as Jamie-Lee retorted:

'Yeah, I'll fucking copy you, shall I, Caroline? Cop off with a married man as soon as I see the opportunity, then dump him just because Santino smiles at you sideways? At least he's not married, eh? At least this time you picked a guy whose wife isn't *alive*!'

There was a loud indrawing of breath from every single watching campmate as these last words exploded from Jamie-Lee's mouth.

'What?' she said angrily, throwing her arms wide. 'What! It's not like he can hear me!'

She turned to point at Santino, who was standing up, examining the fish. Seeing her out of the corner of his eye, he waved at her once more, flashing his dazzling smile, quite unaware, as she had said, that she had just been screeching about his beloved dead wife.

It was a gift to the producers, naturally. The daily online viewer question read: 'Was Jamie-Lee Too Hard On Caroline'? To their mild surprise, the results of the poll were 45% for Yes and 55% for No, when they had expected a huge majority for the Yes answer. Caroline's romance with Santino was proving very unpopular with the female viewers, who strongly felt that a 'homewrecker' like Caroline did not deserve a man as handsome, good-natured and devoted as Santino.

Caroline's face, as those words hung in the air, was a picture of distress. Everyone fell silent: Debbi clapped her hands to her mouth, that very female gesture of shock when the unsayable has been uttered.

Eventually Joe muttered:

'*Babes*, come on. That was too far,' to Jamie-Lee.

Even Veronica said: 'Oh, I say. That's rather harsh,' and squeezed Caroline's hand.

Caroline had been prepared, however. Jamie-Lee's temper was explosive: she could neither tolerate being challenged without lashing out, nor could she control what came out of her mouth when she did. Nothing good could come of prolonging a slanging match with Jamie-Lee; even nastier things would be said, and Caroline, given her situation with Frank, was bound to come off worse.

So, playing the victim, Caroline responded in the most dignified way she could manage, her voice catching in her throat:

'I can't *believe* you'd talk about someone's dead wife like that!'

She turned and walked away. Unfortunately, it was not the most effective exit, as she had to pick her way round several camp beds and then circle the fire pit before finally reaching the woods. A cameraman tracked her steps all the way, and she desperately wished she could cry, but the tears weren't coming, and she knew better than to fake them. Contestants on reality shows always got busted if they covered their face and made sobbing noises to gain sympathy, only for the close-up shot to reveal dry eyes, reddened by strategic rubbing.

So, ducking her head, she put her fist over her mouth as if she were doing her level best to fight the tears away, and, once in the woods, she collapsed onto a big log which the contestants often used for strategic 'private' conversations. Hand still pressed to her mouth, she breathed heavily, chest rising and falling, trying to maintain the pretence that she was struggling not to cry. Caroline was fairly sure that one of the contestants would follow her, and sure enough, in short order Debbi appeared at the head of the path to the beach, looking agitated.

'Caroline? You all right?' she said. 'God, that cow's so bloody vicious! It's not like I took my top off on purpose! I've never seen anyone go off on people like she does!'

This was not who Caroline had been hoping for; nice as Debbi was, she was bound to make the conversation principally about herself. To Caroline's great relief, Santino bounded up the path behind Debbi, took her shoulders and set her gently aside, and then sped towards Caroline, sitting down next to her on the log.

'Debbi, *grazie*, I will look after Carolina now,' he said firmly as he put his arm around Caroline and pulled her close, hugging her.

Debbi stood there for a few seconds, visibly trying to think of a way to insert herself, even briefly, into this scene. Not being the brightest lightbulb in the chandelier, however, she could come up with nothing, and after a short while she realized that to stand there any longer would make her look like a voyeur, as the embrace was very swiftly transforming itself into a makeout session.

Having cupped Caroline's face in his hands, Santino was kissing her by now with increasing fervour, while Caroline's hands were roaming all over his naked back. He was only wearing a tattered old pair of shorts, and by now, with his dark Calabrian skin, he was tanned a deep glossy brown, his skin deliciously warm to the touch. Debbi opened her mouth to say something about being pleased that Caroline was feeling better, but, lacking the wit to come up with a snappy line, closed it again and trudged away.

By this time, Santino had swung a leg over the log to straddle it and was guiding Caroline to do the same. This enabled them to face each other fully, pressing their upper bodies together, her breasts to his bare, wet chest. Caroline lifted her legs to wrap around his waist, bringing their crotches into direct contact. Santino's big tanned hands closed over her thighs, pulling her into him, letting her feel his cock rising against her pelvis.

Caroline moaned. This was more intimate than they had ever been before; they had been sneaking off now and then to kiss in the woods, but this was faster, stronger, much more intense. It was the first time that, if they had genuinely been in private, there was no question that they would be scrambling to pull off their clothes, finding somewhere that they could couple like animals in the woods. Another cameraman had followed Santino, naturally, and the two of them were scrambling eagerly, making eye contact with each other, positioning themselves to film the scene without crossing the shot, moving carefully to avoid making any sound that would distract from the pants and moans and groans that were issuing from the happy couple.

Santino's hands tangled in Caroline's hair, pushing back her head so he could kiss her throat; she let him eagerly, feeling incredibly sexy, as if she were starring in a passionately romantic scene in an Italian film. He smelt of sweat and sun and salt water, and yes, of fresh fish, but over the last week and a half this had become completely unremarkable. His lips were even dryer now with salt and sunburn, but the sensation was deliciously intense, making her want him to kiss her everywhere, unfasten her shirt, kiss even further down, cover her breasts with his callused hands, kiss them with his sunburnt lips . . .

She ran her hands down his chest, glorying in the feel of his hot, leathered skin, to his waist, toying with slipping her fingers under the waistband of his shorts, hearing him groan at her touch on skin that was concealed and therefore more sensitive, closer to where he really wanted her hand. But this, Caroline knew, was as far as she could go. She was already tarred with the label of husband-stealer: whenever the British public was allowed to vote to nominate candidates for the trials, it inevitably selected Caroline for the nastiest ones. She was the immediate choice for anything that involved eating kangaroo testicles or having stinking cockroaches poured on her. She smiled through them, knowing she couldn't afford to be seen as a bad sport. Besides, the public's appetite for torturing her would, with any luck, keep her on the show when the eliminations started.

But while performing all the nastiest trials might keep her in, acting sluttily was guaranteed to get her chucked out. It had to look as if she and Santino had genuine feelings for each other, rather than just scratching a physical itch. Caroline needed her image to be enhanced by her appearance on the show, not further damaged. Other contestants would be able to get away with sticking their hands down one another's shorts: Caroline the Homewrecker most certainly couldn't.

So she summoned up all the willpower she had and pulled back, gasping, her mouth red and swollen from kisses. Dragging her hands up from the temptation to delve into his low-riding shorts, she pushed him away, mumbling: 'We mustn't! Think of your boys, they shouldn't see this!' – a line she hoped would make her sympathetic to the viewers. Santino nodded in wordless agreement, tilting his head forward to rest again hers, their breath coming harsh and ragged in the quiet forest as they struggled to gain control of themselves.

Meanwhile, back at the beach, Debbi had returned to report breathlessly that Caroline was being very effectively consoled by Santino. On receipt of this news, Jamie-Lee, not to be outdone, had promptly taken Joe's hand and dragged him off to the sea, where she allowed him much more access to her pneumatic curves than she had previously permitted. They cavorted for a while with the water at waist height, putting on a show that would be played in slow motion for the recap: Jamie-Lee theatrically tossing back her mass of hair, water flying from the ends, as Joe buried his face between her bosoms. The producers had great fun with the sound effects.

And then, in a *Celebrity Island Survivor* first, the happy couple moved into deeper water. Able to support Jamie-Lee's magnificent figure in a way even he would not have managed on dry land, Joe lifted her, settled her legs around his waist, and began to start a rhythm that was entirely unmistakeable.

'No *way*,' Debbi breathed, staring at the two of them. 'They're actually *doing* it! In front of all of us!'

'We can't actually see anything, though,' Veronica said, sounding rather disappointed. 'Wish I'd thought to bring binoculars as my special item, don't you?'

'Veronica!' Debbi said, shocked. 'I didn't know you were a voyeur!'

'Oh come on, Debbi,' Veronica said, eyes fixed to the spectacle of Joe and Jamie-Lee, head and shoulders above water, rocking backwards and forwards, Jamie-Lee's arms wrapped around Joe's neck, kissing him passionately as he worked away. 'It's bloody boring here ninety-five per cent of the time, and we're not even getting any of those ghastly trials because Caroline's being put up for all of them! Let me at least have the fun of watching two healthy young animals make the beast with two backs!'

'You what?' Debbi said blankly, as Caroline and Santino, unnoticed by anyone, came slowly down the beach path, hand in hand.

'It's Shakespeare, dear,' Veronica said, eyes still glued to the spectacle. '*Othello*. It means sex.'

'Oh!' Debbi, having thought about the expression, executed a comic look of surprise, eyes opening wide, as she worked it out. 'I get it! I didn't know Shakespeare wrote, you know, that kind of thing? Like, sex stuff?'

Out in the sparkling blue waves, the sun beating down on their heads, Jamie-Lee and Joe were speeding up their rocking movements, Jamie-Lee emitting a surely exaggerated screech of ecstasy which was shrill enough to reach the assembled audience on the beach.

'Never heard anyone sound like a seagull when she comes before,' remarked a comedian who had been part of the Yellow Team, garnering some sniggers.

'*Ma guarda*,' said Santino, stopping in shock as he saw what was going on. '*Stanno trombando!*'

'This was one of the best days *ever* on *Celebrity Island Survivor*!' Pip announced happily in the live recap the next day. 'Seriously, Dan and I could talk about everything that happened for weeks on end, couldn't we, Dan?'

Dan held up his fingers and started to count off the memorable moments.

'Ow!' he said, as he pulled down the first one. 'That's my bleeping finger! What Veronica doesn't know is that we take our jobs so seriously that we do all the bleeping ourselves. I was up till the early hours taking out every second word that came out of Jamie-Lee's mouth, and I think I sprained my finger . . .'

'"Worthy of a Billingsgate fishwife!"' Pip quoted blissfully, as a crew member wearing a white coat and stethoscope dashed in to splint Dan's finger in a carefully rehearsed comedy moment.

'Veronica teaching Debbi the sexy bits from Shakespeare!' Dan continued as he held up his hand to be bandaged.

'I asked Martyn to make the beast with two backs with me last night,' Pip said, referring to his husband, 'and he slapped me round the face and told me he wasn't that sort of boy.'

'Well, you *are* married now!' Dan said. 'Everyone knows you don't do that sort of thing once you're married! Right, what's next? Caroline and Santino's hot log action!'

'Steady on,' Pip said. 'I didn't know we were allowed to say "hot log" on live TV.'

'But hard as they tried, ahem, they were totally beaten for the sauce factor by Jamie-Lee and Joe getting friendly in the sea!' Dan said. 'A *Celebrity Island Survivor* first, with extra seagull imitations thrown in at no extra cost! Which brings us to our top moment of today's action,' Dan said gleefully. 'We all learned how to say "Look, they're having sex!" in Italian. All together now, let's practise it!'

The crew member who had played the doctor now returned to the shot, his white coat and stethoscope gone, carrying a big blackboard which he propped on the desk. On it were written the words Santino had exclaimed on seeing Jamie-Lee and Joe in the sea. Dan picked up a pointer and indicated the first word, as he, Pip and the entire crew chorused:

'*Ma guarda! Stanno trombando!*'

Chapter Thirty-Seven

'I'm *so* excited to meet you, Lexy! I'm your biggest fan!' gushed the hundredth woman that afternoon to say exactly those words on reaching the head of the signing queue.

Lexy, sitting at a trestle table entirely covered with fuchsia material which had been chosen to match the cover of *Lexy on the Loose*, flashed a big smile at the woman and said: 'Thank you *so* much!' as an assistant slid yet another copy of the hardback book, open at the title page, in front of her. Most authors did signings in bookshops, if they were deemed popular enough to make it worthwhile to organize one; the demand for Lexy, however, was beyond the capacity of any British bookshop. This signing was being held at Sweetwater, the huge luxury mall in Essex whose customers were the perfect target market for Lexy. They bought her hair styling tools, her hair extension products, her accessories, her make-up. Now they were queuing almost around the mall to snap up a signed copy of her book.

'I bet everyone says that, don't they?' the fan continued. 'I can't believe I'm actually standing opposite you! You're even prettier in real life, and so tiny! I bet everyone says that too, don't they?'

'Thank you *so* much!' Lexy said, starting to sign the book. To speed up the process, bookshop assistants were working the line, asking each customer for their name and writing them on Post-it notes for Lexy. Until you started doing signings, you had no idea how many different ways there were to write, for instance, all the many, many variants of how to spell 'Jane'.

'Hope you enjoy it, Jessi,' she said, handing it to the fan with another smile even as she turned to the next woman in the queue. It was short and sweet, but there were so many people waiting that Lexy did not have time to have a conversation with each one.

'I *was* hoping to see Frank here with you,' Jessi said, lingering by the table even as the next one came up.

'Oh, me too!' said the new fan excitedly. 'Now that Caroline's shown her true colours, you and Frank'll be getting back together, right?'

'Oh yes, you *must*!' Jessi agreed, looking at Lexy with big puppy-dog eyes. 'You're such a great couple! I'm still looking for my prince in shining armour, and seeing you two together made me feel so good about having a chance of finding Mr Right!'

'I feel *just* the same!' said the new fan, whose name, Lexy read on the Post-it, was Saira. 'I'm like, if *Lexy and Frank* have problems, then it's okay if I do too, but they *have* to stay together, because if they don't, that's so depressing!'

This is what happens when you put your life on reality TV, Lexy told herself for the umpteenth time, gritting her teeth. *People think they know you. They think they have the right to ask you the most personal questions about your love life. And you asked for this. You wanted the fame and everything that came with it. So suck it up and play nicely with the other children.*

'We're working things out,' she lied, signing the book to Saira with a scrawl rather than her usual flourishing signature and handing it to her with a smile that said 'Next!'

To Lexy's great disappointment, Frank had not been in touch since that glorious evening when Lexy and Sophie had watched Caroline and Santino, still chained together, sneak away to kiss in the woods. Since then, they had become an established couple. Of course, most of the *Celebrity Island Survivor* relationships didn't survive past a few weeks once the participants returned to the outside world, but whether 'Cantino' – the horrendous name coined for the couple by the gossip magazines – lasted was irrelevant as far as Frank was concerned.

As Lexy had commented to Sophie, Frank dumping Caroline did not necessarily mean that he would take Lexy back. It had been a week since that first kiss, and Lexy was forcing herself to sit on her hands, not contact him in any way; it was indescribably painful, but she was sure it was the right thing to do. What could she say, after all? *Now that your girlfriend's cheated on you, shall we get back together?*

'I was thinking that now that Caroline's shown what a slag she is, Frank'd come to his senses,' Jessi said eagerly.

'Yeah!' Saira agreed. 'I mean, Lexy was a bit naughty, but Frank knows she's a wild girl, and it was Deacon who followed her into the loo, wasn't it?'

'And then Caroline just nipped in there while Lexy was off sorting herself out in rehab—'

'Fucking *slag*,' Saira said with great venom. 'She needs a right seeing-to.'

Lexy, signing a book to a Lindsey, accidentally wrote the name with an 'a' at the end rather than an 'e', cursed under her breath and grabbed a fresh copy.

'Ladies, if you could move along –' said one of the publisher's PRs, in the kind of tone that turns a suggestion into an instruction.

The fans waiting in line were corralled in the kind of lanes that airports used for passengers going through security, marked out with poles and connecting tape. But there was a generous area at the end of the long signing table that was open to the public, and that created a cosy little spot where fans, clutching their signed copies of *Lexy on the Loose*, could loudly debate the state of their idol's marriage.

The PR was indicating the exit, but Saira, Jessi and Lindsey with an 'e' paid no attention to her at all.

'I was thinking Frank would see that and be all "oh my God, what was I thinking, she's such a slut!", right?' Lindsey said enthusiastically.

'Right!' Jessi said. 'Like okay, we all make mistakes, but he and Lexy are supposed to be together!'

It was clear to Lexy that the women meant to be supportive. But that was only making it worse for her, because she agreed with every word they were saying.

'Ladies, I really need you to move along! We're going to have a log jam building up,' the PR said. It was an unfortunate choice of words, onto which Saira jumped right away.

'Hot log action!' she said gleefully. 'It's so funny how Pip keeps saying that!'

'Cracks me up every time!' Jessi said. 'Did you see yester-day where he brought in a hot dog and said he was having hot dog action?'

'He's hilarious!' Saira agreed.

'D'you think Caroline's getting kicked out tonight?' Lindsey asked. 'It's *so* time for her to go.'

'Yeah, Jamie-Lee hates her,' Jessi said eagerly.

'Called her a stuck-up bitch yesterday,' Saira chimed in. 'I mean, they bleep her but you can see what she's saying!'

'Caroline's *nice!*' said a child's piping voice from behind the women. 'And you're not supposed to say "bitch". It's a bad word!'

The three women swung round to see Laylah and London arriving. They had been taken away by Gareth's assistant to get frozen yoghurt with tapioca bubbles and sprinkle top-pings, as they had been getting restless with nothing to do while Mummy signed books but chase each other round the pillars and try to terrify the fish in the enormous wraparound tank by pulling grotesque faces. Clearly, Laylah had bullied the assistant into getting much larger servings than Lexy would have permitted. The cups were almost as big as their heads, piled so high with toppings that the yoghurt swirls were visibly teetering. London was holding his very carefully with both hands; it was a miracle he hadn't dropped it yet.

Normally, Lexy would never have trotted the children out at an event like this. But under the particular circumstances, the publicists handling the book launch were absolutely insistent that the kids should be available for photographs, smiling and happy, showing how delighted they were to be with their loving, newly sober mother.

Lexy had dressed the children up in matching outfits: they were in fuchsia and white, accessorized with gold stars, to match the book cover. It was Lexy's invariable practice to do this herself when launching her products, dressing up to embody the branding. She herself was wearing a fuchsia jumpsuit with white trim, her hair piled up on top of her head and studded with big gold star pins, her eyeshadow gold and her lipstick the exact same shade of fuchsia. Round her neck was a gold star necklace, and matching stars dangled from her earlobes. Coco Chanel had famously advised that, to avoid wearing too many accessories, you should look in the mirror and take one thing off before you leave the house. Lexy was much more likely to put three more on.

Laylah's outfit was a miniature version of her mother's in every respect, apart from the fact that the gold sandals had a one-inch heel, rather than four, and her face was bare of any make-up but lipgloss. London was dressed in white trousers and a fuchsia T-shirt with a gold star on the front. Lexy had even convinced him to have his short tight curls sprinkled with gold powder, telling him it was magical fairy dust; she couldn't help thinking how much fun it would be to pull these photographs out in ten or twenty years' time and embarrass him thoroughly.

All day, Lexy had been unable to stop smiling every time she looked at her two gorgeous children. Now, however, she was horrified at what her daughter had just blurted out. Her small daughter was frowning furiously at Jessi, Saira and Lindsey over the top of her frozen yoghurt.

'You don't even *know* Caroline, but you said something nasty about her!' she said loudly. 'You're a mean lady!'

The three women's expressions were a blend of consternation and excitement. They had been busted by a ten-year-old, yes: but it was Laylah, who they saw on TV every week! They could boast forever about having met Lexy's daughter. Also, she had mentioned Caroline! This was fantastic gossip, if they could just eke it out a bit longer . . .

'Ooh, that looks like a yummy ice cream!' Jessi said in the kind of high-pitched voice people use to talk to babies.

This approach was met with the contempt it deserved.

'It's not *ice cream*, it's *frozen yoghurt*,' Laylah said coldly. 'You're naughty *and* stupid.'

'Laylah, that's rude!' Lexy snapped, catching the eye of Gareth's assistant and trying to indicate, by rolling her eyes furiously, that she needed to whip the children away immediately. This was the problem with not having a nanny; there was no one to tell Laylah that her frozen yoghurt would be confiscated if she didn't apologize straight away, then whisk her off again to keep her out of trouble.

'*She* was rude first, Mummy! She was rude about Caroline!' Laylah screeched.

'I miss Cawoline,' London said wistfully.

'You *miss* her?' Saira pounced on this juicy gossip nugget, bending down to London's level.

'Is it true Caroline helped you write the book?' Jessi, greatly daring, asked Lexy, thinking that she might as well try the question that everyone in line had been strictly told not to ask. Jessi already had her signed copy of the book, after all: what were they going to do, rip it out of her hands?

'Is Frank going to go to Australia to see her?' Lindsey asked, going for gold. 'Is he upset about her and Santino?'

'*Okay*, that's *enough!*' the PR said, swooping in with a mad stare, her arms outstretched like condor wings to shoo the three women away from the signing table.

If Lexy's PR Emily had been present, the situation would never have got to this point. But Bailey and Hart's publicists were handling this, and skilled as they were, they did not deal with soap actors and reality stars on a regular basis, but much dowdier and less famous authors. They had not anticipated the intense, fervent curiosity which Lexy's fans directed towards every detail of her life.

And then, of course, there was the unfolding spectacle of Caroline to add extra fuel to the flames – not just Lexy's love rival but her unacknowledged ghostwriter, appearing live on television every night, making it clear that she had moved on from Frank by draping herself over Santino every chance she got.

Jessi, Saira and Lindsey were herded in short order through the exit, a loud stream of 'Thank-you-so-much-for-coming-Lexy-really-appreciates-your-support-enjoy-the-book' pouring from the PR's lips. Lexy signalled frantically to Gareth's assistant, wide, sweeping gestures that told the young woman to pull Laylah and London around to the back of the table.

'Eat your yoghurt quietly while I finish up my signing,' Lexy said. 'And don't talk to *anyone*.'

'Why did the lady say Cawoline was mean to Mummy?' London asked through a very large mouthful, brightly coloured sprinkles smeared all over his mouth.

'*Don't say her name any more till we're home!*' Lexy hissed over her shoulder, so vehemently that London's eyes popped wide, the way only small children's do, saucer-like with surprise. Then they stretched even wider in panic: in his shock, he had choked on a tapioca bubble. Laylah exclaimed:

'Oh my *God*, London! Mummy always *says* to chew the bubbles properly!'

She pounded him on the back, blue eyes glittering with sheer glee at being able to both swear and hit her brother without instant retribution. Lexy shrieked even as London let out a massive cough, his narrow little ribcage spasming as he hoicked up the bubble. The waiting fans, having gasped at the sight of London in distress, let out a collective sigh of relief as the tapioca bubble flew out of his mouth and splatted messily onto the fuchsia fabric. Then they burst into spontaneous applause.

Lexy was already dashing round the table to London, dragging him into her arms. If she had spent more time bringing up her own children, however, she would have known that this was a terrible mistake. Her inability to stay calm turned a minor mishap into a full-blown drama. London, seeing his mother burst into tears of relief, started crying too, clinging to her, his yogurt-smeared mouth staining her jumpsuit. It was a total meltdown. The more they hugged, the more they sobbed.

London's mishap, as it turned out, had provided the perfect release for the stress Lexy was going through that afternoon, the humiliation of sitting behind a signing table with a bright smile when every single woman buying her book knew that it had really been written by her husband's mistress. It had been hard enough to hear Caroline's name, let alone tolerate the fact that her daughter was still attached enough to that woman to defend her in public.

Additionally, Lexy was terrified by the fact that Frank still had not been in touch. What if he ended up not even leaving her for another woman, but simply . . . leaving? Wouldn't that be even more humiliating? The prospect of this, always on her mind day and night, was so overwhelming that once she had started crying, she simply couldn't make herself stop.

'*Okay!*' the PR said, eyes still manic, clicking her fingers at the tech guy who was sitting at the far end of the table, laptop open, equipment stacked in front of him. 'We were saving this as a fantastic surprise for Lexy at the end of the signing, but I think we should do it *now* . . . let's *go!*'

Huge TV screens were strategically positioned around the central atrium of Sweetwater, where the signing was taking place. These had been displaying the usual content that ran in a loop in luxury malls: promotional videos for shops and restaurants, catwalk footage of the latest fashion shows, interspersed with fuchsia and gold banners announcing thrillingly that Lexy was signing her book 'RIGHT NOW IN THE ATRIUM!' together with a prominent image of the cover of *Lexy on the Loose*.

No audio accompanied the images, however. Sweetwater had a low-pitched, carefully chosen soundtrack piped through its speakers, calibrated to adjust for different times of day and evening, based on their research into its visitors' shopping patterns. Now, however, the mood music faded away and was replaced by the very familiar theme tune to the number one reality show in the world, *Sugar Girls*.

Heads jerked up all around the atrium at the melody: the name of the show was now blazoned on the screens. The theme tune played out, the volume increasing, even though the opening sequence – in which Silantra, Shanté and Summer each popped up in turn, dressed in white and flashing huge smiles in which their perfect pearly teeth were barely visible behind their hugely inflated lips – did not appear. The music was a tease, to catch the attention of every fan of the show. Finally, Silantra's face and impressive cleavage appeared on screen.

'Hi Britain, I'm Silantra!' she said in her hugely well-known sexy purr, and her hardcore fans screamed in excitement at the realization that this was not a clip from an upcoming show, but Silantra actually talking to the gathered crowd.

'How're you all doing?' she asked, and many of them, eyes wide, actually called back: 'Great!' or 'Fine!' or 'I love you, Silantra!' as if she could somehow hear them.

'So I've recorded this clip to say Hi to my new bestie, Lexy! Hey, that kinda rhymes,' she realized, tilting her head. 'Bestie Lexy! Hah, you can see this isn't scripted, yeah? So, like, I hope the book signing went really well, Lexy. I'm like totally psyched to be appearing on your show. And you should come to the States and guest star on *Sugar Girls*! We had such fun hanging out in London! Everyone, you *gotta* watch that episode of Lexy's show.'

Silantra winked, a slow, sexy gesture that was much more significant to Lexy than to anyone else watching. The straight guys present whooped at its sheer eroticism. Only Lexy knew what Silantra meant: if Lexy was willing to spend another wild night with Silantra and her wide array of toys, Lexy would be granted the prize of a guest appearance on *Sugar Girls*.

It was a huge opportunity. It would open more doors to her in the States than anything else could ever manage. And it was entirely risk-free: there was absolutely no way that Frank would ever in a million years guess that there was a very specific quid pro quo for the tremendous privilege of being in an episode of *Sugar Girls*. Who would?

Besides, although it wasn't Lexy's usual sexual preference, she had thoroughly enjoyed that night with Silantra. It had been great fun; it truly hadn't even felt like cheating, as it was so removed from her day-to-day life. If she were single, she would do it again in a heartbeat.

But she wasn't. She was married, and even though she was currently estranged from her husband, she wasn't going to cheat on him. Which was ironic, considering that she had been perfectly happy to cheat when she *had* actually been with Frank.

Damn it, this is Doktor Weinstein's voice in my head, isn't it? she thought suddenly. In her sessions at Schloss Hafendammer, the doctor had hammered home the point that adults behaved exactly the same way when they were alone as if someone was watching. Children, he had said firmly, sneaked a drink or a cigarette in private, as if it were cheating someone else and not themselves. Adults, however, were able to discipline themselves without the need for observers to keep them in line.

In her sessions with the doctor, Lexy had not talked about her one-night stand with Silantra. It hadn't even occurred to her as something to feel guilty about, and since it hadn't been tied into her drinking in any way, it hadn't seemed relevant.

But it did now.

'And hey,' Silantra concluded, 'don't forget to watch the new season of *Sugar Girls*, starting the seventh of September on Bravo TV!'

She waved a theatrical goodbye. It was noticeable that Silantra, whose speech was usually littered with *likes* and *yeahs*, was perfectly capable of forming a sentence without either when it came to publicizing her show as clearly as possible.

'Miss you, Lexy!' she finished, blowing Lexy a kiss.

The screen flickered and reverted to the usual mall programming. The audience, which was now swelled with the shoppers who had flooded out of boutiques at the sound of Silantra's voice, was buzzing with excitement. Lowering their phones, they checked the images and videos and excitedly posted them on social media.

I'd kill to be on Sugar Girls, Lexy thought. *Funny expression – you say that without thinking. And when you do think about it, you realize that not only wouldn't you kill, but you wouldn't fuck someone to get what you want either.*

Not any more.

Lexy was growing up, and not before time. She was the mother of a nine-year-old and a four-year-old, for God's sake. And by Doktor Weinstein's definition, her choice to turn down the opportunity Silantra was offering truly counted as an adult decision, because Frank would never know that she had made it. 'Hey, honey, I'm so committed to you that I'm not going to fuck Silantra any more, not even to get on her show,' was not a line Lexy would ever be using to convince her husband to come back to her.

Lexy had a sudden, vivid picture of one of the Lego towers London loved to build; once they were as tall as he could possibly manage, he would gleefully knock them down and promptly start to rebuild a different one from the same pieces. That was exactly how she felt – as if she too had been torn down, and now was slowly reassembling herself into a very different shape, from the ground up.

Or maybe she was a Transformer! That was an even better metaphor, and of course it also came via London. He was obsessed with those films, could watch them in an endless loop.

She realized, with a half-smile, that her images were entirely drawn from London's choice of entertainment. That would never have happened just a few weeks ago; back then, she wouldn't have had the faintest idea what toys her son played with, what films he loved best.

She really *had* changed.

Chapter Thirty-Eight

Ten days later

'And the fifth member of the tribe to be voted off the island,' Pip said, pausing as he looked back and forward between Caroline and Debbi, maximizing the suspense as much as possible as the two women held hands in solidarity, the camera zooming in for a close-up of their tense faces, 'is . . . Caroline!'

It was no more than Caroline had been expecting. She was frankly lucky, with her terrible reputation and lack of fan following, not to have been voted off first. Only the miracle of her chemistry with Santino had saved her from that fate, she was sure, and she gained considerable points by frankly admitting that in the exit interview with Pip and Dan. Everything they threw at her she acknowledged, taking the potential sting out of each question.

Yes, she said, she was very grateful to have been voted off fifth, not first. No, she hadn't expected to last this long, not at all! Yes, she couldn't believe how well she and Santino had clicked. Yes, she agreed with the messageboard commenters that he was completely out of her league. No, she had no expectation that Frank would be waiting for her when she left the island. No, she couldn't blame him at all for that.

Unusually, the interview was much less about the details of life on the island and more about the love triangle between her, Frank and Santino.

This worked perfectly for Caroline. It was the ideal platform to state her case: before nine million viewers, she could explain that she had not started dating Frank before Lexy snogged Deacon and then left for Switzerland, that she had gone to Sandbanks to help take care of the kids and then had got swept away by spending time with him, but that she now realized it had been a bad decision to date a married man, even a separated one, and that she truly regretted coming between a husband and a wife.

By the time she stepped onto the boat that would take her off the island, Caroline thought she had done very well indeed. Dan and Pip had been so charmed by her willingness to acknowledge her failings that they had even let her mention that she had a book coming out soon: they usually cut off or mocked contestants who tried to promote their projects too openly.

The mainland was drawing close. Standing in the bow of the boat, Caroline could see the assembled press waiting for her at the dock. Of course, Frank was not the 'friend or family member' standing on the red-carpeted jetty. She had never expected him to come to Australia. It would have been too public a declaration of their relationship; he wasn't even formally separated from Lexy.

So Caroline had nominated her older sister Louise instead. Crammed into a too-small house with a husband and three kids, money chronically tight, Louise had naturally jumped at the chance of a child-free, all-expenses-paid holiday in Australia. There she was on the jetty, waving cheerfully, sporting a very British lobster-pink sunburn and wearing an eye-wateringly bright Matthew Williamson for Debenhams kaftan whose lurid greens and oranges would have been better suited to a woman with much darker skin.

'Oh my God, Caz, look how thin you are!' she exclaimed as Caroline stepped onto the red carpet.

Louise could not have said anything that would have pleased Caroline more. She could only be called thin by comparison to the weight she had been for most of her adult life; Debbi, for instance, who had started the show at a slim size ten, was now positively skinny after the scant rations they were given, her fake breasts looking like tennis balls bolted onto her ribcage. But this was certainly the thinnest Caroline had ever been in her life, and she was hellbent on not putting on a pound. She couldn't help being aware that beside her plump sister, she looked even slimmer by contrast.

'Don't let me eat *anything* but steak and salad without dressing while we're here, okay?' she whispered in her sister's ear as they hugged, too quietly for the boom mikes to pick up.

'But it's all free!' Louise said, wide-eyed. 'Booze too! It's like fucking paradise here, Caz!'

The journalists were yelling questions about Santino, Frank and Jamie-Lee, the breakout star of this season. Caroline kept smiling as she walked back to the hotel arm in arm with her sister, answering the questions that related to the show while ignoring anything to do with Frank, no matter how many times they shouted his name.

The show lasted for six more days, during which time

Caroline managed an entirely carb-free diet. Salad without dressing, grilled protein, an occasional vodka with diet tonic: the fantastic seafood in Australia, the gloriously warm weather, plus the demands of wearing a bikini by the hotel pool, made this diet regime much easier than it was back home. She almost – nearly – just about – if she stood with her legs in a strange contorted way – had the highly coveted thigh gap, and she was determined not to lose that.

Day by day, more contestants trickled back from the island. It became increasingly clear that the top three was going to consist of Joe, Jamie-Lee and Santino, the most attractive and popular members of this year's cast.

Santino's three sons flew in, accompanied by his mother and sister-in-law. The two Italian women, as slim and tanned and elegant as Louise was large, brash and sunburnt, were polite to Caroline when they met in the hotel; this happened fairly often, as there was really nowhere else to go but the sprawling grounds of the resort. They did not, however, make any effort to get to know her, and despite Louise eagerly encouraging her to go over and talk to them as they sat by the pool or sipped drinks in the bar, all Caroline's instincts told her not to force an acquaintance on them when they weren't seeking it out.

After all, she rationalized, they were doubtless waiting until Santino returned from the island to see how he greeted Caroline – with an affectionate hug that would relegate her to the friend zone, or, as she naturally hoped, a passionate embrace that made the strength of his feelings for her very clear. Happy as she was that he was so popular that the British public kept voting to keep him on the island, the longer she waited the harder it became to see him onscreen, laughing and joking with Joe and Jamie-Lee as easily as if he didn't miss her in the slightest.

She filled her time with gym workouts and aquarobics classes, and with proofing the manuscript of *Bad Girl*, which her editor had FedExed to Australia. Re-reading what she had written, all the ways in which she had satirized and parodied Lexy, Caroline could only be glad that things were broken off with Frank, who had not been in touch. She had not realized quite how much fun she had made of her erstwhile employer; there was no question that Frank would be furious at the picture she had painted of the mother of his children.

The day of the finals dawned. Caroline spent the morning first at the gym, then in the hotel beauty salon. The cannier of the women on the show had booked well in advance, knowing that appointments would be in very high demand. As Caroline and Debbi sat side by side in the pedicure massage chairs, watching their feet be buffed to perfection, Debbi babbled non-stop about how excited Caroline must be to see Santino and how romantic it would be to throw herself into his arms.

Having been there right from the start of Santino and Caroline's island romance, Debbi was hugely invested in its success, and her encouragement was a massive boost to Caroline. By the time she was primped and preened, highlights newly done, false lashes discreetly applied, nails perfect, her weight loss on the island almost completely maintained, Caroline was almost breathless with anticipation, and absolutely sure, with Debbi's encouragement, that the reunion would be magical.

478

The eliminated contestants, plus friends and family, gathered in the hotel ballroom to watch the final show. Joe was voted out first, as had been expected. Jamie-Lee and Santino were the bookies' favourites, with very little to choose between them. While Joe's parents and brother were down at the jetty greeting him, the final vote was announced: Jamie-Lee was the Queen of the Island.

To everyone's amusement, Santino's boys bellowed their disappointment: this was captured by the camera crew, who then panned to Caroline, sitting on the other side of the ballroom, not wanting to seem as if she were trying to ingratiate herself with Santino's children before she was an official girlfriend. Having been thoroughly dragged through the mud by newspaper columnists for her closeness to Laylah and London, she was not going to make the same mistake again.

As soon as the winner was announced everyone poured out of the ballroom, heading for the dock. Caroline, flanked by Debbi and Louise, felt her heart beat savagely in her chest as she saw the boat carrying Santino draw away from the island, moving ever closer across the narrow strait of water. It was like a scene at the end of a film, the hero returning from a quest: Santino was standing in the bow, balancing with effortless ease, waving with both his arms at his three boys, his mother- and sister-in-law, as if he were semaphoring an urgent message. He was lean as whipcord by now, barely an ounce of fat on his body, his skin tanned so dark that his resemblance to a Native American was even more pronounced.

'*Papa! Papa!*' the boys were screaming happily, and as the

boat reached the jetty, the tears pouring down Santino's face were proof of his joy at being reunited with his sons. He didn't wait for the boat to be tied up to the mooring. As soon as it bumped against the jetty, he jumped straight onto the red carpet and ran to his boys, dropping to his knees so that he could hug all three of them at once. Many of the observers started sobbing too, the drama so heightened that Santino might have been returning from the wars rather than a reality show on an island just across the bay.

Floods of Italian poured out as the family babbled away to each other. Finally, Santino wiped his face, did the same, with great tenderness, for each of his sons, kissed his mother- and sister-in-law, and then swept the smallest boy up into the crook of one arm. Turning to walk back to the hotel, his free hand was clasped by both of the older boys. It was the perfect picture of fatherly love.

And now, of course, every head swivelled to Caroline, because they had all seen the father entwined with Caroline for days on end. The cameras focused on her face as she swallowed hard, looking into Santino's coal-black eyes as he passed her. He nodded as their eyes met, a brief greeting, and then looked straight back at the little boy whose legs were wrapped around his waist, smiling at something his son had said.

That was it. A nod was all she got. He hadn't mouthed, 'See you later,' or even given her a smile or a wink, and now she was watching him walk away from her. Caroline was unable to move, sweat icy in the small of her back. It was as if, if she stayed completely still, if she didn't even breathe, she could rewind time somehow. Santino would come back, kiss her, draw her into the bosom of his family . . .

'He's with his kids,' Debbi said, doing her best to sound breezy and unworried. 'He's got to be with them for a bit.'

'Yeah, he'll call you later, once he's settled in,' Louise chimed in, making a similar effort to reassure her sister, but her high-pitched tone betrayed her nerves. 'No worries. Bound to happen!'

Caroline knew everyone was still looking at her, whispers of speculation running around the group, catching fast as wildfire. She mustn't look defeated or disappointed; it was very likely, after all, that Debbi and Louise were absolutely right.

'Yeah, bound to happen,' she echoed, managing a smile.

Caroline knew she had to wait on the dock until the boat brought Jamie-Lee over, looking superbly regal in the golden crown and sceptre given to the King or Queen of the Island, as the cameras were waiting avidly to pick up on any hint Caroline gave of disappointment or heartbreak. Instead, she had to look both poised and delighted for Jamie-Lee's triumph.

Trumpets played, fireworks burst over the island: escorted off the boat by Pip and Dan, Jamie-Lee walked down the red carpet waving and smiling like a cross between a monarch and a Miss World winner. All attention was on her, mercifully, or almost all; Caroline knew perfectly well that even as they applauded Jamie-Lee, people were still sneaking looks at her, whispering about how odd it was that Santino hadn't even said hello to her after all of their kissing and canoodling.

She kept that smile on her face as she too clapped and

cheered the Queen of the Island. No one watching would be able to say that she looked devastated by Santino having practically ignored her. The viewers might even, hopefully, think that he and she had discussed this before she left the island, agreed that he would initially give all his attention to the children with whom he was being reunited after nearly a month. If only that were the case! But she could tell herself, as she smiled and smiled till her jaw started to hurt, that he would assume she knew this, that he would be ringing her room later, once the joyful father/son reunion was complete, just as Louise had said . . .

So as soon as Jamie-Lee had led the triumphal procession back to the hotel and started a round of victory interviews, Caroline shot back to the room she and Louise shared and sat down by the phone, willing it to ring. She wouldn't leave until the last moment, when it was time to attend the celebration party that evening. In her fantasies over the last few days, she had entered the party on Santino's arm, his acknowledged companion, her smile stretching almost from ear to ear.

When she heard a knock on the door, she was sure it was him, come to collect her. Jumping to her feet, Caroline practically ran down the hallway – the hotel room was as big as a barn; space was definitely not at a premium in this part of Australia – only to see a production runner standing there, tasked with bringing her down to the party. Her heart sank; a huge lump formed in her throat. And she knew, too, that the runner was there to make sure she didn't duck out; everyone was waiting to see if Santino did more than nod at her this time.

Caroline's only consolation was that, because the clothes she had brought with her were now too loose, she had borrowed a sexy, clinging dress from Debbi that showed off her slim figure and made her breasts look spectacular. She held her head high, laughing and joking with Veronica and Debbi, and when Santino came in she was careful not to move in his direction, even though her every nerve was jangling as she waited for him to come over.

He did, of course. He made his way around the room, greeting everyone; he hugged and kissed her, Veronica and Debbi with the same enthusiasm, keeping up a steady stream of talk to cover any awkward silences; how tired he had been by the end, how great it had been to have a proper bath, how much he had missed his boys, how the one glass of wine he had drunk so far was going to his head. Then Jamie-Lee was triumphantly carried in on the huge shell, borne by topless young men dressed in loincloths, the way every winner of *Celebrity Island Survivor* entered the celebration party, and all the attention was upon her. Santino was summoned to play the runner-up's role, helping Jamie-Lee out of the shell, escorting her to her throne, placing the crown on her head and giving her the papier-mâché orb and sceptre.

Caroline stood stock still as the pantomime was enacted in the centre of the ballroom. She barely knew how to process the shock. After all their kisses and endearments and passionate embraces, Santino had treated her like any another contestant. As if she hadn't felt his hard cock pressing against her, whispered with him about what they would do together when there were no cameras around; as if he hadn't been practically glued to her side for the fortnight they'd been on the island together!

She knew better, however, than to confront him once the photos were over. What if he rebuffed her in public? That would be manna from heaven for the media. Already, she knew that Santino's rejection of her would be a major headline tomorrow, a twist that no one had seen coming.

Or had they? she suddenly wondered. While Santino was on the island without her, had someone – Jamie-Lee, most likely – told him stories about Caroline, chosen the word 'homewrecker' to turn him against her? And if that had happened, was it possible that the editors had deliberately chosen not to use that footage, so that Santino's treatment of her would be entirely unexpected, a spectacularly dramatic shock to Caroline and the viewers?

On the few occasions their eyes met, Jamie-Lee seemed, Caroline thought, to be smirking at her. Was Jamie-Lee relishing Caroline's humiliation because she had caused it herself? This was, for Caroline, a desperately needed ray of hope. If Santino had been misinformed – okay, maybe not precisely *misinformed*, but if he had been given the facts in the worst possible light – then surely there was a chance for her to put her side of the story?

So, when Caroline saw him leave the party without another word to her, she waited ten minutes, told Debbi and Louise that she was going to the toilet, and made her way, in a very roundabout fashion, to a set of lifts on the far side of the hotel. Hopefully from here she could reach the penthouse floor without anyone spotting her and reporting gleefully that she was chasing after him. It was common knowledge that Santino was staying in the penthouse suite so that his entire extended family could be accommodated all together.

As Caroline rang the bell, she was feeling calm for the first time that day. She had managed to convince herself that once she was alone with Santino, she would be able to turn things around; the powerful physical attraction between them would spark once more. As long as it wasn't his mother or sister-in-law who answered the door, and promptly slammed it in Caroline's face because she too had heard about her reputation . . . oh God, Caroline was getting hysterical, this wasn't an episode of an early evening soap opera . . .

The door swung open, and to her immeasurable relief, it was Santino standing there. His strongly defined black brows drew together over that familiar beaky nose, even more prominent now because of the weight loss. Caroline felt faint, her legs buckling, at the sight of him, so handsome, so close to her.

'*Carolina*,' he said, looking at her very seriously. He stood back, holding the door open. 'Yes, I thought you would come.' And then he added those words that never fail to strike dread into the heart of anyone who hears them:

'We need to have a talk.'

Chapter Thirty-Nine

Legs still trembling, Caroline walked inside. The hallway of the suite was as large as the room she shared with Louise, the lounge beyond so gigantic that the furniture arrangements looked dwarfed in the enormous space. Her heels skidded a little on the elaborately inlaid marble floor. As she got her balance, she noticed that Santino did not turn back to help her, as he had always done on the island if she tripped in her flip-flops.

He was heading for the terrace: the sliding glass doors were standing open, and she remembered his often-expressed, vehement views about how Italians considered air-conditioning terrible for the health. If she had been feeling on stronger ground, she would have joked at the contradiction of the soft, humid, warm air around them, so much better for the lungs, and the fumes he was about to inhale; he was picking up a cigarette packet from the rattan table on the terrace.

But she couldn't. She was too nervous to joke about anything.

There was a bottle of red wine on the table. Without asking, Santino poured Caroline a glass of wine and handed it to her, and that made her even more nervous, because it was as if he knew she was going to need it.

'Sit,' he said, gesturing at the white-cushioned armchair. As she did so, he tapped a cigarette out of the packet, lighting it with a Zippo he pulled from his pocket.

'I want to tell you a story,' he said. 'Listen, please, for it is very important.'

There was no need for him to tell her that; she couldn't have spoken a word. Her throat had closed up. She couldn't even manage a sip of wine; she set the glass down on the table so that he would not see her hand shaking with nerves.

'So six years ago, I am on holiday in Barbados, with Ilaria and Giova,' he began.

Ilaria, Caroline knew, of course, was his dead wife. Instantly, Caroline assumed, at the mention of her name, that Santino was going to say that he needed time; that the passion on the island had been wonderful, crazy, but that now they were in the real world and he was back with his kids, he had realized that he needed to slow things right down. It dovetailed exactly with what she had been telling herself, the story she had created to explain his behaviour. Of course she would follow his lead, not introduce herself to the kids until he was ready, stay in the shadows if that was what he wanted, do *anything* not to lose him, not to be humiliated by the gleeful media coverage of her romantic downfall . . .

'And one night at dinner at the hotel,' Santino was continuing, 'we feed Giova some of our food. Ilaria and I are very Italian, we believe that children should not eat different food from the adults, they must learn to have good palates. We teach that to all our boys.'

He was leaning against the terrace rail, not looking at Caroline as he talked and drew on his cigarette, but off into the night, over her shoulder.

'But one bite that we give him – I will never forget, it is some mashed potato, and it has little bits of hazelnut in it – *cazzo*, a stupid thing, why would they do that? *Ma lascia stare* – so yes, there is hazelnut. And it turns out that Giova is allergic to nuts. He gets red, a rash, itchy, he starts to scratch his face. He's only two and a half, he's frightened, we are frightened. Ilaria starts to cry. I hold Giova's hands to stop him scratching, but he cries and fights me and the rash is growing – it happens so fast, so fast – and Ilaria is calling for a doctor. We are screaming now, both of us, screaming for help – we don't want to leave Giova but we need a doctor, we are desperate, we don't know what to do –'

The terror of those moments could clearly be heard in Santino's voice. Caroline had no idea where this was going; she knew Giovanni had survived, of course, but she was still on tenterhooks because she didn't understand why it was so important for Santino to tell her this story now, of all times.

'And then,' Santino continued, 'another hotel guest runs over to us, holding a pill for Giova to take. But she says the dose is too big, so she gets a steak knife and she cuts it up and gets some Coca-Cola so that he will want to swallow it and gives it to him. We are hysterical, sobbing. He is our only son, so young, and we are in panic, and she does everything. Everything.'

He drew a long breath, remembering the fear and panic of that evening, shaking his head in disbelief at how fast it had happened.

'A doctor comes at last, but by that time Giova is breathing better and he doesn't want to scratch his face so much any more. He tells us that the lady has saved Giova's life by giving him an antihistamine. There is an injection the doctor can give, but Giova is still small, the injection is for adults, not children, and maybe it would have been too late, because with this allergy, the throat closes up very fast and Giova maybe chokes to death.'

Santino's free hand clenched into a fist as he said these last words. He took another long breath, then slowly opened his fingers again, running his hand through his black silky hair. Only a few days ago, Caroline had been able to do that herself, twist her fingers into his thick mane, the sense of privilege so delicious it was almost overpowering. Now she would not have dared to touch him; there was a cold aura around him, a force field repelling contact, and that hurt like a bandage wrapped tightly around her torso, a pressure squeezing her lungs.

'So, this woman, this hotel guest we do not know, she has saved our son's life,' he finished softly, stubbing out his cigarette. 'I wonder if you can guess who this lady is, this angel from heaven who Ilaria and I will never be able to thank enough?'

Caroline actually jerked as if she had been punched in the ribcage, realization dawning on her.

'Yes, I see you have guessed,' Santino said. 'She is called Lexy O'Brien. And a month ago, she rings me and she says she is trying to pull strings to get you on this show, and she asks me, if she manages it, will I do her a big favour? And before she tells me what it is, I say, Anything. I will do anything for the angel who saved my Giova's life.'

He looked at Caroline directly for the first time since he had opened the door to her. There was compassion on his face now, and that was worse than anything. Much worse, say, than anger or contempt.

'In Italy, the family is the most important thing,' he said. '*La mamma è sempre la mamma.* I would have done this for Lexy in any case, but when she tells me that you have tried to come between her and Frank, parents of two children, I am horrified. How could you do that? You do not seem like a bad person, Carolina. But you have done this. You tried to take a husband away from a wife. And that is what I will say when they ask me in the interviews why I don't want to see you any more. That I did not know, I did not understand, what you had done. But now I do.'

Lexy had thought of everything, including the simple and devastating explanation for Santino's rejection of Caroline. She couldn't even deny the truth of what he had just said. She dropped her eyes to the table to avoid his gaze, but what she was seeing was the television footage of Lexy trying to get into her own house, surrounded by paparazzi, entering the gate code over and over again before realizing that Frank, at Caroline's very delicate but effective prompting, had changed it to bar his wife. Caroline remembered vividly the moment that it had dawned on Lexy what was happening, the sag of her shoulders, the paling of her cheeks, the long pause before she eventually turned back to her waiting car.

Without Caroline whispering in his ear, Frank would never have locked his wife out. They would almost certainly have reconciled that day. But Lexy, clearly, had spent the time since then not just drying out, giving up smoking and taking care of her own children, but analyzing her downfall and plotting to undermine Caroline just as Caroline had undermined her.

Caroline had been so flattered to be invited on *Celebrity Island Survivor*! She had thought it meant that she was becoming famous enough for people to know her name! But no, not at all. Even that had been taken away from her. She hadn't got the show on her own merits, but through Lexy's clever manoeuvrings.

'Was any of it real?' she heard herself ask the table in a tiny thread of a voice.

He was reflected in the glass top; she saw his shoulders rise and fall in one of the exaggerated Italian shrugs with which she was achingly familiar.

'You are an attractive woman,' he said. 'It was not difficult to make love to you.'

'Well,' Caroline managed, still looking at the table. 'That's something, I suppose.'

She must have sat there for a whole minute before she realized that the conversation was over. Santino had nothing left to say, and nor did she. It took a little more time for her to gain the strength to push back her chair and stand up, and even then she used the edge of the table for support, her sweaty fingers leaving marks on the glass top.

'*Addio*, Carolina,' Santino said, stubbing out his second cigarette, watching her go with the same mortifying look of compassion in his black eyes.

He did not see her out. He left her to cross the sprawling

expanse of living room on her own, the sound of her heels small, lonely clicks in the huge space, as if underlining her single status. From a door on the far side of the room Ilaria's sister emerged, slim and tanned in an orange linen dress, her black hair pulled into a bun, her arms stacked with gold bracelets. Behind her were the two younger boys in pyjamas, clutching soft toys, clearly getting ready for bed. Giving Caroline the most cursory of glances, they bounded across the room in the direction of the terrace, calling:

'*Papa! Papa! Dove sei?*'

The sister-in-law remained where she was, looking at Caroline, her silence indicating that she was waiting for Caroline to leave. As she resumed the long walk to the door, behind her she heard a happy family, the giggles and chatter of the small boys, Santino's deeper voice laughing with them, his sister-in-law speaking in quick, beautifully articulated Italian, sounding indulgent but reproving: clearly, she was trying to get the children to bed, while they wanted to stay up and play with the father they hadn't seen for weeks.

It sounded joyous, cosy, warm. With every step Caroline took, she felt more and more alone. She had been trying, she realized, first with Frank and then with Santino, to enter an already established family, to have the benefits without having done the work, to walk in and warm her hands at a fire someone else had built.

It was very cold, leaving that fire behind. Very cold indeed.

Her hotel room was empty. Louise was still partying happily downstairs, soaking up as much free food and booze as she could cram in. The air conditioner was running, the chilly room a perfect metaphor for Caroline's current mental state. The door closed behind her, and she stood there in the dark, her key card in her hand, not reaching out to slide it into the slot that would activate the lights.

For a long time, she didn't move at all. She just stood there, silently, in the darkened room, slowly, painfully, absorbing the full extent of the revenge which Lexy had inflicted upon her.

Chapter Forty

Three days later

Lexy was so relaxed that it was all she could do not to start snoring. The heated marble lounger on which she was lying in the sheer luxury of the spa at the Corinthia Hotel was the culmination of two hours of total rest and relaxation. Not even a four-handed massage in the Maldives with the sea lapping softly beside her was more restorative than visiting the thermal suite floor.

She had swum in the pool, sweated in the amphitheatre sauna, sunk her hands wrist-deep into the ice fountain and scattered chips of ice all over her heated body, curled up in one of the tiled recesses of the steam room and done two circuits of the 'vitality pool', where you sat or lay on various underwater seats or beds through which powerful jets pounded different parts of you into dazed and happy submission. The heated lounger was the final stage, an ergonomically designed chaise that looked cold and oddly space-age, until you lay down: the warmth of the stone and the cleverly angled shape cradled the body in an instant embrace.

In front of the loungers was a long glass cabinet in which a line of flames flickered and leapt, gold against the black background. This was the only spa Lexy had ever visited which was kept as dark as possible, and she had never failed to fall asleep on the lounger at the end. Earlier that day, she had had a facial at Skin3, so that she had arrived at the Corinthia already in a trance. The effect of the mask going over her face was by now as familiar and comforting as a heavy blanket in winter, snow falling onto a statue, settling gently first on the eyes, then on the mouth. A calm hand smoothed everything down: the current started, tingling, trippy, but becoming the new normal so swiftly that when, after twenty minutes, it switched off, Lexy felt almost bereft as the heavy, rubbery mask was lifted off her face, surprised that the lights flickering before her eyes from the electricity passing through the mask had disappeared. Then came the last cleansing, hands working oil into her face with confident curving strokes, a glass of cucumber water placed on the side table as she lay there on the ridiculously comfortable treatment bed, tucked in under the charcoal duvet, her face gently tingling still.

Lexy had wanted to pamper herself to the maximum today. Not only was she celebrating Caroline's downfall, but this was the first day she was spending away from her children in over a month. Sophie was picking them up from school and taking them for a sleepover at hers. Laylah and London, it turned out, adored Sophie's home, which was like a cross between an Outward Bound course and a very benign boarding school. James and Libby were allowed to run wild in their huge garden all day long, could get as filthy and muddy as they wanted, but were also expected to do chores around the house, help cook and clear up after meals, and do their homework before any TV or tablet watching was allowed.

Lexy was going to make the most of every child-free minute. And she needed to achieve as Zen-like a state as possible, as after this, she was heading over to the Chelsea apartment to meet Frank. It would be the first time she had seen him since he had handed the children over to her in Sandbanks and taken off to London with Caroline. Lexy had no idea what was waiting for her, and the mere thought of the approaching meeting terrified her: the stakes were so high. Every instinct told her that this was make or break. By the end of the evening, she would know whether she was still married, or whether her husband wanted a divorce.

Lexy had barely been able to eat that day for fear of throwing up anything she put in her stomach. Despite her nerves, however, the atmosphere of the spa had worked wonders. The flames flickered in front of her like the lights that had danced on her eyelids during the facial. Wrapped in a thick white robe, her feet in slippers, her body relaxed onto the warm marble, her head propped on a neck roll covered with towelling that supported it at the perfect angle, she closed her eyes and contemplated the triumph of her plan to bring down Caroline, humiliate her as Caroline had crafted Lexy's own public rejection.

Santino had rung her yesterday, telling her that Caroline now knew everything about the situation, and wishing Lexy a successful reconciliation with Frank. She found her thoughts slipping away to that holiday in Barbados, she and Frank and little Laylah sitting on the dining terrace of their hotel in the warm, moist evening air on the first night of their holiday. They smiled over at the table on the other side of the terrace at which a family like theirs sat, with a little boy rather than a little girl, recognizing Santino dell'Aquila from his TV appearances: Lexy speculated on whether the kids might want to play together on the beach tomorrow.

And then Santino and his wife leaned in towards their son. Something was wrong: was he choking? The wife's voice rose, panicky, appealing for help: diners started to look over, thinking that the little boy was choking, a waiter running over to try to Heimlich him. Lexy spotted the blotchy pink bloom of rash forming on the little boy's face, saw his hands rising to start scratching the irritation, remembered a friend of Laylah's who was allergic to strawberries, and knew immediately what was happening.

Santino was calling for a doctor, and if there were one nearby, fantastic. They would know exactly what needed to be done. But if there wasn't . . .

There was no time to lose. Lexy kicked off her strappy sandals, grabbed the room key from the table and took off barefoot at a tearing run, dodging startled waiters, heading for her suite and the medications in the main bathroom, on a shelf too high for Laylah to reach them; once the little monster had eaten an entire vial of Lexy's homeopathic pills and just giggled, completely unrepentant, when Lexy shrieked at her, and Frank didn't help by pointing out that those pills were nothing but sugar in the first place . . .

This was why working out regularly was so important. Add to that having learned not to care about making a fool of yourself in public by shooting outrageous scenes for your reality show. Lexy shot down that corridor like greased lightning, shrieking: '*MOVE! MOVE! MOVE!*' in the kind of piercing tones that most British people would be mortified to use in a public place.

She crashed into the bathroom, tore the zippered pill case from the shelf, shot out again without even checking that the suite door closed behind her: she was entirely focused on getting back on the dining terrace, scrabbling through the pill sheets, popping one out, cutting it up – grabbing the Coke she'd yelled at the waiter to bring, insisting that the little boy swallow the crudely halved antihistamine tablet. In the absence of a doctor with an EpiPen dosed for a two-year-old, it was his best chance.

And the parents managed to keep it together. Lexy had been ready to throw a glass of water in the mother's face, but as soon as Lexy snapped that her panicking could make the kid worse, she understood, took a deep breath and held it till she got some control over herself, squeezing her husband's hand with everything she had as he told the sobbing, scratching little boy to do what the lady said and take the pill that would make everything better . . .

Lexy had no idea of the appropriate dosage for a two-year-old. She knew, however, that anaphylaxis could choke him to death with terrifying speed: so when he managed to swallow that half-pill she almost sobbed with relief, because it meant that his throat was not yet closing up. Ten minutes later, it was clear that the rash had spread no further, and after twenty, Lexy was fairly sure it was receding. The kid was no longer trying to scratch his face, and he was still sipping the Coke, so his throat was obviously fine; he was lying in his father's arms, very drowsy, a side-effect of the antihistamine, but now managing to smile.

A doctor arrived, shone a torch down the little boy's throat, gave the all clear and confirmed that Lexy's quick thinking might well have saved Giovanni's life. The mother started crying again at this, thanking Lexy profusely; Santino swept the kid up to carry him back to their suite, seconding everything his wife was saying, his face taut with the exhaustion and stress he had not yet been able to give free rein.

The dell'Aquilas were scheduled to fly out two days later. They spent most of their time holed up in their suite, recovering from the shock of nearly having lost Giovanni. Santino had met Lexy and Frank the next day to beg them to ask him for anything in the future, anything at all, and invited them to his restaurant as soon as they were back in London.

They had accepted the invitation, of course. But although it would have been natural for the two couples, each with a small child of a similar age, to make friends and socialize together, their lifestyles were quite incompatible. Although Lexy was settled down with Frank, she was not slowing down her hard-partying ways, while the quiet, modest Ilaria was visibly uncomfortable with Lexy's saucy tongue and salty language. Family gatherings were not Lexy's style, and the couples had swiftly realized that they had little in common beyond mutual goodwill.

The incident had never got into the papers: the hotel had comped both families' stays in return for avoiding adverse publicity. So when Lexy had conceived the plan to detaching Caroline from Frank, after she saw that promotional ad for *Celebrity Island Survivor* on the bus coming off the Studland ferry, she had known that there was no way Caroline could be aware how profoundly Santino was in her debt.

Lexy had rung him first, aware that he had already signed up for the show. Initially, Santino had been taken aback by the request to flirt with and then dump a random woman; but once he realized that Frank and Lexy were actually separated, and that Caroline had had a considerable hand in making that happen, he instantly agreed. Lexy had then reached out to the producers of her reality show, asking for a contact at *Celebrity Island Survivor*, and promising them a series of dramatic interviews during the show if they signed up Caroline.

Of course, she had never had any intention of going through with the interviews. But she had had to offer them something, and she had been aware that they would be wary about the idea of a staged, pre-planned romance, worried that it could blow up in their faces if Santino failed to go through with it, or, worse, broke down and confessed on live TV what he had intended to do.

Lexy, of course, had known she could rely on Santino. It was, after all, a very easy task for him: like so many Italian men, he was a natural and instinctive flirt, and to charm Caroline into falling for him had been as simple for him as breathing. And in the post-show interviews it had been very simple for him to explain, his handsome face very serious, that he had very strict views on marriage – much too strict to be comfortable introducing his sons to a woman who he had found out was a homewrecker.

That explanation had been universally accepted. Not only was it entirely plausible, no one could possibly think of any other explanation for Santino's behaviour. He had gone on to say that, though Caroline had clearly not been the one, his flirtation with her had made him realize that it was time, at last, to move forward. He was finally able to contemplate the idea of bringing a woman home to meet his sons who might potentially become their stepmother.

This, naturally, had been greeted with great excitement, and not only by his devoted fans. With considerable amusement, he had told Lexy in their phone conversation yesterday that he had already had two approaches from TV companies eager for him to star in a reality show about him finding love again.

Drifting off to sleep, Lexy found herself wondering if she knew anyone she could introduce to Santino. It was mortifying to acknowledge that among her social circle of reality stars, TV presenters and television executives, there wasn't one who was genuine, unselfish and kind enough to be suitable for a widower who was bringing up three young sons.

Maybe Sophie knows a nice woman, she thought, and as her breathing slowed, as she started to fall asleep, she remembered Ilaria, her thin elegant features, the high-bridged nose and delicate bone structure, the big dark eyes, the absolute lack of any make-up, all very characteristic of a sophisticated Italian woman. She imagined Sophie's friends, Home Counties blondes like Sophie herself, with sturdy muscles from skiing and horse-riding, sensible hair and no-nonsense attitudes: *actually*, Lexy reflected drowsily, *that might be perfect for him. His kids would love her, just like mine do Sophie. It would be a new start for them all, someone as different as possible from sensitive, quiet Ilaria . . .*

And on that thought, Lexy slipped into a deep, peaceful sleep, a gentle snore issuing from her parted lips. The next thing she knew, her face was covered in burning hot coals and she was screaming in shock and fear.

'You *bitch*!' Caroline hissed. 'You've completely ruined my life!'

It had taken Lexy several shrieking seconds to identify that it was ice she was frantically shovelling off her skin, that the scorching sensation was from cold rather than heat. But what the hell was going on? She hadn't signed up for a spa treatment which consisted of having her adrenalin levels spiked by therapists dumping ice on her unexpectedly!

And then, belatedly, the penny dropped.

'What the *fuck*!' she shrieked. Mashing the last chips of ice from her eyelids, blinking the water away frantically, she grabbed the lapel of her robe, wiping her face. 'What are you *doing*, you stupid bitch?'

'You completely set me up!' Caroline yelled. 'And no one believes it! My publicist's rung *everyone* and nobody will run an interview with me about you and Santino taking me down! The *Mail* actually laughed at her and hung up!'

Lexy looked up at Caroline and started to laugh as well. After the scare she'd just had, it was the most enormous relief to let it all out. Big howls bubbled up from deep in her diaphragm, rocking her body like a comic actor clowning for effect.

'Oh, I *bet* they laughed!' she managed to say between the giggles. 'I bet they thought you were a crazy delusional bitch! I can't believe you were stupid enough even to *try* telling them that story!'

This was too much for Caroline, who was smarting from

the humiliation she had endured over the last few days. Her flight had been met at Heathrow by massed ranks of press, all of whom had gleefully shouted one mortifying question after another at her. It was the celebrity equivalent of the walk of shame: she had kept her head down, not saying a word, trying to deafen her ears and blinker her eyes to the prying lenses and invasive stares of bystanders who had seen her being rejected by Santino live on television just a couple of nights ago.

Beside her, Louise, who had dipped very regularly into the drinks trolley onboard, made things worse by swearing at the cameramen. She even pushed one away, to his great delight; he'd recorded her arm thwacking towards him while deftly dodging to one side.

You wanted this, Caroline had kept telling herself. *You wanted fame, and now you've got it . . .*

Caroline had done her hair and make-up on the plane, of course. She'd meant to walk off flashing smiles for the cameras, seeming unaffected by what had happened with Santino. But she had been unable to muster the strength to pull it off. Instead she looked defeated, ground down, humiliated, especially because she was bitterly aware that Lexy would have made lemonade out of lemons, sashayed through Heathrow looking fabulous, lean and tanned, reminding everyone to buy *Bad Girl* when it hit the shelves in a couple of months . . .

Rage surged up in her as she got into the cab, still surrounded by yelling paparazzi. Caroline knew she would have no peace until she had confronted Lexy, the author of all her recent misfortunes.

Posing as one of Lexy's publicity team who needed to get in touch with her urgently about an interview, Caroline rang Jason, Lexy's manager, and asked his assistant about Lexy's schedule. The assistant checked and reported back that Lexy was unavailable that afternoon, as she was booked into the Corinthia Hotel spa; a quick call to the Corinthia ascertained that Caroline could purchase a day spa visit herself. So, having unloaded Louise at Waterloo to catch a train back to Southampton, the cab proceeded along the Strand, into Trafalgar Square and down Northumberland Avenue to the ocean liner that was the Corinthia Hotel.

Caroline had located Lexy easily enough, and revelled in the satisfaction of seeing her genuinely shocked and frightened by the ice landing on her face. But now Lexy was actually laughing at her, taunting her with how she had turned the tables on her so successfully, and it was unbearable, intolerable – she couldn't let it go on another moment, she *couldn't* –

Bending over, Caroline grabbed hold of Lexy's hair with both hands and tugged at it viciously, screeching:

'Fuck *you*! How *dare* you laugh at me!'

The spa manager, who had been standing just inside the entrance door, could no longer stand back. He had been watching Caroline and Lexy yell at each other, too nervous to interfere; it was a highly delicate situation. But once Caroline dug her hands into Lexy's hair, he practically ran forward. It was the first time two clients had ever brawled, let alone two famous ones, and he had absolutely no experience in breaking up this kind of thing, but he knew he had to calm things down.

Lexy, screaming in fury, grabbed Caroline's hands and

started trying to prise one of her fingers free; she got hold of Caroline's middle finger and forced it painfully back. But even as Caroline yelped in agony and pulled her hand away, with it came a chunk of Lexy's hair extensions, and Lexy's cries became bloodcurdling as some of her own hair was ripped out as well. Caroline staggered back, cradling her damaged hand, the hank of hair dangling from her fingers.

Assessing her escape route with one swift, frantic glance, Lexy calculated that she couldn't scramble over the wide marble lounger in the heavy robe she was wearing before Caroline came around it. Instead, she made for the open space beyond her attacker, heading around the fireplace wall; she was intending to put the large vitality pool safely between herself and Caroline, buying plenty of time while the spa realized what was going on and summoned security.

Because Lexy had absolutely no wish to engage in a public brawl with her love rival, let alone on the very day she was supposed to meet her husband and convince him that she had sobered up and was ready to truly settle down! How on earth would this look when the press got hold of it? And even apart from Frank, she was damned if she would give Caroline a smidgen of extra publicity. That bitch had written what, Gareth had warned Lexy, was a tell-all about her life: Lexy would be livid if news of this catfight gave Caroline extra pre-orders for the bloody thing.

But unfortunately for Lexy, her spa slippers were, literally, her downfall. Designed for walking with the slow, relaxed pace of a spa visitor, they were much less useful when fleeing a crazed attacker. With every stride they caught under Lexy's feet, and as she rounded the fireplace wall she found herself tripping, the toe of one flapping disastrously, sending her off balance. She struggled, arms flailing, to get some kind of purchase on the slippery marble floor. The two people in the vitality pool, lying on the moulded beds, bubbles surrounding their elegantly toned bodies, stared over at her, shocked dumb by this intrusion into their very expensive, very exclusive paradise.

And as Lexy desperately tried to right herself, Caroline came up behind her, took hold of her shoulders, and threw her sideways into the pool.

In Caroline's defence, she had never visited the spa before. She had simply dashed around a corner, seen a swimming pool and followed an irresistible impulse to throw Lexy into it. In a normal pool, Lexy would have tipped in, thrashed around in the heavy robe, then either been fished out or managed to unwind herself from its folds. Caroline was quite unaware of the silver bars lying dangerously in wait below the surface of the bubbling water. As Lexy toppled in, her head and shoulder hit the bars with an audible smash. Bouncing off them, she sank like a stone to the floor of the pool.

Caroline screamed, as did the woman in the pool. The man was sitting up, struggling against the force of the jets to climb off the bed and help Lexy. Caroline dropped to her knees, looking down into the water. Everything was black, however: the walls, the floor, the tiles of the pool. All she could see was the white robe, heavy with water, billowing dramatically against the black background, blown back and forward by the jets; on either side of it were silver bars, and Caroline couldn't see how to climb down without stepping on a possibly unconscious Lexy.

The thought that she had injured Lexy, who might actually be lying at the bottom of the pool, knocked out, bleeding, starting to drown – that Caroline could be arrested and charged for what she had just done – was racing through her mind with such terror that she could barely breathe. So when, from the white folds a figure arose, black hair plastered to her face like something from a horror film, dripping with water, the robe discarded, one swimsuit strap slipping down from her shoulder, almost completely revealing one recently enhanced, artificially perky 34DD breast, Caroline barely had time to gasp in shock at the apparition as the creature reached up, sunk its hands into Caroline's hair and dragged her into the water.

Caroline tumbled in awkwardly, rapping her ankle so hard on one of the bars that it immediately started to throb. As soon as she hit the water, the robe she herself was wearing weighed her down like a wet blanket, slowing down all her movements. The pool, it turned out, wasn't deep, and she got one foot under her, unable to stand on the injured one. She brought her fist up to hit Lexy under the jaw, but, since she was trying to undo the tightly knotted belt of her robe with the other hand, neither attempt was successful.

The next thing Caroline knew, the iron grip on her hair changed: Lexy's hands flattened on the top of her victim's head, and, Caroline's face was pushed underwater. She flailed frantically, her hands coming up to try to grab Lexy's arms, nails digging in, trying to force Lexy to let go. Air bubbled from her nose and mouth, and she swallowed some water, her body convulsing as she choked on it. Her eyes bulged out in panic. No matter how deeply she sank her nails into Lexy's arms, the grip on her hair didn't budge. Lexy had Caroline exactly where she wanted her and wasn't planning to let her up any time soon.

Caroline had been underwater for long enough that her breath had run out. She had barely a few seconds left before her bursting lungs compelled her to take in water. In a last-ditch attempt to force Lexy to let go of her hair, she charged forward as best she could in the completely saturated robe, ramming her head into Lexy's chest.

Lexy staggered back and let go of Caroline's head. Caroline bent her knees and pushed upwards with everything she had. After the months of running on the damp sand of Studland beach, her legs were solid muscle, twin pistons driving her torso up as her head broke the surface, water flowing off her eyes, her nose, her mouth – she was dragging in a long, agonized breath, the effort ripping at her lungs. There was a rasping noise in her ears that she realized was her own body: she sounded like a rusty old tractor trying to start up.

But she was breathing air, not water! Around her, she felt pushing and shoving, other bodies cramming in between the bars. Her scalp was aching. She stumbled and felt a body behind her, raised a hand to wipe water from her face, and saw Lexy with her hair matted to her forehead and arms pinned to her sides, the man who had been on the bubble bed gripping on to her to hold her still as she struggled against him. Her left breast had popped completely out of her swimsuit by now, and a considerable part of the right one, but she seemed completely unembarrassed by this. In fact, as she writhed to get free, it was the poor man holding her who was rearing back, doing his best not to touch her impressive bosoms.

Someone caught Caroline, restraining her too, and as the pounding in her lungs began to lessen, she looked around to see, to her great surprise, that it was a fully clad man, his clothes sodden, his expression contorted with embarrassment.

'Miss,' he said, 'I'm the spa manager, and you're going to have to leave this area immediately, I'm afraid—'

'Oh my *God*!'

The woman on the bed was pointing at Lexy, her voice hysterical as she exclaimed in a heavy Russian accent:

'She's bleeding! Look at her! It's all over her head!'

The dark decor of the spa, the black-tiled pool, the dim underwater lighting, meant that the people in the water were shadowy silhouettes to each other. The woman sitting up, however, could see by the light of the fireplace what the others did not: that it was not water matting Lexy's hair to her head, but blood.

'It's going in the *water*!' the woman shrieked. 'Oh my God! François, let go of her! You could get it on you! I feel *sick*!'

François did let go of Lexy, who, frowning, put a hand up to the side of her head. Clearly, the adrenalin rush of attacking Caroline had meant that Lexy had failed to realize how badly she had been hurt when she hit the bars falling into the pool. Her hand came away smeared with blood.

Lexy stared at her palm. It was as if a wide brush had been dragged over it, thick with red paint, glossy and slick. Slowly, she probed her head, feeling for the extent of the damage that had been done when she landed on the bars, realizing for the first time that her shoulder was stiff and bruised as well. Her fingers touched her skull, probed around, and located a deep dent into which her index and middle finger sank right up to the base of her nail.

With blood dripping down her cheek, dark drops falling one after the other from her chin to her bare breast, her fingers exploring a terrifying indentation in the bone of her skull, Lexy was suddenly overwhelmed by dizziness. Her head felt as light as a balloon: her eyes rolled up, her face went pale as a ghost, her legs buckled and she slumped over, her face slapping onto the surface of the water.

François, seeing her fall, managed to step forward and catch her under the armpits, saving her from possibly hitting her head on the bars once more. And then he stood there haplessly, Lexy's unconscious body dangling from his hands as his girlfriend shrieked at him hysterically to let go, get his hands off her, get out of the water *now* –

'Oh *no*,' the spa manager wailed. 'Oh *no*, we're going to have to empty the whole pool!'

Chapter Forty-One

Two months later

'It's a fantastic turnout,' the bookshop manager gabbled excitedly to Caroline and her publicist. 'Really, beyond our expectations. And you're in the *Sunday Times* bestseller list, the first week the book's out! You must be over the moon!'

'I *am*,' Caroline said happily. 'I can't believe it, I really can't—'

'It's been an amazing ride,' the publicist agreed smugly. 'Did you see the interview with Caroline in the *Sun* last week? She got a two-page spread and a great review for *Bad Girl* in their Something for the Weekend review page as well!'

The interview had featured a photo spread of Caroline in the skimpiest clothes they could coax her into, swimwear with a range of elegant, see-through cover-ups: she had reasoned that she was probably in the best shape she would ever be in her life, with her weight loss on the island and her very flattering tan. The photographer, Krystyna Fitzgerald-Morris, was famous for her extremely sympathetic and beautiful portraits of women, and Caroline looked positively doe-eyed, her hair curled and soft around her face. Krystyna had assured Caroline that there would be discreet but effective

Photoshopping if necessary, and certainly Caroline's figure had never looked better, her jawline as tight as if she had had one of Lexy's CACI treatments.

No word of the confrontation in the Corinthia had leaked to the media. That kind of publicity was anathema to a five-star hotel. François had turned out to feel exactly the same: he was a hedge-funder skiving off work for a day with his mistress, something made abundantly clear by the stream of abuse she threw at him once they were both out of the pool and being fussed over by the spa staff.

She had wanted to go shopping, the mistress had complained very loudly, instead of soaking like a prune for hours; he had promised her a trip to the New Bond Street boutiques, where she knew he had taken his wife last week, and instead she'd had to lie around in stupid pools and watch stupid women bleed into the water, which was absolutely *disgusting* and something he'd never make his wife do –

As François and the spa manager lifted Lexy out of the pool, laying her on the tiles to wait for the hotel doctor, the general manager arrived, grasped the situation instantly and offered the unhappy couple access to the best available penthouse suite plus anything they wanted to order from room service, at which point all their complaints magically disappeared. Clearly, neither of them had any idea who Lexy and Caroline were, nor any interest in finding out.

So none of the publicity arranged by Caroline's publisher had been tarnished by news of her bashing Lexy's head in. She had been deluged with interview requests, had even been invited on live breakfast TV to promote her book, an almost unheard-of feat for a first-time author. The crowds today, filling the bookstore, spilling out onto Piccadilly, were proof of how effective *Celebrity Island Survivor* had been in making Caroline a household name. Lexy might have set Caroline up for humiliation, but the side-effect had certainly been to markedly raise her victim's profile.

Caroline was dressed to look as relatable as possible – a word that her editor and publicist had used repeatedly in every conversation with her since her return to the UK. There should be nothing sexy, nothing provocative in her clothes or demeanour that could give off a homewrecker vibe. It was all very well to do a photoshoot in swimwear, to write taboo-breaking racy sex scenes, but in real life Caroline should look like the girl next door.

So, after handing herself over to a personal shopper at Selfridges, Caroline had emerged with the perfect outfit: a silk ruffled chiffon blouse by Chloe over fitted J Brand jeans, and on her feet, blue velvet Charlotte Olympia 'Kitty' low heels, with cat's faces embroidered in gold thread on each toe, playful, fun, and, slightly less relatably, costing five hundred pounds. The personal shopper had described these confidently as an 'investment', and Caroline had bit her tongue to avoid asking how on earth a pair of shoes you were planning to wear could be an investment, because the shoes were adorable, and she wanted so desperately to be talked into buying them.

Simple gold jewellery was draped round her neck and dangling from her ears, her hair loose and tonged at the ends in the current faux-effortless style. Her publicist had nodded approvingly, commenting that she not only looked like the girl next door, but the one you wanted your son to date, bring home for Sunday lunch and eventually impregnate with adorable grandchildren.

And as Caroline signed copies of *Bad Girl*, the reaction from the people queuing up to buy it was surprisingly positive, much more so than she had imagined. Popular as Lexy was, the reality star clearly had plenty of detractors, or wannabes who were secretly envious of her glamour and success.

Just like Caroline. The irony did not escape her. Here she was, making a considerable amount of money by channelling the resentment felt towards Lexy by women less talented and attractive than her: women who were jealous of her many lovers, her handsome husband, her lovely children. Like them, Caroline had wanted to be Lexy, to step into her shoes, take over her life. Instead, she had managed only to ride Lexy's coattails for a while before Lexy contemptuously shook her off and took a devastating revenge.

Well, enough of that! she thought as she smiled and signed the next copy, aware that her hand was starting to cramp. *Lexy and I have done enough damage to each other. After this book, I never want to have to talk or write about her again. I want to pretend she doesn't even exist . . .*

Which made it even more annoying that she could hear Lexy's name now, being murmured eagerly in the crowd; not by the people closest to the signing table, but at the front of the bookshop, by the big plate-glass windows facing onto the street. It was a name that was very easy to distinguish, with that X both hissed and tongued to pronounce it; the word *Lexy, Lexy, Lexy* ran through the bookstore like a wave far out at sea, gathering strength, breaking hard, sending up a spume of white foam, and then crashing hard against the shore with a smack as it rolled into land . . .

And now the sea was parting. Caroline could see ripples at the front of the store, bodies moving, pressing closer together. The crowd was splitting down the centre, creating a channel down which a woman could pass, a woman dressed in a pillar-box red trouser suit cut tight to the body, a sliver of white silk bodysuit showing underneath it, its neckline low to show off her impressive bosom. Her black hair was piled high on top of her head, her heels so high that she positively stalked down the avenue formed for her by the people pressing back on either side.

Lexy's ears were hung with glittering diamonds; a chain of pearls was wound around her neck, dropping down to a larger stone that nestled at the base of her cleavage. Her lips were the same shade of red as her suit, her big blue eyes outlined dramatically in black, and from Silantra she had copied the idea of mink lashes. Caroline could only gawp at how magnificent Lexy looked. She might have been a younger version of Joan Collins in *Dynasty*, confronting a rival in a cliffhanger scene from the legendary soap opera.

Caroline braced herself. She had not seen Lexy since that afternoon at the Corinthia, when Lexy had been treated by the hotel doctor and then taken to hospital for what they had described as an accidental slip and fall in the spa. Caroline herself had been escorted from the premises and curtly informed that she was banned from the hotel for life. For all she knew, Lexy might be out for physical revenge.

Caroline glanced nervously at Lexy's hands to see if she

was carrying anything. She wouldn't have put it past her to be armed with a brimming martini glass, ready to throw its contents dramatically in Caroline's face.

But as Lexy arrived at the signing table, it was clear that her attack was to be purely verbal. Lexy's perfectly painted red lips parted. Looking down at Caroline, she said:

'I'd like a couple of books signed.'

The gasps from their audience were audible. This was the last thing anyone had expected.

'You *what*?' Caroline stammered.

'You heard me,' Lexy said, her tone very clear, aimed to carry to the farthest corners of the bookshop. 'I want two copies. One for Frank, one for Santino.'

Louder gasps resulted, followed by a positive babble as people who didn't even know each other repeated the extraordinary request that Lexy had just made to their neighbour.

Lexy's eyes bored down into those of her former ghost-writer.

'Go on,' she said. 'It's a book signing, isn't it? Get on with it and sign some books!'

In retrospect, Caroline realized she could quite easily have refused. But Lexy's stare, her physical presence, were as warlike and intimidating as an Amazon. Meekly, Caroline picked up her pen again and, her publicist wordlessly sliding the next pre-opened book towards her, wrote the words: 'To Frank, love Caroline' on the title page as if on automatic pilot. As soon as she finished the word 'love', she cringed: but it was too late to change it.

'Now do one for Santino,' Lexy commanded, inexorable.

Caroline didn't understand what was happening: but what she wanted more than anything was to make Lexy disappear. So she took the second book and wrote: 'To Santino, from Caroline', at least managing this time to avoid the word 'love'.

She closed the second book, sliding it over to Lexy in its turn. Lexy picked up the two books and fixed that piercing blue gaze on her victim once more.

'Good luck finding someone else to leech off,' she said. 'You came into my home and tried to steal my husband, and now you've tried to steal my story. Good luck finding someone else to thieve from. Because from where I'm standing, it doesn't look as if you have a man or a story of your own.'

Lexy was no actress, but for years she had uttered heavily scripted and rehearsed lines for her show. This little speech had been thoroughly practised in advance, and she delivered it in heartfelt tones, nailing every emphasis, every beat, pausing to let it sink in before she turned on her heel and swept back down the channel at the centre of the room.

Someone at the back started to clap in appreciation. It was swiftly taken up. By the time Lexy reached the doors, most of the people inside the bookstore were applauding. Lexy stopped, cast a smile of thanks around the room, and then said to the bookstore employee who was standing nervously by the door:

'Can I get a dustbin?'

'I'm sorry?' the young man stammered.

'A dustbin,' she said, and behind her, someone in the crowd said:

'Lexy wants a bin! Is there a bin anywhere?'

The room buzzed with activity, people at the edges turning to look around them to see if there was a dustbin against the wall; over at the cash desk, an employee called: 'I've got one here!' and hoisted it in the air. The person beside her reached out and took it, passing it over his head towards the front of the shop. The dustbin crowd-surfed through the air, held by its base, until it reached the bookstore employee, who reached out, took it and set it down in front of Lexy.

Like everyone else in the bookstore, Caroline's attention had been entirely on Lexy in her red suit and glittering diamonds. It was only now, with horror, that she saw a photographer at the back of the store, busy capturing every moment of this scene; staring more intently, she saw someone else with a professional-looking video camera, holding it high . . . and of course the mobile phones were out, of course everyone was frantically snapping and recording away, capturing Caroline's latest public mortification at Lexy's hands . . .

'Thanks, everyone,' Lexy said, and one by one, she dropped the two books into the bin.

'Trash into the trash,' she said – and, to the bookstore employee: 'Bill Caroline for those. Fuck knows, she can afford it after the dosh she's made screwing me over. She bloody owes me.'

It was the perfect closing line. With a toss of her head, Lexy stalked out of the store, people jumping to open the door for her.

'Wow,' someone in the signing line breathed in awe. 'She's *such* a diva.'

'That was *amazing*,' the person beside him sighed.

Like spectators at a tennis match, the faces swivelled back to Caroline. Lexy had dominated the rally from the start, finished with a smash that it was impossible for Caroline to return, comprehensively won the game; their expressions clearly said that they were looking at the loser. She wanted to get up and run away, back into the stockroom, collapse on a pile of books and burst into hysterical, loser tears. But then she found herself asking:

What would Lexy do?

Caroline sat up straight, bit the inside of her lip to stop it from wobbling with nerves, and pegged her chin Lexy-high.

'Okay!' she said, as brightly as she possibly could. 'Who's next in line?'

Both her publicist and the bookstore manager let out involuntary sighs of relief. As the next book buyer stepped forward, Caroline's publicist patted her on the shoulder encouragingly, saying in a loud voice:

'Caroline's not going to discuss what just happened – we've got so many fans of hers who want their books signed, we need to push on . . .'

As Caroline took the book and asked the buyer for her name, she caught sight of someone at the front of the crowd who she was sure had not been there before. Riz must have taken advantage of the scrum to work his way forward, and here he was, raising a hand to her, smiling shyly as he waved a hello.

She'd moved out of the Edmonton house into a rental flat as soon as she got back from Australia: she hadn't seen him for quite a while. He looked okay. He had lost some weight, toned up a bit, bought himself some more fashionable clothes, maybe even shelled out for what looked as if it could be a Reiss shirt. And he was carrying flowers, a bouquet of yellow roses, now very bashed by being squashed as he worked his way through the throng of people. But still, roses.

Lexy had taunted Caroline just now for not having a man of her own. Well, here was a candidate: he was no Frank, no Santino, God knew, but he was better than nothing. Clearly, also, he was willing to put the past behind them, the way she had dumped him to take up with a married man – overlooking, too, how she had seamlessly moved on from Frank to Santino.

Maybe Riz was just a fame-whore, wanting to be close to the centre of the action. But then, so was she. And given the choice, after this signing, of going back to her rental flat all alone – of googling her name to find gloating online posts about Lexy throwing her books in the dustbin, complete with photos and videos from the paps Lexy had clearly hired – or taking Riz back with her and riding him hard as long as he could last to work off all her pent-up frustration and rage . . . well, if Caroline asked herself *What would Lexy do?*, there was no question that Lexy would pick the option which involved angry sex.

Caroline jerked her head to the side of the room in an easily understandable gesture that said *Hang out there and wait for me*. Beaming, Riz obeyed.

She bloody owes me, Lexy had just said. And it was true. Look where Caroline had been when she first met Lexy, and where she was now; not just with a career earned off the back of writing for Lexy, but a lover willing to hang around while she fucked other men and take her back afterwards . . .

Caroline grimaced. Damn it. Even after the scene Lexy had just thrown, Caroline was still in her debt. She really *did* owe her.

Chapter Forty-Two

Lexy made sure her exit from the bookstore was suitably dramatic. Striding down Piccadilly as onlookers turned to stare, her killer heels struck the pavement with satisfying force, as if she were grinding Caroline beneath them. She kept this up until she had passed the frontage of the bookshop; then she stopped to let the photographer and cameraman catch up to her, reviewing their footage, making sure that they had everything they needed. With this confirmed, they shot off to ring their agencies. The coverage of Lexy humiliating Caroline at her own book launch would be online in a couple of hours, maximum.

Many fans had followed Lexy out of the bookshop, and she happily signed autographs and took selfies with them. Her smile was unwavering as she refused politely to answer questions about the state of her marriage, while encouraging them all to buy *Lexy on the Loose* and watch the premiere of the new season of her show. When the tide of admirers had finally slowed to a trickle, she waved the last fans a very warm goodbye and resumed her progress down Piccadilly, drawing stares of recognition and appreciation all the way to Fortnum and Mason.

Entering by a side door, she wove her way through the store to the Diamond Jubilee tea salon. This was an oasis, decorated in white and pale blue, presumably to exert some kind of calm to balance out the babbling, excited children present who were busily feeding their sugar highs. At the entrance, a piano tinkled away, gentle tunes obviously intended to have the same effect.

Lexy spotted her family almost at once. Frank, Laylah and London were ensconced at a table by the far wall, London kneeling up on the pale blue leather banquette, reaching for a petit four from the top plate of the cake tower, a curlicued white stand layered with white china plates with blue and gold rims. The plate rattled perilously as he grabbed it; Lexy took a moment to relish the sight of her happy husband and children, jam smeared over Laylah's face as she stuffed a cream scone into her mouth, London demolishing the petit four, Frank chuckling at the sight of his kids in the throes of pleasure.

Two tables over, a woman sipping pink Ruinart champagne with a friend, bags from their shopping spree piled around the table, glanced over at Frank. Her eyes softened with that unmistakeable glow typical of a certain type of female when they see a man looking after his children. It was like being broody by proxy: they wanted not just a baby, but the whole package.

Just as Caroline had done.

Lexy had missed the multiple times Caroline must have cast just that dewy-eyed, hopeful, admiring gaze at Frank. That wasn't all Lexy had missed, of course; she hadn't realized the value of what she had till she had nearly lost everything. Her kids, her husband, her home. She shivered with relief when she thought how close she had come to losing it all.

Thanks, Caroline, she thought for the umpteenth time. *Weirdly enough, I owe you. For showing me what I had, for making me fight for it. Even for cracking my head open in that vitality pool.*

Whatever Frank had been intending to say to Lexy later on the evening of that fight in the Corinthia Spa, she would never know. Had he been going to tell her he wanted to reconcile? She had never risked asking him that question. Because once the hospital called him, everything had changed. On hearing that she had a severe concussion, he had dashed over there immediately. Lexy had been groggy, barely conscious, having just emerged from a CT scan which had mercifully been negative; Frank tore into her room, horrified at the sight of her pale face, the bandages on her head. Once Lexy had managed to smile and tell him she was basically okay, that she had been cleared for bleeding or swelling of the brain, he had started crying in relief, which had caused her to start crying too, and then they were hugging and crying together, and after that it had all been smooth sailing.

Thank you, Caroline, Lexy thought quite genuinely, *for shoving me into that pool and knocking me out, so that my husband would realize he still loved me and couldn't stand the thought of me dropping dead from a head injury.*

That's the last thank you I'll ever bloody give you, though.

The woman with the pink Ruinart champagne had been staring wistfully at Lexy's husband for quite long enough.

Stepping up to the table, as London yelled: '*Mummy!*' with ecstatic glee, Lexy bent over Frank and placed a long, thorough kiss on his lips, both children hooting and pointing at Daddy wearing lipstick.

Picking up a napkin, she dipped it into a glass of water and wiped her lipstick from his mouth.

'Sorry, babes,' she said, sitting down next to him and glancing briefly sideways in triumph at the Ruinart woman, who was looking deflated. 'I just can't resist you.'

Frank took her hand and squeezed it hard, smiling lovingly at her.

'I got you macaroons,' he said, indicating the plate.

'Mummy's favourite!' Laylah chanted. 'Mummy loves macaroons!'

Lexy looked at the plate of low-fat macaroons.

'Ah, sod that,' she said. 'I've had a really good afternoon. Give me one of those scones, and pass the cream while you're about it. Hey, kids, I have some news. Mummy isn't going to be shooting her show any more. No more cameras in the house following us around all the time.'

'You told them, then?' Frank asked. Before dropping in on Caroline's book signing, Lexy had been in a long meeting with her TV producers at their Soho offices. 'How'd they take it?'

'Not too well at first,' she admitted. 'But I gave them another bone to chew on. If we can pull it off I'm going to be hosting a new show, called something like *Lexy Knows Best*. I'll be taking the latest reality show winners and working with them so they're not flashes in the pan, you know? I'll decide how to steer their careers, what they should be doing, who they should be dating, how they should be maximizing their fame. I might start with that Jamie-Lee. She's an ambitious little madam – just the kind that does well at this kind of thing.'

'You'll be brilliant at that,' Frank said loyally, releasing her hand so that she could dig into the highly fattening scone. 'It's a great idea.'

'Yeah, it was mostly me who came up with it,' she boasted. 'And you know what? If it doesn't work, we'll try something else.'

'Why aren't we doing the show any more, Mummy?' London asked.

'*Mummy*,' Frank muttered, rolling his eyes. 'Ever since they've been spending time with Sophie, they've got so bloody posh!'

'Your dad doesn't want you kids on TV any more, babes,' Lexy said. 'And he doesn't want to be on TV any more either – not on a show about us, anyway. He never did. I made him.'

Frank's smile of acknowledgement was a beautiful thing to see.

'But I *like* it, Mummy!' Laylah wailed. 'I *like* being on telly!'

Her big blue eyes, so like her mother's, widened in distress as she looked from her mother to her father, begging for some sort of reprieve.

'I've got so many followers on Instagram!' she pointed out. 'They're always asking when I'll be on telly again! And Snapchat too! Mummy, I *need* to be on telly, you don't understand! I *need* it so I can get more and more followers, I want thousands and thousands . . .'

Her voice was rising perilously. In the old days, this meltdown would have been dealt with by a hapless nanny, who would have been expected to whisk Laylah off to the toilets till she calmed down. Now it was squarely on her parents' shoulders. Frank blanched, but Lexy leaned across the table, grabbed Laylah's hand and hissed:

'If you don't calm down *right now*, young lady, your phone's being taken off you for a *week*, d'you hear me? I'm not pissing around!'

Sorry, Sophie, she thought guiltily. *Still got some work to do on not effing and blinding in front of the kids.*

The sob issuing from Laylah's cupid's-bow lips was caught midway as she stared at her mother in utter horror, her eyes now so stretched that she looked positively comical. With animal instincts, she took a swift inventory of her mother's expression and read in it nothing but absolute willingness to make good on her threat.

'Can I *never* be on telly any more, Mummy?' she said piteously, trying a plea since the threat of a meltdown had failed. 'Not *ever*?'

Lexy looked at her beautiful, wilful daughter, a miniature version of herself in so many ways, and her heart sank at the thought of the years of trouble that lay in store for her and Frank as Laylah grew up.

'Oh, I think you probably will,' she said grimly. 'But nothing your dad doesn't approve of.'

Laylah turned to Frank, cast a frantic look of appeal at him and then buried her face in her hands.

'You're ruining my *life*!' she moaned.

'That's early,' Frank said, deadpan. 'Didn't think we'd be hearing that till she was in her teens.'

He shoved his leather armchair closer to Lexy's, put his arm around her shoulder.

'Kids, your mum and I are a team now,' he announced. 'We make our decisions together. No more going behind one of our backs to try to get what you want from the other one. Those days are over.'

It was London's turn to look appalled.

'London!' Laylah said, still into her hands, quoting a line they had recently heard in a film. 'You know what this means? We're *doomed*.'

And her delivery was so perfect that not just her parents, but her younger brother, who didn't usually like to give her credit for anything, dissolved in floods of laughter.

Acknowledgements

Huge thanks to:

The amazing team at Pan Macmillan: my editor Wayne Brookes and his assistant Alex Saunders, Caroline Hogg for her fantastic RTs, my publisher Jeremy Trevathan, sales whizz Stuart Dwyer and designer James Annal. Everyone is such a pleasure to work with and it's a delight to keep building sales together!

Amanda Preston at LBA, my truly engaged, super-smart, active and passionate agent.

Emma at ED PR, for all her wonderful hard work publicizing my books.

Ewa and Davina at IIAA, who, together with Faye, Amy and Charlotte at Skin3 Salon, have been a fantastic resource as I painstakingly researched Lexy's very sophisticated skincare regime. I'm very grateful for their time, trouble and generosity in answering my questions and letting me try out the facials so I could describe the experience! My skin has genuinely improved and I am a convert to the miracle that is Jane Iredale BB cream.

Yvonne Campbell for the link to Lauren Goodger avoiding a puddle, with which I made great capital!

Emily Banyard and Jamie-Lee Nardone for letting me use their names for a pair of hard-nosed bitches – nothing like them of course!

Bettina Hartas Geary for suggesting the name Darrell Rose.

Ilana Bergsagel for 'These Words' by Natasha Bedingfeld for Caroline's ringtone, and for the 'carbs and bikinis' comparison.

Antonio di Meglio for making sure I had the Italian for 'shagging' right. He's the Italian shagging expert.

Victoria Sharkey for the very helpful info on night tube and bus routes to Edmonton.

Dan Evans at Plan 9 does such a superb job with my website and business cards that you should all use him for yours.

Matt B, my reading twin, as always, not only for all his help and support but for making me read *Madness of a Seduced Woman*!

Sarah Weinman, such a great friend and such a loyal supporter of my books.

The gorgeous team of McKenna Jordan and John Kwiatkowski and everyone at Murder by the Book for bringing my smut to Texas.

I couldn't have written this book without the Rebecca Chance fanfriends on Facebook and Twitter cheering me up with delightful banter! Thanks go to: Angela Collings, Dawn Hamblett, Tim Hughes, Lauren O'Brien, Jason Ellis, Tony Wood, Melanie Hearse, Jen Sheehan, Helen Smith, Ilana Bergsagel, Katherine Everett, Julian Corkle, Robin Greene, Diane Jolly, Adam Pietrowski, John Soper, Gary Jordan, Louise Bell, Lisa Respers France, Stella Duffy, Shelley Silas,

Rowan Coleman, Tim Daly, Joy T. Chance, Lori Smith Jennaway, Sallie Dorsett, Alice Taylor, Joanne Wade, Marjorie Tucker, Teresa Wilson, Ashley James Cardwell, Margery Flax, Clinton Reed, Valerie Laws, Kelly Butterworth, Kirsty Maclennan, Amanda Marie Fulton, Marie Causey, Shana Mehtaab, Tracy Hanson, Beverley Ann Hopper, Nancy Pace Koffman, Katrina Smith, Helen Lusher, Russ Fry, Gavin Robinson, Laura Ford, Mary Mulkeen, Eileen McAninly, Pamela Cardone, Barb McNaughton, Shannon Mitchell, Claire Chiswell, Paula Louise Standen, Dawn Turnbull, Fiona Morris, Michelle Heneghan, Jenny Hilton, Kelly Harvade, Vikki Harris, Annie Lancaster, Derek Farrell and Bryan Quertermous, Derek Jones and Colin Butts, the very exclusive (i.e. tiny) club of my straight male readers. Plus of course Paul Burston and the loyal Polari crew – Alex Hopkins, Ange Chan, Sian Pepper, Enda Guinan, Belinda Davies, John Southgate, Paul Brown, James Watts, Ian Sinclair Romanis and Jon Clarke. And the handful of beloved relatives brave enough to read my books – Dalia Hartman Bergsagel, Ilana Bergsagel, Sandy Makarwicz and Jean Polito. If I've left anyone out, please do send me a message and I will correct it in the next book!

And as always – thanks to the Board and the FLs of FB for being there. We are fantastically lucky to have the solidarity of our peers in trying times.

Mile High

by Rebecca Chance

First class can be murder . . .

Pure Air's new LuxeLiner is flying from London to LA – on its inaugural journey – with a first-class cabin packed with A-list celebrities. As the feuding crew compete to impress their famous passengers, the handsome pilot tries to win the attention of a pretty young stewardess.

But one VIP singer is battling something seriously sinister: watching her every step is a very determined stalker, someone who will go to any lengths to get the star to satisfy their desires. At thirty thousand feet there is nowhere to run, and nowhere to hide . . .

Killer Diamonds

by Rebecca Chance

They're to die for . . .

When Oscar-winning beauty Vivienne Winter decides to auction her multimillion-dollar jewellery collection for charity, there's no shortage of people eager to buy a piece of her incredible history.

Young, ambitious Christine Smith is a jewellery expert working for a centuries-old auction house. She's desperate to secure the sale of Vivienne Winter's gem collection, set to be the biggest auction since Elizabeth Taylor's. However, meeting the Hollywood star is just the first hurdle Christine has to jump.

Vivienne's spoilt and sexy playboy grandson, Angel, is the heir to her fortune. The anger and resentment he feels towards his grandmother for selling what he believes to be his inheritance sets in motion a series of events with deadly consequences. Angel is totally unscrupulous, and family secrets cut sharper than diamonds . . .

extracts reading groups
competitions books new
discounts extracts
competitions
books new
events reading groups extracts
events books
extracts new titles reading groups
interviews
events extracts events
discounts books
new books events
events new reading groups
discounts extracts discounts
www.panmacmillan.com
extracts events reading groups
competitions books extracts new